THE ANOINTED ONE

THE
ANOINTED
ONE

BOOK II: TRILOGY OF KINGS SAGA

SUSAN VAN VOLKENBURGH

Creek Bluff Digital books may be ordered through booksellers or by contacting:

Creek Bluff Digital
9005 County Road 302
Kaufman, TX 75142
www.creekbluff.com
1 (817) 427-8755

Edited – Karen Summerville
Cover design – Susan Van Volkenburgh & Ron Van Volkenburgh
Map illustration – BMR Williams

ISBN: 978-0-9600755-0-8
ISBN: 978-0-9600755-1-5
ISBN: 978-0-9600755-2-2

Library of Congress Control Number: 2018914236

CREEK BLUFF DIGITAL REV. DATE: 2/18/2026

To all who stand upon the Rock in a shaky world.

PSALM 62:2

SIDONIANS

ARAM

N

W E

S

• Sidon

• Zarephath

Mt. Herman

• Tyre

Iyyon •

Abel·beth Macaah •   • Dan

The Great Sea

Hazor •

Gennesaret •   Sea of
Chinnereth

Mt. Carmel   Mt. Tabor

Kishon R.

Dor •   *Jordan R.*   Yarmuk R.   Ramoth-Gilead •

• Megiddo   En Dor •

CANAAN   • Jazreel   • Tishbe   AMMON

• Taanach   Beth-shan •
Mt. Gilboa   Bezek •   Jabesh-Gilead •
Mt. Ebal   • Zarethan
Pirathon •   Shechem •   Mt. Gerizim   • Succoth
Yarkon R.   Eben-Ezer •   • Arumah
Aphek •   Tappuah •   *Jabbok R.*
• Joppa   Shiloh •

Lod •   *Aijalon R.*
Jabneel •   Aijalon •   Bethel •   Michmash •   • Rabbah
Gezer •   Mizpah •   Geba •   Heshbon •
Sorek R.   Kirjath-Jearim •   Ramah •   Jericho •   Gilgal •
• Ashdod   Gibeon •   Gibeah •   Mt. Nebo
Ekron •   • Beth Shemesh   • Nob
Elah R.   • Azekah   Jebus •
• Sochoh   • Bethlehem
• Askelon   *Zephathah R.*   • Mareshah
Gath •   • Hebron   Salt Sea
Lachish •

PHILISTINES   En Gedi •   Arnon R.
• Carmel

• Gaza   • Ziklag   MOAB
Besor R.
• Sharuhen   Beersheba •

NEGEV   Zered River

• Tamar   EDOM

CONTENTS

PART THE SECOND

PART THE THIRD

PART THE FOURTH

PART THE FIFTH

PART THE FIRST

I will redeem you with an outstretched arm
and with great judgments. I will take you as My
people, and I will be your God. Then you shall
know that I am the Lord your God.

EXODUS 6:6–7

CHAPTER 1

UNREST

The long-resounding cries of battle were swallowed by a gathering murmur of hooves thundering over the ridge. The Philistine ranks gave way, releasing hundreds of horse riders cascading over the encompassing hills. Across the bloodied field, the enemy spilled like a wave cresting the shore at high tide, bearing down upon the Hebrew lines.

Tiphcar, captain of the Israelite forces, looked on in horror as the battle turned to ruin.

"Pull back! Pull back!" Tiphcar cried as he gestured for retreat. A moment before, the Chosen of God had been winning the day. Now they were being crushed under the hooves of the Philistine beasts. Stunned, Tiphcar pressed his men toward camp, the concussion of the enemy's charge close behind.

Unable to brook defeat, the captain halted.

"No," he spoke as he wheeled about. "We cannot abandon the Ark of God. We must fight!"

Mustering his courage, Tiphcar called to the trumpet bearer, "Sound the advance!"

The lad's eyes were wide with fear, yet he obeyed his captain. Pressing the horn to his lips, he let out a clear note that echoed over the confusion on the field.

At the sound of the trumpet, the Israelites stayed their retreat, their courage renewed as they gazed upon their stalwart leader.

With sword lifted, Tiphcar bellowed in his strong voice:
"Reform the line! Reform the line!"

The horde of horses hung on the horizon, filling the wind with the sound of snorting and hooves pawing upon mud-laden earth. Regrouping, the phalanx of foot soldiers pressed their spear-bolstered shield-wall into action. Shields locked together, spears angled up. They waited for the wave of hoof and rider to break over their lines.

Tiphcar could feel his heart beating to the rhythm of the galloping gait. Perspiration trickled down his face and neck, prickling his skin. He took a deep breath to steady his nerves. Every man looked to him for salvation. The weight of their trust rested heavy upon his shoulders. All this calamity was his to bear.

"Archers, arrows on my command. *Reggah*, wait." Tiphcar raised his arm, steadying the bowmen.

Orach's voice rose above the clamor as he clutched his spear tighter. "Now this is getting interesting!"

Yet the captain could hear nothing save the crashing cadence of the rising tide. For a moment the action seemed to slow as the horses bore down ever closer to the rocky shore of shields. It was as though Tiphcar was watching from outside himself. He looked on with deaf ears as each rider lifted spear or sword above his head, pressing toward his mark.

Soon all would be decided. If the front lines failed, the ranks would be trampled—the day would be lost. The heat of battle coursed through the captain's body. Suddenly audible, the savage roar of battle exploded upon his unstopped ears as the raging flood of horse and rider rushed forward.

"*Attah*! Now!" Tiphcar shouted as he lowered his arm toward the onslaught of the hastening host.

With the twang of bowstrings, a volley of missiles let loose. Men and mounts were brought down as arrows pierced them through. Many foes fell, yet where one left off another took his place so that the wave of horse and rider seemed to have no end.

The front line prepared for impact: heel and toe dug into the rain-soaked earth, head ducked behind bulwark, shoulder pressed against shield-barrier.

The galloping horde broke upon the wall like water over stone. Spears pierced horses. Horses trampled men. Riders jabbing and hacking, sliced through the lines, sending the Hebrew tribes into a mass of agonized confusion.

"The horses! Kill the horses!" Tiphcar called as he lifted his face above the mass of clashing swords and shields.

Obediently, the Hebrew spears focused on the Philistine steeds, piercing many upon the breast.

Within the tangled turmoil, Tiphcar found himself surrounded by many foes, unaided by his Hebrew comrades. Cut off, he fought with all his strength. His destiny now undisputed, the captain resolved to die well, for it was his decision that had led his men to their present doom. He would fight until life was hewn from him. He would die among his men, as one of them.

Yet, just as the last buffer against despair was dismantled, hope unlooked for was revealed. Nagad and Orach rushed upon the scene, their sword and spear striking out against the enemy, their bodies covered in the leaching loam of the nearby swamp. Under their fury, Tiphcar's fate was decided, for by their might the swarming swordsmen melted away.

"Well timed, my friends."

Wiping his forehead with the back of his bloodied hand, Tiphcar turned to the Ark. Seeing the horses of the Philistine contingent rushing over the field toward the Holy Shrine, he shouted:

"To the Ark, to the Ark!"

Before his eyes, the horror of the scene played out. The priests were engulfed by the charging beasts. As many as were able ran to assist as the holy attendants were viciously cut down where they stood.

Tiphcar felt a burning rage rise within him, bloodlust overtaking him so that all caution was lost. No one could withstand the tremor of his might as he threw down all foes in his wake. Yet, the charge of the indomitable beasts would not yield to his thirst. The enemy pressed the Hebrews back from the Holy Coffer. Reaching out, the Philistines seized the Ark to carry it away, back to the fortress at Aphek.

Tiphcar, with Nagad and Orach, raced after the Ark of God. Before they could reach their desired quarry, a sound resonated in the distance.

It was a fell force that bore down upon them: the noise of the rumbling wheels and galloping horses. The jolting chariots and the rearing horsemen wreaked havoc about them.

The icy fingers of fear gripped Tiphcar's heart. Horror struck, the captain stood; his feet frozen in place. His sword, bloodied and dull, slowly lowered as he watched, gaping in despair. Calamity upon calamity weighed down upon him as the earth tilted out of joint.

A mournful wail rose from the Hebrew lines. So haunting was this cry of woe that for a moment all fighting ceased. Even the Philistine forces recoiled at the wound they had inflicted upon the tribes.

"All is lost," went up the cry.

The sky grew dark with a crack of thunder that shuddered through the ranks. Clouds burst open with a torrent of rain that obstructed the vision. And still the captain stood unmoving as the raging chariots pressed around him. Then the enemy was upon him.

He jolted with a start.

Roused from his repose, Tiphcar sat with his cloak flung from his quaking frame. His breath was short as he wiped the cold sweat from his brow. So long it had been since his dreams had been haunted by that memory.

Why do I call to mind that trial now? thought Tiphcar. *All that has been resolved. The Ark has returned, and peace has been restored.*

Yet, the old captain's mind was heavy, for he had heard murmurs of tensions building and a plan put in motion by the elders. Shaking his head, Tiphcar rose and jostled the dust from his cloak. *I am getting too old for sleeping out of doors.*

Throwing his mantle over his shoulders, Tiphcar clutched the woolen cloth across his chest to ward off the morning chill. He was still troubled by the dream as he entered the road. The landscape was serene, a reflection of the present state of affairs.

Even so, the old captain's mind lingered on the thoughts etched upon his memory. Portents of doom pressed into his waking reason, growing more ominous with each step he took.

Twenty years it had been since Mizpah, and peace had settled upon the land. Yet peace never lasts. As the long years waned, a hidden malice grew, rumors of war in the west, whispers of unrest in the east.

It was for this purpose that Tiphcar had received a summons to Bethel, the house of God it was called, to meet with the council of elders, for fear drove them to assemble once more. A high place to

Yahweh had been raised there since the destruction of Shiloh, the holy city. But the Ark of God lay hidden in the house of Abinadab, secluded in the hills of Kirjath-Jearim, forgotten by the people.

Tiphcar rounded a bend in the road as the terrain curved to the northwest. A low rocky ridge lifted the city of Bethel before him.

The town stood between two shallow vales that housed seasonal streams, one on each side of the city, as though the settlement was held in check by the bounding waters. The migratory currents ran the course of the two depressions, which met at the entrance to the city, making a moat on three sides of the rise.

A sluice crossed the small cataract formed by the union of the two rivers. The juncture of the streams produced one watershed that fell toward the southeast, supplying the bountiful pastureland with irrigation, the amount of overflow being regulated by the watergate. Beyond the waters' barrier, the gates of the city rose, lifting the eyes to accommodate large towers on either side of the entrance. Masonry walls encapsulated the town, stones cut to precision and piled one upon another forming a barrier against the outside.

"What is this?" Tiphcar spoke with agitation as he entered the gatehouse. Within the sparsely furnished chamber sat the eleven elders.

"Have you come together without me? I received your summons, but apparently, I have received it late. Have you decided without hearing my case?"

"Tiphcar, my friend, come in, come in." Gadowl, bent and withered by time, spoke as he gestured for the old captain to have a seat. "We have not done anything against you. We simply have gathered to discuss the facts before we present our cause before you."

Tiphcar walked into the room, but did not sit. Still powerful in body despite the passage of time, he towered over the aged elder. Gadowl grew uncomfortable under the shadow of Tiphcar; he laughed nervously, and took a step back.

Turning, the elder council member, with the sweep of his hand, indicated the presence of his fellow conspirators and spoke, "My brother, you are new to this assembly. It is not uncommon for us to debate an issue before including all members. We find it saves time to collect our thoughts."

"You mean swaying the others to your side before they get all the information. Well, *brother*," Tiphcar gathered himself up and spoke these words with malice, "you will hear what I have to say."

"Now, now," spoke Zaqen. "Let us not come to this. We are all brothers here. We must not let our feelings rule our decisions."

"Yes, yes," spoke Gadowl. He wrung his hands as he stepped closer to Zaqen. "Let us not come to spiteful words." Indicating a bench with his outstretched hand, the elder continued. "Please, Tiphcar, join us and hear what we have to say."

Tiphcar scowled, but took a seat upon a bench that rested against the outer wall.

"As you know, there has been some news from the north, just east of the Jordan," began Gadowl. "Our enemies are on the move."

"Yes," interjected Haddabar, who, as he spoke, remained seated across the room from Tiphcar. Leaning forward, resting one hand upon his knee, the elder gestured with his other hand as he continued his address.

"Even now, Captain Nagad has sent word from the north that he and his men have encountered unrest on the borders of Ammon. It appears that King Nahash has threatened to invade our outer cities. And our spies in the west tell us that the Philistines once more grow restless and are fortifying their borders."

"Rumors have come to my ears of the Amalekites to the south," spoke Gadowl. "They too have strengthened their borders. And reports have reached us that the kings of Damascus and Aram Zobah are building forces in the north."

Gadowl walked over to Tiphcar and looked down upon him. "So you see, I tell you now, even weeping, that our enemies have hemmed us in on every side. We must take action, and do it quickly, or we shall face annihilation."

"What do you propose we do?" inquired Tiphcar, yet wary.

"A king," spoke Gadowl. "We need to appoint a king, someone to unify the tribes and go out to fight against these threats."

Tiphcar let out a great sigh. Standing, he addressed the assembly, reaching to them with his outstretched arm.

"All these long years, Samuel has led us well. See how peace has ruled the land. Do you now doubt? Do you think our God will leave us undefended? Has He not provided for us in the past? I tell you brothers, we need no king over us whilst we have the Lord Almighty. In our hour of adversity, we are not without hope. Do not let fear cloud your vision. Do you not remember how the Lord protected us and delivered us? Did not Gideon refuse the throne when offered saying, 'I will not rule over you, nor shall my son rule over you; the Lord shall rule over you'?[1]

"Let us have this mind," continued Tiphcar with passion, standing before the elders with his arms open as if waiting to deliver an embrace, "that no matter what the threat, we will continue to trust in the leadership of Yahweh."

Lowering his empty arms, Tiphcar's voice softened as he shook his head slowly. "My brothers, we are not like the other nations; we have been chosen to be governed directly by God. Why would we desire to put our trust in a ruler? Has not the Lord shown Himself a worthy King?"

"It is a simple matter of good politics, brother," injected Gadowl while extending his hand, palm side up, as though he were showing what he was speaking. "We see how the other nations prosper. We see how they are held together, unified. A king to govern us is necessary to compete in today's world."

Gadowl walked over and placed his hand upon Tiphcar's shoulder. "Times have changed my friend, and we must change along with them. If we do not have proper leadership, we shall face another defeat like Aphek."

Tiphcar regarded the hand upon his shoulder with disgust. Too well he remembered that it was Gadowl who first spoke of taking the Ark of the Covenant into battle, unbidden. And at Aphek it was that the Holy Shrine was lost.

Yet Tiphcar had agreed, so the burden of guilt rested upon his own shoulders. Still, the old captain was slow to trust the counsel of this elder.

Shaking free from Gadowl's grasp, Tiphcar spoke, "Was it not the Lord who redeemed us at Mizpah? Without His intervention, we would not have a nation."

"Tiphcar, this matter has already been decided," growled Gadowl.

---

[1] Judges 8:23

"Zaqen," pleaded Tiphcar, his hand extended toward the elder, "you of all people cannot agree to this."

"Tiphcar, I have pledged my support." Zaqen averted his eyes from the old captain's gaze, unable to bear up to his reproach. "We need someone to unify us, to lead us. This cannot be Samuel. See how he has aged. He cannot long endure as judge over us. To whom then do we look? His sons? They have forsaken their father's ways. They are no better than the sons of Eli, perverting justice for their own gain, taking bribes."

Shaking his head, he continued. "No—we cannot look to the sons of Samuel."

"Then do you all agree to this?" queried Tiphcar as he surveyed the faces of the elders.

"Aye, we do."

"It appears I am outnumbered," Tiphcar spoke with sorrow. "At least we must consult Samuel. It is not right to decide these matters without his input. We must go to Ramah and meet with the prophet. It is he who must decide the fate of Israel."

CHAPTER 2

AT THE GATES OF RAMAH

Samuel sat outside the city gate, looking down at the ground. He heaved a great sigh. He felt old—old and worn. Many years lay between this day and the time he had first become judge over Israel, many trying years leading this band of wayward people. He had spent the better part of his life traveling from year to year on a circuit throughout the territories of Israel, striving to awaken the Hebrew people's fidelity.

Now, age had slowed his body. It was for this cause that he had limited his rotation to Bethel, Gilgal, and Mizpah. But he always returned to Ramah, for this was his home.

As he pondered the long years behind him, the old prophet's heart grew heavy. *They are a stubborn group, these people.* For a great length of time, the western threat had been subdued. The tribes had lived in relative peace. Yet the people grew restless, desiring the finery of the nations in the west.

His own sons, as Eli's before him, were no better, for they did not walk in his ways. Both had been appointed judges over the land of Beersheba to ease Samuel's burden. But, Joel, his firstborn, and Abijah, his second, had given themselves over to their cravings for pleasure and riches, turning from justice and mercy to personal gain.

The heavy burden continually weighed upon Samuel; his influence over the people had begun to wane as his body grew weary before its time.

Concerned for the future, Samuel searched his heart for what should be done. He would not last much longer. His time as judge was growing short. The tribes were a cluster of splintered factions, each tribe providing for its own clan members with little regard for their neighbors' struggles. Uniting these Chosen of God had always been a difficult task.

Adversity had brought them together in the past, but now, peace ruled the land. Without a cause to unite them, the multitude had become lax in their faith and neglected the Lord, withholding offerings and mingling with the peoples of the other lands. *Their wanderings abroad will be their downfall. Their wayward ways will be their doom.*

Samuel let out another sigh; the air escaped without releasing his unease. *A time is coming, a day of reckoning. I can feel it, lurking in the shadows, just beyond the bend, waiting to tear this people asunder.*

Will they be able to endure? Or will they altogether forget the One who is the source for all their needs? How natural it is to lean on the Lord, our Strength and Sustainer, in the presence of danger; yet, how easy it is in times of prosperity, when fear and urgency cease, to become complacent, to forget promises made.

Still looking at the ground, twirling a twig betwixt his forefinger and thumb, Samuel became aware of approaching footfalls.

Now what? Never a moment's peace from these petty quarrels!

Lifting his head, he beheld all the elders of Israel gathering before him. Samuel fixed his eyes upon the elder in the forefront.

Gadowl—the very name left a bitter taste in his mouth. The old prophet could not forget the trouble this elder had caused the people. Many years of sorrow followed that counsel, and many had paid a heavy price.

There was a long spell of silence in which the recipient of Samuel's stern gaze grew restless with discomfort.

Drawing himself up, Gadowl broke the taut air, a wry smile breaking across his wrinkled face. "Behold, thou art old, and thy sons, O Samuel, walk not in thy ways."

The words stung, but the old prophet hid his distress, keeping his gaze unmoved.

Extending his hand to the west, Gadowl continued, "Look at the nations among us. They are strong, and powerful. Their barns are full of grain and their people work as one. They have iron implements and weapons aplenty. Strong armies protect their lands and people. The Philistines stretch out their arms in all directions. It will not be long before they desire the regions returned to us after the battle of Mizpah. Even now, we hear rumors of threats to our security. Peace will not long endure."

With one eye closed against the westering sun, Samuel asked, suspicious of the answer forthcoming. "What is it that you would have me do?" There was an edge to Samuel's voice.

It was the question for which the aged elder was waiting. A smile slid across Gadowl's face, edging through the veil of his restrained countenance, hinting at his hidden agenda.

"Make us a king to rule over us," declared Gadowl, "like all the other nations."

Samuel grew tense. He took in a deep breath, and exhaled as he forced his body to relax. Even so, his expression remained unaltered, his inner thoughts shrouded from those who awaited his response.

Gazing once more to his twig, he raised it before his face, examining it closely. He twirled it this way, then that, narrowing his eyes to bring the scion into focus.

The prophet began to speak, his voice soft and gentle, each word spoken with deliberate intent. Ever his eyes remained on the twig.

"It is said that the trees once went forth to anoint a king over them.

> And they said to the olive tree,
> > 'Reign over us!'

> But the olive tree said to them,
> > 'Should I cease giving my oil,
> > With which they honor God and men,
> > And go to sway over trees?'

> Then the trees said to the fig tree,
> > 'You come and reign over us!'

> But the fig tree said to them,
> > 'Should I cease my sweetness and my good fruit,
> > And go to sway over trees?'

Then the trees said to the vine,
'You come and reign over us!'

But the vine said to them,
'Should I cease my new wine,
Which cheers both God and men,
And go to sway over trees?'

Then all the trees said to the bramble,
'You come and reign over us!'

And the bramble said to the trees,
'If in truth you anoint me as king over you,
Then come and take shelter in my shade;
But if not, let fire come out of the bramble
And devour the cedars of Lebanon!'"[2]

Growing impatient, Gadowl spoke sternly, "What do trees have to do with us? See how you wander in speech. No, we need a king, as the nations around us have their kings."

"I ask you," spoke the prophet, as again he squinted up at Gadowl, "what shade or protection can there be in a bramble? Is not the true purpose of the bramble but to kindle the fire and in so doing destroy the noble cedar? How can the people of Yahweh take shelter under the shadow of a lesser king?"

Surveying the assembly of elders before him, Samuel settled upon Tiphcar. "Is this your wish as well, Tiphcar, old friend?"

"The council has discussed these matters," answered the old captain returning Samuel's gaze. "It is the will of the elders, though not my own desire, but I must heed the wants of the majority."

The old prophet beheld Tiphcar in sorrow and nodded Closing his eyes, he lowered his face and took in a slow breath.

"When you have eaten and are full," spoke Samuel, "beware that you do not forget the Lord your God."[3]

---

[2] Judges 9:7—15

[3] Deuteronomy 8:10—11

Anger festered within him as he pondered the request. "Woeful stupidity!" cried Samuel, turning upon the elders. His brow was furrowed, his eyes aflame. "You have taken the jewels of heaven and cast them at the feet of swine.[4] You have buffed out the glory of their shine and made them dull as the rocks upon the ground. You do not want for a king!"

The prophet lifted a hand toward heaven. "The Lord Almighty is your King. Where does your rejection stop? At the worship of other gods?"

Taking a deep breath, Samuel calmed himself and lowered his gaze. His voice softened. "This thing you ask of me is not for me to decide. Come back tomorrow, for I must speak to the Lord regarding this matter."

"Samuel," cautioned Gadowl, "time is waning. We need an answer. Our enemies will not wait for an old man to make up his mind. We will be answered!"

"And you shall." Samuel spoke with an edge of annoyance, though he kept his voice low and calm. "Tomorrow."

Gadowl growled, but said no more. The elders turned to leave, stirring up dust in their wake. Samuel sat where he was, watching as they walked away, their backs to him.

"So, they do not want me to speak for them any more." Closing his eyes, the old prophet shook his head from side to side. "All my long life, even from my childhood, I have served these people." Samuel looked to heaven as tears welled in his wise eyes. "And now they reject me as judge, for they deem I am old and useless. Maybe I am. I am not as young as I used to be. My body is tired.

"But this thing they request is vile. I know it in my heart."

As he sat there, gall rose within him. "A king! They do not know what they ask!"

Dropping his twig, Samuel gained his feet, leaning heavily upon the wall. He let out an involuntary "O" as he pulled himself erect. Heaviness lay upon his frame as he passed through the gate, taking note that the sun was low in the west.

The fortifications of the city stood strong and high, a vast heap of great stones hewn and set with precision, the very weight of them

---

[4] Matthew 7:6

15

holding firm their place. Along the wall were several openings appointed for the daily traffic to pass into the city. Large towers, one on each side and one directly above the gate, loomed down upon Samuel as upward he glanced. He raised his hand over his eyes to shield them from the setting sun. Great wooden doors, heavy and strong, hung open on either side of the entrance.

It is getting late; soon the gates will be shut for the night.

Gathering a slow breath, Samuel girded his strength and trudged through the city, past the market place, and down a side street, until he reached the path to the high place.

Ramathaim-Zophim, or Ramah, sat upon a hill, the city built on multiple levels. Within the lower section, where the terrain was less rocky, most of the homes were set.

But it was to the highest point of Ramah that the old prophet was bound. As he strove up the steep incline, Samuel came to a flat, stony clearing. It was here that he had raised an altar to the Lord.

Pausing to catch his breath, Samuel leaned forward, resting both hands upon his knees. When he had recovered, the old prophet lifted his head and observed the high place.

Before him stood the large platform made of an unhewn boulder, for no stone cut by human means was permitted as an altar to the One True God. After providing the evening sacrifice, Samuel approached the sacred dais and knelt down before it.

His voice toward heaven, he prayed unto *El Elyon*, the One Who is above all.

"It is for Israel my tears do fall, and for her my prayers are uplifted. Forbid that ever I shall cease to intercede on her behalf whilst breath remains within me. Till all care and strength are lost to me, I will hold her before You.

"These people, whom You have purchased, in their pride and ingratitude, have thus rejected me as judge and You, O Lord, as rightful King.

"They wish to be numbered among the nations, no longer chosen from among the races. No more do they believe that You, O God, will fight their battles for them.

"Lord protect them from their own desires, for they do not understand what it is they ask. This thing they request is evil. Do not grant this, which they seek, for this cure is worse than the difficulties we now face!"

After a time, a voice of one like thunder resounded upon his mind. Samuel knew this voice, for he had heard it before. And in his heart, he perceived that the Lord desired the prophet listen to the words of the people and give them what they asked.

Yet it was not Samuel whom the people rejected, but Yahweh, for they did not desire that He should reign over them. So it has been since the day the Lord brought the people up out of Egypt, even unto this day, wherewith they have forsaken their Lord and served other gods.

Now therefore, the Lord instructed that Samuel should hearken to the voice of the people. However, the prophet was to solemnly protest and show them the ways of the king who shall reign over them. For what they ask was far more serious than even the prophet knew.

Now Samuel, being weary of heart, agreed to do as Yahweh commanded, though it was not his wish.

Betrayed! These ungrateful people will rue the day they desired a king.

Disgust swept over Samuel as he rose. He closed his eyes and drew breath, striving to still the tempest rising in his breast.

They have become a stiff-necked people, looking this way and that. They have forgotten the promise made to the Creator by their forbearers.

Slow steps and with head bowed, Samuel made his way down from the sacred place. He followed the path that entered into the heart of the city. It was late. The sun had set, yet the afterglow of the day-star illuminated the western sky.

Within the fading light, Samuel navigated through the narrow streets of Ramah. The markets had closed for the night. People were hurrying home for their evening meal. He could smell the sweet aromas wafting upon a faint breeze. His stomach grumbled.

Samuel soon approached a modest home, constructed of limestone rock, which had been joined together with mortar made of lime, sand, and water. Though his permanent residence was the Naioth, the prophet's house of instruction, Samuel had taken a humble dwelling within the city so that he could escape the demands of his students. After traveling and ministering to the people, he found it necessary to have the solitude of an abode apart from his duties.

17

He opened the door and slid inside. It was dark within and the air was stale. After a few moments of fumbling, he found a lamp and lit it. Light poured across the chamber revealing a sparsely furnished area that served as eating, living, and sleeping quarters.

Scrolls and parchments cluttered the small table at the center of the room. A reed pen and an inkhorn lay forgotten on an overturned clay pot. Several well-worn mats were strewn across the floor, a bed roll had been flung aside near the wall.

Samuel closed and latched the door. Crossing to the far corner, he bent over the brazier and stirred the fading coals, kindling them against the evening chill.

Despite the coolness of the evening, he drew aside the heavy curtain from the narrow window, permitting a fresh breeze to enter and drive out the close, must-laden air of the chamber. Moonlight slipped through the lattice that covered the opening, casting a mesh of shadow across the floor. The old prophet filled a cup from the jug set beneath the window. For a time he lingered there, gazing through the woven slats, lost in thought, the cup untasted in his hand. At length he stirred from his reverie and drank deeply, the water easing the dryness of his throat.

Reaching for a basket, he grabbed a few dates and a stale loaf of bread. *A meager meal after a trying day.* He ate in silence, sitting alone in his little room, until he was content, and then spread out his bed roll.

He fell asleep as soon as he lay upon the mat.

The darkness of night permeated the room as Samuel awoke with a start. His mind was full of words that flowed deep from his memory, a prayer he had heard before, drawn from a time long ago.

> My heart rejoices in the Lord;
>> My horn is exalted in the Lord.
>> I smile at my enemies,
>> Because I rejoice in Your salvation.
>
> No one is holy like the Lord,
>> For there is none besides You,
>> Nor is there any rock like our God.

Talk no more so very proudly;
>Let no arrogance come from your mouth,
>For the Lord is the God of knowledge;
>And by Him actions are weighed.

The bows of the mighty men are broken,
>And those who stumbled are girded with strength.

The Lord kills and makes alive;
>He brings down to the grave and brings up.
The Lord makes poor and makes rich;
>He brings low and lifts up.
He raises the poor from the dust
>And lifts the beggar from the ash heap,
>To set them among princes
>And make them inherit the throne of glory.

For the pillars of the earth are the Lord's,
>And He has set the world upon them.
He will guard the feet of His saints,
>But the wicked shall be silent in darkness.

For by strength no man shall prevail.
The adversaries of the Lord shall be broken in pieces;
>From heaven He will thunder against them.
>The Lord will judge the ends of the earth.

>He will give strength to His king,
>And exalt the horn of His anointed.[5]

The soft voice of his mother, Hannah, grew within him. It had been many years since he had thought of her. *Those are her words. Why do they come to me now, after so much time has passed?* Pondering this, Samuel lay back upon his bed and looked up at the ceiling.

Tomorrow, everything will change. Shadows stretched long as the night wore on, the moon peeking in through the open window. The air had

---

[5] 1 Samuel 2:1−10

grown still and silent. Soon, Samuel drifted off into a fitful slumber, his mind in conflict even as sleep came upon him.

CHAPTER 3

A KING OVER US

The cock crowed. Beams of light glinted across his face.

"What?"

With reluctance, Samuel opened his eyes and groaned. How could it be dawn when he had just fallen asleep? Stiff he was, his movements slow as he rose from bed. For a moment he stood still, drawing deep breaths to claim his balance and gather his senses. Bending at the waist, he took hold his mat and tossed it back into the corner of his cluttered room. He poured water into a clay basin and splashed it upon his drowsy face, then shook his head against the cold.

"Unwelcome frost!"

He was ill-tempered as he grabbed a morsel of food and headed toward the main gate of the city. He knew the elders would be gathered there, waiting for his answer. Legs of lead he bore as he pushed himself forward. The weight of his burden lay heavy upon him. At this moment, Samuel wished he had never been called as judge over Israel.

Has all my work been in vain? Has anything really changed? The people still look for help from lesser sources. They yet refuse to rest upon Yahweh, and wholly trust in His leadership. So then, what has it all been for?

The morning teemed with activity. Shop owners were busy setting up for the day's market. Voices rose over the sounds of wagon wheels and the unloading of crates. It seemed that goats and children scurried everywhere, around carts and under tables, bleating and squealing with glee.

"Samuel, Samuel!" called several children, running up to him.

"*Shalom*, my little ones," the old prophet spoke with a gentle voice.

They threw their arms around his waist, a few found his legs. He almost lost his balance, but managed to center himself after the onslaught ceased.

"Enough, enough," cried Samuel, patting some upon the head. Despite his mood, he found himself smiling. *It is for these little ones, that is the cause for which I strive.*

"I must be on my way," spoke the prophet tenderly as he stroked the head of a child. "The elders wait at the gate."

Releasing their hold upon him, the children waved as they ran off in various directions. The smile upon the prophet's face faded as he resumed his pace toward the entrance of the city. As he reached the gate, he saw a large group of people waiting.

"*Shalom Aleichem*, peace be unto you," greeted Samuel, his voice solemn.

"*Aleichem Shalom*, upon you be peace, Samuel. Have you come to a decision regarding our request?"

Samuel shot a stern glance at Gadowl. "I have spoken to *El Elyon*, the Almighty, Who was from the beginning."

"And what did He say?" asked Zaqen, standing to his left.

He turned to the elder. "Tell me, my brother, is your heart set on this thing? Do you deal thusly with the Lord, O foolish and unwise people? Is He not your Father who bought you? Will you all forget this and return to your homes?"

"We will not relent. Our hearts are set." All spoke, save Tiphcar who stood aside as though loathe to be associated with the others. His arms were crossed about his chest; his gaze was fixed upon the ground.

Samuel conveyed to the elders all that Yahweh had spoken to him, each word weighing heavily upon his tongue. "This will be the *mishpat*, or manner, of the king who shall reign over you: he will rule with arbitrary and absolute power. He will take your sons and appoint them for himself, for his chariots and to be his horsemen; and some shall run before his chariots as messengers to announce the king's coming.

"And he will appoint him captains over thousands and captains over fifties, and will set them to till his ground and to reap his harvest, and to make his instruments of war and instruments of his chariots.

"And he will take your daughters to be confectioners and to be cooks and to be bakers. And he will seize your fields and your vineyards and your olive yards—even the best of them—and give them to his servants.

"And he will demand a tenth of your seed and of your vineyards, and give to his officers and to his servants. And he will take your menservants, and your maidservants, and your goodliest young men, and your beasts of burden, and put them to his work.

"He will require a tenth of your sheep; and you shall be his servants. And you shall cry out because of your king that you have chosen; and the Lord will not hear you in that day."

Samuel paused to let his words sink into the hearts of the elders. Yet, as the old prophet surveyed the faces of the men before him, their countenances appeared unaffected by his speech.

In frustration he spoke, "So, I ask you again. Are your hearts set? Will you not forgo this foolishness?"

The elders looked upon one another, stern and unmoved.

Gadowl turned toward Samuel. "Nay; but we will have a king over us, that we also may be like all the nations, and that our king may judge us and go out before us and fight our battles."

The old prophet hung his head. He raised his hand to his brow as a dull ache formed behind his eyes. With his lids closed, Samuel shook his head. "Did not Moses tell your fathers in the wilderness not to be afraid? The Lord, your God, has ever gone before you. He has fought for you, according to all that He has done for your fathers in Egypt, and in the wilderness. The Lord carried them."

Samuel walked among the elders, pleading with them, his hands outstretched as he looked upon their faces. "Did not Yahweh say that if you prepare your hearts for the Lord, and serve Him only, He would deliver you from your enemies? Was *El Elyon*, your God, not faithful to deliver you from the hands of the Philistines at Mizpah? He is your true and only King; you need no other."

"Nay, we have spoken!" rebuked Gadowl.

Samuel stood, looking upon the hard countenances of the men before him. Many crossed their arms about their breasts and set their feet wide, as though forming a stout wall of resistance. Unyielding, the elders looked upon the prophet with harsh expressions. The silent stalemate continued as each side refused to give way.

Ashamed, Tiphcar lowered his face, for he could not gaze upon Samuel. *What have I done? There was a time I would have fought.*

I wonder at my decision to join the Council of Elders. I would take a sword any day over this battle of speech. My tongue is not sharp enough to prevail against this enemy. No, I am not made to mince words.

Samuel saw that they would not be appeased, yet he did not yield.

"Come again tomorrow, and I will deliver my answer, for I must consult once more with Yahweh." His heart remained unbent before the command of his God. *Surely, the Lord will relent if I but ask Him one more time.*

"Why do you delay?" Gadowl scowled. "The night will not change our hearts."

"Even so," replied Samuel, "I must ask you to allow me this one favor. It is for my own peace of mind. If Yahweh has nothing more to say, then I will be content."

The group of men turned and dispersed, shaking their heads.

It is a fearful thing they demand, thought the old prophet.

And so, as in times past, the Chosen Race of Yahweh refused to heed the voice of His prophet—the very one appointed by God to deliver His word to the people.

CHAPTER 4

A Changed Destiny

Clouds gathered about the distant summits, lingering until the heat of day could spend the moisture and dispel the shadow of mist. The rise of Ramah could be seen in the distance, north, ascending above the cloud veil. Below, the valley lay, undulating waves of earth, foothills carpeted in golden tassels and unbroken tussocks of green. The coolness of night lingered. Dew clung to the flora like a myriad of tiny white jewels. The face of nature was green and lush after the latter rains, pleasant and reviving, ripening the crops and the awakening verdure of the fields. The sky spread serene, the expanse wide and blue, with wisps of thin white vapor painted across the arch of heaven.

Tall upon the ridge, a lone figure stood, Saul, son of Kish, as was his wont, ever looking over the hills and plains of Benjamin toward the rising of the sun. The ends of his tawny hair, caught in the gentle breeze, fluttered about his face and danced upon his shoulders, teasing the full beard that grew upon his pleasing face. High in stature, from his shoulders upward, Saul stood taller than any of the people. Great was the extent of his shoulders, his size lofty, his strength well-supplied. Strongly marked, he was the splendor of great men of old, brave and valiant. Proud was his bearing, though humble was his heart.

His dark eyes narrowed as the sun shone across his bronzed skin. Saul breathed in the morning air. The musty smell of damp soil rose, bringing with it a contented feeling of good earth and plenteous times. The full force of his happy life fell upon him with a wave of joy as he softly quoted:

> Benjamin, the beloved of the Lord,
> Shall dwell in safety by Him,
> Who shields him all the day long;
> And shall dwell in between the shoulders
> *of His mountains.*[6]

"Saul."

Startled, he turned. "Ahinoam, what are you doing here?"

"It is your father. He is looking for you. I knew that I would find you here."

Saul smiled at his wife. "Is it not beautiful? Almost as beautiful as you, Ahinoam, daughter of Ahimaaz." He reached his arms around Ahinoam's waist, encircling her in his muscular embrace. "It is all I ever wanted, to be here with you, to work the land. Everything we could desire is here. See, you have even given me fine sons. I lack nothing. I am fulfilled to all ends."

Ahinoam looked up into the handsome face of Saul. Goodly to behold, for truly there was not a more splendid person than he among the children of Israel. How fortunate she felt to have such a man to call her own. Many there were who envied her.

"Saul."

He bent his gaze upon his wife, her visage comely and fair. A strand of her dark hair had escaped its plaiting and whipped across her face. He brushed it away, tucking the silky tendril behind her ear.

Suddenly moved, he took her face in both his hands. Saul kissed Ahinoam, his mouth gentle against her lips.

"What is it my love?" he whispered.

Almost forgetting her mission, Ahinoam grasped Saul by the arms and pulled away from his loving hold. "It is your father. He is quite distressed and is asking for you. Please, you must go to him."

A flash of concern swept across Saul's face. Placing an arm around Ahinoam's back, he led her down the ridge. "Let us go then, and see what we can do."

---

[6] Deuteronomy 33:12

Gibeah stood upon the height, northeast of Kirjath-Jearim, twin cities whose boundary line ran along the road leading to the coastal plains. From its summit, the important central Benjaminite Plain could be viewed. Many torrent beds and deep ravines cut through this vast mountainous region, following the watershed, linking the land to the hills of Ephraim.

Kish, son of Ner, a Benjamite descended from Aphiah, a mighty man of power and influence, waited upon the hill overlooking the pasture. As he spotted Saul and Ahinoam coming over the rise, he hurried to meet them, wringing his hands in concern.

"Ah, Saul, my son, there you are."

"*Abba*, what is the cause of your distress? How is it that I can help you?"

Kish lifted his eyes to the devoted gaze of his choice son.

"I have dispatched messengers to seek the donkeys that were grazing in the pastures," shaking his head in wonder, he continued, "but they have been unable to locate them. In all my days, I have not seen the likes of this. The beasts have ever been obedient and loyal to their master, yet today my she-donkeys have wandered off and are lost. Please," Kish spoke in earnest as he took hold of Saul's arms, "take one of the servants with you, and arise, go and search for the donkeys."

Saul placed his hands, one on each of his father's well-braced shoulders and looked down into his dark eyes, still strong and full of life. "As you wish, *Abba*, so shall I do."

Taking leave with the nod of his head, Saul walked over to his wife and, as he ran his hand down her silky hair, his lips brushed hers in a gentle kiss.

Ziba, the servant of Kish, waited, already burdened with the journey's provisions. Saul smiled, his face alight, as he approached Ziba and clapped the youth upon the back.

"Off we go then, a trek across the mountains."

"Yes, *adon*. It is as you say. We are well supplied."

"You are a good lad, Ziba. Lead on."

So spoken, Saul turned to behold Ahinoam one last time. As he did so, his heart lurched with apprehension, the leeward pitch of a changed destiny. And though he loathed their parting, he would not neglect his father in need.

Thus began Saul's wandering and eventful journey in pursuit of the wayward donkeys. Henceforth, a change would be wrought, the course of which was laid out beyond his making, the order of things a fixed path set before him.

CHAPTER 5

QUITCLAIM

The remainder of the day was spent in prayer and fasting. He did not return to the city gate, as was his wont, to make judgments for the people. Solemn was his mood, and as a shadow fell upon him, he withdrew, speaking to none but the Lord.

As the sun sank once more in the west, he set his steps toward the high place. There, upon the hill's height, the prophet gazed beyond the far reaches of the earth.

A magnificent view was the reward for his efforts. Southward stretched the plain of the Salt Sea, its water glinting as crystal across the horizon. North to south, a line of mountains cleaved the landscape in twain, a purple glow illuminating the uplifted pedestal. Westward lay the long coastline of the Great Sea whose waters were aflame in the setting sun.

His breath escaped as he returned his gaze to the altar. All that the people had spoken he remembered, for he had turned it over in his mind the entire day. Lifting his voice, he recounted the words in the ears of the Lord.

Yet, Yahweh did not yield, but commanded the prophet to give the people what they desired.

Samuel dared not argue with the Lord. Reluctant steps led him home, grieving within his heart for the people of Israel.

They do not understand what they are about to bring upon themselves.

Sitting down at his table, the prophet reached for his reed pen and parchment and began writing all that had transpired. When the account was complete, he felt compelled to add a passage at the bottom of the scroll:

> For by strength no man shall prevail.
> The adversaries of the Lord shall be broken in pieces;
> From heaven He will thunder against them.
> The Lord will judge the ends of the earth.[7]

Samuel blew across the page to dry the ink, and leaned back satisfied with his work.

"The record has been set for the generations that follow. The cost of what they ask will be evident to all."

Setting the parchment aside, he laid himself down to rest.

The sun had been up for nearly an hour before Samuel stirred from his slumber. Dreading what was to transpire, he rose to begin preparations. Hunger plagued him, recalling his fast of the previous day.

"I must have food before I face the elders."

Grabbing his cloak from the peg by the door, Samuel journeyed from his home, winding through the narrow passageways between houses built so close one could walk across town without setting foot on the ground.

It was a brief jaunt to the baker's shop where he received bread and cheese, which he washed down with a jar of water. Refreshed, he knew he could not delay the events that were to unfold any longer. He continued his trek through the market street to the main gate.

As before, a crowd had assembled about the entrance, speaking to one another with animated gestures. Upon seeing Samuel's approach, the men rushed forward, some wringing their hands.

---

[7] 1 Samuel 2:9–10

Zaqen spoke as he reached his hand toward the prophet. "Samuel, you have come at last. We have been gathered here since ere the sun rose. We mean to receive your answer today."

"And so you shall, my brother. Patience, while an old man recovers his breath."

The prophet leaned his hand upon the wall of the city. Gazing down at the place where the masonry met the ground, he steadied himself, drawing breath deep. Small sprigs of dry grass strove within the juncture of earth and stone.

"Samuel," Gadowl's voice cut sharply. "We need your answer. The people grow impatient with your delays. I fear there will be trouble if we do not come to a decision at once."

The prophet drew himself up and spoke to the men of Israel, each word measured and deliberate. "I do not hold with what you request. It is folly to desire a king other than *El Elyon*, the sovereign Lord."

"Samuel—" interrupted Gadowl.

Raising his hand to quiet the elder, Samuel continued, "Nevertheless, the Lord has spoken, saying, 'Hearken to their voices, and make them a king.' I cannot refuse *Adonai*, my Master, who rules heaven and earth. Go you every man to his own city. All will be as you have asked."

A smile of triumph crept across Gadowl's face. He nodded at the prophet, and turned to the elders. "So it shall be. Go, do as the prophet says." Fixing his gaze upon Samuel, with narrowed eyes, the elder spoke in a quiet tone. "And Samuel, do not delay in choosing. We will have our king."

Samuel lifted his chin with a grunt, casting his eyes down his nose at Gadowl.

Hands and words were alike in eager motion as the men of Israel departed, obeying the voice of the prophet.

Tiphcar turned, his weary eyes meeting Samuel's. Sighing, the old captain lowered his head and walked away, his hands clasped before him.

That was the last Samuel saw of Tiphcar this side of the grave, for soon after, the long years of conflict bore down upon the old captain. And as the former ways of the Chosen of God perished, so too Tiphcar drew his final breath.

Samuel tarried not, but departed from Ramah that very day, going upon his circuit through the cities, ministering to the people of Israel and waiting upon Yahweh—the One who should have been king.

CHAPTER 6

HOLY SEAT

The weather was fair. A faint breeze wafted across the swelling landscape as the two wayfarers worked their way through the countryside. Unknowing was Saul of the path he was taking and the destination he would find, though in obedience to his father he went, desiring only to fulfill his obligation to Kish. How often it seems that great events are first accomplished through trifling matters. Yet the loss of the donkeys was no small occurrence, but an incident that would bear great consequence. They had set out in a northwesterly direction. For twenty-five miles they wandered, seemingly aimless as the two trekked after the wayward animals.

As they navigated the distant course, Saul made mention to the shepherds they encountered, inquiring after the stray animals bearing the mark of Kish, yet to no avail, for the donkeys remained elusive. Therefore, Saul and his servant passed north through the mountains of Ephraim, across dense woods and fertile valleys. Turning southward, they journeyed as far as Shalisha over the verdant hills where the fruit ripened first among all places east of the Great Sea.

Here it was that three vales converged into a great ravine, a wild and uninhabited region known as the Land of Jackals. The path was desolate and isolated. The hollow sound of the wind ripped through the valley, a moaning wail pursuing the men, haunting their footsteps.

"I do not think the beasts have come this way. It is a quarter that speaks a warning to any who enter. Let us leave this place."

Ziba nodded as he looked upon the high walls that encircled their heads, eager to escape the shadow of the gorge.

The land grew more gentle and green, with sloping hills and vales that swept across the horizon. Saul and his servant walked on through a gap in the mountains and entered into a lush landscape, a secluded retreat. A well-marked path led their approach, gradually rising to the height of an abandoned city. Scattered beside the way were several large cisterns cracked and ruined, no longer suitable for their intended purpose. In all directions, the city clung to steep cliffs and rocky ledges. The tattered gatehouse was the only entrance into the ruins, the walls of which now lay crumbled and burnt.

"I know this place," Saul spoke in a hushed tone as he pushed aside some fallen debris with his foot.

Ziba looked at his master knowingly, for he, too, understood.

"I remember coming here as a child. Three times a year we would come to worship Yahweh, to bring offerings to His house. There, on the hill it was that the Tabernacle stood." Saul pointed with his outstretched hand to a rise on the edge of town.

The son of Kish remained motionless, looking at the leveled city, to the cloven walls of the temple court. Shiloh. The Holy City.

Ensnared, Saul walked as one drawn against his will, step by step, toward the temple mount. A lone gate hung precariously on a single ruined hinge, desperately clinging to the remnants of the crumbled wall. Holes in the ground marked where the canvas roof had been fastened. Several steps led the way up to the place the five brazen pillars had denoted the entrance to the Tabernacle. The threshold was bare, for no columns endured. Before the doorpost was a level platform where once a stool had been set, a place upon which the priest could sit. No priest sat there now. No altar. No sacrifice. No sweet aroma. Just empty space—Yahweh's dwelling place on earth, deserted... desolate.

Saul stood over the burnt masonry, stilled by the sight of the ruined Tabernacle. Grass now grew in the cracks of the rubble. Creeping things crawled where the priests and prophets once trod. Where praises had been lifted to Yahweh, now sickly quiet rested upon the land. A chill ran down his spine. A warning weighed upon his heart. Mute and unsettled, Saul lingered as a hollowness entered his soul.

He was pulled from his reflection as his foot kicked something in the dust. Kneeling down, Saul reached into the ash and lifted out a doll, the fabric faded and tattered, even burnt in places. Carefully, he brushed the dust from the damaged figure. His eyes locked with the painted eyes of the child's toy. *What lives were shattered within this city?* Life for the tribes had changed. The very center of their religious worship had been stripped from them. Now they were a people who had no approach to their God. And he wondered if ever a way could be found to bring Yahweh back to the people.

Saul found his voice and in a hushed whisper he spoke, "He felt so close to us then. Now, He has been driven away."

Anger stirred within his heart and he rose with fervor for the destruction of the Tabernacle at Shiloh. "We turned Him out, and He is gone. He will never come to this hill again, for we have banished Him."

Tucking the doll into his belt, Saul made to leave. Ziba gazed upon his master in awe, for he looked a different man. His jaw was set and he had a driven stare in his eyes, as though he saw into the distance a future happening that only a prophet could attain.

"My *adon?*"

Saul met his servant's questioning eyes. He blinked and the moment passed. "Let us leave this place." He shook his head. "My soul is disquieted within me. I do not wish to tarry. We must return to our duty."

And with that, Saul forsook the temple mount. He walked beyond the ancient fig tree on the west side of the court, past a row of large clay jars that still held raisins charred in the torching of the city, through the gap in the crumpled walls, past the amphitheater and rock-cut tombs, where the High Priest Eli lay east of the city, until he left Shiloh far behind, for there they had made a house for Yahweh, then turned Him out.

As he put his back to the ruined relic of a holy city, so walked Saul, son of Kish, the footsteps of one predestined.

CHAPTER 7

PLACE OF HONOR

Beyond Shiloh and the vales of the Jordan, a day's journey from Shechem, they saw no sign of the donkeys. So they traversed over another day as far as the land of Shaalim upon the west side of the mountain range, along the slopes east of Lod, but they found them not. Approaching again the borders of Benjamin, Saul passed eastward through the land, scouring the territory until they entered into the district of Zuph.

The bareness he had known at Shiloh had not left him. He was altogether downcast, as when fellowship is broken and a friend departs, leaving no word of farewell. Saul could not shake the sense of being empty and alone in a world beyond his control. At length, its burden overcame him, and despair settled upon the wandering son of Kish.

"Days we have been gone in search of these donkeys," spoke Saul, shaking his head. "They are lost to us. Come, let us return, lest my father cease caring for the donkeys and become worried about us."

"Do not lose hope, my *adon*," answered Ziba. "A thought has come to me. Look now." He pointed to the rise of Ramah and continued, "I have heard there is in this city a man of God, and he is an honorable man. His reputation is well known throughout the land. All that he says surely comes to pass. So let us go there. Perhaps he can show us the way that we should go."

"How can this be accomplished? Is it not customary to bring a gift as an offering before one requests a service such as this? But look," reasoned Saul, "if we go, what shall we bring the man? For the bread in our vessel is gone, and there is no present to give to the man of God. What do we have? We cannot approach this seer empty-handed, lest we bring a curse upon our heads."

The servant spoke as he opened his hand to show his master. "See here, I have at hand one-fourth of a *shekel* of silver. I will give it to the man of God that he may tell us our way."

Saul's face lightened as he looked upon the coin in his servant's palm. "Well said. Come, let us go and seek this seer and in so doing, may it be that we will fulfill my father's wishes."

The approach to the city followed the upward grade of the land. South of the road, the village crowned the elevated height of a limestone hill. Cisterns could be seen scattered throughout the surrounding countryside, dotting the undulating landscape. West of the city sat a reservoir, its store of water glittering in the evening sun.

As the two men ascended the rise, they met some young women going out to draw water from the good well, just beyond the gates south of the city. Each bore a clay vessel upon her shoulder, steadying it with upraised arms against her head. At the sight of Saul, the maid-servants whispered to one another.

The son of Kish advanced toward the maidens as they drew near. Seeing how pleasing Saul was, the young women eagerly gathered to hear what he had to say, basking in his attention.

With one eye squinted to ward off the glare of the sun, Saul looked upon the maidens. "*Shalom.*"

"*Shalom,*" greeted the girls in unison.

"Can you tell me, is the seer here?"

"Yes, there he is," answered one of the young women as she turned, pointing in the direction of the gate, "just ahead of you. You must hurry if you wish to speak to him, for today he has come to this city to make sacrifice for the people. The prophet is going up to the feast for all is ready, so you have little time."

"As soon as you enter the city," encouraged another, "you will surely find him before he goes up to the *bamah*, that is, the high place. The people will not eat until he comes, because he must bless the sacrifice; afterward those who are invited will eat. If you make haste you can catch him, for about this time you will find him."

Smiling, Saul inclined his head toward the girls and spoke, "*Todah*, thank you, you have been most helpful." As he turned, Saul thought he heard the maidens giggle. *I wonder what is so amusing.* Casting the thought aside, he turned to Ziba and said, "Come then, let us go up to the city."

As they entered through the gates, Saul and his servant beheld a man coming toward them on his way out of the city. His hair was the color of ashes, whitened by age, his beard full and gray, his eyes soft and venerable.

Saul stepped forward to meet him. "*Shalom uv'racha*, peace and blessing, *adon*, forgive me. Please tell me, where is the seer's house for I have need of his service?"

The elder man stood silent for a time, looking up at Saul as though marking the details of his face. Smiling, he spoke, "I am Samuel, the seer."

"Go up before me to the high place, for you shall eat with me today. And tomorrow I will let you go and will tell you all that is in your heart. As for your donkeys that were lost three days ago, do not be anxious about them, for they have been found."

Saul fixed his gaze on Samuel. Speech fled; his eyes widened, and he stood unmoving before the prophet.

Samuel continued, his face suddenly serious: "And on whom is all the desire of Israel—?" He placed his hand upon Saul's shoulder and leaned toward him. The seer's expression softened. "Is it not on you and on all your father's house?"

Stunned, Saul answered and said, "Am I not a Benjaminite, of the smallest of the tribes of Israel, and my family the least of all the families of the tribe of Benjamin? Why then do you speak to me in this manner?"

"What is your name, son?"

"I am called Saul, son of Kish."

"*Asked of*, you are," Samuel muttered as he rubbed his chin.

Well pleased, Samuel looked upon the great and goodly form of Saul. "Indeed, the very image…"

"I do not understand. I am only seeking lost donkeys, nothing more."

Smiling, Samuel nodded. "Even the smallest trifles are arranged by the hand of God. Now, come, you will dine with me tonight."

Placing a hand upon Saul's shoulder, Samuel redirected his course and walked Saul, and his servant with him, to the high place which lay outside the city proper.

The strength of day waned in the western sky as Saul, guided by the prophet of God, reached the summit of the *bamah*. The altar of the Lord stood upon the highest rise, the evening Peace Offering consumed within the fire. Next to the holy pedestal stood a *cukkah*, that is a pavilion, made of twelve upright poles of wood, one for each tribe, connected by cross branches, binding the beams into one unified structure. The twining vine of the morning flower grew up and over the top of the booth, its leaves, heart-shaped and green. The roof, being flat and covered by a network of twigs and grass wattled together, provided protection from the warmth of the sun

A breeze filtered through the chamber, for the walls remained open, save one thatched backdrop located behind the head table. Seated upon mats around three narrow tables arranged in an open-ended square were thirty people of influence.

"Come, please, sit down." Samuel smiled as he gestured toward the head of the table, the most honored seat. "We have been waiting for you and have saved your place."

"Waiting for me?" Saul again was struck with awe. He did not move, but looked at the favored seat as a shadow passed over his brow.

"Yes, the offering has been made and the guests await the meal. See, I have invited the leading citizens of Ramah to join us."

Saul walked over to the center of the head table and sat as instructed. A ripple of confusion passed through him as he sensed all eyes burning into him.

How strange that these people are here.

Samuel joined Saul and stood to his right. Reaching behind, he plucked a flower from the vine. Pondering the sight of the failing blossom, Samuel spoke to the assembly.

"Woe the crown and grandeur of his splendor, for all flesh is grass and all his faithfulness is like the flowers of the field, whose glorious beauty is a fading flower.[8] The unopened spiral bud of a morning

---

[8] 1 Peter 1:24

flower bursts forth with the new dawn, rising for a day, then fades and is extinguished. Short and vibrant in existence is the waning bloom as it withers in the heat of the sun."

Pausing, Samuel brought the flower close before his eyes and marked the quality of its form. With a quick nod, the prophet smiled and turned to the guests, gesturing toward the blossom in his hand. "Yet its inner life holds a star even as the fading glory curls in upon itself under the unveiling of the day lamp, even as the light burns out its radiance. Truly the light is sweet, and it is pleasant for the eyes to behold the sun."

Samuel hesitated. Turning his focus upon the man Saul, he looked deep into his eyes as though drawing out his soul. "Therefore glorify the Lord in the dawning light, which reveals secret things, that your vision not be in error and your judgment not a stumbling block."

Releasing Saul's gaze, Samuel returned his attention to the crowd. "The flesh of the sacrifice of the Peace Offering has been made for thanksgiving, that we may be accepted by God and may have peace with Yahweh, by the shedding of this innocent blood. We look forward to newness of life and peace through the anointed of God, which He will grant to His people. Eat therefore, and rejoice before the Lord your God, to serve, to give thanks, and to praise. Blessed are those who partake of the feast of consummation. Yet beware, for who can bear exaltation and prosperity."

As Samuel sat at the right hand of Saul, he motioned to Tabbach, the cook. "Bring the portion that I gave you, of which I said to you, 'Set it apart.'"

The cook took up the shoulder, and that which was upon it, and set it before Saul. It was this portion that signified the election of the anointed, for upon his shoulders the weight of government shall rest, borne as a burden, a yoke of bondage for the good of the people.[9]

Saul gasped at this honor, which unlooked for, came. Noting his surprise, Samuel leaned over and spoke, saying, "Here it is, what was kept back. It was set apart for you. Eat, for until this time it has been held for you, since before I invited the people."

"For me? But how?" Saul fixed his eyes upon the prophet, his hands laid out flat upon the table before him, on either side of his

---

[9] Isaiah 9:6

41

plate, as though he was ready to spring from his seat and flee. "I do not understand. How could you know these things? What vow is it that we are fulfilling at this feast of the Peace Offering?"

A glimmer of mirth shone in Samuel's eyes. "Soon, Saul, all will be revealed. But for now, eat, for the day wanes and night will soon be upon us."

So Saul ate with the prophet that day. And as the night shroud was drawn over the eastern edge of the celestial vault, the two men came down from the high place and entered into the city.

Samuel placed his hand upon Saul's shoulder and patted it with affection. "Come and stay with me tonight, for much there is to discuss. You must tell me all there is to know about yourself, and I will teach you of the destiny that awaits you."

Through the winding streets of Ramah they trod, speaking of Saul's family, of their military history, of Kish, his father, and of Ahinoam, until at last the two approached a modest home on the edge of the market district. A stone staircase on the outside of the dwelling led to the flat roof encircled by a parapet. Clay storage jars and firewood lay stacked in precarious piles along the far side. A limestone roof-roller rested in the corner, awaiting the first rains, when repairs to the roof would be made.

Here Samuel spoke with Saul, on the top of the house, of the weakness of the tribal confederacy and the threat the Philistines posed.

"Even now, we hear rumors of war, not only from the Philistines, but also the Ammonites. The people look now for a mortal king to lead them, a king to go out before them against the enemy."

"I understand the threat, for in Gibeah we see the encroachment of the Philistines upon our lands, how they build up garrisons and press ever into our territory. It is time to push back. I am willing to fight for our people." Saul paused, then continued thoughtfully, "but I do not understand what it is you want from me. My family is of little consequence. Our tribe is the smallest and least influential of all the tribes. What can I do to help Israel?"

Samuel gestured toward several mats, offering a seat to Saul, as he, himself, sat down. Saul obeyed, pondering the words of the prophet.

As though he had only taken a breath between thoughts, the prophet continued.

"Even though all of Israel has rejected the Lord God as their king, He will not wholly abandon His people." Samuel gave a slow shake of the head, his visage lifting with a quiet assurance. "He has not wholly stepped down from His throne. You see the Lord retains His control. Yet, the people desire a king, *like all the other nations*, so God will give them what they ask. He has chosen you, O Saul, to rule His people."

Startled, Saul recoiled, his arms spreading wide, his head shaking in protest. "Me? How do you know this? I am just a man looking for his father's lost donkeys. I do not seek after power. I have everything I ever wanted. I need no more."

"The Lord told me of your coming," answered Samuel. "The Lord told me in my ear the day before you arrived, saying: 'Tomorrow, about this time, I will send you a man from the land of Benjamin, and you shall anoint him commander over My people, that he may save them from the hand of the Philistines, for I have looked upon Israel because their cry has come to Me.'

"Then as I was walking out of the city today, when I saw you coming toward the gate, the Lord again spoke to me, and said: 'There is he, the man about whom I spoke. This one shall reign over My people.'"

Saul gasped at this revelation and turned away from Samuel. Gazing out over the city, he thought on what the prophet had spoken. A frown creased his brow. Samuel rested his palm upon Saul's forearm. He would not meet the seer's gaze, but continued to look into the darkness beyond the rooftop, troubled within his heart.

"You see, I gave you my portion at the meal." The prophet's voice softened. "For my time has come to an end. The leadership of Israel has passed now onto your shoulders. You must have strength, for you now must bear up under the weight of the affairs of government. But do not forget that a good king is more than strength. He must carry the affection for his people with him in all that he does; the people must be within your bosom always, for they must be dear to you. It is for them that you serve."

Samuel leaned back, away from Saul. The two men sat in silence for a time. Overwhelmed, Saul drew in a deep breath and sighed. Frowning, he shook his head. "I still cannot see why *I* have been chosen. There must be some mistake."

Samuel threw his head back and chuckled. Saul looked at him and thought, *he has lost his reason.*

"Oh, Saul, my boy, do not try to understand the ways of God. Our ways are not His ways.[10] But look upon thyself. You are the very image of an earthly king. You have a strong military background. The people will follow a man such as you. Do you not see that in you we can unite the tribes and have victory over our enemies?"

"Do I have no choice in this matter?" Saul asked, his hands clasped within his lap, his thumbs working against each other.

"Saul, do you love the Lord your God? Do you not wish to serve Him?"

"Always," Saul lifted his eyes to Samuel and spoke earnestly, "even from my youth."

"Then you will do as the Lord requires."

"What then, must I do?"

"All you need do is to give your heart wholly to the service of Yahweh. Submit to Him as your King, only then will you be a worthy sovereign for Israel."

Saul sat in silence, gazing into the night. The city was aglow; the unquarried brilliance shone as the evening lamps emanated their broken, quavering light through the dark veil. Quietly he brooded, as one losing his bearings through the twists and turns of unmarked paths.

Samuel, perceiving Saul's unease, stood. "Sleep now, for the night grows late. Rest well, for tomorrow you will be shown all that you need know. *Lailah Tov*, good night, Saul."

He looked up at Samuel with questioning eyes, as though the words would not take hold. The old prophet smiled, then turned and descended the stairs, leaving Saul to think upon the words he had spoken.

The night was pleasant as Saul lay there, staring up at the vast dome of the endless heavens stretched above him. Looking into the deep velvet dark of the infinite majesty of creation, Saul sensed the uncorrupted timelessness of the expanse. A sea of ancient starlight. He lay there quietly listening to the stillness, waiting for a word, hoping for hidden meaning.

---

[10] Isaiah 55:8

New realms traversed his inmost being with visions of the future, a future unlooked for and unknown. Careless whispers of half-remembered dreams, of expectation and uncertainty, engulfed his awareness like waves overwhelming the rocky shoreline.

All in a moment, everything he knew and hoped for washed over him, unseating him, and a sense of ruinous foreboding settled as a heavy burden drubbed upon his soul. His self-possession lost, many thoughts raced through his unsettled mind, completely overcome, unmoored for want of a plain path.

Then Saul's meditation turned to Ahinoam, of the touch of her soft skin, and the sweet scent of her neck, of the hollow of his hand on the small of her back, and he longed to lie beside her. His mind calmed with the memory of his fair wife and his home, until he drifted into a fitful sleep filled with dreams of beasts unrecovered and paths unknown.

And so it was that a king was led to the throne by the wanderings of wayward donkeys.

CHAPTER 8

THE ANOINTING

The sun had not yet crested the eastern horizon when Saul stirred, aware of a shuffling sound upon the stairs. Memory of the previous night's conversation with the seer flooded his mind.

As he lay there, languishing in that place between sleep and wakefulness, Saul struggled to distinguish between dream and reality.

I am still asleep.

Asleep, but very aware of himself, of his body in time and space, of the endless horizon stretching out before him.

Was it all a dream? His frame, heavy from slumber, felt as if it was sinking, as though the world was moving away from him and he was no longer a part of it.

"Saul."

He bolted upright and turned toward the stairs, his heart pounding in his chest. *I am awake now.* Samuel stood upon the steps, looking over the parapet. "Get up, that I may send you on your way."

Saul rose and gathered his belongings, then he and Samuel went outside. As they walked beyond the outskirts of the city, the prophet said to Saul, "Tell the servant to go on ahead of us. But you stand here awhile, that I may make known to you the word of God."

So Ziba went on ahead as he was told, while Saul stood alone with Samuel in an open field.

"Saul, kneel down before me."

His heart beat wildly as his chest tightened and his breath came in short, shallow gasps. With trembling reverence, Saul submitted, kneeling before the prophet of God.

Samuel took a flask of oil and poured it over Saul's head, and kissed him upon his brow.

Bewildered, the chosen king gazed up into the eyes of the prophet.

He smiled at Saul's surprised wonder and said, "Is it not because the Lord has anointed you leader over His inheritance?"

The prophet placed his hands upon Saul's shoulders as he looked down at the obeisant sovereign. "Israel belongs to the Lord. They are His inheritance and belong to no other. This task you are about to undertake is of great importance. Yahweh has set you as commander over His people, a people who belong to the Lord God. Therefore, you will take care to rule them—not according to your own will and pleasure, but in keeping with the will and mind of God."

There was no crown, no scepter, no special robe to signify the office. No audience looked on as the king was anointed—only Saul and the prophet stood in the field beside the road.

This cannot be happening, thought Saul. He had been anointed with oil before. In the mornings at home, his servant would anoint him before leaving his house, or as a guest before dinner was served. But this was altogether different. This was more than a blessing. It was a sacred rite.

Oil, poured thusly upon Saul's head, ran down his face and through his beard, flowing even to the edge of his garments.

The field grew silent, motion slowed, and the ground tilted under his knees. A wave of disquiet washed over Saul. Dazed, he cocked his head as he lifted his gaze beyond Samuel to the vacant land.

He wondered at the empty field, barren of life, the open expanse of cleared earth. He could smell the damp soil, and the rich loam. The land lay fallow, its fruitfulness ebbing away. Or was there a loss that prevented the sowing of the field, for was spring not the time of new birth?

And he thought, *the land belongs to God and God's people must trust in His providence.*

"Rise up, my son."

At the command of the prophet, Saul rose slowly to his feet. Spent, his actions were without thought, bereft of strength to direct his own course.

Grasping Saul firmly by the arms, Samuel smiled warmly up at him.

"Behold, the anointed of God. Today begins a new age for Yahweh's Chosen. Be wise, Saul, in all you do, for now you have been set aside for a purpose far greater than tending your father's herd."

Samuel continued, his voice serious with intent. "These signs are given you, that you may believe all I have said is true.

"When you have departed from me this day, you will come upon two men by Rachel's tomb, in the territory of Benjamin at Zelzah. They shall say to you, 'The donkeys which you seek have been recovered. And now your father has ceased caring for the donkeys and is anxious about you, saying, "What has become of my son, for he has been gone many days?"'"

Saul gazed vacantly into the eyes of the prophet. Half-listening, the anointed of God stood, astounded and undone. Trying to focus on the words of Samuel, Saul leaned forward, frowning.

"Then you shall go on forward from there and come to the great Elah tree of Tabor. There, three men going up to worship Yahweh at Bethel will meet you, one carrying three young goats, another bearing three loaves of bread, another holding a skin of wine. And they will greet you and give you two loaves of bread. These you must not refuse, but receive from their hands.

"After that you shall come to Gibeath-elohim, the hill of God where the Philistine garrison is located. And it will happen, when you have come there to the city, that you will meet a band of prophets descending from the high place, returning from where they had been to worship and to pray.

"In their hands will be a stringed instrument: a tambourine, a flute, and a harp, upon which they will be playing songs of praise, and they will be prophesying.

"The Spirit of the Lord will fall upon you. And you, O Saul, will prophesy with them, and be turned into another man. And let it be, when these signs come to you, that you do as you must. Do not fear to act as the occasion demands, for God is with you."

Looking hard at Saul, he continued, "Now remember this, and do not forget. When the need arises, you shall go down before me to Gilgal. I will come down to you to offer burnt offerings and peace offerings. You must be patient and do not act rashly. Seven days you shall wait, till I come to you and show you what you should do. I will not neglect to be there as I have promised."

Samuel fixed his gaze upon the son of Kish, grasping him firmly by both arms, half shaking him to rouse him to heed. "Do you understand all that I have told you?"

Saul's glazed eyes rested upon the prophet, and he nodded, granting assent though he knew not if it be true. The breath within him seemed struck away. All had come to pass with sudden swiftness.

So it was, in the cool of the morning, when Saul turned his back to go from Samuel, southward toward Gibeah, that a stirring quickened in his heart. An awakening. A sense of power encompassed him, within and without. A Presence unknown till now. Fullness pressed upon his chest, beyond his understanding.

As Saul came upon the place where Ziba, his servant, waited, his spirit rose, lifted by the Sacred breath, until he stood taller as though girded for battle.

Sensing a change, Ziba asked, "Are you well, *adon*? What has come to pass to make you look so distant? What did the seer say to you?"

"Nothing, Ziba, nothing at all."

"Shall we make for home?"

"Lead the way," Saul bade him, with a wave of the hand.

In silence, the two men proceeded, empty-handed, for no donkeys had they found. Saul journeyed homeward along the heavily traveled road, passing through the rise and fall of gentle slopes. Deep in thought, with senses suspended, Saul moved in a fixed course, giving no heed to the few scant trees along the side of the road, or the well-worn path beneath his feet.

The rolling foothills lifted into the northern mountains, giving rise to the hill country of Ephraim, the land rich with the history of Israel. Saul felt the eyes of his ancestors weighing down upon him.

Who am I, that I should lead this people? I am not a leader, but a tender of crops and a herder of donkeys. I could not even find my father's animals. How then can I lead a people, and in times like these?

CHAPTER 9

A New Man

"Saul, are you Saul ben Kish?"

"Who else could he be, for look at his mighty stature?"

Lifting his head at the call of his name, Saul beheld two men approaching along the road. "Yes, I am Saul."

"Saul, we have word that the donkeys, which you seek, have been recovered. And now your father has ceased caring about the donkeys and is anxious about you, saying, 'What has become of my son, for he has been gone many days?'"

Saul fixed his gaze upon the strangers, and uttered not a word. For behold, he stood before Rachel's tomb, just as the prophet had foreseen. Beside the simple sepulcher rose a great pillar, wrought of eleven stones laid one upon another, one for each of the children of Jacob, save Joseph who was thought lost.

It was here, in ages past, that the Israelites first rested after crossing over into the Promised Land. In this place, so long ago, Rachel, favored wife of Jacob, died giving birth to Ben-oni, *son of my suffering*. Jacob called him Benjamin, *son of the south*. It was he, Saul's forebear, who had become father of the war-like Benjaminites. This was a story that ran much deeper than a single moment in time.

Now Saul was to take part in the ancient tale of covenant promises, a recital of events crying out for fulfillment down through the ages.

The two men looked at Saul, waiting for a reply. When none came, they shook their heads. "Well, *boker tov*, good day to you. Do not delay long, for your father is sorely distressed."

Ziba inclined his head toward the men as they turned to continue down the road.

Saul remained quietly gazing upon the tomb. A whispered breath swept across his ear. A gentle song of sorrow brushed past him and touched his soul. The voice, a lamentation of future hurt, of Rachel weeping for her children.[11]

Then the veil was drawn open and Saul knew that this voice was not only the voice of mourning, but of hope.

Is it not one of her children who is now called to unite the tribes and fight the enemies of Israel?

"*Adon?*" questioned Ziba.

Saul took in a deep breath. "How close to us draws the unseen world. It is but a vapor that separates us from the invisible. All God need do is to thrust aside the cloud that covers and all we hold in high esteem is turned abhorrent and base."

Ziba beheld his master in wonder, for something had changed in his bearing.

Coming to himself, Saul cast his eyes about and spoke, "How have we come to this tomb? Were we not upon the road for Gibeah?"

"*Adon*, we have missed the path for you were deep in thought and did not hear when I spoke thus to you, saying, 'The road is passed.' I feared to persist, for your countenance was severe, so now we have come to this place."

"Far we have come off the road we at first set out to take," spoke Saul with surprise. "We must return to our way, for I long for home."

Having regained their course, they traveled onward toward Gibeah until the day warmed with the advance of the sun. Then, as the road grew weary, Saul came to a large tree beside the way. Yearning for its shade, he bade his servant stay their journey until they had rested within the shadow of its branches.

It stood in symmetry, each side answering the other as in a perfect design, the reach of its limbs unfurling rounded leaflets as a multitude of fluttering feathers. Each bough held in its hand clusters of ruddy

---

[11] Jeremiah 31:15

berries burgeoning amid delicate crimson flowers. Digging deep, the roots of the long-lived elah tree clung to the ancient soil as its branches, large and spreading, sent forth its resinous odor, teasing the senses with its spicy aroma.

Sitting in the shade of this time-worn tree, Saul lifted his gaze through its branches, moved by the life it held.

I wonder if this tree was planted long ago, a memorial for the dead as is so often done.

He inhaled deeply in the cool of the shadow, taking in the air as he beheld the breadth and height of this lonely pillar.

There is something mysterious hidden within a tree, something unknown. Though everything around it strives to destroy it, yet life remains unseen within its branches, its substance preserved, even when its branches are deprived of its leaves, springing forth in its due season.

"*Adon*." Saul looked up at Ziba, who stood upon the road, his gaze turned south. "Someone approaches."

The son of Kish stood and shook the dust from his robes. Pouring forth its steady rays, the bright beauty of day saturated the sky with brilliant beams of blinding light concealing from view the veiled forms.

Shielding his eyes with his upraised hand, Saul made out the figures of three men. As they drew near, he saw that one carried three young goats, one he held in each arm and the third he carried across the nape of his neck, supporting it upon his shoulders. Three loaves of bread were held by another, and the third bore a skin of wine. Saul stood quietly, watching their advance.

"*Shalom Achi*, my brother," spoke the one who bore the loaves. "Peace to you."

"*Shalom*," replied Saul. "*Le'an atah nose'a*, where are you going?"

"To Bethel, the sacred height, to make sacrifice to the Lord."

Saul nodded, for it was clear they carried with them the articles of offering.

"And you are headed home," returned the traveler.

Saul looked down at the man, his eyes widening. "Yes, how is it that you know this?"

"It is in your bearing. And we have heard of your quest, for indeed, you must be Saul of Gibeah, for there is no other with whom you compare."

"You have heard of my quest?"

"Yes. Here, receive this portion, born of soil." The man offered Saul two loaves of bread. "I give it to you, for I perceive it is needed more by your hands than mine."

Saul reached out and took hold of the loaves baked with leaven, the priests' portion. Yet the man kept his grasp upon the bread.

"But I tell you, remember, that which is freely given can as easily be snatched away. Take care lest you lose that which has been rendered you."

The man released the loaves into Saul's hands. He returned to his companions and the three of them smiled at Saul, waving as they spoke, "Drishat Shalom."

As the men continued north upon the road, one called back, "*Ad me'ah ve'esrim shanah!* May you live to be one hundred and twenty."

Then they departed singing songs of praise to Yahweh.

Saul watched their going in silent wonder, pondering the words of the prophet in his heart. When the travelers were lost to his view beyond the rise in the road, the son of Kish gestured toward Ziba, his servant, bidding lead the way home.

Onward they marched through the healthy hills, well-watered and fertile. Waves of green spread across the distant land. The sun in its prominence, the radiant beams of its splendor, shone favorably upon the long-awaited hour.

The landscape grew intimate and familiar, as the son of Kish and his servant came to *Gibeath-elohim,* the hill of God, Saul's own city. It was on the heights of Gibeah overlooking the surrounding hills that the Philistine watchtower stood. It was a fortified garrison, a standing camp, a reminder that the enemy was ever present.

Saul glared upon the garrison with contempt. "How far these Philistines have stretched out their hands upon the territory of Israel! Though they have cast off the leaves of Israel, the tree still lives. Israel is not yet overcome. We shall rise. And though our history is hidden in shadow, we will be redeemed. We will become a holy seed that sprouts up and is renewed."

Music rose to fill the air with its sweet harmonies, lifting the senses to new heights. Saul looked upon the hill of God and behold, a company of prophets was coming down from the high place, prophesying of the good things of Yahweh, with stringed instrument: a tambourine, a flute, and a harp before them. The people stood watching the prophets, throwing gifts and asking for blessings in return.

An ineffable stirring seized his inmost being, and Saul declared, "It is remarkable how sound can be fashioned into such pleasing songs. It is a special gift from God."

"Beware, my *adon*," warned Ziba, "these are strange and dangerous men, for they dwell within the realms of two worlds, the seen and the unseen, able to view deeper realities extending far beyond mortal apprehension."

When Saul gazed upon the prophets praising God, his heart welled within him. New thoughts quickened in his mind, chasing away the ambitions, aspirations, and hopes of the past. A tumult of feeling raced through him, as a cloud surcharged with lightning.

Being brought near to the supernatural by tokens of Godly ordination, Saul was profoundly moved as he sensed the Divine Presence come upon him. Overcome with ecstasy, he could no longer contain all that had happened. With a sudden swell of emotion, Saul was impelled to join in the company's song. And as the breath of God rushed upon him, he prophesied among them.

Ziba beheld all in fear and wonder.

"My *adon*," spoke the servant as he sought to take hold of his master's arm.

The crowd pressed forward, pushing Ziba away from his charge. Losing sight of Saul, the servant strove to break through the assembly of onlookers.

"What is this that has come upon the son of Kish?" came a voice from the multitude.

Ziba turned toward the sound of the query, but could not make out who had spoken.

"Is Saul also among the prophets?" questioned another.

The servant of Saul continued to press forward, using his hands to part the sea of people. Yet the crowd closed his advance.

On his toes, craning his neck, Ziba tried to locate his master. But the youth could not see above the heads of the people.

"What is the meaning of this? Can one from low degree suddenly come to honor?"

At this, Ziba stopped struggling and fixed his gaze upon the citizen to his right, for it was he who had spoken last. The man was plainly agitated, or rather, disgusted by Saul's outward behavior—as though it were above his station to be among the prophets. Ziba took offense at this indictment, but the servant knew his place and said nothing in rebuff.

"Wonder not at this matter," came a voice on the servant's left, "but give glory to God, for who is their father?"

"What is your meaning, ancient one?"

Ziba found himself pressed between the two men as they exchanged words, the one on his left aged and gentle of face.

"This can only be from the Lord," answered the old man. "For what has birth to do with prophecy?"

In total abandonment, Saul continued in his rapturous state until finally his elation was fully abated. The memory of what Samuel spoke upon the rooftop came to him, of the glorious future of Israel and his part in its unfolding. As a mighty rushing wind, the significance of each meeting at each sacred stead washed over him: the stories represented by each place, of Abraham and the patriarchs, the warrior-chieftains of Israel, the hallowed ground of the illustrious dead, and the eternal truth, that help comes from the Holy Place.

"What am I before so great a God as this?"

His thoughts thus redirected, Saul was made into a new man, elevated by the prospect before him, awed by the sense of God's nearness, his heart now bent toward action. His fervor spent, he went at once to the high place from whence the prophets had come. Conscious of the change wrought within him, Saul desired the solitary communing in the quiet of the *bamah*, to worship the God who had come so near.

As he climbed the steps leading to the stone altar, Saul's uncle, Abner, *father of light*, was coming down from the high place. Though but a few years his elder, he was the younger brother of Kish, Saul's father. His dark hair and full beard framed his pleasing face. A fine cloak he wore, draped across his broad shoulders. Of considerable height and well-furnished in form, Abner, a mighty man of valor, stood not as tall as Saul. Yet he held his agile body erect and proud, having a greater, far nobler bearing.

At the sight of Saul's approach, Abner halted, for he marked a change in his brother's son. Speaking sternly, Abner looked hard at Saul. "Where did you go? Where have you been?"

"To seek my father's donkeys." Saul lowered his gaze, unable to meet his uncle's, for as their eyes locked, doubt touched his mind. "When we saw that they were nowhere to be found, we went to Samuel."

A shadow of alarm touched his uncle's face. "Tell me, please, what Samuel said to you, for I know of this prophet and his involvement in the troubles which now plague our people."

"He told us plainly that the donkeys had been found."

And though Saul longed to confide in his uncle, to whisper to him everything that had transpired, he remained quiet regarding the matter of the kingdom. Yet Abner sensed there was more to the story, but he let the matter drop.

"Do not take too long in returning home. I know Kish is indeed concerned for your welfare."

"I will be but a moment. I want to thank the Lord for safe passage upon the road. I will not tarry."

"See that you do not."

Saul watched his uncle as he made his way down the path that led away from the *bamah*. Again unrest troubled him, and the truth he had withheld weighed upon his spirit.

Lowering his head for a moment, Saul let out his breath before turning to face the ascent toward the high place. The dirt path was set with a few stone steps worked into the soil at the steepest parts of the slope. Taking a deep breath, Saul gathered his robes and made his way up the hill.

There he made sacrifice to the Lord God of Hosts. A spirit of gentleness enwrapped him as he lingered before the altar.

It was as though he could touch the very face of God, so near to Him he drew. With the awe-filled sense that God was everywhere, that His Spirit pervaded even the farthest reaches, Saul stood before Yahweh, naked and exposed, knowing that the secret things in his heart were unveiled, and nothing could be kept back.

"You are so near. I can feel Your Spirit hovering about me. There is no place I can hide from Your Presence. My inward thoughts are made known to You, O God, and all is revealed before Your face."

Struck by the awareness of his flawed nature, Saul held his breath, fearing even to draw air before so holy a God. "Why did You choose me? I am nothing. I cannot do this task You have placed before me. Please, choose someone else. This burden is too great for me."

But the Lord would not be moved. Saul was to be king.

The Spirit of the Most High infused His anointed, washing over him like a river flowing down a rocky mountain. The hairs upon his arms rose. Breath came in short gasps. His heart beat wildly. Tears welled and trickled down his face.

The awe-full sense of God's essence enveloped him. His knees weakened, and he collapsed before the altar of the Lord.

As God's gentle voice whispered within his soul, Saul's life was being shaped, and with every passing moment, he knew he never wanted to be separated from the Lord's will. He was filled up and overflowing.

At that moment Yahweh became his sole regard, his only hope. No longer would Saul labor for his own ends, but wholly entered into the service of the Lord.

"Hide me in Your holiness, O God." His voice was but a whisper.

After a time, Saul rose. He came down from the high place and walked in a daze, unknowing until he came to the hill that looked over his valley. He stood awhile, gazing upon his home. Everything appeared as though nothing had changed, but everything had changed. He had changed.

No more was he to be a tender of field and herd. Nothing would be as it had been. The life he had known was over. Saul could not help but mourn the loss of what would have been. Sighing deeply, he walked toward his house, eager to see his family.

Saul entered into the covered threshold by way of the gate. The shallow receptacle of the footbath rested in the left corner of the vestibule, waiting to fulfill the first obligation of hospitality. After cleansing his feet, as was the usual custom, Saul hurried directly into the courtyard, which was open to the sky.

The central area of the house was encircled on three sides by rooms, bearing white-plastered walls built of roughly-hewn stone blocks stacked one upon another. Stone pillars in two parallel rows supported the upper floor, extending forward from a broad room at the back of the house that served as long-term storage.

In the hearth at the center of the court, a stew of lentils simmered in a blackened cooking pot, tended by the house servant, casting forth its pervasive aroma. Close by, a goatskin churn, supported by three wooden poles for curdling milk, sat unattended, abandoned by the girls, Merab and the youngest, Michal.

Seated on the cobblestone floor, huddled around a board game of twenty squares, Saul's youngest sons, Jishui and Malchishua were heavy in competition. The girls watched intently as Jishui cast the knucklebones to determine his next move.

Saul smiled to himself as he quickened his pace across the courtyard where his children were gathered.

Standing with his hands upon his hips, Saul glared down at his brood. "Ah-hem. What is this, neglecting your duties?"

The children lifted their eyes in surprise, overturning their game. "*Abba!*" they cried all at once. The four leapt to their feet and ran to their father, wrapping their arms tightly about him, so that he staggered.

"Ah now, let me look upon you."

Pulling them aside, one at a time, Saul beheld each of his children. Emotion welled in his soul, for here was the promise of the future, the issue of his life. A change was wrought in him when in the presence of his children, a softening of his spirit. They brought forth in him a tenderness and a gentleness he knew not elsewhere.

No kingship could replace the way he felt when he looked upon his children. He would do anything for them, sacrifice all, and even consent to leading a nation that he might secure a safer future for these, his children.

Kneeling beside them, he gave each a hug and kissed them on the cheek. Lastly, he looked upon Michal, "*Neshama,* my little darling. I have missed you all greatly."

"*Abba,*" Michal said as she clung to her father.

"Little one." Saul's voice was quiet. "I have a charge for you."

Reaching behind his waist, Saul retrieved the tattered doll he had carried since Shiloh.

"She needs some special care. You see, she has been through a terrible time and needs an *ima* to tend to her."

Saul looked into the eyes of his youngest daughter; a serious expression was upon his face. "Will you do this, my little one?"

Gingerly, Michal reached for the doll. Saul released his grip as Michal took it from him. She examined the burnt and tattered cloth, caressing the doll with gentle hands.

"Oh, *Abba*, yes," she cried as she tenderly cradled the doll to her chest. "I will give her comfort."

Saul smiled at his daughter as he ran his great hand over the top of her head. "Good, very good."

Rising from his knees, Saul walked over to the pillared room to the left where Kish and Jonathan were cleaning the stalls and laying down new straw. They had ceased their labors and were watching him.

Extending his hand toward Jonathan, Saul placed it upon the boy's shoulder and kissed him upon the opposite cheek. Then, shifting his hand to the other shoulder, he kissed him upon the other cheek.

Pride welled within him as he looked upon his eldest son, who so favored him, noting that he had nearly grown into a man.

Turning to his father, Kish, Saul greeted him in like manner. "I am sorry, *Abba*, that I was unable to locate your beasts. I have failed you."

"No matter, the donkeys have been found. How is not important." Kish fixed his eyes upon him for a moment as though he had something more to say, then changed his mind. "I am glad you are home, my son."

"Where is your mother?" Saul asked Jonathan.

"She is upstairs, at the loom."

With long strides, Saul strove for the crudely fashioned stairs at the back of the courtyard. Bolting upward, he ascended to the main living area. He cast his eyes toward the loom. There sat Ahinoam weaving.

At the sound of her husband entering, Ahinoam stood wide-eyed, dropping her shuttle, which went tumbling across the floor. Her hands went to her head as she smoothed her hair.

"My beloved," she cried, "and long-awaited husband."

Saul rushed to his wife and wrapped his arms around her, enfolding her into himself. Taking her face in his hands, he kissed her with passion, drank her in as though he were dying of thirst for her. Not a word he spoke, but fulfilled his desire for her, knowing that this was where he belonged. Beside his love.

CHAPTER 10

THE BUZZARD AND THE HARE

The rosy face of morning peeked over the distant mountains, still robed in the silken mist of dawn. Above, with its impressive wingspan, a long-legged buzzard, in its soaring flight, hung on the wind, surveying the earth below. Upon the bend of the bird's wing, dark carpal patches were plain to behold, giving rise to pale flight feathers. The raptor's flaxen head and breast yielded to dark bronze contour feathers, the hunter's herald.

As the early vapors faded from the plain, within the open stretches of scrub and short grass, the swift-footed *arnebeth* ventured from its shallow nest of flattened turf.

Timid at first, the hare loped across the ground, its long, black-tipped ears telling its course. A moment of pause, it scanned the area for danger, ears and nose twitching, eyes shifting across the horizon.

Yet poised above, danger lurked, unawares.

The buzzard cocked its head as it hovered, tracking its prey.

Rising onto its large, hind legs, the hare looked about and sniffed the air, sensing something ill upon the wind. Flat it lay within the grass, belly down and ears back, the *arnebeth* froze, assured of its concealment, for to be still was to be unseen.

As the shadow of the buzzard fell over its prey, the hare sensed its impending doom. Beset by fear, the *arnebeth* sprung, bounding across the plain. Without a beat of its wing, the buzzard did wheel, then swooped down and snatched up the hare in its talons.

The captive screamed a most pitiful cry as the buzzard flew off into the heavens.

Saul watched the scene unfold before him, the fate of the hare and the mastery of the buzzard. Troubled thoughts wrestled within his mind as he stood looking over his valley. Doubt had crept in, clouding his resolve.

"I have become swept up into greater events," mused Saul.

"What events?"

Surprised, Saul turned to find Ahinoam had walked up beside him.

"What troubles you?" The soft brush of her voice reached out to him.

"Am I the hare or the buzzard?"

"A hare or a buzzard? I do not understand."

Saul looked back over the valley below as he shook his head, his brow creasing.

"Why are you so distant, my husband?" Ahinoam moved before Saul, capturing his gaze. "You have spoken but few words since your return. I do not understand your deep silence. What causes you to be so quiet?"

"Do you believe that our future is ruled by fate, that we have no choice? Was it the fate of the hare to become the meal of the buzzard?"

"I believe that our future is what we make of it."

"Did our fathers before us have a choice? Did Abraham or Moses have a choice? Or were their lives preordained by Yahweh?"

Ahinoam moved closer to Saul and placed her arm around his waist. "God lays out the path for us, but we must choose to take the next step. Why do you question so? Tell me what has happened."

"How can one man change the world? Who has that kind of power?"

"Do you not see that we are all connected? Saul, all we do affects those around us, who then in turn affect more people. In this way, yes, a single man can change the course of many."

Ahinoam looked up into the face of Saul. She stroked his brow in a vain attempt to brush away the furrows of anxious thought fixed upon his countenance. "Saul, why do you speak so? Do not keep me at arm's length."

"I do not know what the path holds before me. I have been shown a course I must take, and it is a road of which I want no part."

"Oft when I walk among the hills, I must journey down a precipice. Where the path leads, I cannot see. In faith I must take that first step, blindly anticipating the next. I cannot see where the next foothold is until I step to the one I do see, then is revealed the next step I must take. If it is God who directs your path, there is naught to do but follow His lead. Have faith, my husband, that He will show you your next step in due time."

Saul let out his breath as he took his wife into his arms and, with a gentle touch, his rough hand stroked her hair. He smiled at her and drew her close to him. "I must go to Mizpah."

"But you only just arrived. Why must you go so soon?"

"The seer, Samuel, has summoned all the tribes to meet with him."

"When must you go?"

"I leave on the morrow."

CHAPTER 11

URIM AND THUMMIM

A thin purple haze stretched across the barren country, bleak and rocky, as Samuel stood upon the precipice of Mizpah. Yet upon the lofty slopes, beyond and within the ravines and empty hills, a myriad of brilliant blooms sprung forth, robed in colors of scarlet and yellow and lavender. Away to the north, the land was cradled by the blue mountains of Ephraim, the summits of Ebal and Gerizim visible upon the horizon. An unbroken barrier, the mountains to the south rose as a division beyond the uplands of Gilead and of Moab.

And upon the plain, before the rise of Shen, that tooth-like crag, stood a lone monolith, the Stone of Ebenezer, raised as a reminder of Yahweh's protection for His people. Here it was that Samuel gathered together again the men of Israel, upon the heights of Mizpah, watchtower of the west.

Jonathan, son of Saul, watched with interest. Never before had his father included him in the affairs of the tribes. "A man," his father had called him. With shoulders back and head held high, he stood beside his father, his Uncle Abner, and his grandfather, Kish, within the circle of their tribe.

"*Abba*, which man is Samuel, the old prophet?"

Saul looked down at his son. "There." Saul lifted his hand toward Samuel. "On the rise before you. He is—"

But his words were interrupted as Samuel began to speak.

"Hear me, you turbulent sons of Jacob, for I speak of such things as will rouse you. Thus says the Lord God of Israel: 'I brought Israel out of Egypt, and delivered you from the bondage of the Egyptians and from the grasp of all the kingdoms, from those who would oppress you.' Is it not so that on this very spot, the Lord, your God, delivered you out of the hand of the Philistines?" Samuel pointed to the ground, his voice stern with indignation.

The old prophet turned to the audience, his hand gliding across the air. "But you have today rejected your God, who Himself saved you from all your adversities and your tribulations. Yet now, when trouble comes," Samuel lifted his hand toward the heavens, "instead of looking to Yahweh for deliverance, you look to foreign nations, to Babylon, and Egypt," the prophet swept his hand toward the east, then the west as he spoke, "and yes, even to the Philistines for guidance, saying to Him, 'No, set a king over us!'

"So look to your king—but I fear you will suffer greatly for your disobedience.

"Now therefore, present yourselves before the Lord by your tribes and by your clans, and I will tell you today whom the Lord has chosen to be your sovereign. Bring forth the ephod," commanded Samuel as he gestured to a priest standing beside him.

The Levite brought the apron to the prophet and helped him don the holy raiment.

The ephod, the vestment of the high priest, was made of finely twined linen, the threads of which were blue, purple, and scarlet and embroidered in gold. The shoulders of the garment were secured by two onyx stones, the black surfaces inscribed with the names of each tribe: six on one stone and six upon the other. The breastplate, with its twelve precious stones, was fastened to the ephod by two golden rings. Doubled over, the breastplate formed a pouch in which the judgment stones, *Urim* and *Thummim*, were housed.

When all was in place, Samuel returned his attention to the people. "*Urim* and *Thummim*, Revelation and Truth, shall decide who among you is chosen by God to be king of all Israel. The lot will be cast, to discern God's will in this matter."

Addressing the multitude, Samuel gave instruction. "Now, each tribe pass before me so that the lot might be cast."

As one by one the tribes came forth, the prophet reached into the pocket of the breastplate of judgment and drew out a stone.

It had been a long history of divination and cleromancy for the people of Israel. Often consulted in matters of great consequence, the sacred lot was drawn so to reveal the will of Yahweh. The *Yes* and *No* stones were a source of revelation, manifesting the course desired by the Lord for His chosen people.

Saul stood among his tribe awaiting his clan's turn to receive their destiny. Reuben stood before Samuel as the prophet drew out the first oracle. *Thummim*, the black *No* stone was withdrawn. The chosen king was not to be found within the tribe of Reuben. As the rejected clan filed out, Simeon came forward. Again the stone retrieved was black. It was a *No*. And so, onward the trial by lot went forth through all the tribes in order: Levi, then Judah, Dan and Naphtali. All were turned away, for no king was found among them.

With nervous glances, Saul waited with apprehension, impatiently shifting his weight from one leg to the other. He was eager to get this over with, yet wished it would never come. Secretly, he hoped the *Yes* stone would fall on another tribe. Each time Samuel put his hand into the ephod, Saul's stomach lurched, and each time the *No* stone was retrieved, his anxiety increased. He grew restless, looking for a way to escape what he knew was to be. But the crowd pressed him forward as his tribe moved closer to the prophet. Beads of sweat gathered upon his brow. His life became a watching vigil of the infernal interval of suspended time as the prophet's hand slowly withdrew from the breastplate.

Next came Gad, then Asher, followed by Issachar and Zebulun. Almost through, and still no *Urim* appeared in the prophet's hand. Saul could hardly breathe. Panic rose within him. A throbbing pain pulsed in his head. He reached a trembling hand to his temple and set it against the torment. Saul felt trapped. He had to get out of there, but the crowd was pressing so close. He needed air. The world began to spin. Saul hardly noticed, as Ephraim was rejected. The tribe of Manasseh stepped forward. Samuel reached again into the pouch of the breastplate. Saul's eyes grew wide. There were no other tribes left beside his. The prophet moved to withdraw it. Saul became agitated, pacing in place as he held his breath.

Oh, why so slow Samuel! Hurry up. I cannot take much more of this!

After what seemed an age, *Thummim*, the black *No* stone, was delivered. Manasseh was not chosen. Only one tribe remained. The tribe of Benjamin stood before Samuel. Reaching into the pocket of the breastplate once more, Samuel brought forth another stone. Saul knew without seeing, but still he looked on, hoping. Slowly, Samuel opened his hand. Indeed, *Urim*, the *Yes* stone, shone white within his palm. And so it was that Benjamin was chosen from among the Children of Israel.

Then Samuel caused the tribe of Benjamin to separate into family divisions. Once more the lot was drawn. The family of Kish was among the least of the families, so stood last in the procession. One by one the other families were rejected. When Saul's division, that is of *Matri,* rain of Jehovah, came before Samuel, *Urim*, the white *Yes* stone, shone within the prophet's hand. From Matri, the *lakad,* as a trap, fell to Saul, the son of Kish.

"*Urim* and *Thummim* have spoken," announced Samuel. "Saul ben Kish shall be your king. Let it be according to your desire."

"*Abba!*" cried Jonathan as he spun round to speak to Saul. But Saul was not among them. Jonathan craned his neck, looking this way and that, but still he could not find his father. Turning toward Abner, he asked, "Where is *Abba?*"

The crowd watched in silence, waiting to gain a glimpse of their new king.

Samuel cried out, "Saul, son of Kish, come forth to receive your honor." But no one came forward, for Saul had slipped away unnoticed. Heads turned. The crowd grew uneasy, murmuring their displeasure.

"Where is he?" came a voice from among them.

"I cannot see him," another answered.

"Has the man come here yet?"

"Did I not see him among his clan?"

Samuel, noting how the multitude grew restless, drew away from the people and inquired of the Lord as to where Saul might be found. And Yahweh answered.

"Look for him among the baggage; there you shall find him."

"See, there he is, hiding in the midst of the equipment."

All turned, and behold, their king stooped in his self-concealment among the saddlebags and sundry implements.

"Come, Saul, you are our king."

Men grasped him by the arms and led him out from the place where he was hiding, pushing the son of Kish to the rise of Mizpah, thrusting him into the mighty destiny God had chosen for him.

"Why do you hide, Saul, like a coward among the provisions?" proud-bearing Abner spoke. "For a great honor has been bestowed upon our house."

Then it was that Saul looked into the eyes of his son Jonathan, and he knew he would not again run from his fate. As Saul stood in the midst of the people, he was taller than any, from his shoulders upward, beautiful to behold; and the crowd reveled in his perfection, for his very presence proclaimed a royal dignity, like unto the kings of the nations. He was the image of a goodly king. And the people stood in awe of this most worthy and venerable sovereign.

Samuel clasped Saul's hand and held it firm. Softly, he spoke, "Saul, do not fear the mantle you must wear, though it rest heavy upon your shoulders. Do not listen to the lies of the enemy, for he is cunning. Lay down your baggage and follow the call, for you are the one God has chosen, and He is with you. Therefore, no one is your equal."

Setting his face toward the crowd, the prophet proclaimed, "Did not Moses say that when you came into the land, which the Lord your God gave you, that you would say, 'Let us appoint over us a king like all the other nations around us?' After four hundred years, we gather together to unite Israel under a single monarchy. No longer shall we be divided by our tribes."

Raising his arm toward Saul, he cried out, "Do you see him, that there is none like him among all the people? Who else among you could go before you in battle as this one anointed by God? Here now is your king whom the Lord has chosen from among your brethren."

A mighty cheer rose, and all the people lifted up their voices, saying, "May the king live forever!"

Samuel's words carried above the crowd. "This is the behavior by which the king should rule. Neither shall he have too many horses, nor shall he have too many wives, lest his heart turn away from the people.

He shall not greatly increase silver and gold for himself, nor burden his subjects with unreasonable tribute.

"It shall be that when he sits upon the throne of his kingdom that he shall write for himself a copy of this law in a book, from the one before the priests, the Levites. He shall keep it with him always, and shall read from it all the days of his life, that he may learn to fear the Lord his God.

"Careful he shall be to observe all the words of this law and these statutes, that his heart may not be lifted above his brethren, that he may not turn aside from the commandment to the right hand or to the left, and that he may prolong his days in his kingdom, he and his children in the midst of Israel.[12] These things he must do to become a noble and righteous king."

Samuel stood silent, marking their reaction. Saul remained by the prophet's side, feeling awkward and conspicuous before the people. Nodding, Samuel released an audible sigh. He lifted his hand and dismissed the assembly. "Go now, each to his own home. Watch and see what the Lord will do."

The crowd moved to disperse. Saul stepped down from the rock and walked over to his family.

Kish, his father, clapped him firmly upon the back. "How about that boy? King of Israel! My own son!" Tears were in the old man's eyes as a smile broke across his face.

"Please, *Abba*. Do not carry on so. Let us just go home."

Saul was empty. Drained. He longed to be far from this place and the burden that he now carried.

How ill-equipped he felt. How was he, a simple farmer and herder, to rule a people as vast and diverse as Israel? What preparation had been given? What education?

Taking hold of Jonathan's arm, Saul pushed through the crowd. But he could find no escape, for the masses pressed in on him. Soon his arms became laden as the people gave to him gifts of tribute. He could feel hands stroking and touching him.

Overwhelmed, Saul strove forward until at last he broke through the throng.

"Who is this that claims to rule over us?" jeered a voice above the endless murmur of human babble.

---

[12] Deuteronomy 17:14–20

Saul turned, but saw no one to own the words spoken. So he fixed his gaze and set his face toward home. The mob followed close behind, some cheering, some crying for joy, waving scarves and palm branches.

"Is he our King?" came another sharp voice. "How can this man save us?"

The first voice answered, "Look how he hid among the equipment. He is no king. He is not my king."

"Nor mine, for nothing good remains within the house of Benjamin."

Old wounds linger. The hearts of some men are jealous and proud, for ancient hostilities yet endure, harbored within the constraints of memory past, suspicions made to treason. The age-worn cause of hatred, hidden long within their souls, ruptures, as past injuries, difficult to relinquish, alter the choices of the present. It was no different this day.

Children of *Belial*—*the* worthless lot. Unruly men who refused to be yoked to any cause, be it just or unjust, except their own desires.

Consumed with bitterness, a toxin seeped into their veins, poisoning their souls against the new king. So they despised Saul, and brought him no presents, their hearts hard toward him.

And to these uncharitable speeches, Saul held his peace.

The son of Kish, the king of Israel, simply turned his back to the band of jeering men and quickened his pace for home. Soon the crowd thinned as the people desired their own hearth-stones. With head down, Saul slowed his steps, loathing his new-found fame.

Maybe those ruffians are right? What right do I have to rule? Yet, Samuel believes in me. He says Yahweh chose me. Does not that mean something?

Saul marked a strange rumbling, the sound of heavy footfalls parading behind him, a multitude of marching feet. He stopped and wheeled about. The newly appointed king stood gaping, unable to believe what he saw.

Many men of valor, those whose hearts God had touched, followed after Saul and had overtaken him.

"What is this?" uttered Saul. "Why do you follow me?"

"Why, you are our king, and we would serve you."

Abner spoke to Saul, saying, "Did you think that you could journey home unattended? These are your mighty men of valor. Your army."

Saul stood amazed. "My army?" The thought had never occurred to him. *Will I need an army? What have I gotten myself into?*

Despite being ill at ease, he allowed the men to accompany him to Gibeah.

And the prophet, though he had anointed Saul, did not enter into the service of the king, but stayed behind, wrote it all in a book, and laid it before the Lord.

Here at Mizpah it was that Samuel began his leadership over Israel, and here, when the people had grown tired of his stewardship, was where it ended, for a king was what the people desired. And a king was what they received.

CHAPTER 12

GAMBIT

The sound of the runner's feet echoed through the garrison. His breath came hard upon his chest, his frame worn with exertion. Pressing on, he made his way across the encampment until he reached the tent he sought. The flap was drawn back to let in enough light to see the map upon the table over which three men-of-war hovered.

"*Sar.*"

Nagad looked up. He leaned heavily upon his arms, which were sprawled out one on each side of the table. Helek was at his side pointing to a position on the map. Beside him, Jarib, the Reubenite, frowned.

"Speak," Nagad commanded as he straightened, standing tall, his face haggard and weary from battle. His chestnut hair and beard were now flecked with gray. The once smooth visage was marred, most notable the linear scar across his left cheek. His right hand, which he ran over his mouth and down his beard, bore its own testament. Tokens all of the long years of battle.

"*Sar,*" continued the messenger. "Rejoice! Rejoice! For this day Israel has a king. Saul of Gibeah, the Benjaminite, has been chosen sovereign of all Israel."

"It is done then," Nagad uttered with a heavy breath.

"Yes, rejoice, I say," spoke Jarib. "This is truly good news, for surely he will save us from this great slaughter."

"No," answered Nagad. "We must fight alone. He cannot reach us in time."

Nagad cast his eyes downward, two fingers pressed upon his brow, a sigh escaping as his thoughts ran deep. He paced within the tent, still rubbing his forehead, the limp of his left leg more evident as the burden of battle weighed upon him. The runner stood, waiting, looking at his captain. Suddenly aware of the eyes resting upon him, Nagad stopped and lifted his gaze. "Thank you, you may go."

"*Sar.*" The runner bowed and took his leave.

"Come," ordered Nagad to his men. "We have much to plan. We must outthink our enemy, for their numbers are greater than ours. Some advantage we must seek against them."

"Nahash's army is approaching here." Helek set his finger upon the map. "We are outflanked and outnumbered."

"They fight fiercely," added Jarib.

"Oh, they are fierce fighters," agreed Helek, "but if we can get our men to fight more as a unit, we could more easily overwhelm their forces."

"The troops fear these Ammonites. They hear how Nahash plucks out the right eye of every able-bodied man he captures. Fear stays their hand." Jarib's voice was stern, his visage grim.

Nagad stroked his bearded chin. "We shall hold our most experienced warriors in tight formation in the rear. We put the youngest before. As fear grips them and they turn to flee, the stouter men will spur courage in them."

Indicating a position on the map, Nagad continued, "We must draw out the center forces in order to open their ranks so that we can maneuver past the front lines of the enemy and strike at the very heart of the adversary."

"A gambit then," spoke Helek.

Nagad nodded, his eyes ever fixed upon the spread of the map.

The Israelite forces gathered in close-order across the rise that overlooked the rolling hills of lower Gilead. Facing the ranks, his back to the rising sun, the captain inspected his troops with a critical eye, searching out any problems before the upcoming battle. The early morning coolness caressed Nagad's stern countenance as the northwesterly breeze brushed past him. Beyond the lines of nervous warriors, the undulating swells of green played before him, the verdure of the field not yet disturbed by the summer heat.

Long ago, it was these splendid uplands, with their wide fertile pastures, that roused the great flock-masters of Reuben and Gad to settle the area outside the Promised Land. As the desire of earthly things prepares men for destruction, so Gad and Reuben have paid for their yearning for these lush hills, for long had been the struggle to maintain this vulnerable terrain. For this land lay open to danger, uncovered and bare, with no barrier between the tribes and the enemies that abode to the east and the south. Alone, the brave men of these frontier clans: Gad, Reuben, and the half-tribe of Manasseh with them, stood against the foe, separated from their brothers to the west by the Jordan River.

Nagad nodded in approval, and turned to face the enemy. Across the plain, upon a rise to the east, stood the Ammonites clad in splendid helmets and shields, golden beams of light reflecting off the bronze domes upon their heads. A swath of white linen hung from each soldier's helm, wrapped about their necks and draped over their shoulders. Bronze breastplates, uniform in appearance, adorned the common white tunics, each soldier a replica of the one beside him. The enemy troops, in one accord, chanted a battle cry, as each spear tipped in unison and rose again. The well-disciplined ranks and unified array brought to mind the Philistines. A tremor ran down Nagad's spine.

Casting his eyes upon his own men, he marked their fear. Nagad drew himself up and stood tall, confident before them. "Fear not these incestuous half-breeds. Be glad and rejoice, for we are honored to fight for our God, for our people. The voice of slaughter shall be stayed; weeping shall be stilled.

"All kings shall fall down before our Lord and King. No one can stand against us unanswered. With our blade and spear, we shall redeem the oppressed and set the captive free.

"These Ammonites shall bow down their faces to the earth and lick the dust of our feet. For today we fight for our homes, for our families, for our very existence. We fight for our liberty! Let us fight now for freedom!"

A great shout rose from the ranks as the men rallied their courage. Across the way, drums beat out their rhythm to the tramping of feet. The Hebrew soldiers nervously shifted their weight back and forth upon their legs, gripping their weapons tighter within their hands.

Nagad turned to face the enemy once more. Dust rose as smoke behind the machine of war that bore down upon them. Drawing out his sword, he leveled his blade at the advancing adversary and strode toward their lines. His men followed hard after, catching and enfolding Nagad into their number.

Arrows hissed past ears, over shoulders. Yet onward they marched toward the foe.

"Javelins!" thundered Nagad from behind his shield.

A flight of missiles discharged from the ranks, deadly shafts all, and rained down upon the enemy, dealing many mortal wounds.

"Fight!" cried Nagad as he ran against the host.

Rushing forward, the two sides collided. Shield to shield the struggle was stayed, paused as the trial of strength played out. A wedge formed within the Hebrew lines, pressing through the front ranks of the enemy, splitting the troops like a plough over soil.

Breaking through the wall of shields, the Israelite forces entered into the heart of the adversary. For a time the fight went on in good contest. But the harvest failed—the battle went wrong. The Ammonite lines winged in on the flanks, closing around the Hebrews. The trap so set, the prey was ensnared.

The battle-cry rose round about them, filling their minds with dread. Confusion seized the Hebrew ranks.

Bursting through the lines, advancing like wolves of slaughter ready to devour, the enemy bared their teeth and let loose a mighty howl as they pounced upon their quarry. Fierce was their onslaught, murderous fury in their eyes. Hacking, slicing, the man-slayer swung down. The curved blade of the Ammonite bit hard into the lines of Hebrew soldiers, lapping up the lives of men, their spilt blood staining the face of the foe.

This conflict of spears, this bitter-battle waged, was too much for the young conscripts. They faltered and made to flee the field, only to be routed by their own comrades, those hardened warriors who stoutly fought, wielding their swords. Pressed between the enemy lines and the Hebrew veterans, they had no choice but to turn and fight, for there was no escape.

Spears pierced the doomed corporeal houses, issuing forth the life once contained. Swords sang out their song upon shield-rims, a terrible dirge as the slain fell to the earth.

Sensing the fear and confusion within his troops, Nagad cried out in a strong voice:

"While we have weapons to grasp in these hands, while sword and spear we are able to wield, I say warriors to battle! Stand firm and be not afraid!"

The bitter strife of battle renewed as each heart strengthened. The war-hardened heroes pressed forward into the fight, rallying the youth before them. For a time, the troops held fast against the foe. Then the battle-hedge broke and the enemy, like a wave, washed over the warriors.

Many there were hewn down upon the field, till the slain were more than those who yet held their ground.

Again their captain raised his voice, boldly speaking over the din. "Make use of your weapons, lads! Do not think to turn away from battle!"

But late it was, for fear gripped them hard. The fight gave way, yielding to flight, for they cared overmuch for their own lives. Life and limb seemed more precious than glory in battle.

Helek, in his wisdom, seized his captain's shield arm. "Hope has abandoned us," he cried. "We must flee, *Sar*."

Nagad resisted the strong warrior's grasp.

"We cannot long hold these forces fast," Helek continued. "It is finished. Though I am loathe to say it, let us flee the play of war or we shall have no troops to avenge this slaughter."

Looking up at the clear sky that hung above the gray smoke of strife, Nagad mused, "It would have been a good day, would it not?"

"Aye, *Sar*, that it would."

"Sound the retreat."

At the call of the trumpet, all fled, turning away from the field of battle, seeking a place of safety to escape the bloody carnage. And like a lion that has put the hind to flight, the enemy pursued its quarry, biting at their heels.

CHAPTER 13

Ela Mai?

Michal leapt across the open irrigation ditches lying between the rows of plants, her basket now full of radishes. Shielding her eyes from the afternoon sun, she looked up, her long brown hair falling across her young shoulders. The thin silver sliver of the moon could be seen to the west, leading the golden orb across the azure sky.

"*Ima*, I can see the moon!"

Not waiting for a reply, Michal bounded once again across the channels of water within the garden. Reaching out her small hand, she ran it across the lacy green foliage of the caraway as it fanned its feathery array. Jumping through the young cumin, Michal squatted next to the silvery-green leaves of the sage and stroked the down that covered each leaf. The lemony aroma made her grin with delight.

Ahinoam smiled at the curiosity of her youngest child. She was so full of life and wonder. Though she favored her mother in looks, Michal's mannerisms and expressions were of her father, Saul. Ahinoam's mind wandered, thinking of her husband, hoping it would not be much longer until his return.

"*Ima?*" came the voice of her oldest daughter, pulling Ahinoam from her thoughts. "Where do we plant the mustard seeds? There is space over there."

Merab indicated a place among the leeks and garlic, her pretty face wide-eyed with inquiry.

"No, Merab. We will plant them within the rows of mustard that are already established." Ahinoam knelt down within the lobed leaves of the pungent herb. "Come."

Merab's brown hair caught in a breeze as she crouched down next to her mother.

"See how we do not plant different seeds within the same furrow?" Ahinoam placed the small mustard seed within the palm of her hand. "This seed is Israel. We cannot join with any other. We must remain separate, for it is written that we shall not sow our field with mixed seed, lest the yield of the fruit which we have sown be defiled. We must remain a separate people, set apart for Yahweh."[13]

Michal continued her trek through the garden, leaping over rows of slow-growing parsley, and square-stemmed mint, invasive in nature, contained within the confines of its enclosure. Thyme, pleasantly pungent, its low-growing leaves green and narrow, spread out like a carpet upon the ground.

"See these herbs as they are sown and grow?" spoke Ahinoam. "All are bitter herbs, reminding us of our bondage in Egypt and our deliverance.[14] It was Yahweh who was our salvation, who is our Salvation. And as a garden, God brings forth its fruit in due season."[15]

Moving over to the dark green leaf heads of the leek, Merab and Ahinoam pulled up those that had overwintered and were ripe for use, exposing the long white shaft of bundled leaf sheaths.

"See, my daughters, how the leek is divided into layers?" Reaching over to the row of onions, Ahinoam uprooted one whose stem was tall and green. "We should not be like the leek, for we are not divided, but we should be as the onion." Ahinoam brushed the dirt away from the plant, exposing the white bulb underneath.

"You see, the onion is the undivided leek, connected in successive layers, though many yet one. This is how our tribes should be. So as we tend and keep the garden, we are to tend and keep our people."

The sound of bleating drew Ahinoam's eye toward her boys. Jishui and Malchishua were struggling with an unruly she-goat, seeking to milk her. The doe's long ears hung beneath her backward-curving

---

[13] Deuteronomy 22:9 / 7:3
[14] Exodus 12:8
[15] Psalms 1:3

horns, her glossy coat full and black. Malchishua, his dark head tipped down, held the goat by the horns, striving to keep it still as Jishui sat upon the milking stool. The goat lifted her leg and kicked out in an effort to remove his annoying hand. Jishui fell backward off his stool. The goat stepped into the jug and knocked it over.

"Stand still, you accursed goat. Do you not want to be milked?" cried Jishui, running his hand through his tawny hair, now damp with milk.

Malchishua placed more feed into the trough, then took one of her back legs and tied it to the fence post. This caused the doe to falter, which halted her kicking. Though she continued to move to and fro, the boys prevailed. In the end, both were covered in milk and the jug was only half-full.

Ahinoam laughed aloud, the sound of her glee filling the air. Merab looked to her mother, a smile breaking across her pleasing face. She always loved to hear Ima laugh. But the moment passed as Ahinoam returned to her own task.

As she did so, the pebbles at her feet began to tremble. Thunder rolled against the encircling mountains. A shudder passed through the earth as Ahinoam lifted her eyes. Brown smoke rose beyond the eastern hills, cresting the rise like a gathering storm.

"What is it, *Ima*?" questioned Merab, her voice strained.

The rumble deepened. Ahinoam stood and raised her hand over her narrowed eyes. *No. Not thunder, but wagons, and the marching of many feet.*

"*Mamme!*" Fear looked at Ahinoam through the eyes of her children.

"Boys! Take your sisters inside and bar the gate."

"But, *Ima*."

"Just do as I say."

No more words. The children dropped their tasks and ran for the house. Ahinoam heard the bar go down behind the gate. The sound grew as the war host moved. Ahinoam stepped from the garden, beyond the stone half-wall. Taking the large spade in hand, she stood waiting, looking toward the east.

Sensing the unknown lurking before her, Ahinoam gripped the makeshift weapon tightly. Her palms grew sweaty. As the sound swelled, bile rose in her throat.

Over the rise, a multitude approached, shadows on the distant hills, the threat no longer lurking, but brazen and uncloaked. Several hundred men of war, and many wagons more, advanced upon her, kicking up a cloud of dust in their wake. Her heart skipped a beat and drummed in her breast. All she could think of was her children barred within the house. Fear washed over her like a wave. Her breath caught, drowning her.

There stood Ahinoam, spade in hand, held as a stave, ready for battle, waiting in dread for the host to arrive and engulf her. Only the trembling in her legs betrayed her.

Closer and ever closer the company came, drawing nearer with every beat of her pulsing heart. She could just make out the shape of each shadowy figure. Narrowing her eyes, she marveled to see one who stood taller. There was no mistake. She knew the frame, knew the gait.

Relief washed over Ahinoam as she beheld Saul. Yet a host was with him. What that meant, she could not apprehend. Still, she drew breath again, her chest rising sharply as she watched their approach through widened eyes.

"*Ela mai,* what then, woman?" spoke Saul, his voice touched with amusement. "Was it your plan to take on the whole host of men?" Shaking his head, his voice became stern. "You should have gone in with the children and barred the gate."

Ignoring his reprimand, Ahinoam questioned, "*Mah zeh,* Saul, what is the meaning of this? Are we at war?"

He looked into the eyes of his wife as he reached for the spade yet clutched in her hand. His countenance pleaded with Ahinoam for understanding, but no words did he speak.

"*Ima,*" cried Jonathan, rushing forward in his excitement, "*Abba* has been appointed king over all Israel."

"*Mah atah o'mer,* what are you saying?" asked Ahinoam, stunned. "How can this be?"

"Sister," declared Abner. "It is so. *Urim* and *Thummim* have spoken."

Ahinoam searched Saul's eyes, her head tipped to one side as she struggled for understanding. With her eyes narrowed and her mouth drawn tight, the king's wife accused her husband without a word.

"So, this is the meaning of your silence. You knew of this, did you not?"

Saul nodded.

Her knees gave way as she placed her hand upon her breast. Saul grasped her by the shoulders and set her upon the garden wall.

"Ahinoam."

"Come sister. It is a celebration. Make us some of your honey cakes."

The sound of pegs driven into the ground echoed through the air. Orderly rows of black goat-hair tents burgeoned within the plain before the house of Saul, as the soldiers, preparing for the night's repose, set up camp. Tribal standards mounted on the breeze, signifying the quartering of troops. In the course of an hour, Saul's valley was changed from a simple homestead into a military garrison.

A bird called in the distance, piercing the evening sky with a warning to its mate.

Within the courtyard of their home, Ahinoam and the house servant formed batter by mixing oil, mint, cumin, and cinnamon into flour. Sweetened with honey, the dough was then formed into little cakes and fried in a pan over the fire.

When the honey cakes were finished, Ahinoam placed them upon a woven tray and carried them up the stairs to the central chamber.

She could hear the voices of the men as she drew near. Entering the room, Ahinoam saw Kish, Abner, Saul, and several men whom she did not know, sitting upon cushions on the floor around the table. Small bowls, the remains of their meal within, sat before each man.

The feast, so spread, was now a remnant of its former greatness: mutton roasted with garlic and rosemary, cucumbers with sliced onions and dill, pomegranates, and dates. Whole green onions were served on a plate along with thin flat circles of bread that had been cooked directly on the hot coals of the fire. At the center of the table rested wide-mouthed pitchers of water, juglets filled with olive oil, vinegar, and honey: all to lend savor to the meal.

Ahinoam placed the cakes upon the table, pushing aside the bowls of seasoned vegetables and cheese. Taking the decanter, she slowly refilled each man's drinking bowl, pouring the wine through the spout, listening intently to the words spoken. The liquid ran red, free of the dregs, as the wine poured through the strainer.

Saul smiled to himself, aware of his wife's eavesdropping, their secret audience.

"Now is the time to act," spoke Abner, leaning forward, his hand coming down upon the table with a thud. "We must strike against this emblem of Philistine presence. Too long they have pressed into our territory, putting fear into our people. We must take the Philistine garrison at Gibeah and remove them from our midst."

"That would bring all of Philistia down upon us!" objected Saul. "I cannot lead our people now into open war. We are not yet ready. The time is not right."

Ahinoam melted into the corner, forgotten in the dark recesses of the room. Kish and the others sat quietly as the future of Israel was disputed, watching the debate between uncle and nephew.

"The threat is imminent, the danger great," urged Abner. "If we grasp the moment quickly, we will catch them unawares and our chances will be greatly multiplied." As he spoke, he clutched the unseen enemy with his hand.

"This will not bring an end to the Philistine threat," rebuked Saul, shaking his head, "only provoke them to do more harm."

Abner spread his hands, urgency marking the gesture. "We must act soon against the enemies of Israel, to unify the kingdom." He looked over at Saul, his voice quieting to a stern, but patient, tenor. "The people need a demonstration of your recent designation as king. It is a chance to prove your worth."

"My worth?" Saul mulled over the sound of the word. Lowering his head and gently shaking it, Saul gave reply, his voice subdued, "I am no king; I do not even know how to be a king."

"What then will you do?" scolded Abner. "Return to tending the fields, to shepherding your herds?"

Saul liked the sound of that, to return to life as he knew it: the wind on his face, open valley before him, the grand mountains encircling him. But all that was lost to him now, for there was no turning back. His destiny stood before him like a mighty giant in the shadows. The full force of his new yoke fell heavy upon his shoulders.

Slowly, he raised his head and looked Abner in the eye. His voice was calm. "I will wait and see what Yahweh will do, to see how the matter will fall." Saul turned his gaze to meet the eager faces of the others, nodding in approval of his own decision. "Caution is prudent. If indeed I am king, I must consider the well-being of my people. I cannot lightly send them to harm. We must be careful to plan our course and not rush into a battle we are uncertain we can win. Our people are not ready to have this burden laid upon them."

Abner shook his head, his jaw set hard. "And while you wait and plan, the enemy grows in strength and confidence. What then will you do when they have pushed into the very heart of Israel?" Abner paused for a moment, then added, "Maybe it is you who are not ready to bear this burden."

CHAPTER 14

UNDER SIEGE

Fleeing, they flew well-nigh from the field with ruinous panic, the enemy hard after them. By the arrow's flight, many death received. These, thus marked, became obstacles to the living as they stumbled over their fallen comrades. Weapons became burdensome. Dropping their arms, the demoralized troops dispersed in mayhem across the open country.

Beyond the lowest foothills dashed the defeated warriors; through wheat fields, the tale of their flight was told as paths were laid by the crushing of the tender stalks.

Scattered and confused, the broken Hebrew army surged over the mountainous region of Gilead, past the territory of Reuben, and north into the land of the half-tribe of Manasseh. Fleeing the storm of the Ammonites, the Hebrews ran, treading over the terraced hills, trampling the lush vegetation, speeding through olive trees, and tearing down vineyards.

The murderous hands of the foe had a stranglehold on them, squeezing out their life, devouring the dying Israelite army. For the number of the slain was not yet enough to satisfy the hunger of the enemy.

Hours passed as the pursuit continued and the bloody massacre pressed hard after the retreating troops. Not until the sun went down was the chase stayed.

As many as could sought refuge within the gates of Jabesh-Gilead. Through the dark night, the survivors staggered into the shelter of the city. Yet few escaped. And those not slaughtered were captured and tormented by the enemy.

Breathing hard, Nagad leaned against the wall, striving to catch his breath. As he looked about, he saw Helek coming to his side. Still winded, Nagad questioned, "How many—how many made it to the city?"

With weariness, Helek spoke, "Some seven thousand by my estimation, *Sar.*"

Nagad, his eyes large and pleading, gazed into Helek's dark orbs. "So few! We are all but destroyed. And I sense this is not yet over."

"*Sar, Sar!*" called Jarib as he hastened to where Nagad stood. "The Ammonites are approaching from the south. Even now they are encircling the city!"

Nagad, followed close by Helek, climbed to the top of the wall. The city rested upon the height of the mountains of Gilead, and upon the rampart, Nagad received an extensive view over land and sea. The air was crisp in the predawn twilight, the terrain lush and fertile below. Wisps of clouds lingered overhead as the scent of wheat and good soil clung to the breeze. Turning south, Nagad watched as the Ammonites advanced toward the city, their numbers growing steadily. Crestfallen, Nagad looked on as their fate drew near.

"*Sar,* your orders?" spoke Helek.

"Bring everyone behind the walls with as many provisions as can be found, then shut the city." Pointing along the bulwark, Nagad continued with purpose. "Position troops within the fortifications along the perimeter. Prepare to defend the city from advancement. Protect the walls, spare nothing. It is all that keeps us from destruction. We are in for a long harassment."

Dark memories of the fall of Shiloh filled Nagad's mind: of the bitter conflict, the battle upon the wall, and lives lost. Sighing, the captain closed his eyes to the wounds of old. Yet he knew that these people here, in Jabesh-Gilead, were doomed—and he alone was looked to for their salvation.

With quick haste, the city swept into action. The gate was barred, and the walls were manned with archers, accurate and deadly in skill.

Once closed, the defenders refused to open it, and those not yet within the city were swiftly hauled up the walls with ropes.

The enemy marred the countryside, chopping down trees, digging trenches, scars inflicted upon the land. Soon, fortifications rose round about Jabesh-Gilead, platforms manned with archers and slingers to harass daily all who ventured near. The line of circumvallation drawn, the city was now completely cut off from all relief: of food and water, and with it, hope turned to vapor.

Mist hung low to the ground as Helek walked through the wood. The forest opened into a beautiful grotto. Trees encircled the clearing; dew dripped from the dark green foliage, the air cool and crisp as a fresh spring morning. He was drawn to the other side of the hollow by the soothing sound of a trickling stream. Water flowed freely over the rocks, forming a miniature waterfall, spilling into pools. Ripples played as small cascades splashed over pebbles and circled back into meres of swirling water.

Across the stream, movement caught his eye. Lifting his gaze, Helek beheld a man smiling, robed in white, robust, and oddly familiar.

"*Abba?*" questioned Helek.

"My son. It is I. Come, drink, and your thirst shall be quenched."

Obediently, Helek bent over the stream. As he did, he perceived that he was wearing a fine linen cloth, white as new snow upon a clear winter's day. He looked to the man, who nodded with a grin and extended his palm toward the spring. Helek dipped his hands into the cold water and drank deeply from the pure living flow, a wellspring to his soul. The water revived his spirit, extinguishing the fire of his thirst.

"It is well that you should drink from this fountain," spoke Orach, "for your life is now returned to you. Your task is yet to be fulfilled."

"My task? What is it that I am to do?"

"Come, now." The man, suddenly standing beside Helek, reached up and placed his hand upon his son's shoulder. The warmth of his father's touch soothed him with the sense that all would be well.

Visions of former days filled his mind. His heart was pricked, the heaviness of a long grief stung his soul. He had precious few memories of his father, for he had been killed at the battle of Aphek when Helek was a mere lad.

How can he be here? How is this possible?

Helek searched the dark eyes of his father. They were warm and welcoming. With his hand still resting upon his son's shoulder, Orach motioned with his other hand toward a table spread with a feast that seemed to have appeared out of thin air. "Eat, and your hunger will be satisfied."

Stepping over to the board of fare, Helek was impressed by the opulence before him. A fairer table had not been seen, a carousal of unrestrained indulgence, varied well in taste. Taking a chair at the center of the buffet, Helek sat alone before the bountiful spread. The repast of choice food, delicacies all, was such as he had never encountered. It was the regale of royalty, to sup on rich provisions, plenteous food and drink, well-prepared and abundantly displayed in fine dishes of superb artistry. Many were the junkets of seasoned meat before him. Decanters of hot spiced wine lingered to please the palate and warm the heart.

"Now this is fine," spoke Helek. With eyes wide in anticipation, he filled his plate with various morsels of succulent meat.

As his hand rose to his mouth with that first tantalizing bite, juice dripping down his fingers, a low rumble came from his stomach. Pausing, he listened again, for the sound grew. *Something is not right.* Shaking his head, he made to eat.

Again he stayed his hand as he heard someone shout.

"What is this?" complained Helek. "Disturbing my meal!"

Yet as he returned his attention to the food before him, more shrieks and screams stole through the forest, this time louder. Helek bolted upward, overturning the table. Smoke filled the glade. Reaching for his sword, he found it gone.

"It is time," spoke Orach calmly through the rising clamor.

"Time for what?"

Smiling, Orach tipped his head toward Helek. Smoke swirled about his form, and he was gone.

"Wait! I do not know what you want me to do!"

A loud crash startled Helek. As the grotto faded from view, he found himself trembling within the confines of his little room. The small wooden table was overturned, and the few utensils it held were strewn across the floor. Helek coughed. His eyes burned as smoke filled the chamber. Shaking the fog of his dream from his mind, Helek did not hesitate. Taking up his sword, he ran from the room.

Fire arrows sailed over the walls. A firestorm exploded on impact, setting structures to kindling, filling the air with a burning brume. The blaze burst forth in violent passion. An artificial glow bathed the city, the flames illumining the stricken faces of fear as the conflagration spread. The residents responded swiftly, quenching the fire before the whole of the city could be ignited.

By morning, the city smoked as the final embers put forth their last rebellion. Smoldering indignation of suppressed combustion, the tinder quiet but not dead, waited for the opportunity to reignite and begin anew. The citizens of Jabesh-Gilead picked through the remains of the dying coals, quelling any flare-ups, smothering them with rugs and mats.

"Our water is dangerously low," spoke Jarib as he watched the people working.

Nagad nodded.

"*Sar*, our food is almost gone. Our people begin to hunger. We cannot allow this to continue. We must do something. I do not wish to sit here watching the slow death that is sure to creep through our city."

"What would you have me do?" queried Nagad. "The city is fully invested; the enemy has encamped round about her. There is now no escape."

"Go out against them—take the battle outside our walls," spoke Jarib resolutely, steeped in courage, eager for glory. "We cannot sit here doing nothing while our troops grow weaker with hunger, waiting for our end."

"No," answered Nagad, "we have not the strength of numbers to risk a pitched battle."

"Will you then do nothing?" retorted Jarib. "Our days are numbered."

"It is a waiting game," spoke Helek.

"Ah, but who will outwait whom?" smiled Nagad.

"You have a plan, *Sar*." Helek looked in wonder at his captain.

"We shall destroy the crops. The enemy has an unlimited food supply, while ours runs low. If we put fire to the crops, Nahash will not have the advantage. Soon, the enemy will feel the pangs of hunger. In this we may have hope that they will give up the siege and go home."

"Brilliant," spoke Helek.

"But the crops, *Sar*—they are all we have for the coming winter," uttered Jarib.

"There will not be a winter if we cannot outwait the enemy," answered Helek.

"Find me our swiftest runner, one who is of great courage," Nagad commanded. "Do it quickly, for tonight we set our plan in motion."

CHAPTER 15

BESET

"*Sar*, here is the lad," spoke Helek.

"You are swift of foot, son?"

"Yes, *Sar*."

"What is your name?"

"Boaz, *Sar*."

Nagad looked upon the young conscript with a heavy heart. Before him stood the promise of Israel, beautiful of face with black hair that curled in unruly locks. His eyes bright and eager, his body lean, but strong, though young, too young to send on such a mission as this.

"In silence you can walk, undetected?"

"Yes, *Sar*," answered Boaz. "I can steal upon any game unawares and take him where he stands without him knowing beforehand."

"Good, good. You know the risk?"

"Yes, *Sar*."

"And you are willing?"

"Yes, *Sar*."

The lad stood straight and tall, his chest puffed out with pride. How eager youth makes one willing to risk all. Nagad was loathe to send the boy on so dangerous an errand, but what choice did he have? He could think of no other course to save the city. Either way, the conscript was in peril. At least with this plan, he may have a chance.

"After you set the crops to fire, run and get word of our plight to our brethren. As quick as you can, bring back help."

"Yes, *Sar*. I will do as you say."

In the dark of night, Boaz sat upon the stone wall. Helek placed hot coals within a clay pot and covered it with a lid, concealing the glow within. Taking the vessel in one hand, the youth, in the dawn of his life, was lowered, slowly, over the outer barricade. As the men looked down from the edge of the parapet, Boaz, in silence, reached the ground. Glancing up, he smiled, then turned and disappeared without a sound into the cloak of night.

Minutes passed as Helek watched from the wall. Beads of moisture formed on the stalwart soldier's brow as his chest grew tight with anticipation. Time seemed to lag as he searched the darkness for signs of the youth.

"Come on, lad. What keeps you?" spoke Helek beneath his breath. His stomach lurched as fear gripped his heart. "Far too long—too long he has been."

The men beside him shifted their weight, some tapped their feet, or readjusted their grip upon their weapons. In the distance he spied movement, and then a light.

"There," whispered Helek.

"What do you see?"

"I see his flame—the pot is broken!" Then, like a sail that has lost its breeze, Helek uttered, "It has been extinguished."

The men peered blindly into the dark, anxiously scanning the unseen horizon. But no crops blazed before them. No sound disturbed the night. Nothing. Helek sighed audibly and lowered his head. They had failed.

Nagad climbed to the top of the wall and looked out over the parapet. Darkness reached his eyes, emptiness filled his heart. Hope left him, yet he watched, waiting for a sign he knew he would not see.

In the morning, before the gate, Boaz's severed head was seen fixed upon a spear. Nagad raised his hand to his brow and lowered his head, unable to bear the sight of the butchered youth.

Helek joined his captain upon the wall and saw the gruesome trophy. "May God have mercy on us!"

Against the outer fortifications, a siege ramp had risen under the daily barrage of arrows and stones. Though the defenders strove upon the wall, it was to no avail. Beneath them came the level slope of wood and earth—soon to bear siege engines to strike against the bulwarks.

"They beset us at every turn," spoke Nagad.

"It was a good plan," consoled Helek.

"It was a risk, and the cost was too great."

A hiss flew past Nagad's left ear. He turned his head in the direction of the fractured air as another whirred just over his right shoulder.

"Take cover!"

Stones and arrows shot swiftly through the air, their song marking the rapid passage, as slingers and archers engaged the defenders on the wall. Above the tumult came the sound of squeaking wheels as a battering ram was brought before the gate of Jabesh-Gilead. The men manning the siege engine worked under a sheathed roof, protected from the onslaught of missiles hurled down on them from the guardians of the city.

The large beam, suspended upon the frame, set to work, the heavy plank driven to and fro with great force, colliding with the wooden gate. The concussion rebounded through the walls, jarring the stones, setting some to crumble.

"Reinforce the gate!" cried Nagad above the clamor.

Residents set to work pulling down their houses to strengthen the gate, bolstering the barrier with the ruins of their domains, each shelter becoming a refuge to all, a haven of defense to weather the storm of raging warfare.

Gradually, and by repeated shocks, the enemy worked, laboring to breach the wall. The besieged cast down boiling water and hot oil from above, hoping to slow the progress of the enemy. This, however, had little impact, for the armored ram shielded the foe from the onslaught.

The sound of cracking wood ruptured the air.

"They are breaking through!"

"More wood! We need more wood!"

Nagad looked to the gate and saw the small breach. "It is enough. They will be through in a matter of minutes."

Upon the inner wall, he spied a torch. "Fire the arrows! Burn the battering ram!"

Lighting arrows covered in pitch, the defenders of the gate loosed a rain of fire upon the besiegers. At once, the covered ram was engulfed with flame; the oil-soaked roof of the siege engine had ignited. The enemy scurried from under their armored inferno.

The defenders, the men of Jabesh-Gilead, sent up a mighty shout as they watched the battering ram burst forth.

"We have done it!"

"It is not over! They shall only make another!" called out Jarib from the wall.

"It will be so," spoke Nagad.

Looking up from the gate, the men cried, "What shall we do, *Sar*?"

"Mend the gate." Turning to Helek and Jarib, Nagad continued, "Gather the elders of the city. We have much to decide."

Amid the thrum of wood, and pegs, and hammers, the elders gathered in a small room at the center of town to discuss their present distress with Captain Nagad and his officers.

With emotions kindled, the chamber was filled with a fervent stir, a rushing tide of dread and despair as the naked plight seized all within its grasp.

"We have this small reprieve, but I fear it will not last long." Nagad kept his voice low and even, striving to pierce the pall of unease. "The enemy will return, but this time with more than one siege engine."

"A breach will open and the enemy will rush in and bear down upon us to destroy us," lamented Ezer, his white hair in disarray. "We must surrender."

"No, I say," declared Jarib, "take the battle to them. We gather our forces, all who can bear arms, and fight outside our walls. Fight, I say. We cannot long endure within these walls!"

"Archers, all those who can bend the bow, have encamped against us," added Orel, the elder. "Daily, shafts discharge from these raised stations. None can escape from the city unmolested."

"And if we do this," spoke Yogev, citizen soldier, "who shall defend our families when the men are all dead? For dead we must be. We are greatly outnumbered."

"Our forces lie dead already upon the field," spoke a hardened warrior, Eyal, it was, who stood tall and was known for his uncommon strength and valor.

"Aye, or captured and rendered useless," agreed Helek, who stood by his side.

Orel leaned forward in his seat and gestured with his hand toward Nagad. "Many of our citizens are falling into sickness."

"We have naught but to sit and wait," spoke Yogev, "and watch as death creeps in and takes us all. Whether we fight or no, death will find us."

"Let us look at our situation," reasoned Ezer in his wisdom. "Our water is near gone. Food is in short supply. We have few who are able to wield arms. And now you tell us that siege sickness is running rampant in the streets. Gentlemen, we are out of options."

"I agree," spoke Orel, the elder. "If we wage battle with the enemy, we will be destroyed, and our families will be slaughtered in the streets, or worse. It is better to surrender and petition for mercy. It is our only hope."

"What say you, Captain," spoke Jarib, "do we fight?"

Nagad fixed a stern eye upon Jarib, deep in thought. He remembered a time long ago when he stood behind his captain waiting for him to decide the fate of Israel. Nagad wished Tiphcar were here now to advise him. It is a hard thing to lead a people, to have their doom resting upon your shoulders. But a decision had to be made, and the outcome could be the end of those who now looked to him for salvation.

Raising his hand to his brow, he stroked it as was his wont. "I see little hope of victory if we take on this enemy. How soon you forget the slaughter upon the field." With a nod, Nagad accepted the bitter course. "We must talk of surrender. I will call a meeting with King Nahash to discuss terms."

CHAPTER 16

SNAKE

Standing tall upon the wall, Eyal, leaning upon his spear, called out to the camp of the enemy. "Captain Nagad, head of the Israelite forces, wishes to speak to Nahash, king of the Ammonites. Will you treat with him?"

From below, an Ammonite of distinction answered, "Come forth. By my word, no harm will come to him."

The barrier dismantled, the gate opened to release Nagad. Attended by Helek and Jarib, polished and unarmed, the captain walked out of Jabesh-Gilead and into the hands of the enemy. A band of five soldiers, splendidly armed and with pennants flying, received the Hebrew contingent. The breeze picked up the banners, causing them to bite the air with a sudden snap. A shudder ran through the Hebrews at the sound of the lash.

Without word of salutation, the commander of the troops urged them forward by pointing with his spear into the heart of the Ammonite beast. The three Hebrews followed in silence, perilously exposed and ill at ease. The infernal stroll seemed endless—the walk toward destruction fashioned by their own hands.

Repulsed at being placed within the confines of their mercy, Jarib surveyed his escort nervously, his mind dark with fear of the enemy. Helek scowled at his guard, a low growl sounding within his throat. Reaching out, Nagad placed his hand upon Helek's forearm.

"Easy, my friend," the captain spoke, keeping his voice low.

Nagad glanced through the corners of his eyes at the guards on either side of him, scrutinizing each move for fear of some betrayal. Though it was without incident that they were delivered into the king's abode.

The shelter was a fine billet made of black goat hair similar to those of their own Hebrew tents. Several flaps were pulled up to let in a breeze, which did not help much, for the mid-summer air was hot. As they entered the tent, the guards stood to the sides and across the doorway, blocking any exit, eyeing the Hebrews with contempt.

Fine woven rugs, tapestries of many hues intricately designed, some bearing large plumed birds, lined the floor. A table and a few chairs adorned the center of the tent; upon the board were set decanters of wine and fine drink. Cushions for reclining rested against the walls.

And there sat Nahash, descendant of Lot and his incestuous daughter, centered near the back of the room, upon a gilded throne.

His straight black hair was cropped just below his ears, encircled by a simple band of gold beset with jewels. Golden earrings adorned each ear, a coiled gilded hoop inlaid with a large pearl in its center with two pendants underneath: golden with a fixed emerald, and a smaller pearl fastened below the precious stone by means of a gold finding. His fine thin beard was neatly trimmed into a narrow line that followed the contour of his jaw until it resolved into a point at the end of his chin. A mustache, also thin and carefully kept, hung over his upper lip and traveled down his face to join the slender trace of his beard.

Nahash was bedecked in an embroidered tunic covered with a purple robe.

His left hand rested on the arm of the throne while he leaned wholly upon his right elbow. Slowly, Nahash moved the ringed fingers of his right hand up his throat and under his chin, which was tipped up so he had to look down his long nose as he weighed his guests.

Each movement fluid, each gesture precise, the mere sight of him was overpowering, momentarily unbracing those before him.

This is the man who has dealt such cruelty, thought Jarib. Yet there was something within those eyes.

Though the king was graceful in form and mien, the eyes were those of a treacherous and insidious enemy.

"Welcome. Sit. Have something to drink, for I know you must be thirsty."

Helplessly transfixed by the gaze of the enemy, beautiful to behold, his words smooth and genteel, the Hebrews were compelled to look into those cunning eyes.

Nagad alone withstood the gaze, for when he looked into the eyes of Nahash, king of the Ammonites, he saw a serpent. *Nahash, the old snake, for even your name speaks of your mettle.*

"I will not drink," spoke Nagad, his cadence slow and steady, "until my people are free."

"Free! How very optimistic of you," retorted the Ammonite king.

Nagad and Nahash locked eyes, each pushing against the other's will. The air grew taut between the two leaders.

Helek and Jarib tensed, longing for their blades.

Nahash laughed as he turned away. Gesturing with his arm, he waved aside the strain that had been building.

"Fine, have it your way. But come, do sit. Let us discuss this situation in which we find ourselves."

"We shall stand."

"By the fire of Moloch, you are a stubborn people!" Nahash paused, his eyes narrowed and fixed upon the Hebrew captain before him. At last, he spoke again. "Come, come, there is no need for hostilities. We are all civilized here. Now, for what reason did you desire to speak to us?"

Nagad stood rooted, unable to bring himself to deliver such a vile message. Surrender was not in his nature. He would rather fight, but he had to think of the people. He did not desire their slaughter to be credited to his account.

"Well, get on with it, man," spoke Nahash. There was an edge to his voice. "I have a siege to carry on. I do not have time to sit here as you stall."

Oh, the pride of this man! The more it pains me to give in to this snake! But his pride we shall use against him—it shall be his downfall!

Nagad drew a deep breath, allowing his anger to drain from him. Smiling, Nagad spoke, "Great King, we wish to know your grievance with Jabesh-Gilead. In this, we may amend any wrong that has been committed."

"The city has given shelter to our ancestral enemies, Reuben and Gad. Surrender and we will let you live."

"Yet, Great King, Jabesh-Gilead is far to the north of the disputed territory, beyond the borders that Ammon has claimed."

"It has been taken from us, and we will have it returned."

"O, King," spoke Nagad, "this land does not belong to you, for we have taken it from the Amorites."

"Who took it from us before you," retorted Nahash.

"That is between you and the Amorites. When we came into this land, we did not take any that belonged to you, for we share a common blood."

"That was long ago. We claim no brotherhood with you Hebrew dogs!" declared Nahash as he leaned forward, both hands pressing against the arms of his throne. "You must either surrender, or die!"

Nagad sighed. *There is no other choice, then.* Humbling himself before the king, Nagad spoke these words, as though they were poison to his lips: "Make a covenant with us, and we will serve you."

Nahash raised himself to his feet; a vile smile spread across his smooth face. "Ah, now you have seen wisdom. This I tell you, on this one condition will I make a covenant with you—that I may put out each man's right eye, and so bring reproach on all Israel."

Jarib and Helek moved not, their mouths gaping at this revelation.

Too bitter were these words to endure. *The old snake.* Deadly and subtle was his poisonous character, writhing while yet burning.

Helek spoke softly to Nagad, "*Sar*, make not this covenant with this devil. That would render us useless in battle and leave our people defenseless. This Nahash will only come at a later date and exact the full price of this agreement. Assuredly, he will return to finish what he has begun."

"This is no game where you may contest the rules. Either die by the sword or surrender," retorted Nahash.

Nagad remained calm, making no reply to Helek's pleas. "Great King, this one thing I ask of you. Hold off for seven days, that we may send messengers unto all the territory of Israel. If there be none to save us—we will come out to you and submit to your condition."

Helek and Jarib gazed upon one another with perplexity.

Nahash, looking pleased, sat back down upon his gilded chair. His fingers worked the end of his beard as he pondered Nagad's proposal.

Then it was that his arrogance overtook his better judgment.

"It is as you request. You have seven days. Use them wisely."

With the wave of his bejeweled hand, Nahash dismissed the company, and though he granted them their petition, in time it would prove his bane.

The Ammonite guard escorted the Hebrew companions back to Jabesh-Gilead. As they entered the gate, many came to seek news of their fate.

"*Sar*," spoke Helek, "you cannot do this. We cannot place ourselves at the mercy of that beast."

"I have no intention of surrendering," replied Nagad. "We must deliver our report to these good people, then we must prepare for battle."

Confused, Helek followed his captain and Jarib to meet once more with the elders of the city. Nagad presented the conditions as they gathered again in the small room. The men sat in silence as they endured the news, all the while the shadow of the setting sun crept into the chamber, darkening their faces even as the terms rested heavy upon their souls.

"Oh, it is wretched to see such men tamely rendering submission to so vile a master as this!" cried Orel, the elder.

"It is too severe to be true," agreed Yogev, "this message of despair you bring. It is futile—all is lost. Dark oblivion looms before us; hope is banished and cannot pierce the shade that dims our future."

"All is not forsaken," reassured Nagad, "for though the wind cannot be seen, its cooling caress soothes. So hope springs from Heaven again. Even as darkness surrounds us, I sense that Hope yet abides upon the horizon."

"Do not speak of false hope," spoke Ezer, the wise. "This languid hour is upon us. Help will not come, for old hurts cannot be healed so easily. The prejudices of the past cannot bend the hearts of the other tribes."

"Nahash is counting on this, but we know something Nahash does not." Nagad looked at Helek and smiled. "The closer to destruction a tyrant moves, the more cruelly he behaves. Yet in peril's darkest hour, hope comes on stormy floods. We have a deliverer. A Benjaminite who will not soon forget the help Jabesh-Gilead gave to his tribe, how you supported us in the civil war. Send messengers to Saul at Gibeah; he is our only hope. He will not forget your need, as you did not forget his father's."

"O Great King, I fear this mercy granted is ill-fated."

"Do not fear; help will not come," spoke Nahash boldly. "These Hebrew usurpers are preoccupied with their Philistine enemies in the west. They have no strength to offer these Gileadites. Dread not the emissaries crossing the siege line to seek aid, for the Hebrews have no savior."

"But can we be sure of this, Great King?"

"Who would risk their own people to help another tribe? Save, how better to spread my name throughout the territory? My reputation will be fearsome throughout the whole of Israel, and they will bow down to me without a fight. No, let the messengers go. They will not raise up a deliverer as they hope. These impotent tribes will watch helplessly while we mutilate and humiliate their kinsmen."

CHAPTER 17

Ox Goad

Following behind the oxen, wearied from the day of working in the field, Saul and his son, Jonathan, traveled the well-worn path toward home. They walked in silence, as fathers and sons often do. Saul looked ahead, straight down the path, the dusty road that his father had taken before him, and he thought about his life, the turns it had wrought, and wondered.

Jonathan watched nature as they passed it by: heeding the course of a lizard, marking the flight of a kestrel as it dipped down, soared up, and floated on the breeze, fixed in mid-air as though time stood still. After a moment, the raptor took wing and ascended to greater heights until it disappeared from sight.

Gazing up at his father, Jonathan examined the bronzed face he knew so well, noting the fine lines that now creased the corners of his eyes. Saul sensed his son's gaze. He turned his head and looked upon Jonathan, and smiled warmly at him. Nearly a man, he was: just a head shorter than his father, the lean muscles becoming defined upon his arms. A fine stalwart youth, comely in form, the son of a king.

"*Abba*, if you are really king, why do you still herd the goats and work the field? It does not seem fitting for you to do so. Nothing has changed since you were anointed."

"It is Yahweh who must raise a king over a nation," answered Saul. "The Lord will accomplish this in His time and in the right way. I have no authority to lift myself above the people or to scheme on my own behalf. The Lord will do all, in His own fashion."

The ox on the left of the yoke strayed, leading the other beast off the path. Taking the ox-goad, Saul poked it on the rump as he called, "Gee." The ox heeded the goad and returned to the straightway.

"What is it to be a king?" continued Jonathan.

Saul was quiet, a furrow creasing his brow. "A king must be honest and just."

"You are such a man." Jonathan's chest puffed, a wide grin spreading across his face. "You will be a fine king."

Saul smiled with a nod as he looked at the path before him. "A good heart is not enough."

He fell silent.

"A king must be wise and know his people, his land, and the needs of all his subjects. He must know evil and yet not yield to it. These things will be taught in time; for now, I am just a simple man who tends goats and ploughs fields. So I must wait until occasion is presented. In the meantime, I have a family to care for."

Saul reached out with his large hand and ruffled Jonathan's hair. The camaraderie of good cheer endured as the two, father and son, journeyed home until at last, with the approach of the village, a great wailing rose to meet them. Women, fallen upon their knees, cried out with arms uplifted. Men from the city gathered about the gate, their clothes rent in anguish.

As they drew near to the men of Gibeah, Saul asked, "What has happened to trouble the people that they cry out?"

"The people have lifted up their voices to weep, for these men have come to us from Jabesh-Gilead with a message of woe, for our brethren are in dire need. Nahash, king of the Ammonites, has encamped against them. Bitter terms, he has given them."

"Tell me all that has happened."

The messengers, two there were, conveyed the horror that had befallen the city, and the danger they now faced.

"Seven days," the runner cried. "That is all the time we have. You must help us, O King, or we must face that which is a fate worse than death."

At the hearing of these words, anger burned within Saul. A change came over him, and as Jonathan watched, it seemed to him his father grew even taller. His face burgeoned dark and stern, and in that moment, the kingship awoke as he drew the mantle of sovereign upon his shoulders. For a good leader is afflicted by the suffering of his people.

"So," declared Saul, his voice strong, "Nahash has roused the quarrel that has lain dormant for all these years. Long ago, Jabesh-Gilead paid dearly for its support of our tribe, destroyed by the edge of Israel's sword. Now, they face destruction once more. It is as though some bad fate attends that place. I am amazed that men will be sundered from liberty, even concede to have their eyes put out, to save their lives. This act—this savagery—is an offense to Yahweh and a grievous act against His people.

"It would be wrong to do nothing. We shall not forget how the men of Jabesh-Gilead would not take arms against their brethren during the dark days of civil war.[16] We shall not allow this reproach to fall upon our people."

Thus spoken, Saul took hold of his yoke of oxen. Under his breath, the king uttered in the hearing of his son, Jonathan, "As Samuel has spoken, *to act when occasion is offered*, so it shall be done."

Then in the manner of the Levite who long ago divided his murdered concubine among the tribes and thus brought civil war upon the nation,[17] so Saul, king of Israel, slaughtered the beasts and cut them to pieces, sending them throughout all the territory of Israel by the hands of the messengers, saying, "Your king summons all able to bear arms, even to all the tribes within the borders of Israel, to convene forthwith at Bezek. Whoever does not go out with Saul and Samuel to do battle, so it shall be done to his oxen." For wisely he knew that the hearts of men are moved better by the vision of their eyes than the words their ears have heard.

The threat conveyed, the spectacle stirred a nation that slept, awakening them as sure as a loud trumpet that blasts throughout the heavens. Saul's powerful appeal to fight set the fear of Yahweh upon the people, even to the last man, until all were compelled to follow.

---

[16] Judges 21:8–11
[17] Judges 19–20

Or so he thought, for there were those who resisted, some who did not know disaster was upon them, and turned their backs against their king.

"What? Shall we fight for this common herdsman who calls himself king?" Anger washed across the face of Zalal.

"Who does he think he is," continued Garah, "to lift himself above the other tribes?"

Nodding, Marad agreed. "Who is he among us, that we should follow him?"

"And now he threatens us into submission." Zalal shook his head, a scowl settling upon his brow. "This has gone too far. Something needs to be done."

"I will go and fight," spoke Marad through clenched teeth, "but I will not serve this pretender. He is not my king. I will die before I will bow down to a Benjaminite."

These were the sons of Belial, whose hearts were untouched by Yahweh's choice, refusing to bear their part, and so rejected their king. And as oxen that refuse the yoke, they, too, must be broken.

CHAPTER 18

BATTLE READY

The sun broke over the horizon, casting long shadows across the plain. The wind had picked up from the northwest, bringing with it a cooling breeze. The sky was fair with just a scattering of fleecy clouds drifting here and there over the green countryside. Upon the hill overlooking his valley, Saul stood girding himself for war.

Jonathan watched with eager expectancy, admiring the display of valor presented by his father. With his greaves in place about his lower legs, Saul fastened his bronze-scale breastplate, pulling the straps tight and buckling the armor snug against his broad chest.

The thrill of anticipation grew within the lad as he stood regarding his father. He wondered what it would be like to raise a sword in battle against the enemy. Jonathan, his father's weapon in his hand, felt the weight of it within his grasp and sighed. Saul reached for his blade, taking it from the hand of his son, and slid it into its sheath.

He was ready, suited for battle; his weapon at his side. Saul stared off into the distance with his hands resting on his sword belt. He had thought long about what he was about to do, yet doubt lingered. Even so, Saul knew it was the right move.

Without changing his stance, the king looked down at his son. Jonathan saw something in his father's eyes that made him take note. It reminded him of the time when his father surprised him with a goat of his very own. The beast was to be his charge. And in that act of giving,

Jonathan knew his father saw him as a man, or at least, the promise of manhood, fit to bear the responsibility of the goat's welfare.

"Doeg—the sword." Saul's voice was commanding, but not unkind.

The servant handed his master a blade within a leather scabbard. Saul retrieved the sword from its sheath and laid the naked blade in his son's open palm. In awe, Jonathan gazed at the sharp edge as the bright rays of morning glanced off the polished bronze.

"You shall come with me this day, and see how the Lord will work in this venture."

Jonathan looked up into his father's eyes, his countenance alight with excitement. "I am coming with you to battle?"

Saul nodded and motioned his men to gather. Abner stood tall as he watched the scene unfold, a faint smile touching his face.

And so the king's son was fitted with armor and given a shield. His sword, he strapped to his side. With his head held high, he took his place by his father's side, sensing the full weight of his defense.

Kish set his hand upon Saul's shoulder, kissed his son upon one cheek, and then the other. "I wish I were still young enough to go and fight with you, my son. Be well, and return home safe with the boy."

Before the farewells could be fully attended, Ahinoam ran upon them and positioned herself between Saul and Jonathan.

"Do not take him," cried Ahinoam, clinging to Saul's breastplate, as she held her son back with her palm to his chest. "Not this time. He is just a boy."

"He is old enough to wield a sword."

Ahinoam's visage betrayed confusion and horror.

Saul clasped his wife's hands and held them close. "Ahinoam." His voice softened as he met her eyes. "I cannot ask other fathers to send their sons to fight for me and not take my own. I will look after him."

"Saul." Ahinoam searched her husband's face. She could see that his mind was set. Relenting, she pleaded, "Bring him back to me. Come back to me."

He leaned down and kissed his wife. He took in her face with his eyes and smiled at her. "Do not fear, God is in this. He will deliver us."

Saul lifted his gaze, Ahinoam's hands yet in his, and turned to the gathering men.

"Ziba, I ask you to stay behind. I am entrusting my family into your keeping. Hold them as your own till my return."

With head bowed, he answered, "I will do as you bid, my king."

Saul frowned at the title. "Doeg, you will come with me."

Saul donned his helmet and signaled the men to move out, his son following in his wake.

And so, as women throughout the ages have done, Ahinoam sent her husband and her eldest son to war. Beside her stood Kish, her father-in-law, his hands upon her shoulders, for she was not alone in the wasting hollow of silent waiting. In anguish, she watched, clasping her clenched hands to her gut.

Searing the night sky, the invoking flame of the kindled beacon sent forth its rays like a star upon a dark world. Fiery signals reached out from hilltop to hilltop, calling forth all to arms, answered by the resounding pitch of the trumpet echoing its convocation within the valleys below. Runners drove the message throughout the territory, dispatched in all directions, hastening to the tribal chiefs with word of the summons. In the span of one night, every city and village was thus roused to the general alarm to gird for battle.

And men responded, men from flock and field, each furnishing his own provisions and weaponry, repairing to their ancestral standards under the orders of their tribal commanders.

Able men they were, from among all Israel, drawn out and mustered by captains of thousands and captains of hundreds, ready to march to the rendezvous at Bezek.

Saul advanced with his retinue of mighty men through the countryside, a long march north beyond the Vale of Shiloh, into the open plain of Bezek. With incredible haste, the company had flown from Gibeah, a day and a night, to come upon this tryst of action, to where his fate, and that of Israel, would be determined. Already many had found their way to this general place of assembly north and east of Shechem on the road to Beth-shan, nearly opposite the ford of the Jordan River, and just out of sight of Jabesh-Gilead.

A feat beyond reckoning, not the least of the acts of Saul, four days and a half it was since the call for help was sent out from the besieged city. Even so, the seven-day reprieve was soon to expire.

As they mounted the ridge, Jonathan beheld the plain of Bezek. Men lined up in formation by hundreds and by thousands. From the heights it seemed a patchwork of embroidered cloth. Passing through the ranks of mighty men, the tribal commanders walked, calling out orders and reviewing the troops. Never before had Jonathan seen so many men in one place.

Saul turned his eye upon the multitude of soldiers, a grim look etched on his face. "Some hundred thousand."

"My king," Abner replied, "three hundred thousand from Israel and thirty thousand from Judah by my count. It is a miracle so many have hearkened in so small a time."

Smiling, Saul marked Abner, his kin. "When God stirs the hearts of men, they are moved to action." The king placed his powerful hand upon his general's shoulder. "Come, let us go down and present ourselves. We have much to prepare."

Descending the hill, Saul and his men passed through the camp of the tribes. Many stopped their labors and gazed upon their sovereign.

"We present ourselves to your service, my king," spoke Ma'aleh, one of the tribal chiefs. "All have come in one accord to fight for Saul and for Samuel, the prophet of God."

"Is this all the men?"

"All who have arrived, though men have been trickling in all day, Sar."

Glancing at the sky, Saul squinted against the glare of the sun, now centered within the dome above, as though pausing in its course across the celestial plain before its descent into the abyss of night. The air was still and hot. He felt a bead of sweat as it crawled from his scalp, carving its slow path through his dust-covered cheek before continuing down into the nape of his neck.

Saul regarded this man with a nod of his head.

"Very good. Have your men rest and eat. We will wait until dusk on the second day, then we move out."

He turned to go, then paused and spoke as he looked back over his shoulder. "Oh, and mind, no fires, for the enemy is very near."

CHAPTER 19

A BEACON OF HOPE

His vapored breath circled about his head as he looked to the billet at the center of camp. The night was crisp and still. Shadows lingered, entwining with the silhouettes of tents and men. He could hear the rumored whispers of soldiers speaking, rising for a moment, then falling into silence. Most were asleep, yet a few walked among the dormant camp, keeping guard through the night watches. A lone sentry stood before the entrance to the king's quarters. He hesitated for a moment, but soon decided upon his course of action.

A twig cracked behind him. He turned and searched the darkness. He saw nothing. The rhythm of his heart remained steady. He was calm as he stole closer to his quarry. As he moved through the rows of canvas shelters, no fires lit the night. The darkness concealed his progress even as the Hebrews hid from the enemy. Yet there was an enemy among them, lurking in the shadows, creeping toward his prey.

In stealth, he came upon the king's quarters. He flattened himself against the canvas and leaned toward the front to check the guard. The sentry's eyes were facing forward into camp, his posture straight and unmoving. *So far so good.*

Without a sound, the hunter stole toward the back of the billet. He drew his knife. Silent as he could, he pressed the point into the canvas a cubit from the ground. The blade was sharp, ready for its purpose. With ease it slid into the taut goatskin, opening a small hole.

Slowly, he pulled the knife down the side of the hide until, at length, a gap opened large enough for a man to pass through.

A bird called, shrill, piercing the darkness. He paused and glanced around. None were near. Parting the canvas, he slipped within and entered the king's quarters. He stood blind until his eyes grew accustomed to the dark. When he could make out images, he moved forward, toward the center of the tent. There before him was the silhouette of the king asleep on his cot.

He raised the knife. He could see the covers rise and fall with the regular rhythm of the king's breathing. A smile spread across the assassin's face. It had been so easy—too easy.

The blade was steady in his hand. He had no fear. Driving the knife downward, the assassin threw himself into the purpose of his visit.

Yet the blade never found its mark, for in that moment, Saul reached up and grabbed the intruder's arm. Alarm struck the assailant's face.

The king's grip was fierce and powerful. Saul rose from his cot as he harshly bent his foe's limb.

The weapon fell from the intruder's hand.

He staggered back, straining to free himself from the king's mighty clasp. He struggled. Saul pressed closer and seized his other arm, forcing him aside.

The monarch and the assassin were locked in a deadly grapple. Writhing and twisting, the foe fought until he at last broke loose the king's hold.

Spying the knife upon the ground, the enemy lunged to reclaim it.

Saul kicked the blade aside and hurled himself upon the intruder with such force that both were cast to the ground. Wrestling, they rolled in the dust, each striving for the upper hand.

But it was the king who prevailed. With his foe pinned beneath him, Saul struck hard.

The enemy stretched out his hand, groping for the knife, while the king beat his face with a clenched fist.

In one swift movement, the naked blade lay against the bare throat of the kneeling assassin. Standing behind, Saul seized his hair and pressed the edge into his neck.

"Who are you? Who sent you?" The king's voice was hoarse and dangerous.

The assassin tightened his lips.

Saul pressed the knife hard against the intruder's throat. He grimaced, yet refused to speak.

"Do not push me—I could end you right now!" threatened the king.

"Do what you must." The assassin's voice was taut but without fear.

"Guard!"

"My king!" the guard gasped as he entered Saul's tent. His hand went to his sword.

"Take this filth from my quarters." Saul roughly released the intruder's head from his grasp.

Stunned, the guard looked upon the scene, then his expression changed. "My king, I know this man. He is one of the *Belial* who spoke against you."

"Take him away before I do something I will regret."

The guard took hold the intruder and, after securing his hands, forcefully led the man away.

Saul turned back into his quarters. His tent was in shambles. Blood covered his trembling hands. After pouring water into a basin, the king washed away the crimson stains. The skin had split over one of his knuckles on his right hand. He looked at the wound and let out a deep breath. Even with peril so near, the king's mind was at ease.

He had been called for a special purpose, and he knew that Yahweh was with him. But evil lurks, prowling in the shadows, waiting to spring upon its victim when guard is down. It is as it has always been, for what God puts forth does not go unopposed. Dark forces walk the earth, desiring to thwart the work of righteous acts.

Yet Saul was steeped in peace, though drained from the struggle. Retrieving his covers, Saul lay down upon his cot in the midst of the chaos and fell easily into a deep sleep.

At daybreak, word of the night's encounter spread through the camp, rumors running rife as the story grew in size. Amidst the murmured whispers of trouble and reprieve, the salvation of a city weighed heavy on the hearts of the men. But their king had been delivered, and it was taken as a good omen. Willingly, the soldiers trusted the leadership of their new sovereign, for surely, Yahweh was with him.

A pavilion had been erected within the center of the field, large and open, a place to meet the captains of the battalions. Here, the heads of the tribes met with Saul. Jonathan stood by his father, learning the art of war, listening to his elders as they prepared for battle.

"Bring to me the runners from Jabesh-Gilead," commanded Saul. He looked down, inspecting his wounded hand. The knuckle was sore, but even as he tried his grip, he knew he could yet wield his sword.

Two men, lean and swift, entered into the presence of the king. "My *adon*," they spoke as they bowed their heads, uneasy at being ushered before their new sovereign.

"You have seen the Ammonite camp. Tell me all you know of their position and the surest way through the mountains. We must come upon them unawares."

"*Sar*, several ways lead through the mountains. It would not be difficult to follow the ravines from several points and emerge on all sides of the Ammonite camp, which is set within the open plain surrounding the walls of the city. The difficulty lies in crossing the Jordan. Beth-shan is the best place to ford the great river, but it will be hard to do so in secret, for it lies in full view of Jabesh-Gilead. From the river, the mountains rise on either side to conceal entry into the Vale of Jabesh."

Saul thought for a time in silence, then nodded. He looked from one man to the other. "I have an errand for you. Hasten back to Jabesh-Gilead and give them this message: 'In two days, by the time the sun is hot, you shall have help.'"

The runners stood tall, refraining from smiling in their joy. "My king, so it shall be."

"Very well. Now, go and may God be with you."

Bowing low, the two men took leave of the tent and traced a path through the camp, disappearing from view as the sun tracked its course in the distant sky. The day waned and night fell as the two raced toward the besieged city. While it was yet dark, ere the sun slept deep below the earth, the messengers returned to Jabesh-Gilead, bearing the news of their redemption. Nagad gazed upon them with awe, for little had he hoped his plea would be so fully answered.

"Now we must act our part and play into the hands of Nahash. I send you on one more errand. Rest until dawn, then one of you must take this message to the Ammonite king. Tell him: 'Tomorrow we will come out to you, and you may do with us whatever seems good to you.' For truly, we shall leave this place on the morrow."

CHAPTER 20

A Charging Bear

As the day drew on, Saul walked among his troops, inspecting them with satisfaction. Three battalions he made, dividing the men into equal columns of infantry; for no cavalry or charioteers did he possess. In the still hours of late afternoon, they moved out through the mountains and rough-cut ravines, eight miles north-by-east, until at last they prevailed upon the open plains below Beth-shan, the place of quiet rest. Here the troops tarried on the west bank of the Jordan River, just south of Beth-shan and the stream that flows from the Spring of Harod.

Looming above, Mount Gilboa frowned down from its heights upon the men as the blood-red sun sank behind the western wall. Crescent-shaped, ridge behind ridge, the range reached out its arms, encircling the plain from the Jordan River Valley south of Beth-shan around to the Harod Valley and then on to Jezreel.

Beneath the growing shade of the mountains, the company took their meal and rested. No flames lit the camp; no noise stirred the air. The firmament cooled as light faded and night descended upon the vale. Muted whispers rose from shadowed figures enwrapped in darkness, hidden from the eyes of the enemy.

Jonathan sat huddled beside what should have been a fire, but was just an empty circle of men. He looked at their countenances, shadowy outlines in the gloom. All must have thoughts of the coming battle, of possible death or hurt, yet their faces betrayed it not. Hard and stern they were, accustomed to war.

But he was untried. He had never seen battle, and his heart turned homeward to his mother, his brothers, and sisters. *They are probably sitting down for the evening meal right now, a good, warm meal that fills their bellies and satisfies their hunger.*

He shifted and cast his eye from the men so they could not see the welling tear. He blinked and sat straight, glancing again at the men beside him. Some were sharpening their blades, shields and spears resting at their sides. Others had drawn their swords, giving the edge a final inspection: proving its sharpness, eyeing the lines of the blades, then returning them to their sheaths with a nod of approval.

And so the night waxed until dew settled upon the backs of the waiting soldiers, dampening their shoulders and clinging to their hair.

Quietly, the men were roused, the silent message passed from man to man, for the night was well spent and the time had come. The troops lined up in three divisions. Under cover of dark they moved out, crossing the Jordan in three columns at diverse fords. One battalion, under the command of Abner, journeyed to Beth-shan to cross the Jordan and come at Jabesh-Gilead from the north. Another went down and came across the Jordan at Abel-meholah to attack from the south. Ma'aleh was at the head of this division.

The king rallied the final company to ford the great river at Rehob, traveling southeast toward Jabesh-Gilead to attack from the west.

Saul and his battalion marched along the great ravines that led through the mountains. Three miles east they trod; silently, their steps moved them beyond the hills overlooking the Jordan Valley. A misting brume rose from their damp bodies, obscuring the lines of shade, effacing their features as the men walked on in an eerie veil of muted shadows. Otherworldly waifs they were, creeping noiselessly through the brush; silent footsteps over the dew-laden hills; phantoms wafting among the poplar trees from which the healing balms are wrought.

All was quiet; an unnatural stillness crept into the hills: even the cricket stayed its song, and no beast dared stir the thicket. The very breath of Nature held suspended, waiting.

The highlands opened and spilled upon a wide plain surrounding the city, which rested atop a lone green hill: the mound of witness,

Jabesh-Gilead, hill of testimony. To the south, softly flowing, a waning rill broke into the vale and cut a path to the Jordan River. Terraced hills of olive groves and vineyards lined the valley. Fields of wheat grew on the lower foothills, creeping to the doorstep of the enemy encampment before the gates of the city; there they lay with the Jordan River at their backs.

The Ammonites had become negligent, and the sentinels remiss, for no guards hindered the Israelite forces' approach to Jabesh-Gilead. Saul's main regiment drew upon the rear of the enemy, while the two battalions under Abner and Ma'aleh swept around the sides, sealing off the flanks.

The trap thus set, the prey ensnared: here, undaunted, stood King Saul with his band of men concealed within the folds of the hills, lying in wait, hidden within the tree line.

The soldiers shifted their weight back and forth upon their legs, gripping their weapons tightly within their hands, as beasts waiting to pounce.

Jonathan's stomach fluttered; sweat slicked his palms as he moved nervously from side to side. Uneven came his breath; his heart drummed in his breast. Sure the enemy could hear the sound, he gathered a ragged breath, striving to quell the thundering beat.

"Steady, son. Stay close by my side."

Saul grasped his sword, drawing it to his face, and looked hard at the camp of the Ammonites. A fire kindled within his breast, generous and brave, a king of his people he had become, the fragile unity of the tribes, now bound in single purpose.

Clenching his teeth, Saul spoke these words: "The fear of a king is as the roaring of a lion; whosoever provokes him to anger, forfeits his own life. Let them hate, so long as they fear."

Just as night lightened and an eerie glow rose in the east, Saul raised his sword above his head, and lifting his voice, he pierced the dark silence, "Arise! Awaken! For the night is passing!"

Grounded in faith, lifted in confidence, with courage and resolve, Saul went forth in earnest effort, leading his great army to battle. The king swooped down upon his enemy while they yet lay upon their cots, their dreams of triumph interrupted as the sound of the trumpet and the cry of battle roused them from sleep. The growing light of morning disclosed the awful truth that the shadowy figures of the attackers were on all sides, rushing upon them in full strength.

Javelins pierced the air, hurled from the front lines; whilst from the rear guard, arrows flew, moving swiftly over the heads of the infantry, raining down upon the enemy as they struggled to arm themselves in the frenzy. Many were cut down by the shafts before they were able to grasp their swords. The trumpet blared once more; the war whoop issued forth its taunting call.

A sea of soldiers, with spears lowered and shields raised, ploughed into the Ammonite camp, cutting down all who stood in their path. Ere the enemy could make a stand, the Israelites were in the midst of their host, hemming them in on all sides, crushing them against the walls of the city. For Jabesh-Gilead stood strong against the enemy, blocking the Ammonites from retreat.

Carrion birds, ill-omened scavengers, circled low overhead against the pale light of the morning sky. Axes hacked, swords clashed, and the enemy quailed beneath the fury. The thundering clangor of sword and shield echoed off the changeless hills. Bodies fell, trampled under the feet of soldiers, bloodthirsty and bold. The air was choked with the dust of battle and the yells of men.

Jonathan entered the fray, his father at his side, as the rival ranks mixed in the fight. A single arrow, shot from within the enemy's circle, flew, piercing the man to his right. Lifeless, he fell at Jonathan's feet. Wide-eyed, he gripped his sword tighter and lifted his shield.

An Ammonite, large in stature, marked the king's son in his sights. As Jonathan raised his sword to grapple with the foe, he was knocked down, pressed by the enemy's shield. As he strove to gain his feet, the sharp edge of the enemy gashed his arm. Blood issued from the wound.

Once again, he drew himself up, but he was driven down with a kick to the shoulder. Jonathan sprawled onto his back. He raised his shield above his head as he frantically pushed with his legs against the ground, scrambling backward to fend off another blow.

It was then the king laid hold of the foe and tore him from his son, hurling him to the ground. The Ammonite's turn had come: thrown upon his back by the strength of Israel's anointed. Saul loomed above, the enemy caught in the dreadful malice of his gaze. The man leapt to his feet, weapon in hand, but Saul cast aside his shield and sprang upon him. The king seized the sword arm in his mighty hand, wrenched it down, and smote him.

The sun rose red, peering over the edge of the eastern mountains, bearing its radiance through the valley below. Jonathan lay upon the ground, raising his eyes to his father: breathing hard, his life returned to him. A beam of light broke through the morning twilight, striking Saul—his armor glinted and gleamed in glowing glory, a light borrowed from a Greater Foe than he. His raiment glistened as though he were the rising sun, an ancient strength of stone, sculpted for splendor.

The king lifted Jonathan to his feet. "Come, son. Let us make an end of this." Saul clapped him on the back and took up his shield. Turning once more to the fray, Saul let loose a savage roar and rushed upon the enemy.

Jonathan looked in wonder upon his gentle and loving father and saw instead a bloodthirsty bear charging upon the foe, his ravenous claws tearing through the Ammonite camp, raining down his righteous indignation. It was marvelous and frightening to behold.

Roused by his father's glory, Jonathan's heart burned with a fury he had never known. And so, he rose up a boy no longer, and took hold of his sword. A moon bearing the reflected light of his father's radiance, spurred on by the splendor of his father's might, he entered into his mettle of manhood—the son of the king joined in the fierce fight.

Father and son raked through the enemy with their rapacious grasp, devouring any who stood against them.

As the confusion mounted, the gates of Jabesh-Gilead burst forth, and, good to their word, the citizens came out and presented themselves before the Ammonite camp, not yielding to the adversary but falling upon their rear. The host was now wholly surrounded.

Saul continued his rampage, cutting a path through the foe, seeking Nahash, but the king of the Ammonites had fled the field and could not be found. Undaunted, Saul, with his war-wave, reared up against the adversary. Stroke by stroke, Saul wrought his swift work and the enemy met with Death upon the field.

The besiegers had not the heart nor the time to make a great stand against the onslaught. The fearful execution of judgment continued on in bloody battle until the heat of the day. The enemy groaned out its last breath as Saul ransomed the city with the blood of the oppressor. Their reward was death and hell.

The besieged had won the day, ending the fray before the seven-day truce expired. Nahash and his army were utterly routed; so complete was their defeat that all who survived were scattered, and no two of them were left together.

The anointed of God stood in his glory, a port of refuge to the weary, redeemer of the captive. In all the days of old, there was never a fury like the fury of Saul unleashed, and in his righteous anger, he had thrust his blade in holy retaliation against the foe.

For by swift march, the enemy had been surprised. The Israelite forces had entered into the midst of the camp in the morning watch and killed the Ammonites until the heat of day. So, as Saul had spoken, so he had done, better even than his word, for help had come ere the sun was hot.

His men gathered about their king, raising their bloodied swords to the sky. Shouts of victory filled the air.

"Hail, Saul! King of Israel!"

Jonathan watched the joyful display with pride. His father truly was king of the people. A great stirring of dust rose as the men pressed forward to glimpse their sovereign.

Through the veil, a soldier emerged, worn but noble, a captain of men walking with a limp, bearing a scar down his left cheek. He was followed closely by a younger soldier, shorter and stouter, and stern of face. This captain approached Saul, and with great dignity, went stiffly down upon bended knee. He took his sword and laid it across the palms of both hands and raised it to the Lord's anointed.

With his head bowed, this man spoke in a strong and solemn voice. "Captain Nagad, *adon*. I present to you my men with thanks and offer you our service. We are forever in your debt, my king."

"Humbly, I accept your offer," spoke Saul as he reached out and raised Nagad to his feet. "But your gratitude is misplaced, for it was Yahweh who won the victory. He it was who stood, a wall of fire around us and glory in our midst."

Nagad looked in wonder at his king. In Saul, he saw the promise of a gentle heart, a noble sovereign. In spite of himself, Nagad smiled up at this man in awe, for he was all that one hoped to behold in a great king.

"*Chadesh yameinu kakedem*; may we renew our days like the days of old," came a voice familiar to the ear.

"Samuel," spoke Nagad, grasping the prophet's arm in greeting. It seemed to Nagad that the years wore heavily upon Samuel; age had caught him, and he bore it before his time.

"Captain Nagad, it does my heart good to see you well. It has been many years."

"Long have I missed your counsel, and your friendship."

"Helek," Samuel said as he set his eyes upon the young Hebrew. "I see you yet remain at your captain's side."

"Always." Helek stood a little taller.

Samuel smiled and laid a hand upon Helek's shoulder. The grin faded; a solemnness settled as he turned toward the king. The two regarded one another, their minds searching the depths of the other's thoughts. A faint smile played upon Samuel's lips, and he dipped his head to the Lord's anointed.

Saul grinned at the old prophet. "Thou art late, Samuel; you have missed the fight."

"Not late; I missed not all. Thou hast done well, O son of Kish."

Then it was that the multitude beheld their sovereign with zeal, praising his name, for he had led them to victory.

Some loyal to the king advanced and cried, "Who are they that said, 'Shall Saul reign over us?' Bring forth the betrayers, that we may put them to death, for they have openly committed treason against our king."

Men there were who took hold the sons of *Belial*. Grasping them by the arms, they were forced through the mass of people. Desperate, they struggled.

"It was not us!" screamed Garah. His eyes were filled with terror.

"Wait, I assure you," protested Zalal, "you are gravely mistaken. It has been a terrible misunderstanding."

"We are not without eyes, traitor! We saw you neglect giving gifts to the king, heard your words of complaint," called one from among the ranks.

Taking hold of Marad, the king's guard spoke, "This one was caught in the king's quarters. He is the would-be assassin. Death to him!"

"Kill the assassin!"

"We had no part in our brother's actions," cried Garah. "He did that of his own accord."

"Death!"

"We knew nothing about it, or we would have warned the king!" pleaded Zalal.

The crowd was in an uproar, rising toward riot. Fervor ran rampant, spilling forth as the soldiers pressed to act against the traitors.

Ere Samuel could answer, the king's voice broke calm and clear, cutting through the clamor. "Not a man shall be put to death this day, for today the Lord has wrought salvation in Israel."

Silence fell over the ranks of soldiers. The wind of fury fled from the angry mob. In awe, the men stood, looking upon their worthy king.

"Guard, escort these three vermin to the border of the kingdom," commanded Saul. "Into exile they shall go, never to set foot upon this sacred land again."

The king glared hard into the eyes of the sons of *Belial*. "If ever I see your faces again, death shall be my answer."

"Now," spoke Saul, "take them from my sight."

And so the sons of *Belial* were driven away, stunned and ashamed, slinking back to the hole from which they had crawled.

Saul stood before his men in nobility and strength. "No more shall we speak of death and destruction. Today is a day of restoration!"

Seeing that the people perceived in Saul a deliverer, Samuel grasped the opportunity to bind the fractured unity of Israel. "Come, let us go to Gilgal and renew the kingdom there."

Samuel turned to Saul, taking him by his powerful arm. He leaned close and spoke words of warning. "Do not be remiss to guard yourself now that the kingdom is firmly established in your hand, O Saul. For oft it is said that man's earthly glory blazes brightest just before the dark night of disgrace and woe comes upon him."[18]

---

[18] (Henry, 1997)

CHAPTER 21

A PILLAR FOR HIS PEOPLE

In Gilgal, Saul stood upon a dais looking out over the crowd that gathered to see their king, hero of Jabesh-Gilead. Beyond the assembly, the brilliant sun, radiant across the open plain, wrought an endless shifting of golden hues. A shallow pool rested beside a tamarisk tree. From the bluish-purple bark, ridged and furrowed, its slender branches reached forth gray-green hands adorned with long spikes of pink flowers. Salt secretions clung to the leaves, fashioning an array of tiny crystals that glittered in the morning light.

Upon the wide, vast landscape, twelve standing stones rose in height. They told a tale of vanished years, megaliths of faith and trust. Solitary figures that were set alone, as Israel was to stand apart from the people of this pagan land.

The circle of markers moved the eye to sweep upwards toward the heavens, bringing to mind the mighty works of Yahweh as He heaped the waters of the Jordan aside and the Israelites crossed the river unhindered by the rushing torrent. These witnesses were a testimony of the new beginning Israel was to have in this land, each stone lifted as an emblem of a tribe, pillars of faith in the One True God, sacred stones declaring Israel's covenant with the Lord.

West, on the outskirts of the Palm Desert, three miles east of Jericho, these memorials set forth the boundary of the sandal-shaped enclosure, a sanctified site invoking oaths of fealty and reliance. The

Hebrews' footprint upon the land: this sector marked the start of Israel's control over the Canaanites within this region. Beyond the walls of this stone encampment, a multitude of tents had sprung to house the people, for many had come.

"Witness this stone, which Yahweh has set up as a pillar for His people, Israel," spoke Samuel, gesturing toward Saul.

A cheer rose from the crowd. All waited in anticipation. Though already elected king at Mizpah, the son of Kish was now to be confirmed. No question remained regarding Saul's qualifications as Israel's sovereign, for he had clearly demonstrated that he was a monarch who would go before them in battle.

Within the shadow of the altar of stone, in the presence of all, Saul knelt before Samuel. His palms grew damp as he perceived the eyes of every person upon his back. Slowly, Saul ran his trembling hands down the front of his tunic. The new linen fabric felt crisp and cool to his touch. Unable to attend the coronation, Ahinoam had sent this gift to him, a fine white tunic, smooth and pristine.

His thoughts turned to her now, across the miles, distant yet near. He sensed her, close to him, her arms around him in sweet embrace, as surely as the new tunic wrapped his body in warmth. Saul discerned her love, and his heart grew full, giving him courage. Lifting his gaze to Samuel, he took comfort in the old prophet's calm eyes.

A boy came forward carrying the crown and insignia upon a scarlet cushion trimmed in gold. The crowd pressed forward in anticipation as Samuel raised above Saul's tawny mane the *nezer*, a simple crown of small triangular pediments. The Lord's anointed bowed his face before the prophet, solemnly accepting what God required. Samuel lowered the circlet, the diadem of gold, and set it upon Saul's head. Next, the prophet took up the *édut*, or testimony, bracelets affirming his adoption by Yahweh, and placed the gilded cuffs about his wrists.

"*Meshiah adonai*," proclaimed Samuel in a loud voice, "God's anointed one." Taking hold of Saul's forearm, Samuel motioned him to rise. "Here is your king whom you asked for and Yahweh has chosen."

Behold, the king stood before the assembly, and the trumpets blared, echoing their concord throughout the valley. All the people of the land rejoiced at the sounding of the horns, clapping their hands and shouting: "God save the King," and "Long live the King!" Singers with instruments of music, of flute and timbrel, offered praises to their new sovereign.

Israel had accepted with full embrace the choice Yahweh had made. Well pleased was Samuel, for thus far Saul had acted well, and the kingdom was firmly established in his hands.

Jonathan looked on with pride as his father bowed to the crowd, then took up his seat before the people. The chieftains of every tribe filed forward, their banners in their hands. As each one approached the throne, he laid his insignia at the feet of Saul.

> From the east came forward:
> The banners of Judah,
> With praises to Yahweh;
> Issachar, who shoulders his load;
> Zebulun, a light for his people.
>
> The southern tribes:
> Reuben, bearing healing life and restoration;
> Simeon, a discerning witness;
> Gad, mighty men of valor,
> laid bare their claim of Saul's kingship.
>
> From the north:
> Dan, a judge of his people;
> Asher, bringing the king's delights;
> Naphtali, in the fullness of glory,
> His banner of the hind.
> Clans all, who placed their emblems
> At the foundation of the throne.
>
> The western tribes:
> Manasseh, and the greater of the two, Ephraim,
> Came forward to pledge allegiance to their monarch.
> Benjamin, vicious wolf, Saul's own tribe,
> Laid their banners at his feet.

Twelve in all were brought before him. Confirming the new sovereign by these acts of obedience, showing homage to the king, each chieftain then stood beside the throne.

"I accept your deference thusly rendered," spoke Saul. "Let every man resume his office."

In reverse order, the tribal chiefs retrieved their banners and returned once again to stand among their tribes.

"I humbly take upon me your appointment as king of Israel. I, therefore, proclaim that within the confines of these sacred walls, in the presence of Yahweh, we shall feast for seven days to honor these proceedings."

The people cheered, eager to celebrate their good fortune. To Saul's surprise, Abner stood to address the congregation. He raised his arms, lifting his voice above the assembly to quiet them.

"People of Israel! Hear what I have to say to you this day, for today is a momentous day! Today, we have seen our deliverance."

Shouts of approval rose from the crowd, then a hush fell over them as the troops poised themselves to hearken to their general.

"Here before you is a great and goodly king! He has been driven firmly into place and will be a seat of honor in his father's house. O bounteous joy to serve under so great and victorious a king as this! Hail Saul! King of all Israel! Long may he live!"

Plaudits exploded from the audience as the approbations mounted in harmony. Music played, and dancing erupted, and voices spoke in happy exultation as the celebration broke forth. Many gifts were laid at the dais of Saul, articles of gold and silver, spices and precious herbs. Such that the people had, they gave freely to their savior and king. For all were joyous at this coronation and well pleased with the choice thusly made.

"Hear me, and hearken to my words, O Israel!"

The people turned in surprise as the voice rose loud over the clamor of their jubilation.

"Hear me!" Samuel confronted the people, gazing upon the ones he had served for so long. "For indeed, I have heeded your voice in all that you have said to me. See here, I have made a king over you. Is that not what you desired? And now, here is your king, seated before you—and I am old and gray-headed, and look, my sons are with you, as one of you, deprived of their judgeships, for they were unworthy to serve you. It is all as you desired. But I have walked before you from my childhood, even to this day. Here I am, and here is your king."

With glad acclaim, the crowd responded as Samuel lifted his arms toward Saul.

"Now I ask you, witness against me before the Lord and before his anointed: whose ox have I seized, or whose donkey have I taken? Whom have I cheated? Whom have I oppressed, or from whose hand have I received any bribe with which to blind my eyes? If any, I will restore it to you."

The people looked on in confusion as Samuel spoke. And they answered as one, "You have not cheated us or oppressed us, nor have you taken anything from any man's hand." Many shook their heads or waved their hands.

Then he said to them, "The Lord is witness against you, and His anointed is also witness this day, that you have not found anything in my hand."

In agreement, the crowd answered, "He is witness."

"Was it not Yahweh who raised Moses and Aaron, and brought your fathers up from the land of Egypt?"

"It was," cried the people.

"I have stood judged before you. Now therefore, stand still, that I may reason with you before Yahweh concerning all the righteous acts of the Lord, which He did to you and your fathers.

"You remember, when Jacob had gone into Egypt, and your fathers cried out to God in their bondage. The Lord sent Moses and Aaron to deliver your fathers from slavery and brought them to this land to dwell. A righteous act of Yahweh it was."

The people cheered.

Nagad stood among the crowd, his arm resting lightly about his wife's waist. He cast his gaze upon Riyphah to discern her countenance. She looked with quiet joy toward the aged prophet, and though the lines of her days had begun to trace themselves upon her lovely face, yet the beauty of her youth abode with her still. A soft breath escaped him, and his visage warmed as he beheld her.

Yet Samuel's voice came, parting the stillness, and the sweetness of that gaze gave way to the heralding of a new age, long sought, dearly won.

"And when they forgot the Lord their God, He sold them into the hand of Sisera, commander of the army of Hazor, into the hand of the Philistines, and into the hand of the king of Moab, and they fought against them. Did they not cry out to the Lord, and say, 'We have sinned, because we have forsaken the Lord and served the Baals and Ashtoreths; but now deliver us from the hand of our enemies, and we will serve You?'

"Was it not the Lord who sent Jerubbaal, that is Gideon, Bedan, Barak, Jephthah, and even Samson, to deliver you out of the hand of your enemies on every side, and you dwelt in safety? Rebellion, retribution, repentance, restoration! Was this not a righteous act of God? His discipline as righteous as His deliverance?"

Samuel fell silent, fixing his gaze upon the assembly. In awe, they met his eye, striving to reckon the meaning of his words. The prophet took up again the thread of speech, his voice low and measured.

"And when you saw that Nahash king of the Ammonites came against you, you said to me, 'No, but a king shall reign over us,' when the Lord your God *was* your king."

Within Nagad, a flame of wrath kindled at the name of Nahash. Riyphah's clasp tightened about his forearm, and he knew she was thinking of what had near befallen him at Jabesh-Gilead. The wound dealt by the old snake still rankled within him. He regretted the Ammonite king had escaped Israel's judgment.

Nagad surveyed the faces around him. Astonishment was written upon them all, as they stood mute beneath the prophet's accusation.

Samuel took hold of Saul's arm and raised him to his feet. "Now therefore, here is the king whom you have chosen and whom you have desired."

His voice rang stern, not jubilant, and the people were dismayed, making no sound as they gazed upon the prophet and their new king.

Nagad inclined his head, his arms folded across his breast, endeavoring to grasp the prophet's intent. Riyphah clung fast to her husband's arm, her face likewise troubled by Samuel's words.

"Mind, the Lord has set a king over you. Yet he is not as the kings of the nations round about, but a sovereign who stands before the presence of the true King."

Then Nagad heard in the prophet's voice a familiar charge, and he pondered whether this time the people would remain steadfast.

"If you fear the Lord, and serve Him, and obey His voice, and do not rebel against the commandment of the Lord, then both you, and the king who reigns over you, will continue following the Lord your God, and the Lord will be with you and your king. However, if you do not obey the voice of the Lord, but rebel against the commandment of the Lord, then the hand of Yahweh will be against you, as it was against your fathers.

"Now therefore, stand and see this great thing which the Lord will do before your eyes. Is today not the wheat harvest? And rain never falls in the midst of summer? I will call to Yahweh, and He will send thunder and rain, that you may perceive and see that your wickedness is great, which you have done in the sight of the Lord, in asking for yourselves a king."

So Samuel stood tall before the people, his hands lifted toward heaven, and with a loud voice he called out to the Lord. Dark clouds coiled upon the shoulders of the mountain. Smoldering and churning, they rolled along the sky, shrouding the heavens. Earth exhaled. Its mighty winds wrecked beyond the firmament, whipping the banners, catching them up, and tossing them to and fro. The banner bearers struggled to hold their burdens in the rising torrent. Thunder broke through the skies, rending the heavens with a persuasive rumble. The acoustic blare of battle sounded forth, exacting vengeance in the sky. A curtain of rain pulled across the plain, pelting down in torrential streams. The storm poured out, fiercely it foamed, full-swift and battered broke upon the open plain.

Gilded spears of light flashed against heaven's vault and withdrew as swiftly as they had appeared. Where one peal ceased, another arose. And the people quailed with fear. They fell down upon their faces and covered their heads with their hands, crying out, for the people dreaded His terrible majesty and the power bestowed upon Samuel.

Cowering, the people pleaded, "Samuel, pray for your servants to the Lord your God that we may not die; for we have added to all our sins the evil of asking a king for ourselves."

Then Samuel said to the people, "Do not fear." Waving his hand across the sky as he called on the name of the Lord, the storm ceased.

"All is not lost; your lives are not yet forfeit. Though you have done all this wickedness, do not stray from following the Lord, but serve Yahweh with all your heart.

"And do not turn aside, for then you would go after false and empty things that cannot profit or deliver, for they are nothing. The Lord will not forsake His people, for His great name's sake. He is Faithfulness. It has pleased Yahweh to make you His people.

"Moreover, as for me, far be it from me that I should sin against God in ceasing to pray for you; but I will teach you the good and the right way.

"Only fear the Lord, and serve Him in truth with all your heart; for consider what great things He has done for you. But if you still do wickedly, you shall be swept away, both you and your king."

So it was that there they made a sacrifice of peace offerings before the Lord, and there Saul and all the men of Israel rejoiced greatly. The king himself furnished the animals for sacrifice, the *shelem*, to pay God the praises due Him. For every grace by Yahweh makes man a debtor. And as the sweet aroma rose up into the heavens, joy returned to the heart of the people.

Seven days, the people feasted, celebrating the dawn of an earthly king who would lead them. Never yet has a man been given charge over a people so fair. What tales were told of the deeds he had wrought upon the field of battle, of the defeat of Nahash, and the victory of Jabesh-Gilead; all knew this story was only the beginning of the tale of King Saul and his people.

PART THE SECOND

If you are willing and obedient,
You shall eat the good of the land;
But if you refuse and rebel,
You shall be devoured by the sword;
For the mouth of the Lord has spoken.

ISAIAH 1:19−20

CHAPTER 22

THE LONG WAIT

"How long, *Abba*, are you going to let this go on?" Jonathan stood up and paced restlessly about the chamber. The room was dimly lit by the soft golden glow of an oil lamp that rested upon the center of the table. "The Philistines harass our people, raiding them, and taking their livestock. For two years you have done nothing, whilst our forces dwindle and the enemy grows stronger."

"Patience, Jonathan," spoke Saul, motioning with his hand for his son to calm down. "You do not understand the strength within the Philistines. I would not risk open war with them. We are not ready. I have seen what they can do." Shaking his head, Saul continued, "No, we are not yet ready."

"As the Lord lives, we need not strength in numbers whilst Yahweh fights on our side. I still recall how the Lord fought for you at Jabesh-Gilead. Have you forgotten, *Abba*?"

Saul gazed down at his hands, which were folded upon the table. He lifted his eyes and looked into the troubled face of his son. "No, I have not forgotten."

"Will you then do nothing?" Jonathan's shoulders fell as he watched his father in dismay.

Saul withdrew from his son and stared across the table. A fly was buzzing about a bowl of dates, then settled down upon the rim and groomed its forelegs, drawing them one against the other.

"*Abba.*" Jonathan leaned across the table, standing over Saul. "My king, they are in our land! Even now, the Philistines occupy our city, the city where you, our sovereign, live! It is beyond insult. We must act swiftly, and soon." Jonathan straightened and pointed at the unseen enemy. "Do not let these uncircumcised dogs control our sacred lands another day. I say we fight."

Abner pulled his hand down the length of his beard as he pursed his lips and furrowed his brow in a thoughtful frown. "It seems to me," his words were carefully measured, slow and deliberate, "that with the added three thousand trained soldiers and the mercenaries now in our hire, Jonathan may have a point. Our weaponry, however, remains a great concern. If we could but achieve some iron works, sword and spear, then we would have better advantage. Still, it is a risk."

"I say we go into the Philistine garrison and take their weapons. In this way, we could build up our arms." Heated passion laced his voice.

"Jonathan!" Saul cried out as a father reproving his child. "You are too rash. If we attack now, we risk bringing the whole of the Philistine forces down upon us. Could you stand against three thousand chariots?"

"Not I," spoke Jonathan, "but the Lord."

"Still," continued Abner, as though he had only paused in his discourse to draw a breath, "we cannot allow the Philistines to go unchecked. We must show some resistance, or they will overrun all of Israel. Perhaps we feign a show of arms. Prepare forces at strategic locations merely to give the illusion of preparedness, so as to slow their progress throughout the land, while we gain in strength."

"*Abba,* at least do something, or you will lose Israel forever to these Philistines."

Saul sat for a time, mulling over the matter laid before him. With a deep breath, the king looked to his uncle. "Perhaps you are right. Where now are the Philistines' strongest garrisons?"

"They gather as we speak at Michmash and in the mountains of Bethel," answered Abner. "And of course, there is the garrison just north of here in Geba."

Saul slowly nodded. "Let us split into three divisions. Abner, take one thousand men to Bethel, and I will take another thousand and stand before Michmash. Jonathan, to Geba, you shall go with the other thousand. We will guard these areas from further raids, but..." Saul leaned forward and set his eyes sternly on Jonathan, "but, we will not engage the enemy unless I give the command."

Jonathan let out his breath and looked down at the floor beneath his feet. He gave a grave nod, then raised his eyes to his king.

And so began the long wait, for wait they did. As time weaved its web through the furrows of eternity, Saul waited, afraid or simply patient; Jonathan did not know, as he himself grew ever restless.

Often, Jishui and Malchishua would bring food and supplies sent by their mother to fortify Jonathan and his men as they held fast outside Geba on the northeastern border of Gibeah. The Israelite camp stood in full view of the Philistine garrison, which was located just beyond the city on the far side of the ravine from Michmash. Weeks had passed, and still no word from Saul.

Jonathan cast his eyes across the rolling green hills, over the limestone boulders that mottled the land, toward the enemy's camp. A fortress of stone rose above the plain.

As the king's son kept watch upon the rise, his armor-bearer drew near behind him.

"Any word from my father?"

"No, *Sar*," answered Cabbal.

Before the entrance of the enemy's garrison, a pillar stood proclaiming the Philistines' occupation of the surrounding area: the district of Geba and Gibeah, land of the Israelite king.

Jonathan's blood boiled within him as he looked upon this mockery. He could not withstand this insult any longer.

"This has gone on far too long," growled Jonathan. "The time for action has come."

CHAPTER 23

A PILLAR AT GEBA

No moon rose as the day darkened into night. A few stars peeked through the veil of the swarthy sky. Jonathan waited with his eleven men as they watched, huddled within the folds of a hill. Three outposts of ten men sat guarding the entrance to the Philistine fortress some distance from the gate: one to the west, one to the south, and one to the east. From this vantage point, the king's son and his men looked on as their comrades, split into three divisions, edged toward the outposts. A Philistine stood to attend the fire, golden-red in the darkness. The men froze, suspended in mid-advance. Jonathan held his breath.

Satisfied with the blaze, the enemy sat again among his fellow soldiers. The night was cool and still. Across the cords of Orion, he saw a falling star, a portent of what, he did not know. The fire crackled and popped, then settled down, its light flickering upon the faces of the unsuspecting enemy.

Jonathan gave the signal. The guards had grown careless in their watch. For years, they had maintained the borders without any resistance. If they had looked, they would have seen shadowy shapes creeping up the hill to where they sat. Silently, the Israelites approached, one to each man, and simultaneously clamped a hand over the Philistines' mouths and slit their throats. After hiding the bodies in the shadows, the Hebrews took their places around the fire, assuming the roles of guard within the Philistine outposts. All was set.

"Come, ere the night is old, the fortress will be ours," rallied Jonathan.

The eleven men at his side sprang to action. Slowly and silently, they crept, crouching, crawling through the shadows, advancing toward the crenellated outer wall on the eastern side of the fortress. A sentinel passed across the raised fortification. As one, the quiet company shrank into the pervading darkness of the hillocks. None moved until the guard turned and walked out of sight.

Seeing their chance, Jonathan and Cabbal made their way to the fortress. The others held their ground within the umbral conclave of the hills. The prince and the armor-bearer scrambled up the slope and leaned against the base of the wall, breathing heavily.

Hidden in the shadow, a rope ladder lashed upon his back, Jonathan set himself to scale the wall, seeking purchase for hand and foot in the rough-hewn stone. One foot took a cleft and bore him up while his fingers caught a jut above his brow; the other found a narrow niche. He held himself close to the stone and reached higher for the next purchase. Drawing by the hands and driving by the legs, he gained halfway, when he beheld the guard above.

All at once, the waiting men fell upon the ground, as though stricken by a mighty unseen power. Jonathan shifted his grip. The stone barrier loomed over him as he hid in its shade like a spider on a wall. Cabbal flattened himself against the fortress.

The guard paused, looking out from the bulwark as though searching for a hidden threat. Jonathan dared not breathe. Sweat ran a track down his neck, prickling his skin, causing his head to twitch. High above, some veiled bird called. The guard glanced up and scanned the sky. Satisfied, he turned and paced back to the far side of the wall-walk.

Jonathan closed his eyes and loosed a long sigh.

Taking a deep breath of relief, Jonathan fixed his gaze upon Cabbal below. His armor-bearer returned a look of gaping wonder, releasing his air through pursed lips. As a sly smile spread across Cabbal's face, he nodded. Jonathan grinned back, then turned his attention upward and resumed his trek up the wall. His fingertips were raw and sore, yet onward he climbed. As he reached the top of the fortress, he slipped over the battlement and poised, crouching upon the edge. The outer barricade stood four cubits in breadth. In the depths of the far corner, the guard paced away, his back toward Jonathan. With great care, Saul's son stole behind the guard, placed a hand over the man's mouth, and slit his throat.

In haste, Jonathan secured the rope ladder and let it down over the wall. Just as the first man clambered up the ladder, a guard turned the corner.

His eyes flew wide as he beheld the king's son in the shadows; he drew his sword and made to advance upon the Hebrew. A knife flew through the air, catching the guard beneath the ribs, casting him to the ground. Jonathan leapt upon his foe. He reclaimed his blade and finished the task, driving the blade into his breast.

Jonathan signaled that all was clear; his men followed up the ladder with silent effort until the last of the eleven had achieved the wall. Ghosts in the night, they slipped across the barrier, relieving the fortress of all guards who stood upon the wall-walk within view of the gatehouse.

The outer barricade was a vast structure, rising twofold in height. Each wall was joined by large flanking towers. Encased within the walls, steps led down into the main court. Edging along furtively, the twelve took the stairs, crowding within the narrow corridor.

Air stole through slender apertures set within the casemented walls, giving breath to the confined enclosure. At the bottom of the stairway, a door stood closed before them. Jonathan placed his hand upon the weathered wood and eased it ajar. He peered around the jamb. No soldiers were within view. The twelve entered into the lower court unhindered.

A quick survey gave Jonathan the layout of the fortress. The entire garrison encompassed an area no less than one hundred and sixteen cubits by one hundred cubits. A large rectangular building, with a pillared vestibule running along the face of the structure, rose high toward the back of the inner court. Storerooms were set within the stronghold's outer walls. The gatehouse stood to the left. Two Philistine guards were stationed before the massive wooden doors, each leaning upon a spear, speaking in hushed tones.

Cabbal slid around the corner; his movements silent as he drew behind the enemy and sank a knife into the back of the Philistine. Likewise, Jonathan came upon the other, seizing him in a stranglehold from behind, squeezing until no breath remained. Releasing his hold, the Philistine slumped to the ground, lifeless.

Jonathan and Cabbal cast their eyes about to see if any movement from the enemy could be detected. So far, so good. No Philistines stirred within the citadel. The court was deserted.

With the thrill of danger pulsing in their chests, three set upon the gate. A large wooden beam lay across the great doors. Metal pins with heavy chains anchored the beam in place. The three bent to their task, working the pins from their fastenings. By great force, the men hoisted the bolster from its braces. The beam was passed to those behind. Turning again to the doors, the men pulled with a mighty effort, straining under the weight of the barrier. At first, no movement came. Then the doors gave way, drawing forth without a sound as the men heaved until they could squeeze through the opening.

Some stole inside and thrust upon the gate. With all their strength they pushed until the great doors yielded to the outer way. Inside the gatehouse, four guard rooms, two on each side of the paved passageway, stood open to the inner threshold.

The outer gate was all that now stood between the twelve and the outside. Again, the three worked the pins, laboring to wrench the bolts from their lodging in the massive beam. With blades aloft, the nine closed about them, a bristling wall to guard the toiling men. One pin held fast, unmoved by all strain.

They pressed and pulled at the pin, heaved upon the chain, wriggled and twisted the bolt, but it stood fixed to the barricade. Sweat beaded upon their brows. Frustration mounted as nerves frayed. Time grew short. Soon the whole of the Philistine garrison would be roused to the Hebrews' presence.

"Hurry!" whispered Jonathan, his tone desperate.

"It will not give!"

Cabbal turned toward the gate. Taking the butt of his sword, he struck the pin with a great blow. The sound echoed off the distant walls.

Jonathan loosed an audible breath as he closed his eyes.

Across the way, a door opened. Light streamed from within the room. A shadow of a man was cast across the court; his image larger than life, a phantastic figure stretched out before them.

146

At Jonathan's ear twanged the bowstring. Cabbal loosed, and swift his arrow sped, the foe across the court laid low. But too late the arrow smote its mark; the cry of alarm already rent the air.

Philistines burst through the open door. A horde of soldiers issued from chambers within the walls, advancing toward the twelve. The guards within the gatehouse, roused by the tumult, pressed through the narrow jambs. Yet still the three worked the gate, desperate to remove the barricade. Surrounded by wrathful Philistines, trapped within the gatehouse, the nine companions fought off the advancing enemy in fierce strife. They could not hold much longer, driven hard against the wall. Time was at its end.

At the last, the gate gave way, and a thousand Israelites burst through the threshold.

Outnumbered, the Philistines fell back into the court, unable to withstand the tide that broke upon them. The Hebrews showed no mercy. In righteous fury, the Chosen cut down all who remained within the garrison.

"Look for any alive among the wounded," cried Jonathan as he stood over his last bloodied adversary. "We take no prisoners. Search now also the building, for some may yet remain, cowards hiding in their dens."

The sound of spears rending the stricken and the last gasps of dying men filled the court. Many left the company in search of more prey.

Jonathan and Cabbal, along with several men, entered the pillared building from which the Philistines had issued. The chamber was dark now. A large table stood in the center of a vast hall. In each corner, braziers glowed with embers, the flame having just been extinguished.

A soft shuffling was heard, as though something dragged across the stone floor. Jonathan drew his sword and moved toward the far side of the room. Beneath the table, quaking with fear, cowed a Philistine in fine linen robes. Jonathan stooped down, seized the man by the collar, and drew him forth.

"Look here, what I have found," derided Jonathan. "A jackal cowering in his den, and no less than the governor of the territory."

Several men broke out in laughter at his taunt.

"Please, I beg you," entreated the governor. "Have mercy. I am no soldier. You might obtain a great ransom for my release. There are those who would give much treasure for my safe return."

"Dog," sneered Jonathan. "We have no interest in your gold. It is your life we require. Come, and meet your doom."

Having thus spoken, Jonathan, still holding fast his collar, compelled the governor, half-dragging him, out of the hall and into the court. The Philistine was thrown to the ground, where, on his knees and with hands clasped, he pleaded for his life. Jonathan grasped him by the hair and wrenched back his head to bare his throat. He raised his sword above his head and lifted his eyes to the heavens. Overcome with grief, the governor gave forth a whimper, but struggled no more.

"In the name of Yahweh, Lord of Israel, and Saul the king, I take back this land."

In one fell swoop, Jonathan swung his sword and struck off the governor's head. With his foot, he thrust aside the body and held up the grisly trophy.

"Place this upon a pike before the fortress gate as a sign for all to see: Israel takes back that which is hers. We will no longer suffer these trespassers and usurpers."

A roar of adulation rose from the Hebrews, many of whom had gathered around the scene. The pike was set into the ground before the fortress gate, and the governor was placed upon it, looking out over the territory he had once controlled.

Jonathan glared with contempt at the Philistine pillar. From the men, he took an axe, hewing at the obelisk, the last mockery of occupation. With great effort, the stone column chipped. A large fissure formed at an angle, coursing through the hard surface.

The king's son swung the axe once more. He struck the pillar alongside the gap. A resounding crack ruptured the night and, with it, the object of scorn gave way under the fury of Jonathan's righteous wrath and crumbled at his feet.

A mound rose outside the fortress as the empty hulls of the enemy were piled into a heap. Armor and such weapons as could be found were collected and retained for Israelite use. The Philistines had been only lightly fitted, for the attack had been without forewarning. Nonetheless, some swords and spears of iron were won.

When all the dead had been gathered, Jonathan took a torch and set the mound to blaze. A great conflagration of orange flame and black smoke billowed as a beacon, a signal lit that a deed had been wrought at the garrison of Geba. And so it was that Jonathan, son of the king, in a single night rose as champion of Israel and brought down the indignation of all Philistia upon his people.

CHAPTER 24

KING AND SERVANT

The walls rose, broad and golden; the fire crackled, dispatching shadows across the carved images of winged creatures, of chariots and swords, and bloody battle. Immortalized, the Philistine victories forever sculpted in relief, stood as a testimony to the power of these fierce warriors, frozen in time upon the walls as the runner hastened down the long hall toward the raised dais, where sat Achish, king of Gath.

Leaning upon his right arm, the son of Maoch was deep in thought, his pleasing face stern and weathered with the passage of time. His brow furrowed, drawn into a frown under the golden band that bound his head. Black was his hair, which rested lightly upon his broad shoulders. His body was draped with a fine red robe that hung down about his white linen kilt.

"*Sar*." The runner came before Achish breathless. "Our outpost at Geba—it—it has been overthrown. All have been killed, and the pillar knocked down."

Achish pushed himself up from his throne, his stature infusing the room with his trembling rage. "What is this you tell me! Who has done such a thing?"

"It was Saul, the Hebrew king. It is he who has done this."

The dark eyes of Achish narrowed and seethed. "They have exceeded my patience with this *king* exercise. Too long have I allowed them to play at kingdom building. We shall see who overthrows whom."

"What!" Saul slammed his hands down upon the arms of his chair.

"Our spies tell us that Achish, king of Gath, has assembled the lords of Philistia. They are gathering all forces at Michmash."

Saul sat, glaring at the messenger who stood before him. He made no move to speak further. The wind shifted, whipping against the side of the tent, playing with the canvas as a breeze upon a sail.

"My king, your son has opened the floodgates. The enemy is mustering their full might. We have no hope of victory."

Saul drew in a deep breath, calming his temper. Bowing his head, he closed his eyes and loosed it. "Bring Jonathan to me."

With trepidation, Jonathan approached. Bowing low before the king, he rose and looked upon the troubled face of Saul.

"*Abba...* my king."

"Son, you do not know the full weight of your actions." Saul's voice was stern. "It is as I feared. Your unprovoked attack has launched a war we will not be able to endure. I fear the worst for Israel. What now shall we do to save our people?"

"Unprovoked?" Jonathan spoke through tight lips in an attempt to keep his voice even. "Has not Philistia kept us in check by rendering us helpless for lack of arms, forbidding the smithing of iron? Charging us high fees even to sharpen our farm implements? Have not our freedoms been taken away? Is not the yoke under which they hold us a heavy burden that we, as the Chosen of the One True God, cannot endure? I dare say, we have been provoked."

Saul glared at his son. A long breath left him as he drew his hand across his jaw.

Jonathan lowered his head before the king. There he stood, bearing the full weight of his father's disapproval. Regret nudged at his heart. Perhaps he had been too rash. Lifting his face, he looked into Saul's eyes. "Yet I see that I have behaved foolishly, for I did not seek the Lord in this first. I will not make that mistake again."

"Too hasty you have acted, Jonathan, bringing down all of Philistia upon us whilst we are not yet ready. There is naught to do now but prepare for a war come too soon. You have forced our hand. The time for action is upon us, whether we would have it or no. Therefore, we will not waste our men and resources on petty strife. It is all-out war in which we must engage."

Saul stood, gesturing toward his attendant. "Summon Israel to muster under my banner at Gilgal. We will need all who can bear arms."

And so the shrill voice of the ram's horn pierced the air, and the call went out: "Let the Hebrews hear! Rise up and fight! Our liberty is at hand!"

The sounding horn was answered, first by beacons of fire, swiftly set, followed by a second call of the trumpet. Again, the answering blaze of a more distant fire until, with haste, all the land received their war-summon. As dust filled the air with the rumor of war, the clatter of arms and the tramping of horses rose upon the high ridge overlooking the pass of Michmash as the vast army of Philistia readied itself for battle.

Saul withdrew to Gilgal, to assemble an army. But as the people saw the gathering force of Philistia, they became fearful, and their hearts melted within them. Many fled beyond the Jordan, leaving their land to hide far from the reach of the enemy. Others, seeing the danger and being greatly distressed, concealed themselves among the crags and thickets within the weathered hills. Swiftly ensconced in pits and holes, and tombs, they hid, leaving behind flock and field for fear of the hammer stroke that was to fall.

Yet not all fled. Some there were who followed their king to Gilgal, trembling, yet following nonetheless.

Saul waited seven days, waited for Samuel to come as promised, to teach him what the Lord would have him do. For the prophet had said, "You shall go down before me to Gilgal, when need arises; and surely I will come down to you to offer burnt offerings and make sacrifices of peace offerings. Seven days you shall wait, till I come to you and show you what you should do."

And so Saul was tested in his obedience to tarry and do nothing. At the renewal of each day, fresh rumors ran through camp of a growing host being drawn up to wage war against Israel. Fearing the well-appointed army of Philistia, soldiers crept away in the moonlight, so that each day's muster revealed a dwindling host. Need waxed desperate, and still Samuel did not come.

Entering the king's tent, Abner and Ma'aleh approached Saul, bowing before him as he sat upon his seat. He gave them no notice. A shadow rested upon his brow as he gripped tight the arms of his chair.

"My king," spoke Abner, "we come with today's report."

Saul started at the sound of his voice. He turned his gaze on his generals, yet gave them no answer.

"My king," Abner continued, "the people lose heart. They are scattering. Many are fleeing across the river, abandoning their homes, their fields, hiding in the mountains and in tombs, taking refuge beneath the earth within cisterns and granaries. Each day, your forces grow thinner."

Still Saul spoke no word, his shoulders bowed as though a great burden lay upon them. He passed his hand down his beard.

"By drawing our sword against the Philistines, we have merely snapped at the hand of our master. Now we will be routed without mercy," spoke Ma'aleh. "You have brought calamity upon us all, for we have no strength of arms to fight against this beast."

Abner raised his hand to quiet Ma'aleh.

Saul fixed his eyes on his uncle. "Samuel, has Samuel arrived?"

"No, my king."

"It is the seventh day?"

"Yes, my king."

"How many were numbered at today's muster?"

"Six hundred who bear arms, my king," answered Ma'aleh.

Wide-eyed, Saul leaned forward in his seat. "Six hundred?"

"It is so, my king," returned Abner.

Saul loosed a deep sigh as his hand went to his brow, his head swaying slowly from side to side. The king sat in quiet deliberation. For with each passing day, their chance for victory waned. Was he to sit and do nothing while the whole host of Philistia came down upon his people?

"My king," Ma'aleh ventured. "It is a vast army; as the sand is upon the seashore, so is the army of Philistia. It is a force beyond reckoning. Three thousand chariots we have counted and six thousand men on horse. Will you do nothing?"

Saul broke his silence, his gaze fixed upon a point somewhere in time, beyond the confines of the tent. "All my life I have seen these cruel marauders mistreating our people, beating, enslaving at will. I have seen our land and livelihood taken without mercy. It has long been my desire to free our people from this oppression. Yet, I have sat here in fear and doubt, and have done naught. Then my son, in his brave daring, attacked the Philistines without dread, without weighing if he could overcome these men of war. He has succeeded where I have failed. The time for debate is over. We must act and finally rid ourselves of these Philistines."

Standing, Saul girded himself in confidence, speaking in a strong voice. "We can wait no longer."

With great strides, he hastened from the tent and entered into the inner quarter of the enclosure. His long legs bounded up the steps of the dais to stand beside the altar.

"Bring a burnt offering and peace offering here, to me."

"My king?" questioned Abner.

"Do as I say."

As the day drew to a close and the westering sun shone red over the distant mountains, a young bull, perfect in form and without blemish, was brought before the king. Saul laid his hand upon the animal, acknowledging its part in taking his place upon the altar. With this act of worship, Saul so presented himself before the Lord, desiring acceptance, a cover, and a blessing for Israel.

Taking hold the knife, he slit the throat of the bull, collecting the blood within a vessel, its death a symbol of complete submission, a laying down of life to the will of God. The blood poured out in sacrifice, he sprinkled against the sides and at the base of the altar.

As a memorial to the death of the offering, the beast was skinned and the hide put aside, this robe of righteousness, a reminder of the provision God has granted, that everything, be it great or small, is given by the will of the Lord.

Saul then divided the sacrifice into pieces, portioned with precision, its body broken, and laid the head and the fat on the altar. The inner parts and the legs he cleansed with water; thus prepared, they were placed within the sacred hearth and set to flame, burning all parts, sending the sweet aroma up to Yahweh so that He might look favorably upon them.

So it was that Saul, king of Israel, weary of waiting for Samuel, invaded the priests' office, offering the sacrifice to the God of Jacob.

With the final oblation complete, Saul looked up, and behold, Samuel stood upon the horizon, his silhouette rising over the ridge. The king's countenance burned red, and his inward parts lurched within him as he made haste to meet him, that the prophet might bless him.

The sacrifice wholly given and wrapped in the rising aroma, Samuel saw the blood that was shed and the exaltation of ascending smoke, and his heart fell.

"Samuel," greeted Saul, "my old friend—"

Pushing past him, the prophet fixed his gaze upon the altar of sacrifice. His mind seethed and his visage aflame as he turned on Saul.

Grasping him by the arm, Samuel fixed his fierce eyes on the king. "What have you done?"

Saul recoiled and shook away Samuel's hand. "What have I done! Where were you? When I saw that the people were scattered from me, and that you did not come within the days appointed, and that the Philistines gathered together at Michmash... I feared that the enemy would now come down upon me at Gilgal. Our numbers are too few, and without making supplication to Yahweh, how were we to defend ourselves? I had no choice but to offer sacrifice to the Lord. You should have been here; you should have come as you had promised!"

Samuel's eyes widened. "You have usurped divine authority that was not yours! You should have waited. The seventh day is not yet over. You have done foolishly. It would have been better to have waited on the Lord."

"I would have, but you did not come," reasoned Saul, his arms outstretched in surrender. "And I feared lest the people turn from me and none would fight for the Lord."

"O Saul," cried Samuel, his head bowed and his shoulders sank. "You should have been more concerned with pleasing God than pleasing men. With what unqualified duplicity and distrust in Yahweh you did act! You have behaved presumptuously and in contempt of God's authority and justice! Did you think He would call you to lead His people, then leave you without His Divine protection?"

"It was His protection that I sought," answered Saul. "The people were fleeing and all would be lost." The king's voice grew loud and stern, his face waxed hot and his muscles tensed. "There were too few left to fight!"

"You forget your place, that God is King and you His servant! There is defiance in your heart, Saul. Could you not but trust the Lord to deliver from so many with so few? You have not kept the commandment of the Lord your God, which He required of you. The Lord would have established your kingdom over Israel forever."

Samuel looked sorrowfully into Saul's dark eyes. "But now your kingdom shall not continue. The Lord has sought for Himself a man after His own heart, and the Lord has charged him to be a shepherd for His people, because you have not kept what the Lord commanded you."

Saul gasped as he beheld the prophet. "I am king of Israel. You have made me so. I had to do what I felt was best for my people."

"Your people!" Samuel met his eye with an unflinching stare; and there, pity stirred. "Saul."

The edge in his voice softened as he rested his hand upon Saul's shoulder. "Why are you angry and your countenance fallen? You must rule over it. Guard yourself lest calamity fall upon you, for it waits to pounce upon you as a lion to its prey. Be still and wait. Do not forget your upward call."

Saul cast his face to the ground, a furrow graven in his brow. The prophet laid his hand gently upon the king's arm.

"Come, hope yet remains," spoke Samuel with quiet assurance. "Come with me to Gibeah. I will not abandon you. But you must return home, for Ahinoam has need of you. She is soon to be delivered of a son. You must go to her."

Saul wavered, for the Philistine threat remained. Perceiving the king's reluctance, Samuel spoke, "Fear not, there is still time. The Philistines will not yet attack in full strength; they are not ready. There is naught for you to do, but go and be by your wife's side."

So Saul, brought low and with no will to fight, turned toward home with Samuel, from Gilgal to Gibeah of Benjamin. Jonathan took the remnant of the king's army to Geba, to take up residence within the Philistine garrison that had been overthrown.

CHAPTER 25

ORACLE OF THE PAST

"Great King." The messenger rose from before the throne. "Saul has departed from Gilgal."

"Ah, at last," declared Achish. "Now we shall proceed with this undertaking."

"My king, the Hebrew sovereign has returned to Gibeah."

"Gibeah?"

"Yes, my king."

"Gibeah? Why Gibeah?" Achish sat on his throne upon the dais, stroking his chin with his ringed fingers. A frown creased his royal brow. "We do not understand. Why does he delay? Did not Saul begin this conflict, and now this false-king refuses to come out and meet us in battle? Is he afraid to fight? Is this the same man they call the hero of Jabesh-Gilead?"

Achish rose. "What does he want?" His voice bellowed, echoing off the stone walls. "What game is he playing?"

The messenger cowed beneath the glare of the sovereign's fury. He knew naught if Achish sought an answer or but spoke his thoughts. Working his hands, the messenger glanced about as though seeking rescue.

The king gestured wildly, pacing as he ranted. "He puts a crown upon his head, and he bethinks it bestows power. As though by placing a gilded circlet atop his brow, he is bequeathed the privileges of monarchy!"

His words flew as a savage snarl. "We shall show him the measure of his power!"

The flames flickered above the brazier that sat in the corner of the dais, drawing the king's eyes toward its wavering light.

"You have no power to contend with this Hebrew."

Stunned by the words, Achish wheeled forth and cast his eyes to the far end of the throne room. There he beheld an aged seer walking toward him, attended by a man of great stature. Achish was struck by the size of the diviner's man. He appeared to the king as one descended from the giants of old, the Anakim.

Gathering his robes about him, Achish sat upon his golden chair.

"How dare you speak to your king in this foul manner! By what authority do you address your sovereign so boldly?"

"By the oracle of the past, my king," bowed the seer as he approached the dais.

"What are you called? What is your purpose?"

"I am one who has seen the future through the events of the past. I come to you this day to offer you a warning, for I have looked into your future, and I saw only grief. Beware of what you seek. It will be your ruin."

"What do you know of these matters? I have told you naught of what I seek."

"You look for answers to questions you do not wish to have revealed. Yet, the answer is set before your face. But I fear that this revelation is one you would not bear to know. There is no hope in what you desire."

"You know nothing!" Achish leaned forward, flaring his nostrils as his hands gripped the arms of his throne. "By the power and authority of all the gods, I will have the head of this false-king before this conflict is over!"

"This Saul has all authority. Your gods have no power against this Hebrew's Deity."

"What do you know of this?" spat the king.

"I have seen His power. I have looked into the eyes of this great God, and I am undone. You cannot stand against Him."

Achish noted the mournful glint within the seer's eyes. There was a moment's hesitation as the king sensed his confidence waver. Then Achish's furrowed brow grew dark and severe.

"Speak no more of this to me!" roared the king. "Get thee gone from my sight, or else you will feel the full wrath of my blade!"

"So be it."

The seer and his companion bowed to the king, and walked down the aisle. Achish watched their leave-taking with indignation. He shook his head and scoffed as though brushing away an ill-bidden feeling.

"Old fool. What does he know?"

Looking to the messenger who yet abode before the dais, the king spoke, "Who was that man that he should come thus to me? Have you any word as to what authority he has to foresee the seasons yet to be?"

"My king—I—I have heard that he was at the battle of Mizpah and that he had an encounter with the Hebrew God. He returned a changed man."

"Well, I care little for his speech."

CHAPTER 26

MARAUDERS IN OUR MIDST

Rising through the sheltered valleys stood the rocky hills of the land of Shual. Wild and mountainous, this region was the home of many Bedouin shepherds and small villages surrounded by a patchwork of well-established crops. On the margins of these communities, small single-roomed homes linked their outer walls to form a meager defense. A few small acacia trees grew about the confines of the open-air enclosure within the compass of the stone buildings. Cattle lingered within this inner court; stores of grain rested beside a common threshing floor. Shepherds often gathered around these villages beyond the folds of the communal cultivated fields.

Upon the rise beyond a village, a lone shepherd leaned against his staff, watching the grazing flock. Scant black goats stood within the fold of white sheep, heavy with their woolen coats.

The sound of bleating and the deep tones of brass bells rose as they foraged for the precious green grass that overspread the hillsides. The varying thickness of the bells produced a strophe and antistrophe of different inflections, composing a symphony of sharp tinkles and sonorous full-toned clunks, quietly resounding as the sheep grazed with lowered heads. On occasion, a peal of rude harmonic dissonance rose in sforzando to intrude as a sudden wave upon the score as a sheep shook its head, then the tone receded as the animal returned to its grazing.

"*Abba, Abba!*" daughter of the shepherd cried, as she ran to him carrying a fresh water jug.

"Daughter," the shepherd greeted the child as he took up the jug and drank the cool draught.

The child looked at the flock and listened to the sounds of the bells. Deep in thought, the tender youth cocked her head as if to make sense of the music wrought before her.

"*Abba*, why do the sheep wear bells?"

Father grinned. "Why, it is to tell where my flock is bound, or by what way." A sly smile stole across his face as he bent low and whispered into his child's ear. "To tell the truth, it is because I like the song of the bells. A shepherd's lot is lonesome. It is the bells that keep me from feeling so apart. They are company to me."

"If you are lonely, *Abba*, why do you stay up here all by yourself?"

"To feed my sheep. They must graze always to fill their bellies with grass."

"Why do they eat grass?"

"It is how Yahweh has made them."

"Where does the grass come from?"

"Yahweh provides for all His creatures."

"Where did sheep come from?"

Ruffling the child's hair, the shepherd smiled at his daughter. "You have many questions, child."

"*Abba*, you did not answer my last one. Where do—"

"Hush, child." The shepherd stood still, listening, his body stiff. The hair on the back of his neck bristled.

"What do you hear, *Abba?*"

"Nothing, absolutely nothing. No bird, no beast, nothing. Something is not right."

Out of the thicket came a clamor of hooves and shouts of men. Raiders on horseback charged across the pasture, crying out their fierce war call, swords swinging overhead.

"Run!"

Too late, for in a moment the marauders were upon the flock. The symphony of bells changed, turning frantic as the Philistine raiders rushed out, driving the flock, scattering them to every quarter. Spying the shepherd, the invaders bore down upon the helpless pair. Father took daughter in arms and fled, rushing away, but still the men on horseback closed in on them. With one fell swoop, the blade reached out, slicing the neck, relieving the shepherd of his flight. His body fell to the ground, his child yet within his arms as the angry marauders pressed forward, trampling the lifeless shepherd and his precious burden.

Charging through the scattering sheep, the invaders carried forth their rampage, thundering over the hills until they reached the village, where their savagery broke anew. With cries of terror, the inhabitants cast down their bundles and fled for their lives. Pell-mell, the people darted in confusion and fear, a tumult of chaos raging through the streets.

Spears flew and swords slew, biting at the heels—no time, no weapons with which to stand and fight. None were spared: not women, nor children, nor the aged. All fell at the hands of the Philistine marauders

Stores of food and provisions, the Philistines seized with greedy hands, plunder to build their own hoard. No need to labor when the Israelites laid up such ample fare, theirs for the taking. The final movement, as the crescendo of crashing cymbals, structures were set to flame. All that remained of this once-lively village was a remnant written in ash.

Then they were gone.

The morning light filtered through the lattice-work window, weaving intricate patterns of sunbeams across the rude wooden table. The meal lay scarcely touched, for the hearts of the men were low. Saul and Abner, Ma'aleh, Nagad, and Helek all sat in silence with heads bowed. Even after much talk, their plight seemed no less dire.

"Without more men," continued Ma'aleh, "we cannot dare go to battle. It would surely be our undoing."

"Samuel does not believe our numbers are of importance," Nagad affirmed. "We have won other battles with but few men. I have seen how Yahweh fights for those who serve him. If He chooses, He can overcome these Philistines. All we need do is trust in Him."

"Trust?" returned Abner. "Who can have faith when six hundred are pitted against some tens of thousands? It is beyond what any man can be expected to do."

"We are in a hard strait, my friends," spoke Saul. "The answer eludes me. Yet I wonder, how long can we sit here with the Philistines amassing their great army? More come every day. They grow ever bolder…" The king's voice trailed off, his hand playing across the line of his mouth. "How long?"

Silence rested heavily upon the room. It was as though all who gathered about the table were bound in the moment.

Helek cast his eyes upon the others, awaiting some decision. Restless in nature, to sit long at table in discourse wore on his patience.

All this talk—what good is it? Let us rise and fight. Battles are not won with words, but by might!

Hurried footfalls resounding upon the stairs rent the stillness.

"My king!" Doeg burst into the room, breathing hard. "My king, marauding bands of Philistine raiders have issued forth from their encampment at Michmash, ravaging through the land. One company turned west to Beth-horon, another set upon the road that overlooks the Valley of Zeboim, eastward toward the wilderness. And yet a third entered the way to Ophrah and on into the land of Shual.

"They have come to kill, burn, and destroy all who are in their path, the women and children, all. Yet at Geba, Jonathan has held the pass to the south."

Saul looked at Doeg, his faithful servant, and gasped. Long he sat, stroking the end of his beard.

Ma'aleh stood and bent toward Saul, gesturing with his right arm. "They have been sent to vex us, to drive us into a pitched battle."

"If the Philistines gain control of the pass at Beth-horon," warned Abner, "they will hold the hill country."

"Not only the hill country, Uncle," spoke Saul, lifting his gaze, "but all roads that lead west to east and north to south."

Nagad leaned forward, resting his arm on the table as though he intended to rise, but never completed the act. He fixed his eyes upon the king.

"The longer we allow these marauders to go unchecked, laying waste wheresoever they go, the more dire our plight. If we do not stem

166

this onslaught, and drive these Philistines from our land, there will be much trouble ahead for Israel."

"There is but little choice," spoke Saul, "we must gain control of the Pass."

Heads nodded in agreement.

"But how should such a charge be accomplished in our present condition?" asked Ma'aleh.

Once more, silence fell upon the room, only to be disturbed again as footfalls mounted the stairs in haste. Cabbal, Jonathan's armor-bearer, rushed into the presence of the king, breathless and pale.

"My king, I have word from your son. The men are frightened. Many have deserted. But a greater evil has taken place. Some have laid hold the iron weapons gained by our victory at Geba and crossed over to the enemy, joining forces with the Philistines that they might be spared when the battle is fought. Jonathan bids you come and fight, for surely, soon the battle will be waged."

"We lost the cache of weapons?" spoke Ma'aleh, stunned. "Now none but the king and his son have iron swords. What hope remains?"

Again, swift tread echoed in the hall. The king turned to see who entered, dread pressing hard upon him. "What now?"

Ziba, chief servant of the house of Saul, came forth, wringing his hands. "*Adon*, it is time. Ahinoam will soon be delivered of the child. She calls for you."

The king rose, all else forgotten, as he followed after Ziba, leaving the debate unanswered. He entered into the bed chamber of his wife, who lay in much travail upon her cot. Pale and drawn she looked, moisture beading upon her tender brow. Taking her hand, Saul bent low and laid a gentle kiss upon her. He stroked her hair as he looked into her eyes.

"Ahinoam," he whispered.

"Saul." She smiled as she spoke his name. "Saul, you must go."

"My love, I have only just arrived."

"Saul, listen to me—" the pain of childbirth gripped her as she halted, squeezing his hand tightly until the moment passed. Deep concern etched upon Saul's face as he watched his beloved so labor.

"Saul, you must go to Geba, to Jonathan."

"I cannot leave you." He grasped her hand firmer. "Not now."

"My love, you must, for in my heart I feel something is about to happen. You must go. Jonathan needs you. I fear for him."

"Ahinoam, you ask too much of me. I cannot leave until I know you are safe and the child delivered."

And so it was, at this time of turmoil, that Ahinoam gave birth to a son, and they called him Eshbaal, fire of the ruler, the fourth son of Saul, king of Israel.

"Come." Saul burst through the doorway, tall and stern of face. "No more sitting and debating. We go to Geba. Call for the priest Ahijah."

"And what of Samuel?" pressed Abner.

"Ahijah is who we shall call. Make haste, for the battle draws near."

"And our weapons, my king?" questioned Ma'aleh. "We have no ironworkers in Israel. How then will we arm ourselves against those who bear iron swords and spears?"

"We shall fight with the axe, the sickle, and the mattock; we shall pound out our ploughshares into spears, that in doing so, the very tools the Philistines sharpened for the harvesting of crops, to despoil Israel, will be used against them in battle."

CHAPTER 27

INTO THE PASS

Cabbal climbed the steps of the bulwark on the northern wall. The dim form of his captain stood in silhouette against the moonlit night. His gaze was set beyond the stone face of the fortress, past the open plain, across the gorge toward Michmash. Cabbal stepped near and joined Jonathan at his post.

"My *adon*, why do you stand here in the night? Why do you not sleep?"

"Cabbal, sleep eludes me. My thoughts grow restless, waiting for the tide to turn. I have been wrestling with this matter, which in my rashness I have caused. Still more soldiers come every day, swelling the ranks of the enemy."

Jonathan leaned forward and rested his arms on the wall, his gaze fixed upon the Philistines' camp.

"Then it came to me. Shamgar. Do you recall, how long ago Shamgar killed six hundred Philistines single-handedly with an ox goad? Had not Yahweh promised that 'Five of you shall chase a hundred, and a hundred of you shall put ten thousand to flight; your enemies shall fall by the sword before you.'[19] Is God different today than yesterday? Surely, He has not utterly forsaken us. It is to Israel that Yahweh gave this land, not Philistia. He has fought for her in the past, many times. Why not now—today? Why not by my hand?"

---

[19] Leviticus 26:8

Jonathan straightened and looked upon Cabbal, his loyal and brave companion.

Cabbal's face melted with concern. "*Sar?*"

"The Philistines will not tarry forever. Soon they will attack. My father has come, yet still he does nothing. We cannot forever wait, discouraged, on the edge of battle, yet afraid to engage. Since I have brought this upon Israel, I will do all I can to end this. Come; let us go over to the Philistines' garrison that is on the other side."

"My *adon*, do not rashly throw your life away."

"My life is all I have to give. But do not fear. I will not do anything the Lord does not require. No longer will I take matters into my own hands, but will do as Yahweh instructs. We must go over to the other side to see what the Lord would have us do."

Cabbal stood tall, placing his hand upon the pommel of his sheathed sword. "It is a wonderfully noble thing you do. Surely I will go with you, to whatever end."

Jonathan clasped Cabbal upon his well-braced shoulder. "Either we live or die at the hand of God, but we will trust Him to bring Israel out of this."

Just before the break of day they went, Jonathan, son of the king, and Cabbal, his armor-bearer, climbed down into the Pass. The terrain south of Michmash acted as a barrier to all who wished to enter the territory. Scrub brush and acacia trees, thorny branches reaching from wide boles, sprung above thistle thickets. The green hills rose and fell, flecked with great limestone boulders. Swiftly from the main road, the valley broke off sloping eastward into a great gorge. A crude track descended into a narrow defile, leading to a broad place within the canyon that afforded an arduous approach through the lofty and precipitous crags, for steep were the cliffs that rose upon each side of this deep ravine.

The Pass was but a slender corridor traversing the chasm, the only way of reaching the other side. It was upon these heights to the north that the Philistine garrison was pitched on a flat field where the ground gradually sloped northward from the edge of the gorge. Michmash, hidden treasure was its name, for within the maze of peaks and ridges the land was scarred by deep ravines, caves and pits, and holes, sunken fissures within the rocky soil.

Down into this great breach, Jonathan and Cabbal went. Two dread cliffs rose on either side of the chasm, Bozez and Seneh they were called, one to the north and one to the south. The two companions descended the steep path where Seneh rose on the southern face of the cliff. The passage led past the thorny bushes upon this shelf, dark as coal, for the bluff ever remained in shadow, sheltered from the sun. In silence they journeyed on, careful not to place a foot on loose gravel for fear of plummeting into the ravine. The way was interrupted at times by cracks and ledges, vertical, overhanging sides that impeded their trek down the face of the baleful slope.

The morning light dimmed as the image of Bozez and Seneh, their grim shade woven together, cast an umbral mantle down upon the two men as they came to the bottom of the gorge. The valley of shadow it became; a foreboding picture of despair as the companions rested, seated for a time beneath the watchful malice of these two giants.

Yet Jonathan soon rose, for despite the overshadowing rocks bearing down on either side, he remained undaunted, even eager. Across the way, he looked up at the ascent of Bozez rising as a beacon in the north; the rays of the eastern sun caught upon the chalky heights, its crown gleaming white above the ruddy and tawny hues of the rugged cliffs.

Reaching out a hand to Cabbal, Jonathan helped him to his feet. "Come, let us go over to the garrison of these uncircumcised; it may be that the Lord will work for us. For I know nothing restrains the Lord from saving by many or by few."

"Do all that is in your heart," spoke Cabbal. "Go then; I am with you."

"Good." Jonathan adjusted his breastplate. "We will show ourselves to them. If they say to us, 'Wait until we come to you,' then we will stand still in our place and go not up to them. But if they say, 'Come up to us,' then we will go up. For in saying this we will know that the Lord has delivered them into our hands. This will be a sign to us."

The two men climbed the broad face of the beacon's base. On hands and knees they first ascended, drawing and driving up the height of Bozez. Still onward they trudged, first went Jonathan, then Cabbal, for even he remained steadfast in his endeavor. It is how it often is when persecuted men are roused to defiance; their blood, being stirred for magnificent battle, is emboldened to greater deeds than if they had never been pressed into action.

And so it was with Jonathan, as he pulled himself onto a shelf just beneath the ridge, under the watchful eye of Bozez. From this outcrop of earth, the king's son cried out, showing himself to the enemy, and there the challenge was given.

"You up there! Come and see, for I have something to show you."

"Hey, look what we have here, gentlemen," guffawed a Philistine soldier as he looked over the ridge. "The Hebrew dogs are coming out of their holes."

Two other Philistine heads appeared, hair spiked and eyes fixed upon the two Israelites below.

"So, they have tired of cowering in shadows and have come forth to deliver themselves to our mercy."

"Hey, you there, come up to us, and we will show *you* something." The Philistines laughed as they drew out their swords.

The sign confirmed, Jonathan's heart leapt within him. To Cabbal, he spoke, "Come up after me, for the Lord has delivered them into the hand of Israel. Let us now set right our cause."

On hands and knees, the two Hebrews clambered up the slope while above them the Philistines hurled down their taunts and jeers. When Jonathan gained the crest of the precipice, the soldiers drew back to make room before him; yet in stepping aside, one caught his heel upon a stone and toppled, striking hard upon his back.

As he did so, the others, startled by his cry, turned to look at their stricken comrade. Jonathan, seizing the moment, unsheathed his sword and fell upon his foes. In that same instant, Cabbal reached the summit; beholding the fray, he lifted his blade and finished the work his master had begun, striking down the wounded even as Jonathan slew the third.

At the sound of the fray, the outpost roused. Twenty stalwart Philistines came forth from behind the crags, running upon the two Hebrews with blades drawn. As each man approached Jonathan, he slew or wounded them, causing a mound of the fallen to heap up on either side. Cabbal swiftly followed, ending any who yet had life within.

Soon, all in the forward outpost were laid low, their bodies scattered over half a yoke of land. The carnage spoke of a multitude. Yet but two had stood against them.

Jonathan and Cabbal found themselves standing alone upon a flat plain surrounded on three sides by a bulwark of large stones. Careful not to make a sound, they glanced around the rock wall and looked across the expanse of land. Two hundred cubits was all that separated them from the Philistine encampment. Their senses keen with caution, Jonathan and Cabbal stepped from the outcrop.

The intrusion upon the field of Michmash had not gone unnoticed, for within the garrison the struggle had been heard. A multitude of soldiers lined up before the battlement, their naked blades within their hands. The Philistines came on, an unseen enemy before them. As they drew near, those at the fore espied two lone Israelites standing, their swords drawn, waiting to face the whole host of Philistia.

The enemy paused. Some broke into broad grins and soft chuckles, shifting their weapons within their hands, as the spectacle before them was made plain.

"Two have come to take on thousands!"

"They have lost their minds!"

"Or come to seek death!"

Cabbal breathed hard, his palm made slick with sweat. He gripped his sword tighter.

"What are one thousand or even ten thousand," spoke Jonathan, "when the Lord is on our side? Courage."

The prince and the armor-bearer braced themselves, ready to pounce on the enemy as they approached. The earth filled with the sound of advancing feet. Louder and louder the cadence progressed. Jonathan's heart beat wildly. Cabbal's breath was audibly ragged. In a moment, the horde of Philistine soldiers would be upon them.

CHAPTER 28

MICHMASH

The veil of night was fast receding as the sun cast its glow across the cool morning sky. Upon the ridge, the solitary figure of the guard stood watch as the lambent embers of the fire faded. His gaze was to the east as the dawn pulled the distant plains from shadow. The stillness of daybreak settled over the Pass. The enemy camp was silent on the other side of the gorge. Out of the corner of his vision, the guard could but make out a fire along the border of Michmash, and he knew that the Philistines were watching him as he was watching them.

Something caught his eye, north, across the ravine. He turned his head to take a closer look. Shadowy figures moved in the distance, but through the dim light of morning, he could not determine what they were.

Metal clashed against metal. With haste, he stood at attention, straining to see the cause. Something was happening. There was no mistaking the sound of blade striking blade. Conflict raged within the Philistine garrison.

From Saul's outpost at Migron, upon the southern brow of the ravine, on a precipice west of Michmash, the king's men had watched as the desolation wrought by the enemy raiders spread throughout their land, and yet, no action had been taken. But now, as the guard looked on in the growing light of day, there seemed to be a multitude engaged in battle, many falling or scattering as though the whole of Philistia did melt away.

The watchman came to Saul and found him sitting, reclining under a pomegranate tree that stood outside his tent. Here, the king sat at a loss, for he knew not what to do to end this stalemate. The Lord's displeasure weighed heavily upon him.

Has God utterly abandoned me?

"My king," spoke the guard, "someone has attacked the Philistine outpost. A great battle is waging as we speak."

With a start, Saul lifted his head.

Now Jonathan had not told his father what he had planned, for Saul had stationed his men on the outskirts of Gibeah. Six hundred men-at-arms were with him, sheltered by the Rock of Rimmon. It was this very rock that sheltered six hundred Benjaminites long ago, Saul's ancestors, during the civil war with the other tribes.

"The main camp is on full alert," continued the sentry. "The lines have been drawn into battle formation. Something has moved them; many fall where they stand."

The king stood and brushed the dust from his hands. "Call the roll and see who has gone from us; also do this at Geba, for then we will know who has caused this trouble."

The men were roused and gathered together, drawn into rank and file, preparing for the roll to be called. None were missing from Saul's company. Then the messenger from Geba arrived.

"My king," he spoke. "It is Jonathan and his armor-bearer, for they alone were not among those counted."

"My son?"

"My *adon*, it is how I said."

A flush rose upon Saul's face, and his brow grew stern. Fear washed over him.

What should I do? I have been mistaken about God's will before; I shall not be again.

So he sent for the priest Ahijah, friend of Yahweh, he was called, to bring with him the ephod to consult *Urim* and *Thummim*. In this way, Saul sought to appease this great God whose command he had disregarded.

And so the young priest came to attend his king. Saul spoke to Ahijah, that is Ahimelech, son of Ahitub, Ichabod's brother. He was

High Priest at Nob. Now this priest, he was the grandson of Phinehas, Eli's son, who had been the Lord's priest in Shiloh.

"Now do as I bid, priest. Inquire for me the will of Yahweh. See if we are to go to battle. Perhaps we might retrieve the Ark ere we fight, to go before us as once we had. May it be that this would please the Lord?"

Noise erupted from the Philistine camp, a rumble that grew until the earth quaked beneath Saul's feet.

"Stay your hand, priest," spoke Saul. "I have no need of you. I have been given my answer."

Jonathan and Cabbal stood their ground as the Philistines drew near. Under the cadence of advancing footfalls, a low rumble rose to join the rhythmic beat. The earth lurched violently, then a tremor tore through the land.

The ranks of the Philistines reeled. Some faltered, their blades thrust into the backs of their own as, with weapons drawn, they lunged forward. Thinking the enemy was at their rear, the lines turned and, in the confusion, fell upon their comrades.

Jonathan beheld the tumult of the Philistines and turned to Cabbal with a nod. They, with swords held firm, ran into the midst of the enemy and joined the fray, cutting down all within reach—two against thousands.

The tramp of marching feet drummed from the northwest. A trumpet sounded. A cry rang out from the Philistine host: "Behold, behold, the king comes!"

All stayed their hands mid-strife and lifted their gaze.

Beyond the hill, around the bend, Saul it was who first appeared: his head held high, his stature great, a herald of his coming. Nor was he alone, for after him there advanced a gathering host. At first but a few, yet ever more strode, until the ranks of Israel filled the rise. Saul and his six hundred.

Glorious they came, a spectacle grand of mighty men looming above the horizon. With swords aloft, the sun flashed upon their armor, and dust arose to wreathe them in cloud. It was as though the gods themselves descended from on high, and the hearts of the Philistines misgave them to see this divine panoply.

At sight of the adversary, the Hebrews quickened their pace. Once more the trumpet sounded; the war whoop issued forth. Full stride the six hundred ran, headlong into battle. Wreaking havoc, they broke with a mighty clash of arms into the ranks of the confounded Philistines. Struck with dread at the wonder of Saul, the Philistines turned and fled.

"It is Saul—the deliverer of Israel!"

And then it happened that the mercenaries, those Hebrew traitors, hearing the trumpet of the king and seeing the turmoil of the Philistines, turned on their masters and fought beside their Hebrew brothers. The Philistines were pursued, the Chosen of God close on their heels as they fled north.

The men of Ephraim, perceiving the call of the horn and the sounds of war, sensing the time for deliverance had come at last, picked up their swords and spears, and descending from the mountains of the north, joined the battle. Then all Israel issued forth from caves and holes, from every hiding place, and taking up arms, poured into the fray.

Hemmed in and harried, the Philistine host collapsed into chaos. Wholly routed, the enemy cast off all thought of battle and broke north to Beth-aven, west through Bethel, and down the slopes of Beth-horon into the Aijalon Valley. And still Saul and his army, their ranks now swollen, pressed hard after them, striking all who fell behind.

So the Lord saved Israel that day. Six thousand Philistines lay slain as the battle shifted a day's march westward. Yet the trial was not over, for the Israelites held fast in heated pursuit of the fleeing foe. It was to Saul that all looked, for upon him now rested the charge to complete the victory and bring the Philistines to ruin.

Yet it was not to be.

CHAPTER 29

THE OATH

The hunt pushed on through the countryside, uprooting the quiet in the valleys. With feral shouts of triumph, the victorious soldiers gave chase. Flocks scattered, disturbed from their grazing, as the men fanned out across the green hills. The fleeing Philistines were continually harassed, taunted by shafts shot into their confused ranks. Arrows let loose and spears flew, striking down the hindmost as they fled.

The sun was high in the sky, bearing hard upon the contest below. The heat of battle, borne on the day's burning breath, took a toll upon the Israelite troops. Sweat streamed down their sun-struck faces and over their heaving chests. Limbs glistened beneath the bright of noon. Yet nothing could dampen the mood of the king. The thrill of action elated his spirit; the fervor of victory coursed through him like flame.

"We shall hunt them down and kill them," rejoiced Saul. "They shall not know rest until we have destroyed each and every Philistine."

The tall grass whipped across the legs of the men, causing raw lines to form upon their skin. Limbs grew heavy; breath was labored. Sinews burned and trembled from unbroken battle. And the unrelenting sun bore down upon them.

"My king," spoke Abner, "the men need food and rest. The troops are exhausted and grow faint from their toil."

Saul said nothing in reply. He, too, felt the toll upon his person. Yet the consuming drive to achieve his goal pressed hard upon his mind.

The company of soldiers entered into a sheltered valley. Trees of oak and poplar dotted the hills, lending some relief from the fierce heat. Feeling the coolness of the glade, Saul relented.

"We rest here for a moment. We cannot afford to delay, or our chance to wholly subdue the Philistines will be lost."

Abner tipped his head toward the king and raised his hand to halt the troops. As the men drew up and gathered together, the joy of deliverance shone upon each face. Many laughed and spoke with gladness as they laid down their weapons. The water jugs were passed. Many uttered words of praise, uplifting Jonathan, for brave were his deeds.

"Jonathan has wrought us a mighty victory!"

"Yahweh has fought for us, and His favor rests upon the king's son."

"Praise be to God!"

As he listened to his men, Saul's face burned hot and his countenance fell, for he perceived that the glory did not belong to him. And in his heart a seed of jealousy grew, for twice now Jonathan, his son, had put him to shame and acted when he dared not. A snarl curled his lip. No longer was his mind exalted with thoughts of triumph, but with disgrace and loathing.

Abner brought the king a jar of water and gave it into his hand. Saul claimed the vessel from his uncle and drank in silence, his gaze fixed, brooding upon his son. The fire in Saul's eyes dimmed to scorn; he snorted through his nose and turned his eyes upon his general.

"We must altogether rout this enemy. We do not halt to rest; we do not halt to eat. We must strike them a mighty blow—one they will not soon forget. We shall pursue our enemy until not a one stands. Nothing will distract us from this task."

Saul lifted his chin, his jaw set. One hand rested upon the hilt of his sword, the other upon his hip. "Therefore, this oath we shall take: none shall eat a morsel of food this day until *I* have thrown down the last of *my* enemies."

"But, my king," spoke Abner, "the men are weary and hungry, and we still have far to go. Surely you will reconsider?"

"Cursed is the man who eats any food until evening, before I have taken vengeance upon my enemies. For the day wanes, and we must make haste; the enemy draws away even now. We shall not cease from pursuit, lest the Philistines escape from our grasp and the Lord's deliverance be squandered. This vow shall stand. My men I consecrate to God through this fast, that they may press the harder toward swift victory."

Though faint and worn, none dared break the fast while still the sun hung within the celestial plains. Thoughts grew dull, vision blurred.

Even the king felt the pangs of hunger, yet he did not relent.

So it was that as the soldiers followed hard, they entered a forest that led down into the central ridge before the western gates of Aijalon. Upon the trees, honeycomb hung rich with its sweet nectar dripping even unto the ground, golden bounty of sustaining grace. Despite their weariness and hunger, none put his hand to his mouth nor tasted the flow of honey, for the men feared the oath.

"The oath is rash," spoke Nagad. "See how weary the men grow. They labor with increasing difficulty. Their pace slows, and still the king yields not."

Gazing with desire upon the amber-hued flow, Helek nodded. "If we have gained any time by not staying our march, we have lost in the strength of our pursuit, for the men suffer."

Nagad made reply with halting breath, for a hitch bit at his side. "So it is that a man cannot sustain his labor without his daily bread. And lo, Yahweh has graciously provided for us, and yet we are commanded not to partake of it."

Vexation mounted as they ventured through the forest, temptation looming all about them.

"Look!" one cried at last. "God has met our need. See how the honey drips from the wood. It would be nothing to reach out our hand and take, and strength would return to us this day. Yet our king has withheld this gift and has caused us to hunger and grow weak in pursuit of our enemy."

The disheartened troops, embittered and disquieted by their forced fast, grumbled amongst themselves. Many looked upon their king with scorn.

Saul felt their disdain reaching toward him. A dull ache formed between his brows, yet he pushed on, his visage furrowed against the gathering pressure.

Just as the front lines of Saul's army broke through the edge of the wood, Jonathan and Cabbal entered into the forest and caught up with the rearguard. With awe, Jonathan looked upon the sweet outpouring of honey, bountiful and golden, dripping richness onto the verdure of the wood. A smile spread across his weary face as he reached out the end of his spear and dipped it into the honeycomb.

The king's son watched as he raised the golden nectar to his mouth, the thick liquid flaunting a play of colors like that of iridescent amber. His countenance brightened as the honey floated across his tongue, evoking memories of verdant, rolling pastures, the soft and smooth texture delighting the senses with the sweet, robust dew.

And strength returned to the battle-worn soldier.

Then one of Saul's army said, "Your father strictly charged the people with an oath, saying, 'Cursed is the man who eats food this day.'"

Now the king's son had not heard his father charge the men with the oath, for he had been in heated pursuit behind Saul's troops.

Jonathan withdrew his hand as a quiver of fear struck his heart. Shaking his head, he said, "My father has troubled the land. Look now, see how I am restored because I tasted a little of this honey. The men grow faint on a day when they should have been made strong. We cannot keep this pace without food. We will have no strength left to fight when we catch the enemy. How much better if the men had eaten freely today of the bounty of Yahweh's provisions! For now would there not have been a much greater slaughter among the Philistines?"

The men nodded at Jonathan's words and said nothing to defend their king.

So as the Philistines continued their retreat toward their own land, none of Saul's men tasted food. And they were troubled and sorely pressed as the battle spread south beyond the mountains through the western passes of Aijalon, which led down into the Philistine plain. The pursuit continued without respite over steep hills, giving rise to grievous hours of toil.

At last the oppressive day closed in Aijalon, and with it ended the obligation upon the troops. Saul's men looked upon the spoil: the sheep, the oxen, and the calves, taken from the Philistine camp; and their desire was aroused. Their mouths watered. Inflamed, their hunger spurred them to action. And so in desperation, they rushed upon the herds and slaughtered the beasts, taking the meat without due preparation, eating the blood with the flesh.

Helek watched the grievous breach unfold. Speaking in a low tone, he addressed his captain. "Our great king has caused the men to lay aside the commandment of Yahweh, inducing them to sin before God."

Nagad nodded, but said nothing. Disgust seeped into his being. He closed his eyes, for he had seen disobedience before, and he was loath to see it again. *Will we never learn that our actions have grave consequences?*

It was not long before others took notice and a murmur rose among them, for not all had disregarded the commandments of Yahweh. Some yet stood above reproach.

Soon, the king heard the rumblings in the camp. "What is happening that so great a disturbance flows through the valley? Tell me."

Pointing toward the plain, those untainted by desire declared: "See, the men are sinning against the Lord by eating with the blood!"

Saul looked on in horror as he beheld the trespass committed by his men. His frame trembled; his face grew hot as shame flooded his heart, for his own guilt struck home. He knew this breach in conduct was born of his rash oath. The king felt himself sink. What lack of honor his men had; what small resolve that they should so easily fall from grace.

Raising his voice above the throng, Saul spoke, "Halt! Stop what you are doing!"

The king stormed into the thick of his troops, waving his arms to draw their attention. "Do you not see your own actions? Did not God command us not to eat the blood with the meat, for the blood is the life? Do you not recall that to eat the life with the flesh separates you from the house of Israel?[20] You have dealt treacherously. What you do is an abomination to the Lord."

As though stricken, the men raised their gaze from their frenzy, blood dripping from their mouths. They cowed beneath their king's

---

[20] Genesis 9:4

stern eye, bending low that they might ward off the retribution of Yahweh.

Turning toward his officers, to Jonathan, Nagad, and Helek, Saul brought forth this command: "Roll a large stone to me this day. Disperse yourselves among the men, and make proclamation throughout the camp, and say to them, 'Bring me here every man's ox and every man's sheep, slaughter them in the presence of the king, and eat; and do not sin any more against the Lord.'

"Tell the men this, for as you know, God hath plainly commanded Israel that they should always drain the blood from a beast before they eat of it. The flesh must be cooked, but the blood is to run forth onto the ground for the life belongs to God."

"As you have said, so shall it be, my king," uttered Jonathan, bowing his head before his father.

So each man did as he was commanded, and brought his ox that night, and slaughtered it there before the king. Then, as the patriarchs had done in times long spent, Saul set up a stone altar to appease Yahweh with sacrifices, with meat properly prepared, to cover the sin of his men. This was but the first altar that he built to the Lord. For Saul, the king, was zealous, as men are wont to be, in preserving the form of worship, though by his deeds he denied the power of Yahweh.

Well pleased he was with the reparation of faults, Saul, seeing the men had taken food and were rested, brought forth an impetuous decree. Laying upon the men yet another hardship, the king said, "Let us go down after the Philistines by night, and plunder them until the morning light; and let us not leave a man of them."

Nagad cast his gaze upon the ground, troubled by this charge. Thus far, the deeds of the king this day had been heedless and unbridled, as though his sovereign were governed by mere inclination.

As the captain raised his eyes to give voice to his concern, Jonathan spoke, "Do whatever seems good to you."

"My king," Ahijah, the priest, entreated, "if it please you, I urge you first to consult the Lord in this matter. Let us draw near to God here."

"This pleases the king," answered Saul.

Now Ahijah had the ephod upon his breast, so Saul turned toward the priest and asked of God, "Lord, will You give counsel to us this day? Shall I go down after the Philistines? Will You deliver them into the hand of Israel?"

Ahijah reached into the ephod to inquire by *Urim* and *Thummim*. But no answer came.

Perplexed, Saul replied, "Ask again of the Lord."

Ahijah extended his hand once more within the ephod; again, no reply came. "I am sorry, my king, but the Lord does not answer this day."

"Why is it that the Lord refuses to answer me?"

Stricken by Yahweh's silence, the king sensed the void stretch wide between him and the eternal realm. Called by God he was, and yet abandoned, forsaken, he stood before his men. Drawing his hand across his beard, the king's eyes swept over his men as they gathered about him. Guilt was written upon every brow.

Then it came to him: *the oath must have been broken.*

And as oft it is when one harbors a proud heart, Saul looked not to himself but to others for the cause; for surely the fault was not with the king.

"Come over here, all you chiefs, and know and see what this sin was today."

The men gathered before Saul, eyeing one another with fear. Saul perceived that the burden lay with his men and, in his rashness, Saul swore another oath.

"Assuredly, we shall bring this matter to light and reveal with whom the guilt lies. For as Yahweh lives, who delivers Israel, though it be in Jonathan, my son, he shall surely die!"

CHAPTER 30

RASH DEEDS

An evening breeze picked up from the west, sweeping across the broad Aijalon Valley, the place of the deer. The lowlands broke open before them, leading toward the approach to the Judean Hills. To the east lay the ascent of Gibeon. West, the path journeyed on past the towns of Aijalon and Gezer, then down to the coastal plain. Upon this swath of land, the Israelite army stood tense and exposed. The men, loyal to their king, had followed his command though vexed in spirit. Now they waited in silence, their eyes cast with reproach, for they knew the answer, but spoke not a word.

Saul strove before his men as the sun sank below the western rim of the valley. "Who has broken the oath this day? Speak now!"

Jonathan's face turned downward, his heart beating wildly. Swallowing hard, he made to step forward, but Cabbal caught his arm and held him back. Jonathan looked to his armor-bearer and met his steadfast resolve. Cabbal shook his head. The king's son stopped and lifted his gaze to his father. He trembled to see the countenance of the king, for it was stern, and his eyes, full of rage.

No one spoke of what they knew, for no one desired to betray Jonathan, whom they loved. Such rash and violent words, if answered, would condemn their young hero to death. Was it not Jonathan through whom the Lord had wrought so great a victory that day? So the men attended in uneasy silence. The fitful glare of torches awakened dark shadows upon the watchful warriors who leaned forward, breathless, casting cautious glances to either side.

Then Saul spoke to all the men of Israel, his men who fought with him, "You stand to one side, and Jonathan and I will stand to the other side."

The men did as their king wished and set themselves together.

"Ahijah," commanded the indignant king, "come between us, for you shall draw out the oracle stones."

Saul then raised his voice to heaven and said to the Lord, "O Jehovah, God of Israel, who has broken the oath this day? If this fault be in me or in Jonathan, my son, give *Urim*, and if it be in Your people Israel, give *Thummim*. Provide us a perfect lot."

Thus the simple invocation was pronounced. Saul looked upon those whose fate was to be decided, as Ahijah reached into the breastplate of the ephod to receive Yahweh's choice.

Within the pocket, Ahijah felt the cold smooth stone. He enclosed the oracle within his grasp and held it fast. A wave of reluctance hung between him and its liberation. Slowly, the priest drew back his hand and brought forth the lot. He unfurled his fingers and gasped. The judgment fell to Jonathan and the king, for it was the white oracle of *Urim* that was withdrawn. Within his trembling palm, Ahijah presented the stone to the king.

Saul's face grew ashen, for he had been sure of the innocence of his son, yet the curse remained between them.

"Cast the lot between my son, Jonathan, and me."

But he knew the answer before the lot was cast, for he had not broken the oath. Saul's countenance held firm, yet he trembled as he awaited the judgment. Too late it was to regret his rash oath. The words were spoken; the command given. There was no way out. Saul lifted his chin as he stood resolute in his purpose.

The priest returned *Urim* to the pouch and proclaimed, "If it be the king, then *Urim* will be withdrawn. But if it be Jonathan, it shall be *Thummim*."

"So be it," spoke Saul in rising agitation.

He laid his hand into the breastplate and grasped an oracle, his hand faltering as he took up the stone. Beads of sweat gathered upon his brow.

Saul rocked from side to side, his hand passing again and again along the edge of his beard. But Jonathan moved not, save his chest heaved with each breath as in silent dread he waited.

With trepidation, the priest brought forth his hand. He looked at the king. Saul inclined his head toward the priest. Ahijah extended his arm and released his grasp upon the stone. Within his palm rested *Thummim*.

The lot had taken Jonathan.

A gasp broke from the host of anxious men. Jonathan staggered as though struck, yet quickly steadied himself.

But to Saul, the force of it was as a heavy blow. For a moment, the king stood, his feet rooted and his breath stayed.

How can this be? My own son has shamed me! And now what is to be done?

Saul's heart hardened as he spoke to Jonathan, "Tell me what you have done."

"*Abba*." His voice was laden with sorrow. He was as a child caught misbehaving. His father had always been a loving and just man. But now, as he looked into the eyes of the king, he found there naught but cold accusation. "*Abba*, I only tasted a little honey with the end of the rod that was in my hand. So now I must die!"

Saul fixed a stern gaze upon Jonathan. "This fight, which you have begun, we cannot finish for your disobedience!"

As a lion lets loose a snarl, Saul glared at his son, wrathful at Jonathan's defiance of the king's word. *After all, is not the king's word law?*

With gall rising, Saul put forth his verdict. "God do so and more also; your blood will be spilt this day—though you be my son, you shall surely die."

It was as though the very air around him was drawn away. The weight of the words pressed upon him, and the earth tilted beneath him, yet he did not waver.

"Take him."

None moved.

"Take him!" Saul advanced toward Jonathan as he drew his sword.

Cabbal and Helek stepped forward, hands upon their weapons, and set themselves betwixt the king and his son.

"Shall you destroy your own worthy son?" spoke Helek.

"Surely his ignorance excuses him from this sin," contended Cabbal. "For he did not know of the vow my king decreed. No offense has been committed."

"Move out of my way!" He raised his blade, wrath kindling in his eyes. "I am your king! You must obey my word! Now stand aside!"

"Shall Jonathan die," reasoned Nagad, "who has accomplished so great a deliverance for Israel? Certainly not!"

The men unsheathed their swords and, as one, stood a bulwark about the prince of Israel, an anchorage safe from the raging storm of the king's mighty wrath.

"As the Lord lives, not one hair of his head shall fall to the ground," uttered Nagad, "for he has wrought with God this day."

A low growl rumbled through his curled lips. Saul, seeing that all were against him, narrowed his eyes. Gall seared his throat, yet the king put up his sword. With anger still aflame, he wheeled about and strode from the field.

Jonathan's breath rushed out, and with it relief poured through him. How near he had come to death, how close the gates of Sheol had pressed—and how wondrously he had been rescued. Israel's deliverer had himself been delivered.

Then Saul gave up his pursuit of the enemy, and the Philistines went to their own place unhindered. Though the victory stood not in full, the freedom won at Michmash gave rise to a spirit of hope in Israel. But some hurts are slow to heal.

PART THE THIRD

I am the Lord, that is My name;
And My glory I will not give to another,
Nor My praise to carved images.

ISAIAH 42:8

CHAPTER 31

OF FATHERS AND SONS

The walls of the imposing citadel loomed above, shading the courtyard below. The soft, warm air was dry as the morning sun increased in its upward advance. Shadows of the workers upon the wall cast strange images of beasts and monsters that moved across the paved court. As one caught up to her, Michal giggled as she turned and ran from the dark image. Noise transgressed the otherwise silent courtyard.

For years, the incessant punch of the hammer on chisel and stone drummed through the air, over the walls and into the surrounding countryside. Men yelled to and fro, giving and receiving orders for their labors. Great white blocks, hoisted by the lifting tackle, were placed carefully upon the grim limestone wall, creating foreboding battlements upon the old Philistine fortress at Geba. Fashioned for its future, the fortress, now in the possession of King Saul, was littered with wedges, plumb lines, and levels. Aged rock-blocks, darkened and embossed, mixed with the clean white of the newly laid stonework, as sawyers and masons worked to unite the old limestone walls with the new additions.

Out of the shadows sprang a dark form, reaching out, taking hold of Michal's arm. She screamed in surprise.

"Eshbaal!"

"Ah-ha," laughed he. "I scared you!"

"You only startled me," retorted Michal, "that is all."

Michal skipped lightly away from her younger brother. She spied something growing out of the corner of the old wall. Lifting its pale blue head, a single flower, its slender stem graceful and erect, rose from the outer fortifications. Michal reached down and picked the blossom. Five petals surrounded the yellow star at its center. Michal smiled as she lifted the flax flower to her nose and inhaled its soothing fragrance. With flower in hand, the young girl, upon seeing her eldest brother, skipped over, and handed the bloom to Jonathan. He looked down at her as his full beard creased into a broad smile.

Handsome in form and appearance, Jonathan had grown into the image of his father. His dark eyes peered through a mane of tawny hair that rested upon powerful shoulders. Having delivered the flower to Jonathan, Michal turned with a giggle and skipped along toward Eshbaal. The two ran off together, seeking new adventures.

Jonathan fingered the flower, cupping his strong hand about the tender bloom. He was lost in his thoughts as he sifted through his mind, rehashing old hurts of father and son estranged. Yet even after all that had transpired between them, Jonathan still looked upon his father with awe and wonder: his own hero. Though always he had tried to honor him, to be a loyal and true son, Jonathan knew he had fallen in stature in the eyes of his father.

"What do you have there, *Nesicha*, my princess?" Jishui bounded upon Jonathan's shoulders, wrapping his arm around his brother's neck and rubbing his knuckles into Jonathan's head.

"Are we collecting flowers, my dear?" teased Malchishua as he snagged the flower from his brother's hand.

Jishui released Jonathan and took the bloom from Malchishua and feigned to smell it, then ran the flower across Jonathan's face. "Let us put it in thy lovely hair."

Jonathan smiled at his brothers, shaking his head at their jest. As he retrieved the flower, he spoke, "It was a gift." Taking care not to damage the delicate bloom, he tucked the flower into his belt.

"Oh… a present from your *girl*-friend?" sparred Jishui.

"Does Jon-Jon have a sweetheart?" continued Malchishua.

"Not Jonathan," taunted Jishui. "He has no time for such frivolities."

Once more Jishui grabbed Jonathan and wrestled him. Jonathan took hold his opponent with his powerful arms and flipped him to the ground. Jishui lay flat on his back, laughing. Extending a hand to his brother, Jonathan reached down and helped him to his feet. Jishui stood, smiling as he brushed the dust off his clothes.

"Well, Jonathan," spoke Jishui as he put an arm around his brother's shoulders. "It is about time, do you not think, to settle down and find yourself a woman?"

"Yes, and the village is the perfect place to start, is it not?" encouraged Malchishua.

Jonathan cocked his head, narrowing his eyes. "What is it that you want, brothers?"

"Come now," spoke Jishui. "We desire to go to town."

"Yes," added Malchishua, "and we want you, brother, to ask for *Abba's* permission."

"Me?"

"Of course, who else?" spoke Jishui.

"Go on," continued Malchishua. "Ask *Abba*."

Jonathan shook his head. "Not I. He will not respond favorably if it is from me."

"Come now, Jonathan," spoke Jishui. "We all know you are the favored son."

"Maybe once." Jonathan looked down, his voice low. "But he hardly notices me any more. He cannot forgive me."

"Forgive you?" repeated Malchishua.

"What could so beautiful a boy as you do to offend our father?" Jishui reached up and ruffled Jonathan's hair.

"Seriously, Jonathan," spoke Malchishua. "He may seem tough, but his hopes rest on you. After all, is it not you who shall be king after him?"

"That will never be…"

"What are you talking about?" asked Malchishua. "Of course it will be. The kingdom always passes to the eldest son."

"King Jonathan!" Jishui bent his body, flourishing his hand toward his brother. "Shall we bow down to him now?"

The two young men bowed before their older brother. Jonathan's face flushed. He smiled and shook his head. Jishui and Malchishua both placed their arms on their brother's shoulders. "How about it then?"

From a balcony overlooking the inner court, Ahinoam watched as her children played. She half rested her head upon one of the great stone pillars that supported the roof above her. Gentle breaths of a cool breeze blew, breaking the warm morning, stirring wisps of hair to flutter as strands escaped her dark plaits. Her eyes turned toward her grown sons as pride welled within her. A faint smile spread across her face, though it was clouded by a hidden sorrow. She could not understand the distance that had grown between Jonathan and his father. Something had happened between them, yet what it was, no one spoke. So it lay in the midst of the family, a wedge that separated. It was always a source of grief to her, lying heavy upon her heart.

"Nearly there."

Ahinoam felt a flutter of surprise. "I'm sorry." Turning toward the sound of Saul's voice, she looked upon him and smiled.

"The work is almost done. Just the final level of the tower, then all these years of labor will be over."

"It will be nice to have peace and quiet again." Ahinoam put her arms around her husband's waist, lifting her gaze as he stroked her hair. "You must be very pleased to accomplish so grand a project."

Saul looked down into Ahinoam's face and smiled. Turning his attention toward the outer wall of the fortress, Saul beheld his boys wrestling in the court below. His heart stirred as he observed their rough-housing. Ahinoam watched Saul's expression as his gaze fixed on Jonathan. His smile vanished and his eyes grew hard.

Her heart sank.

"Saul, what has happened? Why does the sight of Jonathan trouble you so? Why are the two of you so distant? You used to be inseparable."

He frowned but did not speak, his gaze still fixed on his eldest son.

"Saul, he loves you and looks up to you."

196

Saul's chest burned with sorrow and doubt. A wave of guilt welled within him. Shaking his head, he pushed it away. "It is in the past—it does not matter now."

"But it does matter—"

"Forgive me."

Ahinoam and Saul turned. Abner had entered the room and stood at attention behind the royal couple.

"Uncle," spoke Saul.

"Samuel the prophet is here. He wishes to speak with you."

Just off the inner courtyard, a covered porch with a large double door at the end stretched across the front of the building. Two guards were stationed at the entrance. Standing aside, these sentinels opened the great doors and motioned for Samuel to pass therein.

Through the doors, the prophet entered into the throne room from the side, to the rear of the northwestern wall. To approach the king, he advanced a few paces, then turned left, facing the dais, and walked down an aisle bounded by two rows of pillars.

At the center of the room, a large open fire pit sent up flames. A small column of smoke swirled through an opening in the roof, which afforded ventilation and light.

Samuel could not help thinking that these massive, unpainted stone walls brought to mind a dungeon instead of a palace.

Two steps led to the dais upon which the king was elevated. Stationed on either side, a pair of guards stood at attention, spears in hand. In the far corners of the platform, small brass braziers cast forth a warm glow.

The prophet approached Saul as he sat upon his throne, his crown upon his head.

"Welcome, Samuel. To what do we owe this pleasure?" Saul reclined upon his gilded chair, his large arms thrown over the side of each armrest. Lifting his hand toward Samuel, he motioned him forward. "Come, speak with us."

Samuel raised his left brow as he beheld the man upon the throne. O how changed. How altered from the humble soul who once hid among the baggage to this king whose heart swelled beneath the prophet's gaze.

"The Lord sent me to anoint you king over His people, over Israel. Now therefore, heed the voice of the words of the Lord.

"Thus says the Lord of hosts: 'I remember that which Amalek did to Israel, four hundred years ago, how he ambushed My people on the way when they came up from Egypt. I will punish Amalek for what he has done.'

"For remember what the Amalekites did along the way when our fathers came out of Egypt, how he met Israel and attacked our rear ranks, all the stragglers who fell behind, when we were tired and weary; and he did not fear God. Did Israel not promise that when the Lord gave us rest from our enemies and gave the land as an inheritance to possess, that we would blot out the name and memory of Amalek from under heaven?[21]

"Now go, Saul, and attack Amalek, and utterly destroy all that they have."

As he spoke, Samuel drew near to Saul, stepping upon the stairs of the dais and slowly advancing until he stood directly before the king. Saul shrank from the encroaching prophet.

"Spare no one, be he great or small, but wipe them from the face of the earth, both man and woman, infant and nursing child, ox and sheep, camel and donkey, for surely the voice of the Lord will be fulfilled in this."

Samuel backed down the stairs and looked hard into the king's face. "Will you accomplish the will of Yahweh?"

Saul sat up straight and blew out his breath. Shaking his head, he let fall his gaze to the floor beneath his feet.

The king rested upon his elbow, his bearded chin cradled in his hand as he rubbed the coarse line of his jaw. "Can we never have rest? For ten years I have fought against our enemies on every side, against Moab and the people of Ammon, against Edom and the kings of Zobah, and against the Philistines. Wherever I turned, I have harassed my enemies to deliver Israel from the hands of those who plundered them. And though I have gathered a great army, taking in every mighty and valiant man from among my people, yet still the enemy persists.

---

[21] Exodus 17:14 / Deuteronomy 25:19

Will there never be rest from all these peoples? Will they never let us live our lives peacefully in this land?"

Deep weariness settled upon Saul as he wrestled with what should be done. He was tired of war. Yet the bitter enmity between Israel and Amalek had never been resolved.

"Do not grow weary of your good work, Saul," counseled Samuel. "Amalek is the very embodiment of evil. If given leave, they will sweep the Hebrew people from the face of the earth. Their desire is to blot out Israel's light from among the nations, to destroy the Chosen of God, and to draw the world after their idols, that they might continue in their abominations unrestrained."

The king looked blindly into Samuel's eyes.

"Saul... my son, if you do not do this, your failure will echo down through the ages."

Saul drew in a deep breath and released it. The earth pressed heavy upon his shoulders as the king slowly rose to his feet. His stature upon the dais towered over the aging prophet.

"This thing you ask of me is a great burden. Yet, as the Lord lives, it shall be done."

CHAPTER 32

AMALEK

The Negev it was called, hot and dry. Saul and his men trekked south to the very border of the Promised Land. To the doorsteps of Edom, they traveled. The midday sun rose hot over the arid desert of southern Judah. The sun seemed hotter here, its beams radiating off the white sands, scorching the skin, burning the eyes. The vast desert landscape stretched out before them, an endless, barren country. It was a desolate and lonely land.

The men appeared as small dots against the grand, steep cliffs, whose sharp and angular sides cut through the landscape. Sculpted by rain and wind, these rocky plateaus loomed on all sides, casting pink streaks through the white sands. It seemed they had been traveling forever. No clouds transgressed the vast azure sky. The air was translucent; the horizon shimmered, blurred by the waves of heat. A beautiful stillness settled upon this land, tasting eternity as the endless earth stretched on as far as the eye could see, empty and yet a wonder to behold. A haunted place, echoing of those who traveled the road before, of Abraham and Jacob, of Moses and Joshua. Time stood still in the Negev; generations came and went, but life remained unchanged.

Shields were flung upon their backs. Wagons followed close behind. The endless column of men snaked across the vast wilderness, a living beast propelled by a force unseen. Gathered from every region of Israel, men pressed into service, summoned by messenger or trumpet, all those able to bear arms were called forth to assemble at Telaim to be counted.

One of the uttermost cities of the tribe of Judah, Telaim lay on the border between Israel and the land of Edom. The perennial stream to the south ran through a channel eroded in the land. Small trees and scrub brush lined the borders of this wadi, clinging to the only source of water, leaving a pallid green track through the sallow terrain.

As the slow and toilsome progress came to a close, row upon row of black tents sprang from the open plain at Telaim. Each soldier stood before his king, shields forward, in groups of ten, every rank dressed and covered, five abreast, and two deep. Side by side, the men stood, impressive lines in open columns. Saul walked among the ranks, along the paths between the men, as they poised now in rigid attention.

With keen eye, the king looked upon each soldier, inspecting front and rear, surveying weapons and armor. The impassive profiles of the men faced forward, as their eyes bore into the distance before them. Young and old there were. Many veterans with hard faces, yet even more new conscripts, countenances shining, inexperienced and innocent. All men cut from the earth.

And so the count was made, two hundred thousand foot soldiers and ten thousand men of Judah. Saul's own sons, Jishui and Malchishua, along with Jonathan, now numbered among the men, willing warriors rising to be marked. So stood Saul, transfixed before his troops, his hands upon his hips, his chest inflated with pride. It was a grand army bred for the mission at hand, devoted to destruction.

Opening his voice, the mighty king sent out his words, inflamed with purpose, the righteous call going forth. "A sound of battle is in the land, and of great destruction. Up to this day, Amalek has been spared until the measure of their sin has been made full. Today, this cup is overflowing. No longer will these bands of bandits raid our settlements, killing and maiming our people. Judgment now comes upon them. This day we begin our duty, charged to us by Yahweh Himself. It is a call we must all fulfill. We must seek out the Amalekites, these shepherd kings, and destroy all we find down to the last child. So men of God, I say, anoint your shield and draw your sword, for judgment without mercy we bring upon the enemy of God."

The cheer rose, the men rallied—the battle ready to rage. Over the varied landscape, furrowed by rain and wind, they trod, over steep cliffs of chalky ground, through ravines and craters, across salt flats and the endless sea of sands, seeking these bands of Bedouin bandits who roamed the Negev. A rocky desert, born throughout time, brought forth by travail, as the earth writhed and groaned its birth pangs.

Years passed as the army of Saul reached out its arm and swept away these camel-riding nomads. From Havilah even to the far reaches of Shur, Saul attacked the Amalekites, smiting all he met with the edge of the sword. Upon the noise of his coming, many fled, seeking shelter until the storm passed.

Yet the Tempest raged over the land, unchecked, until all but a few of the ignoble race remained. The sun hung low in the sky as the host of Israel reached the ravine of *Nachal Besor*. Good news it was called, the largest water source in the Negev, which ran a course from the mountains east of Beersheba through the western plains until finally draining into the Great Sea to the west. The land was better here, more fertile. Tall grass covered the sweeping expanse, swaying as the air breathed over the open fields.

Well-fortified upon the ascent to the south, overlooking the heath below, rose the stronghold of the Amalekites, Sharuhen, refuge of grace. Eighteen miles west of Beersheba, between the Way of Shur to the east and the Way of the Philistines to the west, this bastion controlled trade upon these two routes between Egypt and the Levant. It was from Sharuhen, the capital of the Amalekites, that marauders were sent out to plague the land, plundering the people of Israel, maiming any who fell into their hands. Now, the remaining peoples of this robber nation were holed up within the walls of this mighty fortress.

Hiding within the deep and winding river bed, Saul and his men advanced through the twists and turns of *Nachal Besor*. Lush vegetation lined this basin, the land rising on either side of the river, granting the large army approach to the city undetected. As the sun crept below the horizon, the desert chilled, cooling the men as they lay in wait just beyond view of the city.

Saul knelt in the shallow stream, the cool liquid lapping at the hem of his tunic. A shiver ran through him as his tawny hair fluttered in the breeze. Ma'aleh edged forward until he drew beside his monarch.

"My king, these Amalekites have been well supplied with iron weaponry. It was the Philistines who gave them strong implements, so as to engage the Amalekites against us, maintaining this level of pressure upon us, their common enemy. How is it that we shall overcome these people of Amalek now that they have banded together within this stronghold?"

Saul turned his head to look into the eyes of his chief. A sidelong smile spread across the king's face. With a nod, he spoke, "Is it not so that it is futile to stand against the Chosen of God? Come now, for I have a plan that will exact judgment upon these ignoble cowards."

Then Saul gave instruction: "In secret, send word to the Kenites, those metal workers who dwell among Amalek, for they are the people of Jethro, the father-in-law of Moses. Declare to them that Saul, king of Israel, says, 'Go, depart, get down from among the Amalekites, lest I destroy you with them. For you showed kindness to all the children of Israel when they came up out of Egypt.'"

"My king," spoke Ma'aleh, "these Kenites have formed an accord with the Amalekites, and you desire to spare them? The city, which stands before you, was given to our enemy by them, so as to maintain peace with this fierce nation, harboring them as they torment our people. They even dwell among the Amalekites."

Saul stood firm. "This judgment is not for them but for Amalek only; therefore, we will not lay a hand upon their people. For those who show kindness to Israel shall not be cut off with those who smite the feeble from behind. Here we are, at the final leg of our journey. With this battle, our obligation is complete. *Cherem* is accomplished, and the judgment appointed long ago is over."

And so it was that the Kenites departed that night, in secret, from among Amalek, and were thus spared.

As the morning light rose over the meadow, a quiet breeze tossed the tall grass, dancing with white daisies and golden asters. Now and then, the red anemone turned its fair face to brush against the azure sky.

Then, from the river basin below, Saul's army lifted its shadowed head, and out they climbed onto the plain, advancing upon the city of Sharuhen. The rolling cadence of heavy footfalls shattered the quiet morn; the rumor rushed across the land. Thundering. Thundering all.

Ten thousand strong, they came. When all had entered upon the field, the men fell back behind their shields, taunting the enemy, to draw them forth from behind their towering walls.

Agag, king of the Amalekites, with a wary eye, glanced over the stone masonry of his stronghold. In scornful malice, a smile spread upon his haughty visage. "Look how bold this king of Israel is. He comes to us with but few men. Greater are we than he. Let us leave these walls and meet this insolent king face to face."

So they came, uncivilized desert people, those craven and rapacious warriors. Warriors, but impious and ignoble cowards, all, for when they fought, they fought with dishonor: nipping at the heels, preying upon the infirm, the weak, on women and children.

Fiercely they came, with bow and scimitar, their bronze skin shone in the morning light. Every head displayed thin golden bands upon dark, cropped hair, and beards of black that sharply traced the jawline of grim-faced men. Each muscular form was covered only by a white loincloth loosely wrapped about the waist. Their shields, small and rectangular, were held before bare chests. Skilled in the use of the bow, the men of Amalek let loose their arrows upon the Chosen of Israel, whose lines stood firm against the onslaught.

Encouraged, the Amalekites came forward, for they had the high ground, which overlooked the Hebrew position, bare and open upon the plain. The advancing regiments crashed into each other, the concussion arresting their forward momentum. Staunch resistance flared anew as the battle pressed back with wanton vigor. Well matched the two armies were, as the companies mixed into a confused amalgam of friend and foe. The conflict spread through the valley, crushing the flora of the field as the mass of tangled men were drawn away from the city.

Malchishua, newly come of age, fought with determined celerity, enduring the race with strength of arms. His brothers, Jishui and Jonathan by his side, bandied with the enemy, the controversy contended. With a sudden thrust, the enemy pushed forward, separating the brothers, pulling the youngest aside to battle alone, a foe on every side.

Seeing his peril, Malchishua lifted his shield close to his frame, his eye just over the rim of the barrier. His sword he raised at the ready. Drawing back, his eye ever watchful, the youth, retreating from the van, strove to rejoin the safety of his ranks. An Amalekite spied the young conscript and, with spirit uplifted, sought out the boy to try.

"Ah," quoth the enemy. "What fun we shall have. You are but a youth, far younger than first I deemed. How is it that you stand here alone, unattended, child?"

"I stand not alone."

"Let us test what mettle lies in you, boy."

Marking his youth, the enemy set himself to toy with him, taunting him with feigned thrusts and counterfeit lunges. Exerting his baleful influence over him, the Amalekite circled his prey, driving Malchishua to dart and turn to avoid the blade. Worn by the opponent's game, he faltered, gasping.

The enemy raised his sword, his will bent on destruction. Down and across the blade came, in one fell sweep, seeking to make contact with the boy's belly.

Time slowed, distorted by senses that had been awakened by fear. The somber cry of a kestrel cut through the air, echoing across the sky a song of lamentation. It was a lonely strain that trailed off as the great bird circled over the field. And still the blade came.

Malchishua looked into the eyes of the enemy. Blinking, the son of Saul shook his head, clearing his mind. The blade bit. A cry of pain escaped as the sword spliced his flesh, laying open his belly. His body pierced, blood flowed, but the wound was not deep, for in that moment, Malchishua had pulled back his midsection just as the blade made contact.

Staggering, Malchishua laid his sword arm across his hurt, his eyes wide with surprise. The Amalekite smiled with pleasure as he beheld his wounded foe.

"You should have remained behind your mother's skirt, boy."

With his sword lifted above his right shoulder, the enemy cut through the air. His aim was high, slicing toward the head to exact a fell stroke upon the youth. Malchishua closed his eyes, awaiting the bite of the blade.

There was a sound of metal clashing, then rang out a familiar voice.

"Maybe, *Sar*, it is you who should have stayed home."

Malchishua opened his eyes—and there stood Jonathan, his sword holding off the enemy's stroke.

The Amalekite's eyes widened, then narrowed in rage as he glared upon the king's eldest son. Pressing against Jonathan's blade, the edges scraping as they slid past each other, the Amalekite turned sharply to the right and drove his elbow into the left side of Jonathan's jaw, sending him back a step as he planted his leg to keep his footing.

The foe, once more with sword uplifted, made to bring it down heavy upon his mark. Jonathan raised his weapon before his face, his blade resting on his left hand, and blocked the descending blow. Struggling under the weight of the enemy, his legs buckled and he dropped hard upon his right knee, his back arching under the force of the adversary. Jonathan fell to his left, rolled out from beneath the press of the enemy, and sprang to his feet. Swords clashed in even battle, sliding against each other until sparks flew, as the two contested the will of the other.

"How you rave," taunted the Amalekite, "yet near is your fall."

Jonathan swung his sword over his head as he roared out his wrath. Catching the hilt of his adversary's blade in his left hand, the king's son slammed the pommel of his own weapon into the face of the Amalekite. The enemy stepped back and shook his head. Blood trickled from his mouth, as grinning, he drew closer to Jonathan, his sword at the ready. The king's son set his rival's blade aside with the forte of his weapon, dragging it down. Laying the flat of his sword in his left hand, Jonathan drove the edge toward the Amalekite's neck.

Still the enemy smiled his taunting sneer. With a powerful thrust, the Amalekite kicked Jonathan in the gut, forcing him to stumble back, releasing his hold on his opponent's life. Seeing his foe raise his sword to strike, he slipped under the guard, between the adversary's sword arm and chest, and drove his blade into the enemy's belly, ending his life.

The king's son pressed his foot against the Amalekite's chest, wrenching his sword from the enemy's corpse as it fell to the ground. With powerful arms, Jonathan took hold his brother and shoved him back, striving to pull him from the fray. But the opposition closed in on all sides. Jonathan contended with one enemy after another. Agile, strong, and quick, the king's eldest fought off all who tried to draw sword against him. The relentless charge of the adversary pushed the two sons of Saul toward the Hebrew ranks. Malchishua, now beyond the shock of his wound, rejoined his brother against the foe. Jishui rushed in to fight alongside them.

At the sight of his brother renewed, Jonathan struck out, forward, into the van, seeking another foe to fell. Perceiving an Amalekite charging toward him, Jonathan ran upon the man and, with closed fist, dealt a blow to the face. The foe off balance, the king's eldest arced his blade as he set his right foot behind the man's left leg, bringing him hard upon his back. Arms flailed as the enemy fell, and Jonathan took his advantage. With the point of his sword, he thrust him through.

Catching a glint from the discarded blade, Jonathan took up the sword. A weapon in each hand, he came at the foe, cutting first with the left, then with the right, again and again he struck, until the earth was strewn with the slain. Holding firm each sword, he continued his deadly barrage, delivering baneful bites with the dual edge-sharp blades.

Two Amalekites pressed upon him, eager to end the young Hebrew's rampage. With a mighty leap, the prince of Israel rose above the enemy, his swords crossed before him. As he descended upon the two, he drew his blades apart in one measured arc, cleaving down and outward, and the last of the Amalekites fell who had dared transgress his path.

Jonathan paused and with his eye, beheld the carnage he had wrought. Then, with the sweep of his bloodied arm across his brow, he turned.

"Well done, my son," spoke Saul as he looked upon the warrior prince.

Jonathan's breath caught as he met his father's eyes. A thrill of joy rose within him—the weight of long-lost favor dawning nigh.

Smiling up at his father, the king, Jonathan gave a quick and heartfelt nod.

The clear, sharp sound of a trumpet broke the air, stealing Jonathan from that brief communion with his father. Renewed, the battle resumed in earnest. The enemy advanced, attacking on all sides with great strength and fury. Thrusting their main force upon the field, a new terror was loosed into the fray. A great horde of armored camel riders appeared above the rise and, in furious charge, thundered over the plain.

Saul's host could no longer stem the tide. The front lines foundered, and like an avalanche, the remaining ranks gave way. Hard-pressed, the Hebrew forces collapsed.

Not content with victory, the Amalekites emptied their city of men to glut vengeance upon their adversary. Nearer and nearer they came, with savage cries that resounded from a multitude of fierce throats, turning cold the heart of Israel. This last was too much.

"Pull back! Pull back!"

The Chosen of God broke and ran, back toward the ravine, the enemy nipping at their heels.

CHAPTER 33

AGAG

"Retreat! Retreat!"

Saul's voice rose above the din of battle. His men fled, north, across the plain, back over the field of daisies and golden asters, back beyond the tall grass, even to the lip of *Nachal Besor*. The Israelites skidded to a halt, the men pressing from behind as the army collapsed upon itself. Saul stayed his forces with his outstretched arms, barely keeping his feet from sliding over the edge of the ravine.

All the while, Agag and his men raced upon their heels, gnawing at their rear as a ravenous wolf, and, oh, how Amalek rejoiced as they drove after them, until at last they were caught in their own snare. Saul's army had but one choice: scramble down the ravine with the enemy upon their backs or turn and face Amalek. Yet then, through the dust-clouded air, the clear call of the trumpet was heard. The enemy turned to see the cause, confused to behold the threat behind.

From within a fold of hills south of Sharuhen, Saul's main force sprang to action. The company of men was split into two divisions, Abner and Ma'aleh at their lead. Each detachment skirted the city, flanking it on either side. It was an easy matter to seize, for the bait had been taken, and the city lay open and bare before them. In their haste to devour Israel, Amalek had left the gates ajar and the stronghold emptied of men.

Sharuhen was now marked for ruin.

Rushing forward, the Hebrew forces poured through the gates and took the undefended city. With haste they set the buildings to flame, sending plumes of smoke into the sky.

The men of Amalek looked and saw their city ablaze, how the smoke ascended into heaven.

Saul's division cheered at their brethren's triumph.

Torn, the enemy wavered, and knew not which way to flee. Many turned back to the city, but too late; they possessed no power to save it. For in that moment, seeing the rising smoke, Saul's men ceased their flight, and struck the fleeing Amalekites with the edge of the sword. Then the Hebrew soldiers, those who had lain in ambush, came forth through the gate and fell upon the foe, so that Amalek was hemmed in by Israel.

Saul's army became a tower of strength against the enemy. With no escape possible, the host of Agag fought for the life they loathed to release. Spears cut through the air, swords and shields clashed, as with equal skill, the battle-play unfurled.

"Bring down the beasts! The camels, bring them down!" cried Abner over the heads of his men.

Spears flew as the Israelites let loose their sharp pointed shafts. The beasts went wild, running this way and that; a great number broke free and fled the field, their riders holding on, striving to keep their seats. Many a man jumped from his mounts. Others were cut down by arrows, so that none escaped the carnage wreaked upon the field.

Agag looked on in horror as he watched the desolation of his army, crushed as grist between two millstones. In despair, he turned, abandoning his men, as on the brutal battle raged.

Furtive and abject, Agag, king of the Amalekites, skulked away from the contest. Glancing back over his shoulder, he took one last glimpse at his army's death throes before he climbed down the ravine toward the river. When he reached the bottom of the gorge, Agag made to turn toward the north, hoping to cross the stream and flee to Philistia. As he altered his course, the Amalekite king came to an abrupt halt, for his way was barred, stayed by the presence of a large soldier towering over him. So near was he that Agag well-nigh hurled against him.

"Leaving so soon?" the soldier spoke as he leaned his head down toward the cowering king.

Agag backed away, his heart racing. Before him stood Saul, king of Israel, a bastion against him, his shield drawn up before him, his spear at the ready. Seeing no way out, Agag gripped his own spear and pulled his shield close to his frame.

Sneering, the Amalekite taunted, "So, Saul, it comes to this. Two kings pitted against one another. It shall be a good day to see the end of you."

"Ah," spoke Saul with grim confidence. "You have forgotten what the prophet Balaam spoke, 'Israel's king shall rise above Agag, and his kingdom shall be exalted!'[22] Today, it is fulfilled."

Startled, Agag shuddered at the words that had been spoken long ago, and in that moment his courage failed. Saul, seeing the king of Amalek shaken, took his advantage and leapt into the air. He held his *shelet*, that is shield, tight against his chest, as he lunged with his spear leveled toward the Amalekite king.

He made no delay, but raised his shield and, with a clash, turned aside the point of Saul's spear. The two kings charged, shields crashing with a thunderous din. Growling, with teeth bared, they strove till the bucklers gave way, and both were cast back.

In haste, Saul responded, thrusting his spear low, his arm straight out by his bent knees. Bringing his *shelet* down, the king of Amalek once more turned aside his enemy's weapon, leaving his breast perilously exposed. Saul raised his spear, grasping it over his right shoulder, and while Agag's shield was yet low, he drove the point for his enemy's head. At once, the Amalekite king ducked; the stroke grazed the air before his face.

Agag's fury burned as he swung backhand with his spear, striking the Hebrew king upon the right cheek. Saul reeled aside, staggering back a pace to regain his footing. With all his strength, Saul struck forth with his *shelet* toward his adversary's neck. Agag bent beneath the shield. Sweat dripped from his brow as he brought up his buckler, barely in time to knock away Saul's spear. In a single, swift motion, the Amalekite king lunged with his own weapon.

Roaring, Saul brought his shield around and struck Agag's spear from his hand. The king of Amalek gasped in dismay, but little time did he have to recover, for Saul followed with a strong thrust toward

[22] Numbers 24:7

the soft flesh of his belly. With desperate vigor, Agag slammed his shield down and caught Saul's spear by the shaft, pinning it to the ground. He stepped forcefully upon the shaft and broke the spear in two. His hand grasped the hilt of his sword as he withdrew the blade from its sheath. Swinging out, he slashed at the Hebrew king's throat. Saul pulled his head back, the blade just missing its mark.

With a snarl, Saul threw away his broken spear and drew out his sword. Agag, eyes narrowed and jaw set, charged for the Hebrew king. Saul stepped aside, and the Amalekite stumbled into the stream. Saul turned and tipped his head as he gazed upon his enemy. Gathering his strength, the Israelite king paced toward Agag.

"Get up and face your doom!" ordered Saul as he circled his foe, who, gasping for breath, struggled to rise.

Agag heaved himself upward, lashing out with his blade. Saul swept it away with ease.

Within the stream the battle renewed, water playing about their feet. Once more Agag crossed blades with Saul, and the two strove knee-deep amid the cool waters of the river. His feet felt like tree trunks, heavy and slow. He gasped for each breath, yet Israel's king seemed to have no end to his endurance. Standing tall, Saul held his head high; his breath came easy. Years of battle had made him strong.

Their blades ground together, the cross-guards locked as each sought to unbalance the other. Saul leaned into the bind, driving the edge toward Agag's bare neck, snarling against the strain.

Agag could feel Saul's warm breath upon his face. He looked into the fierce eyes of his enemy, resolute in his charge to destroy him. The Amalekite king pressed upon him with all his might, his face flushed red, but the king of Israel was too much for him.

With a sudden snap of his arm, Saul wrenched his blade down and flipped his sword up, freeing the weapons. Agag's sword flew from his hand. Saul sprang toward his foe, blade in hand. The thrust was caught upon Agag's shield, but the force of the blow knocked the Amalekite king to his knees.

Saul stood over Agag, looking down in grim satisfaction as the enemy dropped his shield by his knees and lifted his hands in surrender.

"It is enough," spoke Agag.

"Prepare to meet thy doom."

Letting fall his shield, Saul grasped his sword with two hands. He raised the blade and brought it down toward Agag's undefended chest. Agag's countenance contorted as he realized, in yielding, his life was forfeit. Only death at the hands of Israel's king awaited him.

The sword drew closer to the groveling king of Amalek. He flung up his hands to guard his face, closing tight his eyes, the river flowing over his legs as he knelt before Israel's king.

Then nothing.

The blade never reached its mark, for in that moment, Doeg the Edomite, servant of Saul, grabbed hold of the king's sword with two hands and stayed the blade's descent.

Saul beheld his servant in dismay.

"No, my king," cried out Doeg. "Look and see what a prize you have before you."

Saul stood suspended, his hands still grasping his sword, poised above the Amalekite king.

"My *adon*," continued Doeg, "is it not written that the young and the old shall not be killed on the same day.[23] Yet here you are, committing such an offense, for you have cut down the people on the same day you would take the life of their king. Is it not enough that all of Amalek is destroyed? And here you stand, king of Israel, who has led his people to victory. Now take that which is rightfully yours and in triumph lead your captive before your troops to honor all you have done this day."

Wavering, Saul lowered his sword. And as he pondered the words of his faithful servant, the pride of Israel's king was pricked.

"Bind him."

---

[23] Leviticus 22:28

CHAPTER 34

THE PRIDE OF KINGS

Then it was when Israel had made an end of slaying, and the Amalekites had been struck with the edge of the sword, that the Chosen of God entered again into the city of Sharuhen. Blood filled the streets as by the blade they consumed any who remained. All were slain; none escaped. And like the sin of Achan,[24] who took the spoil from Jericho after the ban, so too did Saul's men gather the plunder of Amalek: the best of the sheep and oxen, the fatlings and lambs, and all that was good, unwilling to consign anything of worth, though marked by God for destruction. But everything that was vile and refuse, that, they utterly devoted to ruin. Then the city was laid waste by fire so that it became an ash heap for generations.

Three years from the time the command was given, Saul conquered the power of Amalek, striking a mortal blow at the center of the Amalekite Empire, bringing their kingdom to collapse.

With great exultation, the Israelite forces, in pomp and power, marched from the land of Amalek toward Gilgal. A grand pageant of honor and glory, the jubilant men trekked through the desert to the sound of the pipe and the timbrel, celebrating their victory and the spoils they had won. Saul advanced ere his troops, a splendor of kingship as his prize was displayed before him. Agag, king of Amalek, bound and forced to march, was paraded in a spectacle of defeat to grace

---

[24] Joshua 7:1

Saul's triumph as he journeyed home to Israel. The Hebrew soldiers taunted their captive as he struggled in his bonds to keep the pace of the well-tempered host. Carts full of plunder, with livestock behind, were driven at the army's fore, touted to sanctify Saul's great military success as though shouting out: "See what I have accomplished!"

Saul, his heart uplifted and his spirit proud, spoke, "We shall go to Carmel, to proclaim my victory, for see I have brought away a living captive and all of Amalek is destroyed."

At this Nagad raised his eyes in wonder at his king. His breath caught in his throat, and his heart sank within him. Loosing a weary sigh, he lowered his gaze. Helek marked the change upon his captain.

"*Sar*, what is it?"

But all Nagad answered was a shake of his head.

The Hebrew contingent journeyed east, through southern Judah and across the sweeping uplands south of Hebron. Upon a small mount, just west of the Salt Sea, where the watercourse flowed over the green hills, Saul halted his men to rest. Looking out over the land before him, the king noted the sun reflecting off the waters of the sea. The mirrored surface cast back a myriad of tiny crystal jewels, shimmering golden hues in the glassy pool. A warm breeze caressed the king's face, teasing wisps of his tawny hair.

Saul smiled. "This is good. My triumph shall be recorded here. We shall set up a pillar to proclaim Israel's mark on the land for all to see."

A cool breeze brushed across Samuel as he lay sleeping upon his cot, a welcome reprieve from the heat of the previous day. The face of the land rested, quiet and still as the moon rose; its aspect nearly full, the orb bathed the earth in soft light. A single cricket chirped in a dark corner outside Samuel's window. At first, the rhythmic melody was soft, then grew in volume until the air was filled with its measured strain. For a moment, the cricket's song stilled as though awaiting reply, then lifted again its gentle cadence.

Samuel tossed in his bed. A furrow creased his brow. He groaned in anguish and bolted up in bed.

"Samuel."

Startled, the prophet glanced about the room, sweat beading upon his face.

"Samuel."

The voice was strong, cutting through the night, like streams of living water running over a dry and thirsty land, yet there was a sense of brokenness in its tone. He knew the voice; it had long spoken to him in the watches of the night.

"Here I am, Lord. Speak for your servant hears."

The Word of the Lord came to Samuel, and his soul grieved. For Yahweh spoke, sorrow heavy upon His word: He repented that He had made Saul king, for Saul had turned back from following Him and had not kept His commandments.

Samuel groaned under the weight of it. "O Lord, say not this dreadful thing."

As a great waterfall crashes over rocks, so Samuel wrestled with God, crying out to the Lord all through the night, broken of heart, for greatly did he love Saul.

Then as the glow of dawn began to rise, Samuel lifted himself upon his feet and wearily left his home, traveling east. The road was long, for the prophet loathed his undertaking. Great had been his hopes for the man Saul. Years ago he had traveled this road with the humble donkey-seeker to Gilgal, there to renew the kingdom and confirm Saul as king of Israel. Now, all had come to ruin. Samuel was spent, heavy-laden, and with little sleep, yet he pressed on, searching for the king.

Along the way, he came upon three men traveling on the road north. Seeing Samuel, the men greeted him, "*Boker Tov.*"

"*Boker Tov*, brothers. I seek after Saul, your king. Have you received word as to what place I might find him?"

"Why, yes," spoke one. "Saul went to Carmel, with his army. A grand spectacle they were, too."

"Indeed," added another. "He has set up a monument for himself there; and he has gone on around, passed by naught a day ago, and has proceeded down toward Gilgal."

The prophet's heart misgave, and his countenance fell. "So it has come to this."

Samuel's head ached. He closed his eyes tightly and pressed his fingers into his brow. Releasing a long breath, the prophet looked upon the men. "*Tov Me'od, Todah*, very well, thank you."

"*Shalom uv'racha leYisrael*, Peace and Blessing to Israel."

"May it be so." Samuel turned and walked away, his head cast down and his shoulders bowed.

Oh, how Samuel's heart grieved at the tidings, for Saul, the once humble king, had lifted himself above the will of God and exalted himself in pride. And now with reluctance, yet in obedience, Samuel traveled toward Gilgal to discipline a king.

CHAPTER 35

THE REPROACH OF ISRAEL

Gilgal, the very place where the pride and strength of Israel were cut away. For it was here that God commanded Joshua to circumcise the people before entering the Promised Land, afflicting their flesh in the presence of the enemy, trusting wholly in the Living God.[25]

Henceforth, the ordinance of circumcision was a reminder that to follow Yahweh, there was a price. The cost was life itself: the right to govern one's own will, the death of self-determination and pride. Yet though man lost something of himself, something was gained of God. It was a powerful act of consecration, indeed, a symbol stating that Israel was not like any other nation, but a people set apart, sanctified to Yahweh, lifted as a special treasure. It was a stepping out in faithful obedience, renouncing the entrapments of the flesh and of the world, rising to a higher purpose. And so the site is called Gilgal, even unto this day, for it was on this very ground that the reproach of the people was rolled away.

As Samuel trekked the slow march toward Gilgal, he saw the wrath of God advancing. There was no escaping what was to come. He could not turn it aside. The course was set. The words given by the travelers lay heavy upon the old prophet's heart.

Pride: Saul's haughty spirit has overcome his sense of duty, raising a monument in his own honor, even before he has offered sacrifice to Yahweh.

---

[25] Joshua 5:2–9

Samuel wrestled with his sorrow as he journeyed farther east, until he entered into the lowland below Gilgal. As the prophet climbed the last rise into the Jordan River Valley, the sound of bleating reached his ears, and he knew that what was told him was true, and his heart broke anew.

Upon the plain, Samuel intercepted Saul's army as it was marching in all its grandeur. He stood before the company of soldiers, gazing upon the columns shrouded in their dismal display of rich regalia.

Saul raised his hand, halting the procession; a thrill of trepidation ran through his frame. Casting it aside, the king smiled broadly. Samuel looked, and behold, Agag stood bound before the host of Israel. When he saw the prophet of God standing before him, Saul hastened to him, glad of heart to see his old friend.

"Blessed are you of the Lord!" spoke Saul with happy proclamation. "I have performed the commandment of the Lord."

Fire kindled in Samuel's countenance as he fixed his eyes upon the king. "What then is this bleating of sheep in my ears, and the lowing of oxen, which I hear?"

Stunned, Saul recoiled from the accusation. "They." The king stretched forth his hand toward the men. "They have brought them from the Amalekites; for the men spared the best of the sheep and the oxen, to sacrifice to the Lord your God; and the rest we have utterly destroyed."

Samuel's brow creased, and with a stern voice, he spoke, "Say no more! Suffer me a moment, and I will tell you what the Lord said to me last night."

Shaken by the prophet's tone, Saul replied, "Speak on."

Drawing a deep breath, Samuel calmed himself. "When you were little in your own eyes, were you not head of the tribes of Israel? And did not the Lord anoint you king over His people? Now the Lord sent you on a mission, and said, 'Go, and utterly destroy the sinners, the Amalekites, and fight against them until they are consumed.' Why then did you not obey the voice of the Lord? Why did you swoop down on the spoil, and do evil in the sight of the Lord?"

Saul heard the disappointment in Samuel's voice. His brow creased as he shook his head. "But I have obeyed the voice of the Lord, and fulfilled the charge whereto You sent me, and brought back Agag, king of Amalek; I have laid waste the Amalekites. Yet the men took of the plunder, sheep and oxen, the best of that which should have been utterly destroyed, to sacrifice to the Lord your God in Gilgal."

"Oh, how is the hammer of the whole earth cut asunder and broken,[26] for you have been proud against the Lord! This war was not for plunder. You might have restrained the men if you would, that they might not love war by obtaining the spoil, but would do this dreadful undertaking out of duty and obedience to God alone, and not for their gain.

> Has the Lord as great delight
> in burnt offerings and sacrifices,
> As in obeying the voice of the Lord?
> Behold, to obey is better than sacrifice,
> And to heed than the fat of rams."[27]

Then Saul spoke with growing agitation. "Is it not so that the Law requires a sin offering for one that is found slain,[28] and here, so many have been slain?" With a sweeping gesture of his arm, Saul continued as though showing Samuel all the fallen of Amalek. "If the old have sinned, why should the young suffer;[29] and if men have been guilty, why should the cattle be destroyed?" Saul took a step closer to Samuel, towering over the old prophet. "We would not lay innocent blood to the charge of God's people, Israel, and not make sacrifice."

Samuel raised himself up and put an accusing finger before Saul's face. "The time for mercy is over, and you, O king, are not the judge. This fight cannot be settled by peace talks and treatises. The only means of overcoming this evil is utter desolation. We must destroy the entire nation of Amalek, down to the last cow! If one of these Amalekites survives, the generations that follow will cry out against you, Saul, for the trouble you have brought them."[30]

The king stood silent, stung by the prophet's words. He looked upon Samuel and spoke not, his mind undone. His shoulders rose and fell with each breath, wrath smoldering within.

[26] Jeremiah 50:23
[27] 1 Samuel 15:22
[28] Numbers 6:11
[29] Ezekiel 18:20
[30] Esther 3:1−6

Samuel drew near and set his hand upon the king's arm. Lowering his head, the prophet shook it slowly. "Saul, as Abraham was willing to sacrifice his only son, so too, O king, you must sacrifice yourself in complete obedience to Yahweh. Do not listen to the whispered voices bidding you to stay your hand."

"Yet one must not muzzle an ox while it treads out the grain,"[31] retorted Saul.

"You have wearied the Lord with your words!" Samuel's voice was sharp, and Saul felt the edge of its blade. "Saul, you have a proud and rebellious spirit. You have done evil in allowing this root of wickedness to remain. You do not reflect God's heart in this judgment, for Yahweh's heart is broken when His wrath is invoked. Yet here you are, jubilant in spirit, rejoicing at the downfall of others. In this you dishonor the Lord of all life."

Samuel lifted his arm toward Agag, who stood bowed, his gaze fixed in wonder as the old prophet scolded the king. "Would not God have rather these Amalekites repented than to run headlong toward destruction? Does He not grieve for their souls? And now I see Israel delighting in their rack and ruin. Be of great care, lest you be cast down with them in your pride and arrogance."

To his full height the prophet rose and lifted his arms above his head. Speaking in a strong voice, he quoted:

> For behold, O king, the day is coming,
> Burning like an oven,
> And the proud, yes, even you,
> Shall be as stubble.
> The day which is coming shall burn you up.
> And no branch nor root shall remain.
> Only ashes shall you be, under the soles of feet.
>
> For from the rising of the sun,
> Even to its going down
> All you build, God will throw down.
> While this is being done by your hands,
> Will He accept you favorably?[32]

---

[31] Deuteronomy 25:4
[32] Malachi 1 / 4:1–3

"But you have departed from the path, O king, and have caused many to stumble. Turn now from your evil ways and evil deeds.

> For rebellion is as the sin of witchcraft,
> And stubbornness is as iniquity and idolatry.
> Because you have rejected the word of the Lord,
> He also has rejected you from being king."[33]

Grieved at these words, Saul thought, *Have I not done all that Samuel has wanted? I did not go out seeking to be king, and here I am declared no longer king. As though I ever desired the crown. I was content with the life I had. I did not ask for any of this! Yet perhaps there is some truth to what Samuel says. Have I grown proud?*

Saul glanced about and saw his men watching in dismay, and his chest grew tight. "I have sinned, for I have transgressed the commandment of the Lord and your words, because I feared the people and obeyed their voice. Now therefore, please pardon my sin, and return with me, that I may worship the Lord."

Samuel met the eyes of the king, and in them he saw a haughty spirit, and Samuel knew that Saul was lost. "I will not return with you, for you have rejected the word of the Lord, and the Lord has rejected you from being king over Israel."

Unbridled rage welled within Saul. His frame trembled, his heart quickened; and as the prophet turned to go, Saul grasped forth and seized the edge of Samuel's robe, tearing it.

At the sound of rending cloth, Samuel turned upon Saul. "The Lord has torn the kingdom of Israel from you today, and has given it to a neighbor of yours, who is better than you. The Strength of Israel will not lie nor relent. For He is not a man, that He should change His mind."[34]

In anguish, Saul reached out to Samuel's heart. He burned with shame that his men should see him so chastised. *How shall I stand before my men after this?* With as much humility as he could muster, Saul entreated Samuel. "I have sinned; yet honor me now, please, before the elders of my people and before Israel, and return with me, that I may worship the Lord your God."

---

[33] 1 Samuel 15:23
[34] Numbers 23:19

Samuel beheld the king's distress, and his heart ached for him, for even though Saul had been rejected by God, Samuel loved him still. So Samuel turned back after Saul, and Saul worshiped the Lord at Gilgal.

The sun burnt orange in the west as the sacrifice smoldered and smoked to heaven. Samuel set his face toward Saul. "The matter has not yet been resolved. Bring Agag, king of the Amalekites, here to me."

Agag, his hands yet bound, was brought before Samuel. Fear took hold of the Amalekite as he saw the prophet bore a large blade. "Surely the bitterness of death is past."

"As your sword has made women childless, so shall your mother be childless among women."

Samuel raised his blade, the very knife used to prepare sacrifice for Yahweh. The Amalekite king trembled as Samuel grasped the neck of his robe with a firm hand. Saul watched in horror as the old prophet brought the knife down again and again upon the proud and violent king until he had hacked Agag to pieces before the Lord in Gilgal.

Then Samuel went to Ramah, and Saul, his heart yet unhumbled and unchanged, returned to his fortress at Geba. Samuel went no more to see Saul until the day of his death. Nevertheless, Samuel mourned for Saul, and the Lord regretted that He had made Saul king over Israel.

PART THE FOURTH

Where is your king, that he may save you?
Where are your rulers in all your towns,
of whom you said,
"Give me a king and princes"?
So in my anger I gave you a king,
and in my wrath I took him away.

Hosea 13:10–11

CHAPTER 36

THE BEST OF MEN

"Samuel, you must eat. You cannot go on troubled so. You are growing weary."

Nagad laid a bowl of dates before the old prophet, then sat down across the table from him. Samuel looked up and smiled, a deep sadness set within his eyes. His face was gaunt and pale.

"My friend, you have always been good to me. Yet I have not the stomach for food. My heart is broken. I have no strength to do anything. I cannot bear the loss I suffer. Such plans we had. I thought Saul was to be a great king. Now, by his own folly, all is lost."

"Yet, even men of high degree are still just men. We fail, and some do not rise again."

Samuel's lips curved with gentle sorrow. "See how the student teaches the wise."

The prophet lowered his head and shook it. "Offenses must come, but woe to that man by whom the offense comes![35] Yet I wonder if there was something I should have done. Some words I should have said. Could I have prevented this tragedy and saved Saul from his unbelief?"

"Samuel, each of us has to walk his own path. You or I cannot force someone to walk the right one. Saul alone is to blame."

"He was a good king for a time. How humble he was."

---

[35] Matthew 18:7

"It is how it always is with power. One loses himself in it. Can anyone stand beneath prosperity?"

"Yet," spoke Samuel, "by his reckless example, he has weakened the faith of the people. And for that, he has paid a heavy price."

Nagad looked down at his hands folded upon his lap. "Is there no hope now for Saul? I cannot forget how he came and rescued us from the hands of Ammon. I have pledged my fealty to him, and I mean to hold to my oath." The captain lifted his gaze to meet that of the prophet's. "Cannot this wrong be righted?"

"Too far has he traveled down this path without remorse. He has deceived even himself, forgotten from whom his strength comes. He fears the people more than the Lord, the true Strength of Israel. Saul can no longer see aright through his own disobedience. His heart is hard and he is lost to us. No longer is he reigning for God, but Saul now rules against God."

In silence, Nagad sat, gazing absently at his hands, deep in his own thoughts. So much had changed since last he had sat at this table. Then it was that Tiphcar had been with him, and the nation was at the dawn of a new beginning. And now...

"We are getting old, Samuel. I do not know how much longer I will be able to fight for the Lord, but I will do so for as long as He grants me strength. I must go today, back to Geba, to stand beside Saul. There I will wait to see what the Lord wills for Israel."

"You must do as you are compelled."

Nagad nodded, his heart heavy with sorrow. At the sound of approaching footfalls, the captain lifted his gaze.

"*Sar*, it is time," spoke Helek as he entered the court. "The troops are readied."

Pushing back his chair, Nagad rose and went to where Samuel sat. He placed his hand upon the prophet's shoulder. It felt frail under his strong hand.

"Take care, my old friend. And eat something. I do not believe the Lord is finished with you yet. I will come again as soon as I am able. *Shalom*." Nagad turned to walk away.

"*Shalom, Na'ar*," called Samuel after him. Nagad paused for a moment, a smile upon his face. Then he departed from the court with Helek by his side, leaving the prophet alone at his table.

For a long while Samuel sat in silence, pondering all that had happened. A heaviness pressed upon his breast. Reaching across the table, he picked up a date. He looked at it and his stomach lurched. The old prophet tossed the fruit back into the bowl as he turned his face from it in disgust. *How can I eat when all has gone amiss?*

In thought he returned to the rooftop meeting he had with Saul so long ago. *Doubt has always plagued him. Oh that he could have trusted the Lord to see him through!* Samuel sighed.

Within his head, a voice resounded, powerful and true. Samuel sat upright, leaning his ear forward as if to hear clearer. These words echoed within his mind, *"How long will you mourn for Saul, seeing I have rejected him from reigning over Israel?"*

"Lord?"

And so Yahweh gave instruction, for the prophet had too long sat in sorrow. What the Lord required stirred Samuel's heart to fear. Nevertheless, he would be obedient, and do as he was commanded. Yet he knew that if word of his charge reached the ears of the king, it would cost him his life.

The opening of day spread forth its lambent wings across the azure plain. The dew-laden plants wept, their heads bent under the weight of their burden. And as Samuel set out, so too was his heart heavy as he journeyed south toward the small town of Bethlehem. This region of Israel had been the home of Ruth, the Moabitess, who, after the death of her husband, had come to Israel with her mother-in-law, Naomi. There she had met Boaz, and they married, giving rise to Jesse's line. Now it was Jesse whom Samuel sought in this hilly, grain-growing region.

Bethlehem, house of bread it was called, stood upon the sloping side of a prominent limestone ridge within the Hill Country of Judah, just beyond the Canaanite city of Jebus. The village had a commanding view over the terrain, sitting within the midst of rolling hills wrapped in a tapestry of vineyards and orchards: the silver-green olive, the spreading almond canopy, and the brightly flowered pomegranates.

The long, dim mountain range of Gilead and Moab, purple-tinted in the morning twilight, stretched like an endless wall along the horizon, north and south, straight and unbroken, until it disappeared from view, far exceeding the reach of mortal eye.

To the east, beyond the north-south ridge route, lay the Wilderness, a vast wasteland of chalky slopes that sprung to life, green and verdant after the former rains, providing pasture to graze sheep and goats. Between the Wilderness and the city, rich fields carved into the hillsides transformed the landscape into a lush patchwork of varied grains. But with the passing of spring, the summer sun and the dry eastern winds would wither the land, turning the lush green of life into brown, dry stubble, a land waiting to be renewed.

Yet, while Samuel journeyed through this region, spring endured and a remnant of richness clung to the land. Beyond the fields of grain, the solitary figures of shepherds stood watch over their flocks. The countryside spoke in whispers, of gentle breezes and bleating sheep, distant and faint as the sun warmed the face of the old prophet. Behind him trekked a heifer chewing her cud at ease, unknowing of her purpose.

As Samuel approached the town, the elders came out to meet him. Blocking his entry, the men stood within the road. One raised his hand, thrusting his palm forward, and spoke, "Strange it is to see you out so far from home. Do you come peacefully? For we have heard what you did to the Amalekite king, and how you have fallen out of favor with Saul, our king. We desire no trouble here."

The prophet looked upon the elders, surprised by their trepidation. "Peaceably, I have come to sacrifice to the Lord. Sanctify yourselves, and come with me."

In particular, Samuel paid heed to one man. "Come, Jesse, son of Obed, I will join you in your preparation, that you and your sons may make sacrifice with me unto Yahweh. Then we shall eat before the Lord of that which has been offered."

Jesse bristled with surprise to be singled out by the prophet. Yet, who could deny a request by such a man as he?

As he lowered his head, Jesse extended his hand to show the way. Samuel followed him down a long street that crested the white chalky ridge. Left behind were the murmurings of displeasure.

On either side, narrow alleys led off the main strip, paltry corridors lined with small clay-brick houses. Along these winding paths they traveled until they reached the edge of town where the houses were less crowded. There, Jesse directed Samuel through an opening in the low barrier that surrounded the city. The wall, more a boundary marker than for any defensive purpose, stood but waist high and was wrought of stones stacked loosely upon one another. Just beyond the barrier, a dwelling was set upon a swath of land, which gave way to rich fields lined with sheep folds.

A little gate led into a courtyard where an open hearth glowed with the remains of a fading fire, its smoke rising in spiraling curls. Here Samuel left the heifer cropping at stubbles of grass that rose in sparse patches upon the ground. Jesse led the prophet across the threshold and into the house. The ground floor had three parallel rooms, partially separated by two rows of wooden pillars. These extended forward from a narrow room at the back that ran the width of the house. The walls were of sun-dried mud-bricks set upon rough limestone foundation blocks, their surface covered in a protective coat of mud plaster that gave the home a smooth, white appearance.

After washing their feet in the footbath to the left of the doorway, Jesse guided Samuel through the lower level, past the paved stable where a crude ladder rose toward the second story. As they entered the upper level, a large room opened before them with a low table at its center. A loom sat silent against the side wall, the shuttle suspended within the partially woven cloth, waiting patiently to resume its work. Here it was that the family of Jesse ate, slept, and received guests.

"Come, refresh yourself, and I will call the family to join us here." Jesse bade Samuel to the table, and after pouring him a bowl of clear water, descended back down the ladder.

The old prophet sat quietly, listening to the sounds of the home as he sipped the cool draught. Distant voices could be heard, yet what was said was beyond reach. As he waited, his thoughts wandered.

He had spent much of his life waiting. *How much time*, he wondered. *I am nearly spent; my time is quickly coming to a close.* Moments later, feet tramping through the lower level brought the prophet back to his present charge.

Soon the chamber was full of activity and people, for Jesse had many sons. Samuel stood as they all flooded into the room, overwhelmed by the sudden crowd that crashed in upon him. Laughing aloud, the prophet smiled as he saw the many comely, youthful visages, all strong, lithe figures of manly vigor.

Indeed, one of these, thought the prophet.

After some time, as the stir settled, the old prophet took Jesse and his sons and, having them change their clothes and wash their frames in pure water, he sanctified them with prayer and instruction, that they might have a spirit of sacrifice.

When all preparation had been accomplished, within the seclusion of Jesse's home, Samuel looked upon Eliab, Jesse's eldest son. The prophet was taken by his fair form, for the young man was strong and tall, well-favored in his semblance.

So it was that when Samuel beheld the son of Jesse, he thought, *Surely the Lord's anointed is before Him!*

"Bring Eliab, your son, to me."

Jesse motioned to Eliab, unknowing the prophet's intent. His eldest obeyed and drew near with an air of assurance, expecting some peculiar honor would be bestowed upon him, having been set apart from the rest. The old prophet took hold of Eliab by the arms and turned him this way and that, taking a careful measure. Well pleased he was with his appearance.

But then it came to Samuel from the Lord, a whispered voice within his ear, that he must neither look at his countenance nor at his frame, because Yahweh had refused him. For God does not see as man sees; for man looks at the outward appearance, but the Lord looks at the heart.[36]

Samuel turned away from Eliab, shaking his head. "It is not he. Bring me another of your sons, so that I may look upon him."

So Jesse called Abinadab, and made him pass before Samuel. He too was comely and strong, pleasant in stature and form.

"Neither has the Lord chosen this one."

Jesse summoned Shammah. Again, Samuel spoke, "No, neither has this one been chosen by the Lord." Thus Jesse made seven of his sons pass before Samuel. And the prophet said to Jesse, "The Lord has not chosen these."

---

[36] 1 Samuel 16:7

Samuel looked about the room, for all had passed before him, yet none had the Lord chosen. Samuel sat down and sighed deeply. *Have I made some mistake?* The old prophet thought for a long moment in silence, his chin resting within his hand, his brow furrowed.

At length he rose and went to Jesse. "Are all the young men here?"

Jesse gazed wide-eyed upon the prophet. "There remains yet the youngest. He is in the field, keeping watch over the sheep."

Samuel laughed aloud and clapped Jesse on the back, delight shining in his aged face.

"Well," spoke Samuel, "go get him and bring him to me. For we will not turn away till he comes here."

CHAPTER 37

THE GOOD SHEPHERD

The sheep grazed peacefully, unaware their shepherd was not present. Short-sighted, they enjoyed the tufts of green grass within their view, having no care to the danger that may be lurking. Yet safety lies in numbers, and the shepherd knew this, for otherwise he would not have left them unattended. Resourceful and trustworthy, the boy cared for each of his sheep. But one had gone missing, and for that reason, the shepherd had left the flock to seek out the one that was lost.

Keeping the sheep was usually a servant's job, but the family was not wealthy and servants came at a price, so the job fell to Jesse's youngest son. A lowly position, shepherds were held in little regard. Yet the boy did not mind. He was content out of doors, roaming the hills with the bleating beasts he had grown to love.

So it was to this boy that the task of caring for the flock had been placed, a serious task, full of danger and constant care, for sheep are helpless, depending wholly upon their shepherd for all their needs. Without someone to guide them, they would surely perish. Their poor eyesight and meager sense of smell kept them from finding good grass and clear water. Many wander astray, falling into crevices or landing in the clutches of a lion or bear.

And so with great diligence, the son of Jesse left the flock to seek the one that had wandered off, hoping to find the lost lamb before some calamity befell the hapless creature. He searched the surrounding rocky slopes, looking deep into any fissure he could find, calling the sheep, for he knew the lamb would know his master's voice. Retracing the steps up the rugged slope whereupon he had led the flock before, the young shepherd continued his search until at last he heard a faint bleating. Following the sound, the lad looked and, behold, the white coat of the little lamb could be seen on a ledge just below the next ridge.

The boy stood over the stranded sheep and spoke, "Well, well, well, now you are in a fix. How did you get down there, little lamb?"

Lying upon his belly, the boy reached and lifted the lamb with the crook of his shepherd's staff. He took the trembling creature into the fold of his arms and sat a moment, cradling the frightened lamb.

"Now then, we must return to the fold, before some other one wanders off."

Rising, the shepherd boy laid the lamb across his shoulders. With rod and staff in hand, he trekked back down the slope to where he had left the rest of his flock. As he lifted the lamb from his shoulders and set it near the other sheep, he spoke tenderly to the lamb.

"Always going your own way. Do you not yet know that to follow me is your protection? Will you not have choice grass if you let me lead you? Come, little lamb, and join the fold, for there is safety here; I will guard you with my life. Now back to the others with you."

With the side of his staff, the shepherd shooed the lamb toward the rest of the sheep. The lad stood for a time looking over the flock, counting the sheep to see that all were present. Satisfied, the boy turned and gazed across the green pasture. The faint sound of trickling water reached his ear. Large rocks covered the ground giving rise to tufts of pale grass.

He climbed upon a large boulder and surveyed the countryside, checking for signs of predators. The peaceful land stretched before him as he gazed across the steep slope within the fold of verdant hills. A distant shimmer caught his sight. Shielding his eyes from the glare of the sun, with his hand to his brow, the lad looked east and beheld the Salt Sea glistening in the distance. Clouds lingered over the water, broken as rays of light streamed down from above, striking the clear green surface. The glint of the crystalline shore sparkled like a myriad of precious jewels. It seemed to him that the glory of God shone down through a window in the heavens and his heart swelled with awe.

Overwhelmed, the shepherd leapt down from the boulder. Taking up his harp, he sat upon the ground with his back resting against the very boulder on which he had stood. As he strummed a tune upon the strings, words formed within his mouth as he sang from the depths of his soul. No human ear could hear and no eye was present to admire his skill, yet he sang with his all, for One alone was his auditor.

> The heavens declare the glory of God;
>   And the firmament shows His handiwork.
> Day unto day utters speech,
>   And night unto night reveals knowledge.
> There is no speech nor language
>   Where their voice is not heard.
> Their line has gone out through all the earth,
>   And their words to the end of the world.
>
> In them He has set a tabernacle for the sun,
> Which is like a bridegroom coming out of his chamber,
>   And rejoices like a strong man to run its race.
> Its rising is from one end of heaven,
>   And its circuit to the other end;
>   And there is nothing hidden from its heat.
>
> The law of the Lord is perfect,
>   converting the soul;
> The testimony of the Lord is sure,
>   making wise the simple;
> The statutes of the Lord are right,
>   rejoicing the heart;
> The commandment of the Lord is pure,
>   enlightening the eyes;
> The fear of the Lord is clean,
>   enduring forever;
> The judgments of the Lord
>   are true and righteous altogether.
> More to be desired are they than gold,
>   Yea, than much fine gold;

> Sweeter also than honey and the honeycomb.
> Moreover by them Your servant is warned,
>> And in keeping them there is great reward.
>
> Who can understand his errors?
> Cleanse me from secret faults.
> Keep back Your servant also from pride
>> and presumptuous sins;
>> Let them not have dominion over me.
> Then I shall be blameless,
>> And I shall be innocent of great transgression.
>
> Let the words of my mouth
>> and the meditation of my heart
> Be acceptable in Your sight,
>> O Lord, my strength and my Redeemer.[37]

The words ceased, yet the lad continued to play his harp softly. A smile lingered upon his lips, as the soothing sound of harmonious melody floated through the air. Peace settled there. He took a deep breath, his heart content. Yet the boy knew that peace did not last long in the hills. Always he had to strain his ear listening for signs of coming trouble.

Far off, a sound drew near the shepherd. The lad stayed his hand above the strings of his harp, as though the moment held him fast, poised for the next note. He strained his ear, listening.

Yes, there it is again.

It was the footfalls of rushing feet, growing ever louder, marking a path toward him. He laid the harp at his side, the song it carried silenced. With rod in hand, the shepherd leapt to his feet. The sheep scattered this way and that, as someone broke through the midst of the flock.

"David, at last I have found you!"

"Abinadab?"

A sudden pounding filled his chest, fearing some trouble at home. His brothers seldom paid him any heed; almost never did they come

---

[37] Psalm 19

into the fields to speak with him. Yet something had brought his brother here now. Urgency gripped his heart.

"What is it, brother? Is it *Abba*?"

"David, you have been summoned by the old prophet, Samuel."

He lingered in place, his gaze drawn across the pasture to the sheep entrusted to his keeping.

"Never mind the sheep, David. Go, I will tend to them."

He nodded, handing Abinadab his rod, and hastened toward home. Swift he went, his thoughts racing as he trekked across the rugged hillside.

The prophet Samuel—summoning me? What could he want with me, a shepherd boy?

At last the lad entered his father's house. He was winded; and as he climbed the ladder, his stomach fluttered in anticipation.

As he gained the upper floor, he sprang into the room. They all turned toward him, scorn set in their eyes.

What have I done?

Then he saw the old prophet standing beside the table. The boy came forward and looked in earnest upon Samuel, his blue eyes bright and piercing.

Blue eyes, thought Samuel, *how unusual.*

"This is David, my youngest son," spoke Jesse.

"David," repeated Samuel, "whose name means *beloved.*"

The prophet looked the boy over, for he was but a youth, not yet showing the promise of manhood. His hair was brown and wavy, a mess of wild, coiled locks cropped short about his ears. His complexion fair, his cheeks ruddy, pleasing was his countenance. David stood before him with sweetness in face and spirit, and quiet majesty in his stance.

Samuel rose to his feet. A smile broke across the old prophet's face as he took hold the lad's arms. David did not flinch, but stood, his eyes unwavering upon the prophet, his head canted to the side. Still holding him, the seer studied the visage he beheld, overwhelmed by the wisdom of God to know the heart of man.

"The Lord has unveiled to me this day the one He has chosen to lead His people Israel." Samuel chuckled softly as he patted David's shoulder.

The room was quiet. Jesse looked upon the prophet as though he were mad. The boy's brothers stole disapproving glances at one another, unwilling to believe Samuel's words.

"There is a king in Israel yet," spoke Jesse, fear pricking his heart. "How then can you say Yahweh has chosen one to lead His people?"

"The king has been disavowed," retorted Samuel.

"You have brought danger into my house."

"Do not fear, Jesse, son of Obed," replied the prophet. "What the Lord has purposed shall not be thwarted. When His hand is stretched out, who can turn it back? He will see it fulfilled."[38]

So Samuel took David and his father from the midst of his brothers and led them without, whereupon he had the boy kneel down before him. David's heart leapt within him, yet his mind was strangely calm as he looked with eyes wide in wonder upon the gentle face of the old prophet.

Moved by the boy's quiet awe, the prophet smiled, for here was one unquestioning in his willingness to do all that was commanded him. He blessed the boy, then took the horn of oil, a horn made by God's own hand, a symbol of power and might, and poured the oil over David's head, infusing him with the strength of Yahweh.

Within his heart David felt a flutter, a filling of the Lord's Spirit, raising him to grace and wisdom, to an understanding of God's purpose. His dark hair glistened as the sun shone bright upon him; his eyes lifted toward heaven, reaching beyond the corporeal realm. A light breeze brushed against David's face, caressing his tender cheek. As he noted the green carpet upon the hills flecked with blue flax flowers, peaceful quiet touched his soul. Nature, the bounty of the Lord's blessing, the promise of life and rebirth. And he knew that anything was possible with God.

Samuel placed his hand upon the shepherd boy's head, tenderness pervading his soul as he looked down at the innocent face of David, and his heart was full. The grief of Saul cast aside by the wisdom of Yahweh.

"Blessed is the Lord's anointed. Hallowed may his days ever be."

The prophet rejoiced, for even though Saul had been rejected, a king had been found, humble and yielding, with a heart bent for God's

---

[38] Isaiah 14:27

service. And so it is that Yahweh often chooses the most unlikely of people; for a lowly shepherd, least of the sons of Jesse, a servant among men, now stood lifted up as a priest and a king unto the Lord Most High. Many there were that in times to come would wonder at the secret of his strength.

With the purpose fulfilled for which Samuel had set out, the most joyous of all sacrifices to Yahweh, the peace offering, the sacrifice of completion was presented. A season of glad communion followed as the festivities began, celebrating a secret vow. Sumptuous feasting, accompanied by the music of the double pipe, filled the room with a jubilant tenor.

The old prophet sat back contented, watching the young of Jesse's house dance and carry on in youthful vigor. A smile spread across Samuel's face, his heart full and light. And though he knew that if the king discovered his cloaked charge, he would be killed, the old prophet feared not, for goodness comes to those who obey the voice of the Lord.

As the evening wore on, the festivities burgeoned into a loud and spirited night. Countenances flushed with merriment. People filled the small house. Upon a chair at the table, which had been pushed to the back of the room, the old prophet could not contain his joy. He threw back his head and laughed, the sound resonating throughout the chamber. David looked upon Samuel. Seeing the light heart of the old man, he giggled with delight. The prophet gazed upon God's anointed and knew—out of sorrow, hope springs.

CHAPTER 38

TEMPEST-TOSSED

The restless wind of anxious thought raced through Saul's mind, pacing endlessly in fictitious imaginings, fables of his own making. As a beast in his cage treading an endless gyre, the impatient traveler parceled his measured steps. Driven by some distraction, his rampage of erratic passages grasped for understanding of some hidden meaning, the issue known only to himself. In perpetual agitation, Saul meted out his endless flight, muttering inaudible reflections, gesturing with hands wild. Ahinoam looked upon her husband, the unquiet wanderer warring within, his spirit vexed. She rushed after him, striving to subdue the turbulent king, but his pace was quick and she lagged behind.

Pausing but a moment in his trek, the king ran his hand through his hair as he cast his gaze from the balcony. "My soul groans within me!" He grasped the back of his neck. "My life unravels as I yet weave." Sighing, he picked up his pace, wringing his hands, muttering anew.

Ahinoam took hold the king's arm. But he recoiled at her touch, as though repulsed, and shook off her grasp. Again, she rushed upon Saul, throwing her arms about him in a desperate hug. The king's progress was stayed. Saul melted into her arms. Falling to his knees, he collapsed within her embrace. Ahinoam cradled her husband's head, stroking his untamed mane, as he grimaced in agony.

"Saul, my love, what troubles you?"

"I do not know," answered the king through clenched teeth. "I harbor a sense of impending doom. Something is at work, a threat hiding in the shadows. I cannot apprehend what it is, but it is ready to pounce at any moment."

Ahinoam kissed his face, smoothing back his hair as tears flowed down her cheeks. She could not bear to see the man she so dearly loved reduced to this forlorn soul. They sat there for a time, clutching in desperation to each other, tortured and without solace.

Saul drew himself up and held Ahinoam's face in his hands, looking into her frightened eyes. "There is something missing," he said, his eyes feral and desperate.

"Missing?"

"Something within me. I feel hollow, empty, as though my very soul has been removed." Saul leaned his head into Ahinoam's arms, his frame trembling. "It is hard to bear. There is a terror within me. I cannot explain it, yet it is there."

Ahinoam lifted his face between her hands. Saul looked at her. With a quavering hand, he traced a tear track upon her cheek, gazing deep into her eyes. In that moment, a connection was made. Ahinoam could feel his body relax. She smiled at him and kissed him on the brow, breathing deeply, peacefully, as she sensed the storm passing.

Saul sprang to his feet, tearing himself from his wife's arms.

"Saul!"

He turned and, with his countenance full of rage, he thrust a finger in Ahinoam's face. "Do you not see? They are out to get me." As he spoke, he stretched forth his hand indicating that the enemy was just beyond the door. "There are those, I know, who plot against me."

Saul paced, agitated, looking about the room, wringing his hands.

"You know? How do you know? Who do you think is plotting against you?"

"I do not know. I just know. I see it in their eyes. They whisper behind my back as I pass by. They are plotting in the shadows."

"Whispering behind your back? Plotting in the shadows? Saul, listen to what you are saying."

Saul rushed over to Ahinoam and grabbed her by the arms. He pulled her to her feet, squeezing her arms in his strong hands.

Ahinoam winced. "Saul, you are hurting me."

"Do you not see? It must be Jonathan; he has always desired my throne."

"Saul, you speak nonsense. Jonathan does not seek your throne."

"Guh!" Saul pushed Ahinoam aside. He turned and strode away from her. She stood staring after him, rubbing her bruised arms, her eyes wide with terror.

"If not him," continued the king, his arms cast about in vehemence, "then it is his friends. They wish to depose me and place him upon the throne."

Ahinoam backed toward the wall, keeping her eyes fixed on her king. He was a stranger to her. Desperate, she thought, *What do I do?* Glancing to her left, she espied a servant lurking in the shadows, watching the scene unfold in horror. Ahinoam motioned for the lad to attend her. Leaning toward the youth, she whispered, "Send for Abner; tell him to come at once. The king is not well."

The servant hastened away, eager to flee the terrible spectacle. Moments later, Abner rushed into the room, out of breath, concern etched across his face.

"Abner!" gasped Ahinoam with relief.

Abner looked upon the restless king, pacing and muttering. The general went swiftly to Ahinoam, startled to see her so undone. He took her hands in his. "What is it, sister?"

"Abner, call for the healer. The king is not well."

Upon hearing his uncle's voice, Saul halted in his tracks; he turned about and glared through narrowed eyes at the general. Striding toward him, Saul thrust an accusing finger in his face. "I suppose you would have my crown also?"

Calmly, Abner replied, "I would never presume to hold such an esteemed office, my king. I am only here to serve you."

Wild-eyed, Saul jabbed his finger at Abner. "Hah!" he laughed in a crazed voice; then turned away, wringing the back of his neck, falling again into his endless trek across the floor.

Abner watched his nephew, beholding the madness before him. He set his eyes again upon Ahinoam. Reclaiming her hands, he spoke, "How long has he been like this?"

"Ever since he returned from fighting Amalek. He has been restless and fierce of temper. Oh, Abner, what has happened? I am so afraid!"

"Steady, sister, we will see what the healer says."

Abner motioned toward the servant who had returned to his shadowy lookout. "Summon the king's *rofe*. Tell him to make haste."

Taking hold of Ahinoam's hand, Abner patted it tenderly, striving to quell the fear that yet lingered upon her face.

Abruptly, Saul turned and glared at his uncle. Surging toward him, the king seized Abner by the mantle with both of his mighty hands, severing his connection with Ahinoam. Saul's eyes fixed on Abner, burning, pleading, "What do I do? Please tell me! We have peace—I have nothing to do. No one to fight."

Thrusting Abner away, Saul staggered back in despair. "My mind is so restless." He raked his fingers through his hair, then threw his arms down to his sides. "I need action to fill my days."

Steadying himself, Abner approached, his voice calm and low. "My king, you must rule your people well even in peace. Though war has ceased for a time, there is still labor to be done in establishing your kingdom. Peace will not last—it never does. Turn your mind to bolstering your defenses. Train your forces. Center your thoughts on the work of kingdom building."

Saul stood still, staring far-off, as though he was weighing his general's words. Shaking his head, he released a long breath, weary from his toil. At last his hollow eyes found his faithful uncle. "My soul is pensive; I feel dry and parched."

Abner looked toward the servant who had just returned from his errand. "Get the king some water."

Nodding obediently, the servant crossed to a table set against the far wall and poured water into a beautifully fashioned brass-and-silver goblet. Warily, the youth brought the vessel to the king and presented it to him.

"No!" Saul struck the cup from the servant's hand, spilling it upon the ground, and turned his face away.

Looking to Abner, the servant waited, stunned. Abner dismissed him with the wave of his hand.

"General."

Abner turned at the word. The royal healer, a *rofe* from the tribe of Levi, entered the king's chamber. Aged and bent, the healer walked over to Abner with a slow gait. In his hand he carried a case containing the implements of his trade: *terufot*, medicines wrought from the earth—root cuttings, herbs of healing, poultices, soothing ointments and salves, and instruments of surgery.

"Come, my king," spoke Abner as he motioned with his outstretched arm, "you are ill, not of yourself. Let the healer have a look at you."

Saul glanced at Abner, then at Ahinoam. He saw his wife's sorrowful eyes, red from weeping, and he relented. With care, the healer inspected the king's person as he rested upon the cushions of his gilded couch. The *rofe* stood shaking his head. "I can find no infirmity of the flesh." Addressing the king, he spoke, "It is a troubling spirit from the Lord that afflicts you."

"What are we to do?" asked Ahinoam.

"Let the evil spirit which troubles him be charmed away," answered the *rofe*.

Ahinoam took a step closer. "How can this be accomplished?"

"It is thought that music can soothe during times of distress. That is what I would recommend. However, this is but a passing remedy; only Yahweh has power over these spirits. See to the priest to provide the king's offerings and supplications. Call on me again if anything changes. *Barchot ve Tefillot*, blessings and prayers."

"*Todah*, thanks to you," spoke Ahinoam, finding little solace in the tidings she had received.

"My king," spoke the servant with trepidation.

Saul sat upon his couch, his head down, spent. He looked up with empty eyes, gazing at the servant who bent low before him. With the wave of the king's hand, the servant continued, "Let our master now command your servants, who are before you, to seek out a man who is a skillful player on the harp. And it shall be that he will play it with his hand when the distressing spirit from God is upon you, and you shall be well."

"This pleases us." Saul waved his hand again as he gave command. "Go now, provide me a man who can play well, and bring him to me."

As the servant bowed and withdrew from the king's presence, Saul turned away from Ahinoam and Abner.

"*Azov oti*, leave me."

Abner and Ahinoam bowed and departed, leaving Saul alone.

With effort, the king raised himself from the couch and stepped over to the balcony. Looking out at the empty sky, Saul breathed deeply, yet his chest felt no relief. "The air, how still it is. Does it not move? How long will this stifling vapor linger? Can I not have air, for my soul hungers for a breeze?"

Abandoning the balcony, Saul returned to his chamber, distress written upon his face. "The days are endless; will they not cease? Must I continue in this languid air of dismal thought? How can I enter each new day when around me all I see is the dark hollows of night?"

Saul stood for a moment, as though seeking some way of escape. His head lowered, and a long sigh escaped him. He shook his head slowly, the motion itself a burden. "But to give in to these thoughts would mean an end to this world and an entering into the next, and the thought of that prospect brings such a terror to me that I cannot scarce venture toward that mark. For what does Sheol hold for me, but more misery? How can I face that which in my folly I have shunned? Yet to continue on is only to confront the endless gloom of disjointed thought."

Burying his head in his hands, Saul shuddered in despair. He drew his hands down the length of his face, pulling at his features as he breathed in.

"I could end this. It would be so easy: a sip of poison or a dagger to the heart. My knife. Just a cut to the throat and it would be over."

Saul took hold of his dagger and placed it to his neck. He could feel the cold blade against his flesh. Sweat beaded upon his brow. His breath came short and quick. Trembling, he pressed the sharp edge into his throat. Slowly, he drew the blade across his flesh. He felt the knife bite. With a start, pain struck; he withdrew the dagger. His shoulders slumped.

"No," he spoke as a trickle of blood issued down his neck. "That is what they are hoping for. I will not relinquish the throne quite so easily."

Saul returned to his couch. Three days he lay there, languishing between reflections of revenge and bouts of despair. Far off his thoughts roamed in distant fields, wandering wearily in wastelands of endless dread.

"Saul, you must eat something," pleaded Ahinoam, her sad eyes looking upon her despondent husband, her voice full of concern. "You have not eaten in days."

He lifted his gaze at the sound of Ahinoam's voice. After a weary breath, the forlorn king made reply, "I have not the stomach for it."

Ahinoam was near undone when a servant entered into the chamber and bowed tentatively before the royal couple. Saul lay upon his couch, listless, resting on his side with his head propped on his elbow. He made no move to acknowledge the one before him.

"Speak," said Ahinoam firmly.

"I have seen a son of Jesse the Bethlehemite, who is skilled in playing the harp, prudent in speech, and a handsome person; and the Lord is with him."

Saul lifted his head at the servant's words. Sitting up, he leaned forward, his hands upon his knees, his face toward the floor. "Bring me parchment on which to write."

The servant fetched the king parchment, a reed pen, and ink, and handed it to his master, then backed away, for of late the king's moods were unpredictable.

Saul wrote upon the parchment.

"What is the lad called?" questioned Saul, his voice hoarse from lack of use.

"My king, he is called David; he is a shepherd."

Saul turned again to the parchment. When finished, he held it up and inspected the contents. He gave a slow nod and blew upon the page to dry the ink. The king rolled the script, and pouring wax upon the seam, he pressed his royal seal into the soft wax.

"Send this to Jesse of Bethlehem. Wait for his reply, then return to me."

Receiving the scroll, the servant bowed low. "As you wish, my king."

CHAPTER 39

THE UNFOLDING

"At last!" exclaimed Jesse as the split *owphan* came free from the axle of the ox cart. Rolling the damaged wheel aside, Jesse let it fall to the ground with a thud. He then took up the new, solid *owphan* and rolled it over to the cart, which was propped so that it leaned heavily upon its remaining wheel, with the tongue of the shaft balancing upon a large stone. With a mighty effort, Jesse lifted the large disk into place upon the axle. Grabbing his mallet from the cart bed, he struck the wooden linchpin into place.

On the edge of his sight, Jesse caught a cloud of dust rising, slowly traveling toward the yard. Standing up from his labor, Jesse ran the back of his arm across his brow, mallet still in hand, as he watched the stranger drawing near.

The young man approached and bowed before him.

"*Shalom.*"

"*Shalom*," Jesse replied with a slight bow of his head.

"Tell me, please. Are you the sheep keeper, Jesse, son of Obed, the Bethlehemite?"

"I am he."

The young man reached into his cloak and withdrew a scroll. "I bear a message from the king." He presented the writ to Jesse.

Laying aside his mallet, Jesse put forth his hand and clasped the rolled parchment. Fear gripped his heart as he noted the royal seal upon the scroll. With trembling hands, he broke the embossed emblem as the messenger looked on, waiting. Jesse took a deep breath, then, slowly, unfurled the parchment. His stomach lurched as he read the sweeping script of the king.

> *It has come to our ears that your beloved son, David, has skill in the playing of the harp and the making of music. Now, send us your son, who is with the sheep, that he might delight us with his song.*

The letter was signed: Saul, King of Israel, Defender of Yahweh's people.

The pace of Jesse's heart quickened. *What could this be? How is it that the king knows so much about my family? Has Saul somehow found out that Samuel had come to Bethlehem and anointed David? Is the boy in danger?*

Jesse breathed deep, then rolled the parchment and handed it back to the messenger.

The young man received the scroll and stood waiting for Jesse to reply.

"It will be done as the king requests," answered Jesse, *for who may refuse a summons from the king.*

So Jesse sent for his son, David. Then took a donkey and loaded it with gifts of bread, a skin of wine, and a young goat, a token of homage to the sovereign of Israel, as was the custom. Turning toward his son, Jesse placed a hand on each shoulder, speaking words of kindness to the youth.

"Though you are the least of my sons, I love you well, David. Go, and be not afraid. Speak nothing of the prophet Samuel, or his visit to you. Do all that the king asks. Trust in God."

"I will, *Abba.*"

He looked into the eyes of his father and saw fear.

"*Abba*, do not be afraid, for the Lord is with me. Yahweh is the master of all that comes to pass. Why then should we fear? Do you not see, His plan is unfolding before us?"

Jesse smiled down at his son. "You are a most remarkable boy." Taking the lad into his arms, he kissed David farewell.

And so Jesse sent his son, not with weapons of war, but with tokens of goodwill, to attend to Saul, king of Israel, whose star was falling.

CHAPTER 40

BECALMED

From the hall to the left of the dais, Abner entered into the throne room. The pungent odor of paint stung his nostrils. On the large stone walls, several artists were hard at work creating murals, the warm hues bringing to life many of the king's battles. Saul sat upon his lofty chair, his chin resting within his hand as he leaned on the arm of his seat, watching with scrutiny as the painters worked.

Abner bowed. "My king, a word, please."

Saul rolled his eyes to look at his uncle. With a motion of his hand, he bade him approach the throne. "What is it?"

"I have word from King Nahash of Ammon."

"The old snake."

"Yes, my king. He wishes to extend his arm in friendship by a pledge of peace between our two kingdoms. To seal this pact, he has offered his daughter, Zeruiah, to you in marriage."

Saul stood. "No! That is not how I told you! Pay attention!" He stormed over to the artist and shoved him aside, seizing the brush. "Like this!" Saul painted upon the wall, enlarging the image, now crudely wrought in rash strokes.

Abner paced behind Saul. "My king. Please, can you not focus? This matter is pressing. The offer will not be extended indefinitely."

"What?" Saul continued to direct the artist.

"King Nahash," spoke Abner, "his pledge for peace. What say you?"

Saul tossed the brush, still loaded with paint, at the artist standing by him, splattering pigment across the man's face. Leaving a trail of paint as he wiped his hand down the front of his tunic, Saul turned, his demeanor calm, toward Abner. "I have a wife yet; I have no need for another."

"It would be wise not lightly to look upon this pledge of peace."

Saul laughed. "I do not need treaties or pledges of peace. I have made known what will happen to any nation that stands against Israel. Who would oppose me, Saul, King of Israel?"

"My king."

"Ah, not a word more about the matter. I have spoken."

Doeg entered the room to find the king and his general facing each other in heated debate. He bowed before the two men, stilling their contention.

"What now!" cried the king. "How am I to attend to matters with all these interruptions?"

"My king," spoke Doeg, his voice measured beneath Abner's watchful gaze. "If it please you, the boy, David, is here. Shall I send him in?"

"It does please us… Well, what are you waiting for? Send him in." Saul strode over to his throne and sat, adjusting his crown upon his head.

Shortly thereafter, David was guided into the court of the king, his lyre strapped to his back. As he turned left, the boy walked down the aisle bounded by pillars, followed by Ziba, the king's servant. The grand throne room was strewn with scaffolding and paints and tarps and artists. A man was washing a misguided stroke off the wall, some figure with which the artist was unsatisfied. In the center of the floor, a flame burned within the open fire pit, softly illuminating graceful spirits dancing upon the walls. The massive stones harbored half-painted scenes of Saul's victories, the images coming to life by the flickering points of flame.

Step by step, David approached the dais. The king, looking down from the platform, sat with solemn gravity upon his throne. Guards flanked the royal seat; each holding his spear at attention, motionless, living statues.

Every eye turned toward David. The artists froze mid-stroke. All movement within the court ceased as the boy presented himself to the king. Ziba brought forth Jesse's gifts: the wine, the bread, and a young goat, its feet bound; all these he laid at the sovereign's feet.

David nodded his thanks to Ziba, then bowed before the king. "Greetings from Jesse, son of Obed. He sends these gifts to honor your greatness, O King."

Saul smiled, his chin raised so that he had to glare down his nose at the boy kneeling beneath him. "Arise, my son. We thank your father for his generosity."

David stood with his face toward the ground, fearing to meet the gaze of so powerful a man as Saul.

"Look upon me, so that I may see into your eyes."

With guarded care, the boy raised his face and met the king's stern gaze.

For a time Saul beheld the piercing blue eyes of David, unable to turn away; for in those eyes all the king's hidden thoughts were revealed, and he shuddered. With a jerk of his head, he looked away, a strained smile upon his lips. "It is told us that you are skilled in the playing of the harp."

"There are some who have said so," spoke David, unsure how to answer. He had never played before one who held such station and power among men.

"Come, play for me."

"As you desire, so shall I do."

The boy reached behind his back and unlashed his *kinnor*. He then sat upon the stairs of the dais, at the feet of the king, with his instrument upon his lap. The two curved arms of the harp he cradled in his left arm, resting the instrument against his chest. With a gentle touch, he strummed and plucked the strings toward his heart with the tips of the fingers of his right hand.

The beautiful, delicate sound of the lyre sprung forth, tranquil and transparent, yet the floating tones of a thousand colors hung upon the air, until the next chord sung, blending, then hushing the last, as the muted tone, suspending, was filled with the next, floating, floating... deeply breathing, inhaling, melting Saul's spirit.

As the song ended, Saul opened his eyes and beheld David. Calmness had settled upon the king, and he smiled. "Tell me, do you sing as well?"

"It is my wont to sing as I bring forth melody from my harp. If it is pleasing to others, I do not know, but it is pleasing to me to give voice so."

"Please, sing to me."

So David lifted up his song, raising his sweet voice before the king, who had been sick of spirit without the grace to bear it.

> Hear my cry, O God;
> Attend to my prayer.
> From the end of the earth I will cry to You,
> When my heart is overwhelmed;
> Lead me to the rock that is higher than I.
>
> For You have been a shelter for me,
> A strong tower from the enemy.
> I will abide in Your tabernacle forever;
> I will trust in the shelter of Your wings.
>
> For You, O God, have heard my vows;
> You have given me the heritage of those who fear
> Your name.
> You will prolong the king's life,
> His years as many generations.
> He shall abide before God forever.
> Oh, prepare mercy and truth, which may preserve him!
>
> So I will sing praise to Your name forever,
> That I may daily perform my vows.[39]

Floating upon the flowing notes, Saul listened, taken by the sound of David's music. He leaned his head back and closed his eyes. Letting go a deep sigh, Saul allowed himself to drift upon the melody. With wings, the mingled tones captured his soul, stealing his mind away on a mystic chord, as though he were a feather wafting upon a gentle breeze. His frame relaxed, his thoughts ordered and whole. An internal calm swept through his mind as the melancholy that had

---

[39] Psalm 61

taken hold of him vanished. His air came deep and steady; he could breathe again.

A single tear rose full from Saul's eye and traced a tender course down his cheek. Lines of strain eased from his visage as a serene spirit drew a quiet smile upon his face. And what could not be cut with the sword, nor quenched by water, nor blown out by the wind, was closed up by the melodious chords of David and his harp.[40]

As the boy continued to hold the mind of the king, he caught sight of a young girl peeking around the corner from the hall to the left of the dais. Her long, dark hair framed her pleasing face, falling about her shoulders and down her back. His eyes met hers, and for a moment they lingered; then she giggled and turned, disappearing into the darkness of the hall. He knew not why, but he longed to run after her. Yet he remained as he was, soothing the king's mind.

When the music ceased, Saul opened his eyes and looked upon David, and he loved him greatly for the blessing he had bestowed upon him.

"My son, you have given to me a gift beyond measure. I will send a message to your father, requesting he give me leave to detain you in my service, for you have found favor in my sight. You shall sing to me daily until such time I have no need. You shall have all of your cares supplied. Your time will be your own until I call for you; then you will come and attend to me."

Saul turned his face toward his uncle and, with his hand, waved him over. Abner strode with heavy steps beside the king.

"General, see to his needs, take him to Ahinoam to find a room for him."

Abner motioned for the boy to rise. David bowed before the king, and followed after him.

"David," spoke the king, "you will be happy here. You shall see."

---

[40] (Henry, 1838)

CHAPTER 41

THE PASSAGE

The hallway was dark and cold after the warm glow of the hearth fire that blazed within the throne room. Abner's steps were slow and deliberate; even so, David had to hurry to keep up with the long strides of the king's general. Their footfalls echoed off the masonry. No other sound could be heard.

Looking upon the empty passage, David felt drawn away into a far-off land. Before him lay the unknown, a realm wholly foreign to him. How remote the sheepfold seemed. The walls were so close, for he was used to the open countryside. Now he was hemmed in by stone walls. Yet he could smell the grass of the field through windows cut in the eastern side of the corridor. His heart lifted as he noted the sun filtering in, casting patches of light upon the floor and the opposite wall. The western side of the hall was lined with doorways, each shut to those passing by, as though saying, "The way is barred; you cannot enter here."

As he progressed down the hallway, David knew that, with each step, his life was changing. He was on a journey wherein his entire future hastened near with every footfall. To continue meant he would never be the carefree shepherd boy again. He was in a passage between two states of being, and he had a single choice: turn back or move forward. Yet David knew he had but one way to go. Providence had chosen his path. And he was determined to follow wherever Yahweh would lead.

He heard the tread of approaching feet, unlike the bounding cadence of the general's steps, echoing along the passageway. Two sets: one gentle and the other light and quick. Rounding the corner from the west, Abner and David came face to face with a lovely woman, and there, at her side, was the girl he had seen watching him. She had a strange effect on the boy, as though she could see into him. Her gaze came to rest upon David, and she smiled coyly. He returned her smile and looked at the ground, running his sandaled toe along the seam between two flagstones.

"Ah, sister," spoke Abner, breaking into the silence of the corridor, "I was on my way to find you."

"General," the woman spoke, tipping her head. She turned her eyes toward David and smiled. He liked how she looked at him.

"Sister, this is the lad, David. He has come to play his lyre for the king. He is in need of a room."

"*Shalom*, my dear boy." Her voice was soft and warm. David was drawn to this woman. As he looked into her eyes, the ache of parental separation eased. He smiled at her, his large blue eyes alive with warmth.

"This is Ahinoam, wife to the king. You will go with her. She will show you where you will be staying."

"Thank you, *Sar*."

"Come with me, David," Ahinoam spoke. "We are so pleased to have you with us."

He walked behind this gentle woman as she led the way. The girl stayed beside her mother, but glanced back at David from time to time. Soon the trio came to the north corridor of the palace. Ahinoam stopped at a door and turned. As she opened it, she spoke, "Here we are, David. This will be your room."

Gingerly, the boy entered. The chamber was a simple cell with large stone-block walls. A single large window was set into the north wall. He was glad for the window. There was a real bed in the room, not just a pallet, but a mat resting on ropes stretched across a frame. He had never slept on so fine a bed. As David stood there, he forgot he was not alone until Ahinoam spoke again.

"Please, David, make yourself at home. A servant will come to give you instruction on your duties and daily requirements." The king's wife went to the boy and took his hand in hers. Her touch was soft and tender; her eyes warm. "David, I thank you for your service to the king. I am in your debt." Her smile thrilled his soul. All he wanted at that moment was to please this woman, to fulfill all her hopes.

The moment passed and she took her leave. The girl followed her mother from the room, but turned just before the doorway and smiled once more at David. Warmth coursed through his chest. As he watched her depart, he stood perplexed by the effect she had on him.

Silence settled upon the room with the absence of his escorts. He looked about the chamber again. A slight breeze filtered in through the window, drawing his gaze to the view. Unstrapping his lyre, he laid the instrument on the floor in the corner, carefully propped against the far wall. He went to the window. It faced north, overlooking the gorge below. Michmash it was that lurked in the distance. He could see the old Philistine fortress across the ravine.

This was the garrison that the king's son had taken. He had heard stories of the feats of Jonathan, how he risked all for the good of the people. A national hero he had become. David imagined scenes of battle and glory that must have taken place just beyond where he now stood. He wondered if he might meet Jonathan here at the king's palace.

He was startled out of his reverie by the sound of light footsteps entering the room. Thinking it must be the servant come to give him instruction, David turned to greet them.

But it was not the servant. The sight of the girl took David's voice, and he stood gazing at her.

"You sing well." She entered the room casually, looking about as though weighing the care with which he kept his chamber.

David inclined his head in silent thanks.

She drew near, her face but a breath from his. A thrill ran through his frame, robbing him of air.

"My name is Michal. I am the king's daughter."

David smiled.

Michal stepped away, inspecting the lyre that rested against the wall. "This does not look as beautiful as it sounds." She turned her head and fixed her eyes on David. "You do not say much."

David's face flushed. Clearing his throat, he strove to speak. "Good to know you, Michal." To his horror, his voice broke, rising higher than he intended.

Michal grinned. She came toward him, leaning close. David's eyes widened, and his breath caught in his chest.

"So you were a shepherd boy. Baby lambs are cute. We used to have goats. I like sheep better."

David nodded.

"I have something for you." She reached into a bag at her side and drew out a blue flax flower. She raised it to her face and breathed in the bloom's sweet scent. Her eyelids fluttered. Looking through half-closed eyes, Michal handed the bloom to David.

He carefully received the flower from the girl, noting the five blue petals with a striking yellow star at the center.

"Did you know that the flax flower represents fate?" Michal wheeled away, her dark hair swinging after her as she stepped to the open doorway. She stopped and turned, smiling at David. "You see, we were destined to be friends."

With a wave, she was gone.

As the days turned to months, David did find a friend in Michal, the king's daughter. Whenever they were able, the two came together, passing the time in quiet conversation, walking in the fields and hills—their young hearts knitting to one another. And each day, David played for the king as the sun rose over Geba, and the king had peace within him. Saul was well pleased with David; happy fate had brought the boy to him.

Yet it was not chance that had led David to Saul's side; for Providence had carried this lowly shepherd that He might prepare the youth for his destiny, placing him within the king's court, where his reputation rose among those who dwelt there. Well thought of, he was, as one who knew the Lord and stood in gentleness and integrity. David grew, learning the art of governing a people, and the ways of kings, as he served Saul well with his music.

In this manner, David waited upon the king. Often he returned to his father to tend his sheep. Yet whenever the unsettling spirit came upon the king, Saul called the shepherd boy back to court to attend to him. David would return, take up his harp, and play it with his hand.

The distressing spirit would depart Saul, and his mind would be made whole and at peace. And so it was that King Saul, unknowingly, came to depend upon the one who was chosen to supplant him, anointed in his stead to sit upon Israel's throne.

CHAPTER 42

BENAYIM

Time passed, and once more, the Philistines took up the sword and gathered to do battle against Israel, deeming it a good time to avenge themselves upon the Chosen of God, for word of Saul's troubles had reached their ears. They had advanced deep into the marches of Israel, as far as Sochoh; this region belonged to the tribe of Judah, just west of Bethlehem. The Philistines encamped in Ephes Dammim, called *Happas-dammim*, the end of bloodshed, which lay between Sochoh and Azekah.

Now Sochoh, called *Givat Ha Turmusim*, or Lupine hill, for in spring the rise was covered with wild blue lupines, lay along the southern hillside of the Valley of Elah. Two miles to the northwest, Azekah rose two hundred and thirty cubits above the west end of the valley, affording a commanding view of the length of the entire vale. Southwest of the Canaanite city of Jebus, the Valley of Elah, *Emek ha-Elah*, the valley of oaks, opened within the hilly region that separated the mountains of Judah and the plain of Philistia.

This battle of old, being thus renewed, brought forth the question posed. By rights, who had claim to the land of Canaan? And Israel gave reply. Saul and his men arrayed themselves upon the northern ridge opposite the enemy encampment and made ready to give debate. The Philistines held the rise on one side, and Israel the rise on the other, each upon high ground overlooking the valley between them.

From camp to camp was heard the hum of dreadful preparation. The lines were drawn and kept, while whispering men in arms waited every night by watch fires ablaze. Each face saw through the piercing dark the boastful flame of the enemy, betraying their flint-hard looks. As the sentinels kept vigil, seeking for threats, both sides listened for the sound of moving feet. Yet none looked to start the argument, but fixed their gaze upon the adversary to set the contest to action. For the army that attacked would have to forsake the high ground and descend into the valley, then climb the ridge of the enemy under the eyes of the watchful foe.

So it was that after long delay, a *Benayim*, that is champion, whose name was Goliath, went out from the camp of the Philistines. Upon the mountain he stood, this *Benayim*, towering before the Israelites, for his stature was great, one of the Anakim of old, whose height was six cubits and a span.[41]

His helm was of bronze, feathered as a crown, with scales of burnished metal that shielded the back of his neck and the sides of his face. The dull buff of bronze plates, scales overlapping each other like those of a fish, guarded his breast, a corslet reaching to his waist and warding his back. His arms were at full liberty, for the armor was held fast by straps about the shoulders. The weight of the coat was five thousand shekels of bronze.[42] Greaves of burnished metal he had upon his legs. Betwixt his shoulders, he slung a javelin of bronze, waiting there until need arose. But in his hand, a spear he held, the staff of which was as a weaver's beam. Upon the tip, the *Lehabah*, flame of his spear, a head of iron flashed like fire in the morning light. Large was this spearhead, whose weight was six hundred shekels.[43]

Clad fully in bronze, the panoply complete, Goliath needed little the shield borne by his armor-bearer. Nevertheless, in state, the armor-bearer went before him carrying the *tzinnah*, the great shield.

Forward the giant stalked until he set himself in the valley between the two armies. Strong and sonorous, Goliath of Gath cried with a loud voice a taunt toward the ranks of Israel. His great stature was

---

[41] nine and a half feet
[42] one hundred and fifty-six pounds
[43] fifteen pounds

such that his very shadow loomed over the enemy host, his speech rising upon the hill where stood the Chosen of God.

"Why have you come forth arrayed for battle? Know you not that it is vain to stand against Philistia? Am I not a Philistine, that led the van when we destroyed our foes, trampling them beneath our feet?"

Goliath raised his spear and brandished it in threatful gesture. "And you, men of Israel, what mighty deed has Saul, the son of Kish, done that you should make him king over you? If he be a man of valor and courage, let him come down himself and fight with me. But if he be weak or faint of heart, then give me a man from among you, the servants of Saul, that he may come to me, that we may fight together and decide the controversy between us. If he be able to fight with me and slay me, then we will be your servants. But if I prevail against him and slay him, then you shall serve us."

Awaiting Israel's answer, Goliath stood, pouring out fresh torrents of abuse to provoke them to wrath. Yet none stepped forward, but trembled at the thought of engaging such a man as this mighty Benayim. With impatience growing, the Champion spoke with such strength and tone of voice, upbraiding them with cowardice and disdain, saying, "Is there not a man among you who dare meet with me in combat? I defy the armies of Israel this day, whom I have stripped and made bare. Give me a man, that we may fight together."

For forty days, both morning and evening, the Philistine drew near to the camp of Israel and presented the challenge. Yet even with so many valiant men among Israel, the summons went unanswered, and so shamed, they came before Saul, their king.

Two advisors he had: Captain Nagad, the Benjaminite, and Abner, the king's uncle. Together they entered into the king's tent, where they found Saul upon his seat. Within his hands, he held a doll, burnt and tattered, squeezing and twisting it, for Saul knew that all looked to him to answer the challenge. Stricken, the king could answer naught. He had not the resolve of heart as afore, for God's Spirit had departed, and a spirit of fear and doubt troubled his mind. Jonathan stood by, yet even he, who had been so faithful, possessed not the courage to deliver Israel as once he had.

"My king," spoke Nagad, "there is no man able to accept this challenge."

"No one?" questioned the king. "Out of all these valiant men, not a one?"

"No," spoke Abner, "not a one. Fear and dread run rampant throughout the armies of Israel. No, there is no one to answer the call."

"My king," spoke Nagad. "What would you have us do? I would that I were young again, but I have not the strength of youth to stand against so great a foe."

Saul, who had been a fierce and noble warrior, now was dismayed by the summons of Goliath. He sat on his seat, leaning upon his elbow, stroking his beard, the doll clutched in his hand.

After a time, Saul sat aright and spoke, saying, "This doll I have kept all these years to remind me of what the Philistines have done, how they laid waste to our Holy City. That offense cannot go unanswered."

"My king?" questioned Abner.

"Send forth word, for this is how it shall be. To any man who slays this Philistine, to him the king will reward with great riches. He also will be given the king's daughter in marriage, and to his father's house will be granted freedom from the burden of all taxes and tributes levied throughout Israel. Send forth this word and watch and see who will accept this challenge."

Abner's face enlightened with much-wandering hope. "It shall be done."

Bowing low, the two advisors took leave of the king's pavilion. The day was warm and dry. The sun reflected sharply off the pale ground, worn bare from the activities in the camp. Abner squinted against the bright contrast, raising his hand to shield his eyes.

"It might work."

Nagad nodded, yet kept his eyes downcast, whether from discouragement or the blinding light, the general could not ascertain.

"Many men will be tempted," said Nagad after long silence, "for the prize is beyond measure. Yet, I doubt any of these men are up to the task. For more than a month, they have sat about their fires, growing complacent and unfit."

Abner looked about the camp. It was as the captain spoke. Around every fire, men sat, leaning upon their elbows, toying with twigs, tossing objects into the flame. Their arms lay at their feet, cast off and left in the dust. As the two walked on, Abner's mood darkened.

"*Sar*," called Helek as he approached Nagad.

The captain lifted his head. "Speak your heart, brother."

"What is the word from the king? Will he meet the challenge? Will our king save us as once he did?"

"My dear Helek," answered Nagad, his voice low. "Our king cannot find his heart. He will take no action."

"Shall this *Goliath* defeat Israel on fear alone?" The words were bitter upon Helek's tongue.

Abner regarded the captain with growing impatience. "It is a task that must be accomplished by one of our mighty men of valor. The king has offered a handsome reward. Send word throughout the camp. Surely, a champion will be found among so many valiant men."

News of this great honor soon spread from one end of camp to the other. Many were stirred by the boon so offered. Even so, the call went unheeded. And as the spirit of courage had departed from Saul, their king, so too had it fled from the mighty men of Israel.

CHAPTER 43

VESTMENT OF A KING

The light was pale as David stood upon the rise, for the sun had not yet broken over the distant ridge. His heart was heavy even while he looked beyond the remnants of the dismal night. Objects had no distinction, just silhouettes in purple shadow. A heavy fog lingered in the valleys, not yet burnt away by the heat of the sun. Yet as he watched, the gloom of twilight yielded its reign to the advent of day.

Sighing deeply, David allowed his thoughts to wander across the lonely hills, north toward Geba. King Saul had not called upon the boy for several years; therefore, he had resumed his task of tending his father's flock. Though David was happy, for that meant the king was well, it left him with an aching heart. His mind of late had been fixed on Michal, the king's daughter. Something in the way he regarded her had changed during the last year. He took a cloth out of the pouch at his side. Carefully, he loosed its folds. Within lay a single flax flower, dried and flattened, yet the bloom retained its blue hue. David touched a petal with his finger. How far Geba seemed. His chest tightened.

Heartache, that is what they call it. And that is how it feels.

Yet even as he beheld the sun break over the eastern hills, he was taken by the dawn. Moved by the beauty, his soul stirred. At the moment of the sun's rebirth, the mystery of the ages was revealed in its entirety, if only for an instant. His heart was uplifted, as though on the edge of some profound understanding.

The moment passed. The full morn had arrived, the shadow cast off, and revelation dissolved into the reality of another ordinary day.

"David."

The sound of his father's voice cut through his thoughts. David lifted his head and turned toward the path where his father stood beside a beast of burden.

"Yes, *Abba*, I am here."

"David," spoke Jesse as he tightened the cinch strap under the donkey's belly. "Come, take these provisions to your brothers and bring back word to me of how they fare. Long have they been gone from me in service to the king. Take now this *ephah*[44] of dried grain and these ten loaves and replenish them, for I deem they will be in need of food." Jesse marked each item as he spoke, as though counting the supplies one final time. "And these ten cheeses; carry them to the captain of their thousand and present them to him to secure his fair courtesy toward Eliab, Abinadab, and Shimea, who are under his command."

"I will do as you say, *Abba*." David stepped over to the donkey and scratched the spot between its eyes.

"Now, make haste to the Valley of Elah, for there you will find King Saul, your brothers, and all the men of Israel drawn up against the Philistines."

David nodded. He kept himself calm, but a secret thrill ran through his frame.

Jesse laid his hand upon the boy's shoulder. "And David, do be careful. War is upon us, and I have too many sons in harm's way. Be not hasty in your actions. Yahweh has chosen you; He will be with you."

David hugged his father. "Oh, *Abba*, what of your flock?"

"Do not worry about the sheep. I have arranged for a servant to watch over them."

Smiling at his father, he then took up the donkey's harness and started down the road. He was eager to fulfill his father's wishes. Jesse, being well advanced in years, was unable to go to war, but had sent his three eldest sons to serve Saul in his stead. So David bore his charge and went, as Jesse had commanded him, and set out west toward the

---

[44] approximately one bushel or about 33 liters

Valley of Elah, a journey of four miles. The terrain was rough but for a narrow path that led through the mountains. Trees grew more prevalent as he trekked deeper into the wilderness.

When David entered the camp of Israel, the host was going out to set themselves in battle array against the Philistines, as they had done these forty days. Seeing the company hasten to form into ranks, David dispatched the vessels into the hands of the quartermaster, whose charge it was to care for the army's provisions, and ran to the field of strife, making his way to the standard of Judah.

"Eliab, Eliab!" cried David.

Turning on his brother, irritation darkened his face. "David, why are you here? This is no place for a boy. Go back to camp before you get hurt—or worse, get in the way, causing someone else harm."

"Eliab." David steadied his voice. "I come in the name of our father, Jesse. He sends word, and inquires how the three of you fare. How is it with you? Do you want for anything? I have brought supplies to replenish your need."

Glancing about, David noted that the two armies faced one another; yet no call to battle was given. The ranks simply stood, each gazing upon the other, waiting.

"What is the meaning of this, brother? Why do we stand in this manner, without action? For is it not so that these two great armies are prepared for battle? Yet still we stand."

A stir within the Philistine ranks caught David's eye across the field. For at that moment, as he had done so before, Goliath, the Philistines' champion, came forth. David gaped at this giant of a man as he drew near the battalions of Israel.

Out of the mouth of this *Benayim* burst taunts, and threats, and blasphemies against Yahweh. "Send me a man so that we may decide this debate and be finished with this stalemate. Or do you lack a man of courage among your ranks?"

None came forth to face the giant. Not a one moved from his place, but all stood in terror, watching and waiting for a champion of their own to save them from this humiliation. And as the stalemate continued, even until the sun was at its full height, the men of Israel slunk away, until at last, the ranks gave way and each man returned to his tent in shame.

So it was that the whole host of Israel, those elite peoples whom God had chosen, were turned and put to flight by just one Philistine, for they had indeed forsaken their Rock and were thus sold and shut up.[45]

Young David heard these taunts, and the arrogant challenge made by this champion, and witnessed how the men fled, their hearts being filled with fear, and he wondered at their lack of faith in the Holy One of Israel.

"What cause is there," questioned David as he followed his brothers back to camp, "that no one has answered the call of this heathen?"

Shimea, exasperated and embarrassed before his little brother, spoke in bitterness. "Have you not seen this man? Surely he has come to defy Israel, to challenge us to fight with him, and condemn us for cowardice, knowing there is none in Israel his equal."

Then David, being filled with zeal for the Lord, spoke to the men who stood near him, saying, "What shall be done for the man who slays this Philistine and takes away the reproach from Israel? For who is this uncircumcised Philistine, a profane man, who has no true religion, that he should defy the armies of the living God?" David fixed his gaze upon the troops around him, his blue eyes accusing, shaming them with his passion. "Does he not know that he does not disgrace mere men, but it is the One True God that he scorns? It is Yahweh whom he challenges. And yet, who will answer his call?"

One that stood beside David gave reply, saying, "He who kills this Goliath shall receive great honor by the king, for he has promised his daughter's hand in marriage. Also he shall be enriched with great wealth, and his family shall be free from taxation. But none will accept this challenge, for there is no one who can defeat so great a man as this Philistine."

Eliab looked upon his brother with scorn, taking that which was the domain of God, and judged young David's heart by his own, for having heard the question put to them, Eliab thought he perceived his brother's intent. Anger burned within him, roused against David. "Why did you come down here? With whom have you left those few sheep in the wilderness?" Lifting his finger toward the face of his brother, and

---

[45] Deuteronomy 32:30

with a scowl upon his brow, Eliab drew closer to David. "I know your pride and the insolence of your heart. You are not content with your lowly calling, but you do aspire to lofty things. Does it give you great pleasure to look upon bloodshed? Is it not for this cause that you have come down to see the battle?"

Misunderstood and rebuked, David bore the insult well amidst the mocking laughter of Abinadab and Shimea, and the other soldiers who witnessed the public upbraiding. He cared not for their high opinions. Though hurt, yet unhindered, David responded, his voice confident and steady. "There is no reason to bear so hard upon me; for what have I done? I have spoken but a word. Should a man be made an offender for a word?[46] Is there not a cause?"

Undeterred, David turned from his brother, Eliab, to another who stood by, and again asked the question, "What shall be done for the man who kills this Philistine and takes away the reproach from Israel?" In like manner, this soldier answered, as the other had done, regarding the king's reward.

While David and the soldiers were yet talking, Helek came to the lad. "*Na'ar*, the king wishes to speak with you, for your words have entered into his hearing. He wishes to discuss this matter with you."

Eliab glared at his brother, yet even as David nodded his assent and made to follow the battle-worn soldier, a tremor of fear ran through Eliab. He stood quiet as he watched the youngest of his brothers leave and approach the king's tent.

Helek held open the pavilion's flap, allowing the shepherd boy to cross the threshold of the king's quarters first. David looked upon this soldier, for he was strong of body, full-bearded, scarred by battle, and he wondered again at the lack of faith these valiant men had in Yahweh.

With unhurried steps, the lad walked toward the king, who sat upon his seat. Saul seemed much as he had been when last David saw him. Yet he had no look of recognition in his eye, for the youth had grown into the dawn of manhood. David bowed low before him and rose to meet Saul's eye. It was good to see the king again, for great was David's love for this man he had so faithfully served.

---

[46] Isaiah 29:21

Saul's eyes widened, and his mouth stood agape as he gazed upon the lad. "Long have I waited to hear the words spoken by this boy, and now I see he is but a youth, not yet grown into his full manhood. What is the meaning of this? Do you mock me to raise my hopes only to have them brought low again?"

Then David said to Saul, "Let no man's heart fail because of this champion, large and mighty though he may be; your servant will go and fight with the Philistine."

Saul shook his head, gesturing toward the lad. "How is this possible? You are not able to go against this Philistine to fight with him; for you are only a boy, and have neither strength of body nor skill in battle. This Philistine is a man of war from his youth, trained in the affairs of battle. Do not let the pride of youth mislead you, for you are no match for him."

"My king," began David, his voice quiet and humble, "a shepherd, among the sheep, has your servant been to his father. When a lion came upon my flock, and seized a lamb to carry it off, I, with haste, did follow after it. As I approached the beast, it dropped the lamb and turned upon me. With fierceness, it rose against me, yet I seized hold its mane about the jaw and smote the beast and delivered the lamb. In the same manner, a bear did come and I also slew this beast."

David extended his open hands toward the king, as though showing him the strength that lay within them.

"See now how your servant has killed both lion and bear, who were but adversaries to me and my sheep, and I only attacked them in defense of the flock. Yet this man, whom I am to fight, is a Philistine, uncircumcised and unclean, an enemy to Yahweh and His people. It is for their honor that I do fight, seeing that this heathen has defied the armies of the true and living God."

David paused, moved in his spirit by the words he spoke. Gathering himself, he drew in a deep breath and stood a little taller, raising his chin in determination as he looked upon the king.

"This battle is the Lord's; and He will stand by me. The Holy One of Israel, who delivered me out from the jaw of the lion, and from the paw of the bear, will deliver me out from the hand of this Philistine. The enemy will be like one of them, is not the foe by nature likened to them, savage, cruel, and unclean? So he will, in his end, be as they. I have nothing to fear."

Astounded, Saul spoke, "How is it that this shepherd has more courage than all the men of Israel, so mighty as they are? Go then, and the Lord be with you!"

The king stood. "Bring armor to the boy so that I may clothe him in it."

Helek retrieved armor from the king's coffer, for the king did possess many chests filled with vestments of war. David removed his shepherd's clothes, and Saul placed a clean tunic upon the youth's body. The garment hung loose. David ran his hand down the shirt, feeling the cool linen cloth against his skin, and marveled at the smoothness of the fabric. Saul then began outfitting the boy, thinking little upon whom he placed his kingly apparel. He set a bronze helmet upon the lad's head; also a breastplate he put upon his frame.

David took up the king's sword and fastened it to his side.

So it was that King Saul clothed the shepherd boy in royal armor, the same boy that Samuel the prophet had anointed to bear his robe and crown.

Taking a step back, Saul beheld the youth as he stood there before him, clad in the king's armament. Awkward and ill at ease, David bided, the armor an ill fit, for it was not made for his person, but for the king's.

"Go on then," instructed the king, "walk a little, and see how it suits you."

David ventured a few steps, but soon found it difficult to move. The armor was large and cumbersome. Yet, he tried it, as the king insisted, for Saul placed his trust in the security of human industry and wisdom. But David stumbled, and his movements were restricted by the rigid breastplate. The sword was heavy and unwieldy.

"I cannot walk with these, for I have not tested them. This armor is not made for me."

"But you cannot go before this champion unprotected," argued the king. "He will overwhelm you. It would not be right for me to send you out so exposed. You will surely come to harm."

"My king," David reasoned with an unwavering voice. "I cannot rely on another's provisions, but must don the armor meant for me.

Do not fear. I do not put my trust in earthly stores. This fight is the Lord's. He will be with me."

So David put off the royal vestments, if only for a time, renouncing the king's armor, and went forth unarmed, clad only as a tender of the flock.

Taking up his shepherd's staff, David left the king's tent and stepped to the edge of the valley. Saul and his men followed close behind. There stood Goliath, the colossal brute, chiding the Hebrews for their lack of courage. David looked for a moment into the face of this giant. Then with unflinching faith, he made his way down the side of the rise.

CHAPTER 44

GOLIATH

As he reached the valley floor, David lifted his eyes across the vale. A warm breeze touched his face. Summer stroked the ridge beyond with the purple spears of the lupine, their whorled banner rising high above a keel of gray-green leaves. The sweet scent of honey filled the air. In the midst of the broad and open plain, a stream trickled, whose bed cut into the valley floor, strewn with water-worn pebbles.

The valiant men on either side stood watching as David stepped into the valley and came to the stream. Five smooth stones he spied on the edge of the brook. He gazed upon them, for it seemed to him they cried out to him, "By us you shall overcome the giant!" So he reached down and took the stones, and placed them in his pouch. With his sling hidden in the fold of his hand, David drew near to Goliath.

The king beheld the boy walk boldly toward the Philistine champion. "Abner, whose son is this youth?"

"As your soul lives, O king, I do not know."

"Inquire to whom he belongs."

Goliath saw that one approached; therefore, he moved closer, with his shield bearer before him, drawing near the youth. As the two stood apace, the Philistine expected to behold one like unto himself, hardened by war and weathered by time, yet he who came forward was but a youth, fair and untried. With contempt, Goliath looked upon

David and put forth his accursed speech, full of allusions and epithets, a most shameful testimony to perceive.

"Am I a dog that you come to me with sticks? The god, Dagon, shall devour thee! May Moloch destroy thee! Come to me, and I will give your flesh to the birds of the air and the beasts of the field!"

Goliath's deep voice reverberated across the hills, echoing in the valley. The men of Israel quailed under his proclamations.

Yet David leveled his eye upon the giant, his voice calm, his face untouched by fear. His courage was brought forth in obscurity and nourished in solitude. "You come to me with a sword, a spear, and a javelin. But I come to you in the name of the Lord of hosts, the God of the armies of Israel, whom you have defied. Today, the Lord will deliver you into my hand, and I will strike you and take your head from you. And this day, I will give the carcasses of the camp of the Philistines to the birds of the air and the wild beasts of the field, that all the earth may understand that there is a God in Israel. Then all this assembly shall know that the Lord does not save with sword and spear; for the battle is the Lord's, and He will give you into our hands."

A ripple of laughter echoed from the Philistine ranks.

"What is he doing?" cried Eliab. "He cannot win this fight!"

Nagad regarded David and smiled, well pleased by the faith this young man possessed. Memory filled his mind of an earlier conflict when the hearts of Israel relied solely upon their faith in the Lord. Here, in David, was one who remembered the lesson learned at Ebenezer.

"Do not fear for your brother," spoke Nagad. "For he carries a greater weapon than all the armies of Philistia."

With wrath and fury as large as his stature, the Philistine lumbered forward to strike the boy. His steps were ponderous, for his armor was thick and unyielding.

Swift David came.

Yet the youth had no intent to meet him blade for blade. He had told the king of lions and of bears; even so he meant to face the giant. He was a slinger; that was his chosen weapon. He bore no weight of bronze, but went forth light and unencumbered. Though he seemed weak, he knew the strength he carried, and he knew how to wield it.

Ere Goliath had time to draw his sword, David reached into his pouch and brought forth a stone. Placing the polished pebble within his sling, the right end of the strap fixed firmly to his hand and the left between his thumb and middle finger, David swung the sling above his head. Faster and faster the sling whipped above his ear. The sound of rushing air sung. His hand was calm, his aim careful.

Little fear had Goliath as he looked upon the youth with disdain. But soon, his countenance betrayed the truth that the rules of combat had changed. He had readied himself for the clash of blades, his body girded in unyielding bronze, his spirit clothed in pride.

But the shepherd bore no sword.

Goliath's spear was poised to strike, to pierce the lad through. Easy prey, the youth bore no defense.

Yet David drew not near the giant. He stood afar, his sling circling in measured rhythm, beyond the reach of the Philistine's mighty arm.

Goliath's strength became his snare; the weight of his armor bound him fast, his movements heavy and slow. He stood transfixed as fate closed upon him.

David loosed his grasp upon the strap. The stone sang as it cleft the air, swift and true.

With a mighty crack, the stone found its mark and struck deep within the giant's brow.

For but a moment, the Philistine stood unmoving, his eyes wide with dread. Then, as a mighty cedar teeters before the axe, Goliath swayed and toppled forward, casting forth a cloud of dust as the earth shuddered beneath him.

And so, in the vanity and proud presumption of fools, Goliath fell headlong to his ruin. For none who harden their hearts against Yahweh shall prevail.

The world was still. Dust drifted through the sunlit air, and before David stretched the giant's desolation. Swiftly his feet bore him to the place where he lay. Though he had fallen, yet there was life within him; therefore, David drew forth the Philistine's sword. He felt its heaviness, and the might that had once borne it aloft.

Even so, the boy brought the blade down with all his strength, and cut off the enemy's head and slew him. With the sword in one hand, David reached down and lifted the Philistine's head, the token of triumph, that all might behold how Yahweh had wrought the victory.

Now when the Philistines saw that their champion was dead, they were filled with fear, for how could so great a man as Goliath fall before a shepherd boy? Bound by their own challenge, yet undone by terror, the armies of Philistia turned and fled.

Saul unsheathed his sword, his courage restored, and cried, "After them! Not a one escapes this day!"

The men of Israel roused, and with a mighty shout surged after the Philistines and pursued them through the Vale of Sorek. Over the hills and across the valleys, they followed hard after the enemy, striking all who transgressed their path. The slain of Philistia lay along the way to Shaaraim, as far as Gath, even unto the gates of Ekron.

When all who found no refuge within the fortified cities had fallen, the men of Israel left off the pursuit of the Philistines. Seeing the enemy's tents, they entered the camp and plundered the spoils: armor, gold, and store of provisions.

David returned to the body of Goliath. He loosed the armor from the giant's frame, yet it was too heavy to bear away. So he went back to the Philistine camp and entered a tent, where on the ground, he found a pallet. Taking it up, he came again to the fallen *benayim* and laid upon the mat each piece of armor, and the head of the champion.

Goliath's sword, David placed into his own belt. With difficulty, the shepherd-hero hauled the pallet, struggling to drag it up the ridge to the Hebrew camp. He turned aside by a longer path, for the armor was burdensome. Yet he bore his prize onward and took the ridge.

Lifting his gaze, David beheld Abner approaching.

"Come with me."

David obediently followed.

The king stood as David entered the tent, his son Jonathan at his side. "Come in, come in. Your actions have been justly marvelous in our eyes, and we thank you for our deliverance."

David bowed before the king, laying the trophies of battle at Saul's feet. The king looked upon the armor, and the head of Goliath, and grinned with pride.

"Now tell me, whose son are you?"

"It is I, your servant David, son of Jesse the Bethlehemite, who played the harp before you. See now, they have prepared a net for my steps, they have dug a pit before me, but into the midst of it, they themselves have fallen.[47] Yet it was not I who won this fight, but the Lord. To Him the victory belongs."

Then the eyes of Saul were opened, and he beheld the countenance of the one who had graced him with song. "David, well pleased am I with your conduct. The Lord has preserved you and our people this day. No more shall you tend your father's sheep nor return to your father's house."

The king drew near to David. Placing his large hands upon each of the boy's shoulders, Saul smiled down at him. "Surely you will not leave my side, but from this day forth, you shall be my armor-bearer."

Saul motioned to Abner. "See to his comfort."

Returning his gaze to the boy, the king continued, "Go now. Refresh yourself. I will call you again. Until then," the king made a sweeping gesture with his arm, "enjoy the benefits of your victory, for well you have earned them."

Abner beckoned. David bowed before Saul, "My king," then took leave of the king, followed by the general.

As David turned to go, Jonathan was drawn to him. "My king." He bowed, then he, too, followed after the boy.

The sun took his sight for a moment. Raising his hand to shield his vision, Jonathan spied David a few paces ahead.

"David... David, tarry a while, please."

David and Abner turned and looked at the king's son. There stood Jonathan, smiling.

"Abner," spoke Jonathan, "I will see to the boy's comfort. Leave us."

The general bowed before the prince. "As you wish."

Jonathan and David, together, watched as the general strode back toward the king's pavilion.

"David, my heart is filled with gladness for this great deed. You have restored my faith in Yahweh, as in former days. And now let us make a covenant, for God's hand is upon you, and I hold you as my own soul."

Jonathan removed his robe and his armor, even unto his sword, his bow, and his belt. Handing them to David, he spoke thus, "These I give to you, for by right they are yours."

---

[47] Psalm 57:6

David lifted his hands in protest. "How can I receive this token of highest honor? For I am only a shepherd boy, and you, the crown prince of Israel."

"Take them," insisted Jonathan, as he pressed the articles into David's hands. "I know your destiny. I have no ambition but to serve the chosen one of God."

David took the garments of the prince, and humbly bowed his head. He was amazed by the genuine love he saw in the eyes of the king's own son.

"Come," spoke Jonathan, "let us make a covenant between you and me."

David nodded, hugging the garments to his chest.

So Jonathan took a heifer and cut it in twain, splitting the animal down the backbone into equal halves. The costly price fulfilled, he set one half on one side and the other half on the other side. The blood flowed from each, passing between them, to form a single course that hastened on its path, soaking deep into the soil they had fought to save. As David and Jonathan twice walked through the pool of blood, they swore an oath together. The blood flowed freely beneath their feet.

With their hands clasped as one, Jonathan spoke, saying: "I pledge myself, my life, loyalty, inheritance, and protection, to you and your descendants, forever."

"And I you," replied David. "Even in death, all I am is yours."

"Brothers of the same family, the same blood. May we be cut in pieces as this heifer, if ever this covenant be broken."

Fully they entered into the oath, the holy pact, ratified in the pouring out of life. Jonathan, the crown prince, and David, the least son of a shepherd, their souls knit together in an inseparable bond of friendship, lasting and indelible, written in blood. And of this oath, they would both be tested, a pact of love and obligation put on trial by the ravings of a madman.

CHAPTER 45

ARMOR-BEARER

"Do not hold back!" cried Saul, his sword flashing as he charged into battle.

David strove to keep pace with the king, bearing the royal shield and weapons. For weeks now the Israelites had waged war against the Philistines, uprooting and pressing them out of the land. Ever faithful, the shepherd-hero stood by King Saul, behaving bravely as his armor-bearer.

Saul, elated with the action of war, rushed without thought, headlong into battle. Every sword was drawn as the Israelites sank deep into the enemy ranks. Spying the Israelite king, the soldiers of Philistia pressed hard toward him, hoping to unburden the troops of their sovereign.

So swift had the king run before the army that Saul and David found themselves cut off from the Israelite forces. Philistine warriors surrounded them. With truculent attacks, their fiery blades licked at them, driving the two to stand as one. David held the king's shield before him, turning aside the encroaching points of iron that sought to mar the royal flesh.

King Saul growled. He had had enough. Lunging forth with his fierce frenzy, the king let loose a torrent of blows upon the enemy.

David, seeing Saul strike, drew his sword and rushed forth in his own storm of fury, his humble spirit kindled in the fray. The king and the shepherd wrought havoc upon their foes, until but a few remained to hinder them.

As the two fought side by side, the tumult of battle came between them. David labored beneath the might of the Philistine who strove against him. Springing forward, the shepherd feigned high, turning the enemy's guard aside. The Philistine raised his blade to ward the blow, but the youth's sudden reversal caught his foe unawares. The strike lost, the enemy's breast was without defense. David took his advantage. Lunging forward, his blade sank deep. As the foe fell before his feet, David looked to the king.

There stood Saul, king of Israel, surrounded, vying with four stout Philistines. The king turned one way then another, blocking each blade thrust upon him. The pommel of a Philistine sword made contact, clouting Saul upon the pate, sending his helmet flying. Stunned, the king took a step back, catching his heel upon a rock. He stumbled and fell hard upon the ground, senseless. Thus made vulnerable, one of the Philistines raised his sword above the king, intent to slay him.

As the sword fell, young David sprang between the king and death, his own blade flashing up to meet the stroke. Teeth clenched beneath the power of the Philistine's arm, David drove back his foe with the edge of his blade. He took up the royal shield and planted it before Saul, a wall shielding the king from peril.

Grasping tight his sword, David drew the enemy away from Saul, tempting them to follow with jabs and thrusts, until the four had moved after the youth. Smiles were upon their faces, deeming the shepherd boy easy prey. David held his sword close to his face, set to withstand whatever stroke should fall. One Philistine lunged forward, his blade whistling past David's ear, shearing several curls from his head.

The near stroke sent him reeling, yet he shifted right and steadied his blade. He raised his sword, sweeping left above his head. With both hands firm upon the hilt, he brought it down and out—edge to edge, iron clashed against bronze, grinding the space between.

A quick flick of his wrist and David disarmed the foe, sending the sword hurtling into the air. He sank the point of his blade into the chest of the Philistine, dropping him to the ground.

The king's armor-bearer stood for a moment, taking in the field about him, aware other dangers lurked. The air was still and acrid; the smell of battle hung heavy.

He sensed movement from behind. Before him, he caught a sudden shift. Two enemies there were who closed in upon him. With his sword held at his side, the hilt facing forward, David thrust the pommel toward the oncoming foe, smashing it into his face. Without hesitation, David drove the blade back over his shoulder, taking the enemy behind. Crossing his sword over his frame, David wheeled about, arcing his blade, and laid open the belly of the Philistine before him. In swift haste, he swept the blade around, rending the wounded foe across his back, thus ending two enemies in quick succession.

David turned and beheld the fallen pair. Yet another Philistine advanced, his blade leveled at the youth. Fire kindled in those eyes, a hatred thirsting for blood. Dust rose at the nearing of his tread. But the shepherd stood his ground.

Strength for strength, the weapons met, testing will against resolve. Time grew long, and still they strove, the contest pressing sore upon them both. The earth groaned beneath them; the rocks quaked in answer. Yet in unbroken courage, the two fought on, neither willing to yield.

Upon the flat of his blade, David caught a blow, staying the enemy's stroke. Together they grappled, their crossed swords locked, gazes fixed in defiance.

Baring his teeth, the Philistine spat, "Go back to your flock, shepherd. You are no match to my skill."

David did not flinch, but answered with unshaken calm. "As the Lord lives, today, your life shall be delivered to Sheol."

"Agh—" grunted the enemy as he pressed hard against David's sword. The blades broke free, driving the two apart.

Circling, each stalked his foe, poised for the other's strike. Impatient with his rival, the Philistine lunged in blind fury. Down the blade descended, and ere the strike did land, the shepherd turned aside.

The cold edge of the boy's sword found the Philistine's naked side, cleaving through bone and sinew. There was a moment of spluttering blood, of gore and gasping breath. The shepherd's hands, once gentle, now bore the marks of violence, marred in defense of one he loved greater than his own life. With one last gasp, the Philistine toppled.

The shepherd-hero stood gazing down at the carnage wrought by his own hand.

At the sound of approaching feet, David turned. King Saul drew beside him, blood trickling down his royal visage. A great smile broke across his face, baring white teeth beneath the grime of war.

He placed his powerful hand upon the boy's shoulder. "Well done! A true armor-bearer of the king!"

No words did he speak, but in humility, David bowed in homage to the king.

Saul clapped David on the back and took up his sword. Looking to the faltering Philistines, the king spoke, "It is not finished. Onward we go, to the enemy. Drive them out of our land."

With their weapons drawn, the Israelites pursued the Philistines away from that place. Beside the king, David fought. Valor without pride, his duty he fulfilled. All fell before him; no sword could touch him.

A cold and searching wind swept over the wreckage of the Philistine host. Dark, thick clouds rolled across the sky. Thunder sounded in the distance.

"'Tis enough," spoke Saul as he looked to the ominous heavens.

That night the rains began. The season of war had ended. Summer had waned and autumn edged toward winter. The Philistines were routed for a time.

The Israelites gathered their arms and turned for home, their spirits high. Saul's heart swelled with gladness. The day cleared as they drew near to Geba.

Seeing the company of soldiers marching homeward, bands of women and children came forth to meet them, dancing with sistrums and tambourines, and with joy, for word had reached their ears of David's victory over Goliath and his valor upon the field. The triumphal procession broke into song, the women singing as they danced.

> Saul has slain his thousands,
> And David his ten thousands.

So it was that in one great act, David had cast himself before the people. No more would he be a nameless shepherd, but a national hero, lifted up in the hearts of Israel as their savior. Yet little did the people know that in what they did, they had committed a great indiscretion, being the cause of so much grief for their worthy deliverer. For in that moment, the heart of the king grew cold toward his armor-bearer, and a dark cloud rested upon his mood.

From a window in the palace, the young girl Michal looked down upon the young champion. Her eyes called to him, stirring his soul. Lifting his face to the silent heights, he found her watching and fixed his eyes upon her. Hair, dark as night, caressed her cheek, touching the wonder of her fair face. Something quickened within him, a painfully sweet intensity that transfixed him. The beating of his heart soon eclipsed the sounds of the music. David smiled at the girl. She turned and disappeared into the shadows.

CHAPTER 46

CLOUD BURST

Storming into the palace, Saul threw his cloak down onto the couch. He paced the room fuming, consumed with anger, his armor sounding as he walked. Ahinoam hurried to him, grasping his strong arm in her delicate hands, striving to stem the violent fury of his rage.

"What is it that has you so vexed, my love?"

With seething sighs, Saul growled, "They have ascribed to David ten thousands, and to me they have ascribed *only* thousands. David has been lifted up higher than the king. The people did not even address me as King Saul; they neglected my royal title as though I were a commoner. More honor do they give to my armor-bearer than to me, their sovereign. Now *what* more can he have but the kingdom?"

Then Saul knew that in this son of Jesse stood the one Samuel had foretold would be a threat to his throne, the intended neighbor that would be given the kingdom. With suspicion in his heart, Saul weighed all David did and said, his every deed and motive, seeing if anything tended to disloyalty and could be used against him to prove treason. So Saul gave way to his jealous thoughts, the progenitor of the blackest and darkest of evils, which burned as a fire in his chest, gnawing at his entrails.

The sky darkened. The wind whipped in from the west, bringing with it the cool breath of winter. The rains came in earnest. Thunder rumbled in the heavens. War rose in the skies as lightning rent the aerial domain. And so the weather of the world turned to swarthy omens, raging as the king's mind darkened and his mood turned again to bitter turmoil.

Saul, the malefactor of wrath, lay in wait, watching as snares he set tested young David, hoping to provide a pretext to war against him lest the foreboding utterance of the king come to pass and David take the kingdom unto himself. From that day forward, Saul looked askance at his armor-bearer, eyeing him with suspicion, as distrust arose in the heart of the king.

It happened that Saul, as he thought upon all that had passed, was struck with melancholy severe. With idle ravings, he betrayed his distempered mind, as one possessed, uttering unintelligible incantations. Ahinoam caused David to play once more upon his harp as she, with her daughters Merab and Michal, knelt before their father. Here, they made silent prayers. Saul sat upon his couch, leaning heavily upon his spear, mumbling incoherent imprecations, pleading with Yahweh to preserve his life and destroy his enemies.

While David strummed with his gentle hand the instrument that had once soothed the king, Saul held violence in his hand, for his spear he gripped tight as his heart burned against the lad. Fear rose within the sovereign. As he eyed David, Saul perceived that indeed the Lord had departed and now did dwell with the young musician. A searing frenzy smoldered within him, rising up, taking control of the king's spirit. The royal mind seethed with stormy agitation. All sense of composure slipped away. In one swift motion, Saul cast his spear at his armor-bearer. The shaft missed its mark and stuck into the stone wall of the chamber. David ceased his playing and stood wide-eyed at his king.

"David!" cried Michal in horror. The women drew in a single, sharp breath, their hands rising to their mouths.

"I will pin him to the wall!" Saul grated through clenched teeth.

"No!" gasped Ahinoam as she reached to grasp Saul's arm, yet he was quick.

With haste he took up another spear and hurled it with great might.

David ducked, the spear just missing his head. His heart beat wildly, his breath drew short, and in that moment the realization struck—the king sought his life. David turned and fled from the chamber.

"Saul!" cried Ahinoam. "What is this that you do? He is your faithful servant, and yet you seek to take his life!"

Saul glared at the place David had stood. Turning toward Ahinoam, a snarl still upon his face, he spoke, "Leave me."

Ahinoam and her daughters gaped at the king, astounded.

"I said leave me! All of you! Or feel my wrath upon you also!"

Shaken, they withdrew, fearful of what next he would do.

Saul stalked over to the balcony and looked upon the stormy heavens. "Why do You torment me so? What have I done that is so terrible that You have abandoned me and come to this young upstart! Well, we shall see what becomes of this shepherd who would be king!"

"David," cried Michal as she ran to catch up with him. "David."

He stopped walking, his back to her.

"David," her voice brushed against the sharp edge of his restraint as she placed her hand upon his arm. At her touch, he turned and looked into her dark eyes. The blue of his eyes shone against the red-rimmed lids. Michal reached up and placed her hand upon David's cheek. He took her arms in his hands and smiled at her lovely face.

"David, please forgive *Abba*. He is not in his right mind."

"I know, Michal. I bear him no malice. Though, I think I will stay out of his sight for a time." He chuckled.

"David, do not joke. This is serious. I am fearful of his temper. He used to be so lighthearted, but of late he flies easily into these dark moods. He is so—"

"Unpredictable," David finished her sentence. "Michal, do not be anxious. Everything will be all right. You shall see."

"He fears you, you know."

"There is no cause for him to fear me." David's tone turned grave. "I desire nothing but to serve him well, and in so doing honor Yahweh. Now go. It is not wise for you to be seen with me. Give it time, Michal."

Michal thrilled at the sound of her name formed upon David's lips. She knew he was right, yet all she wanted was to be with him, by his side always.

David released his hold upon her and shooed her away. As she made to leave, he called out to her. "And do not worry. The Lord will work it out in His time."

Michal smiled at David, yet she doubted the truth in what he said.

CHAPTER 47

NOBLE EXILE

Saul paced with long strides about the room, erratic paths round the chamber, as though reworking the weaver's thread, trying in vain to mend the unraveling cloth. He was alone, and his thoughts turned inward to the unquenchable enemy of his mind. Unable to release the anxious disquiet within his frame, Saul went to his couch and sat. Rocking to and fro, pressing his fists into his aching brow, Saul was throttled by torment.

Thunder rumbled in the west.

Saul marked movement in the corner of his sight and looked up. Before him, the balcony curtain was caught in the billowing wind, fluttering in restless waves of flowing cloth that reached into the room. The king rose and crossed to the balcony, gazing out at the dark sky.

Taking the drape into his clenched fist, Saul spoke to himself his doleful soliloquy. "What augury is this that the heavens do speak? It is day, yet it looks of night. Never have I seen a day as this prodigy of fate. See how the heavens storm. The very atmosphere is a brooding dread. 'Tis a portent of things to come."

Casting the curtain aside, Saul turned back into the chamber. The room quivered with shadows as the flames danced upon the braziers. "I cannot keep silent, my anguish speaks, my soul complains in bitterness.[48] My spirit wanes; my reason wavers."

---

[48] Job 7:11

A clap of thunder sounded, the rumble lingering, rolling away into the night-clad sky.

Saul, startled by the concussion, wheeled about and looked out the balcony. A shudder ran through his frame. "David, the very name is as a poisonous dart that devours my soul in bitter strife. God has given him wisdom; it is plain to see. That thought gives me pause, yet the disquiet of my mind increases, the dread of him rages within me."

Turning back into the room, Saul stood transfixed by his own tragic tale, frozen in place by his dark imaginings. "He gathers the hearts of men like summer's fruit.[49] Even my own son is knit tightly into the folds of David. And yet to me, he is a killing frost that cuts off life from me before my fruit is full ripe. O that someone would clip this bud before his time, and prune my life of this thorn. See how he pricks me, and I do bleed. My own fears, my thoughts are certain and dependable, though many think me mad. My own pain clarifies my mind; it does not deceive me."

Drawing in a deep breath, Saul frowned. "What then shall I do? Lie in wait until the full measure of this contest be wrought? Nay. I shall, with love's counterfeit, feign true friendship, lay up noble exile and send him from my face, lest I go mad to see him daily pace before my presence. By this, it may be that his daring spirit will lead him to destruction by some intrepid actions against the sword of the Philistines."

Saul smiled at his own resolution. "My own hand shall be innocent of his blood. 'Tis a perfect plan."

The king's armor-bearer stood upon the wall, looking north across the gorge to Michmash. The wind whipped from the south, quieting the raging sky. Spring was on the horizon, and with the coming season, the time of war would be renewed. Yet would the king require his service? For of late the king had no desire to be near the shepherd-hero.

---

[49] (Kitto, 1859)

"David," spoke Ziba, "my *adon* summons you to come to him."

Concern washed over David's face as his heart sank within him. "Where is he, Ziba? For surely I will go to him."

"He sits upon his throne, waiting."

David climbed down from the wall and entered into the court of the king. There sat Saul, regal in all his royal finery, with his crown upon his head. As the shepherd-hero approached, the king waved him forward, a smile upon his handsome face. The king appeared calm and in his right mind, though there was something in his grin that put David ill at ease.

"David," spoke Saul. "Come forward and let me look upon you."

He hesitated, fearful of the king's purpose.

Saul peered down his nose at him, his mind composed. Yet when he laid eyes upon the youth, a surge of bitter wrath newly arose within him. Shrugging aside the rising tenor, the king smiled the more to cover the intent of his heart.

"Do not be afraid, my son," the king spoke with gentle words. "I have good news for you. I am going to bestow on you a great honor."

He came forward. "My king," bowed David. "I am at your service."

"Good, good." Saul rose, standing upon his dais so that he towered over David.

The king stepped down to the floor where his armor-bearer waited and set his hand upon David's shoulder. "I have need of your service." Saul let loose of David and began pacing about the room. The air was thick and warm. The fire crackled within the hearth.

"As you are aware, the Philistines are a constant threat, pressing in upon our borders. We must not let them breach our lands."

Saul, still smiling, turned and looked at David. "I am placing you as captain over a thousand. You shall take your company to guard the frontier from the advances of the Philistines. You must do whatever it takes; make whatever sacrifices necessary to prevent their encroachment. These uncircumcised dogs must not set foot upon the land given to us by God. Are you willing to serve your king in this?"

"Always I seek to serve you well, my king. I will do all that is required of me."

Saul clapped David on the back, then ascended the dais, and sat once more upon his throne. "I knew I could count on you." Saul took a deep, satisfying breath and let it out. "*Tov me'od*, very good. Go now and perform your duty well."

So David left the presence of the king and made preparations for the journey to the western borders, even the far reaches of the kingdom. Word spread of the honor bestowed upon the shepherd, turned musician, who became the king's armor-bearer, and now had been lifted up to be a captain of a thousand. Pack animals laden with supplies waited, stamping their hooves as men gathered for the trek beyond the mountains. David walked over to the company, fully arrayed in his armor, bearing his person with a vesture of strength and honor.

"David, wait, do not go!"

He turned to find Michal running toward him. Taking her aside, out of sight of those nearby, David reasoned with the king's daughter in the shadow of the courtyard.

"What choice do I have? The king has decreed it. It is an honorable banishment."

"Oh, David," Michal whispered in his ear, unlocking his heart and setting his spirit free as a new morning peering over the distant horizon. "You know how I feel. I cannot bear to think of you gone."

"Michal, I too will miss you. But I have to go. I cannot defy the king, your father."

She leaned forward upon her toes, making to kiss David upon his lips. David reached out and stayed her.

"Nay," spoke he. "I shall not kiss you upon your mouth and, in so doing, dishonor you. In truth, I do love the king your father, and am loath to abuse his trust."

Michal looked down, her tender lips drawn into a pout. David reached up and stroked Michal's cheek, smiling at her. "Farewell, my love. I shall return as soon as I am able." He bent and kissed her brow. Then he turned and was gone. Michal covered her face, and wept.

CHAPTER 48

MARRED

The cold stones of the corridor spoke softly under the light foot of Ahinoam as she walked down the empty hall of the palace. The fine linen fabric rustled in her arms as she carried the cloth, newly purchased. Rendered flax was usually reserved for the priestly garments inasmuch as the fineness of the unadulterated white fabric represented the moral purity and separateness of the priest. Yet, Ahinoam believed it fitting that the sovereign of God's people should be outfitted as such, for truly, was he not the Lord's anointed? So it was that Ahinoam had planned to make new royal robes for the king.

Her lips curved at the thought of the soft linen resting upon the stalwart body of her husband. She caressed the fabric to her cheek, enjoying its cool silkiness. Eager to set her hand to the work, she picked up her pace.

Voices came to her ear as she drew closer to the king's chamber. Ahinoam looked up and saw her husband standing outside the doorway. The vision of his pleasing form brought a smile to her face. With enthusiasm, she started toward Saul. She opened her mouth to call to him, but the words stuck in her throat.

Just then, Rizpah, the handmaid, appeared in the doorway. Ahinoam halted, frozen where she stood, her mouth gaping.

"Come inside, my king," the maid spoke as she ran her hands through Saul's hair.

The king snatched her into his arms, pressing his lips against her neck, laughing as she taunted him. His hands were upon her hips, kissing her forcefully on the mouth. He backed her into the room, closing the door behind them, his heart diverted by the triumph of wanton cravings.

Horror-struck, Ahinoam stood there, transfixed. The sound of muffled giggles seeped through the door. Her chest tightened as though she had suffered a sudden and violent blow; she could not breathe. Her mind whirled beneath the weight of loss, as memories of years spent together, a husband and wife living life as one, pressed through her, rushing upon her inward thought until she teetered. Her hand reached for the wall. The linen cloth dropped to the floor as she rested her palm upon the cold stone.

"*Ima*, are you well?" Jonathan rushed over.

Ahinoam's heart leapt. Glancing up at him, she managed a weak smile. "Yes, yes, all is well."

Jonathan surveyed her with a doubtful frown, noting the color had drained from her face. He bent down and gathered the bolt of fine linen and handed it back to his mother. She reached for it, brushed the dust away, and saw that the once-pure white was marred.

"*Ima*, what ails you?"

"I am fine." Her voice was hard.

As he was about to protest, he heard the voice of his father through the closed door. Jonathan turned toward the king's chamber, listening as another voice, that of a woman, replied. Sickened, he placed his hand upon his mother's back. "*Ima.*"

"It is nothing, Jonathan. Go; have no concern over me. Truly, I am well."

Smiling, Ahinoam looked at her son, placing her hand on his cheek, a deep sadness within her glistening eyes. She turned and resumed her trek down the hallway and was gone.

Jonathan stood there, looking after his mother, seething with disgust toward his father, the king. With a hurried pivot, Jonathan stormed from the corridor.

CHAPTER 49

OF HONORABLE SERVICE

"David is back!" cried Amah. "My *Sarah*, David has returned."

Michal grabbed the hands of her maid, overjoyed with the news. Giggling with delight, the king's daughter released her handmaid and ran from the room. She swept swiftly down the stairs into the fortress court, where the warriors, worn from battle, were gathering. There amongst the wearied soldiers stood David, dusty from his trek across the wilderness.

"David!" cried Michal as she hastened to him, her heart quickened with delight.

She meant to cast herself into his arms, forgetting all restraint in the rapture of reunion; yet David caught her hands in his, holding them fast, his thumbs moving softly upon her skin.

Smiling down at the fair Michal, his gentle gaze reaching into her, David breathed his words. "I told you I would return."

The two stood there, each transfixed by the vision of the other, willing captives bound in tender obedience.

"*Sar* David," bowed Ziba, "the king seeks your presence."

"But he has only just returned," cried Michal.

David placed his hand upon Michal's arm to quiet her.

"Take me to him."

"Our most worthy and excellent captain," spoke Saul as David entered into the throne room. "How our heart rejoices at your safe return." Bitter were the words upon his tongue.

David bowed before King Saul. "It is good to be back, my king."

"Tell us then, how you have fared upon the field. Give a full report of all that has come to pass."

And so David revealed all that had befallen, of his going out and coming in, how he stood before the Philistines and turned aside the onrush of their host. Well-furnished was the account of all deeds, abounding in examples of valiant endeavor to preserve the nation whole. All David's actions were marked by valor, for with stout-hearted charges he had driven back the enemy ranks and restrained the inroad of the Philistines.

Saul could scarce keep his mind upon all David recounted, for his thoughts were overthrown by jealous imprecations. As the king looked with contempt upon the shepherd-captain, he could not help but see how the boy had changed. The youth's frame had hardened, muscular and stalwart after months of battle. His stance was noble and his bearing well-born. David looked a man, fully grown.

"Nothing could daunt us," David continued, "as on we fought. With courage my men did strike down our foes. Not only did we hold back the tide of invasion, but we pressed into the enemy's land and plundered their supplies, bearing away such stores as we could carry. Not a man was lost whilst we fought, for Yahweh was with us."

The report was made full in honesty, without haughty praise, but in homage to the true Deliverer of men. Yet no act of valor could redeem him in the eyes of the king, for as Saul listened with growing impatience, his fear of David grew to overflowing. Perceiving how all the shepherd-captain did prospered, a plot was forming in Saul's mind, a snare to expose him once more to harm.

"David, well pleased are we with your valiant deeds," Saul spoke as he looked with narrowed eyes upon the source of his distress. "You have grown into the full stature of manhood. It is time to uphold our obligation to you, for was it not promised that whoever defeated the giant Goliath, to him would be offered the hand of the king's daughter in marriage?"

Then Saul said to David, "Behold, here is our eldest daughter."

Merab entered at his bidding. She was beautiful to look upon, the image of her mother, though beyond David in years.

"She, will we give thee to wife. Only by this dowry we demand of you, be stalwart, a son of valor for us, and fight the Lord's battles."

David stood astonished by so high an offer bestowed upon him. "Who am I, and what is my life, or my father's family in Israel, that I should be son-in-law to the king? Therefore, I will indeed fight for you in the Lord's battles and prove to my king that I am worthy of this great honor."

Saul, the clever manipulator, smiled.

"Very good. Go now and serve your king well."

"My king," bowed David.

As David left the presence of the king, Michal appeared before him, tears streaking her fair face. He halted, concern upon his countenance.

She rushed over to him, took hold his arm. "What is this that you do? What have you done?"

"Michal."

"I heard what you agreed to do. How can you so carelessly discard our love as useless, cast it off as imperfect?" Her words fell into sobs. She covered her face with her hands.

David tucked her hair behind her ear, and cupping her face in his hands, raised her chin to meet his gaze.

"Michal."

Looking into his eyes, Michal stifled her sobs, trembling under the burden of emotion.

"Michal," David said again. "Do not shed a tear for me. I cannot bear to cause you pain. Daily I am racked with the sorrow of not possessing you. But I have not command of my own life, for I am only a servant to the king, pressed to do his bidding, to come and to go at his leisure. It is my duty; I cannot break faith with the king."

"Duty, faith, love—which is the more valuable? How can you just spurn the love we have and give it to another? Has your heart withered for me?"

David's eyes darkened, hurt that Michal would doubt his feelings. Taking her arms in his hands, he leaned close to her, speaking in earnest, his voice but a whisper.

"I am undone by you. Like a flame, my love for you consumes me. My heart is impoverished by the absence of you. My love will always belong to you. But it has always been a dream. My life is not my own to choose as I desire."

Their eyes locked, fixed upon each other. Longing drew them closer, their lips nearly touching. David's heart burned within him. With all his strength, he pulled away, his lids closed tight against his desire. Breathing hard, David leaned his brow upon hers.

"Do not do this," pleaded David, "or I will not have the courage to do what I am commanded."

"David, do not marry Merab. Do not throw away what we have. Do not take my father's offer."

"The day is not done. We do not yet know what is appointed to us. But I must obey the voice of the king, or it will be counted as treason. Michal, you are above my reach. Forget me and find joy."

He released her from his grasp and left her, for he could no longer bear her presence.

So Michal remained alone once more, watching David depart. As a wild beast caged, she was desperate at their parting. Her heart thundered in her breast, stealing her breath. She trembled at love's scorn. Her soul was sinking into a depthless abyss, and she cursed her allotted portion.

CHAPTER 50

PLIGHT

"Long has David been gone from us."

"Yes, my king," returned Abner.

Saul, with his hands clasped behind his back, paced the floor of the throne room as his general stood upon his guard. "The unbroken conflict with the Philistines has been waged without end," continued the king, "the border of our two lands in constant debate. Each passing month without word from our son, David, causes us to fear he has fallen to the enemy, that by some drive toward valor, he has revealed himself to danger, and been undone."

"It may be as you say, my king." Abner's calm voice resonated. "Or it may be he has merely been delayed by much action. Word may come any day."

"No… we believe too much time has passed."

The king stopped his pacing and stood looking off in the distance as though witnessing something in a far-off place. "There is this man, Adriel, the son of Barzillai the Meholathite, who makes pledge for Merab's hand. He is a worthy man, and Merab is well past the age for marriage. We mean to accept his offer."

"My king knows best," Abner spoke, treading lightly on the matter. "Though I would remind my king of his pledge made to our worthy David, who fights for you toward this purpose. May it be that if we wait a little while, he will return to us in honor? The people hold him as dear to them. To break faith with him could turn against his majesty's favor."

"You speak the truth," Saul spoke with fire on his tongue. "We do know best. When we seek your advice, Uncle, we will ask it of you." Dismissing the general with his hand, Saul commanded, "Go, before we lose our patience with you."

Bowing, Abner left the throne room, sighing softly to himself.

"Thou faithless King!"

Saul wheeled about to see Ahinoam in unaccustomed fury. Disconcerted by her temper, he took a step back as she hastened toward him.

"What say you?"

"First me, then Merab." Ahinoam gestured vehemently with her hands. Her brow furrowed with emotion. "Your words have no meaning!"

"What is this you speak?" Saul looked upon Ahinoam, confused by her tenor. He took note of how pale and gaunt she had become.

"Is this the substance of your love? To speak tender words out one side of your face, only to turn and speak something else from the other? To turn away and give yourself to another?"

"We know not of what you speak."

Ahinoam lifted her accusing finger to the king's face. "I saw you with her. And now I hear she is with child."

Heat rose beneath Saul's skin. "It was nothing. Merely a moment of weakness."

Ahinoam quieted her voice, a deep sadness washing over her face. "What has happened to us, Saul? Has your heart turned cold for me?"

"Of course not, my love." Saul's tone softened. "You will always hold my heart. Nothing can change that."

"What is it then that causes you to treat me so? Is it that I am not as fair as once I was? How can I take up youth, when it has fled, and be your fair bride again? What power to compete do these lips still hold, to turn again the head of the king? Time has undone me." Ahinoam lowered her face into her hands and wept.

"Ahinoam." Saul reached for his wife, moved by her grief.

Looking up into the troubled face of Saul, Ahinoam spoke, "My husband, there was a time when your heart was humble and your actions gentle. But that was long ago. Now I fear your heart is hardened by pride. You hold onto your kingdom with an iron grip. Too much you fear the future of your throne."

Saul stiffened at the reproach. "You know what that old fool, Samuel, foretold. What choice do we have but fight for our place over this kingdom? God Himself gave it to us. We would not have it taken away!"

The king turned his back on his wife.

"Do you not see?" spoke Ahinoam with urgency, desperately pleading as she grabbed his arm, forcing him to look at her. "You are the cause; it is your own pride that has usurped the throne. Your vanity sits over all your actions and designs, corrupting all you do. Even now, your passions have mastered your reason. Do you not see what hurt you are causing? You even use your own daughter as a vessel in this game you play. I know what is in your mind, how you would break faith with David, to rouse in him an offense against the crown."

"You dare correct the king!" Saul's voice rose as he thrust himself away from Ahinoam. He turned on his wife, gesturing wildly as madness seized him. "Life is a game that must be played. Each move must be weighed and measured, then put into action. As king of these tribes, we must play our part to preserve them in unity. We were charged to lead this people, and yet you ask us to mask our strength, to subjugate our power, to act with kindness when harshness is necessary. We cannot cloak our deeds with weakness, any more than you can cover your womanly frame." Saul drew away, sulking.

Ahinoam, overcome with grief, reached out to the king, crying, "O Saul, though the kingdom may be lost to you, you still have us. Please do not rashly cast away your family. There is still time to save yourself. Do not lose yourself as well; do not lose us."

Saul grunted as he shook off Ahinoam's hand and stormed out of the room.

CHAPTER 51

THE BEST LAID SCHEMES

Dust rose as the flagging soldiers trudged on their advance toward home. The enthusiasm of the metered journey was growing thin as before them the tiresome miles stretched, though many lay behind. Plodding heavily along, each man counted every step, pining for his own hearth.

For a time, the Philistines had ceased to trouble the people, and the land rested fertile before them, surrounded by hills and higher ridges, green with the pleasant residue of spring rains. The song of birds whispered over the leaves of olive and acacia trees. Purple thistle lined the road, noble crowns lifted up, as little creatures scampered about the sharp prickly leaves.

The day's march began from the west as the sun lifted its head in the east, casting long shadows behind the procession of troops whose hearts kindled with an eager air. Now the sun stood in its descent to the west, its hot rays resting on the soldiers' backs, raising beads of sweat that trickled down their necks. Though the journey was weary, the hearts of the men were lifted up in victory and the knowledge that home lay just beyond the hills. David led his thousand with purpose, intent on claiming his prize, yet a hollow thought of untrodden paths lingered, love shrouded in duty, as though placed in the grave.

Limestone boulders mottled the rolling green hills as the king's stronghold ascended before them in the distance. Tents had sprung on all sides of the palace. A great noise of revelry rose from within the fortress. People abounded with excitement, full of merriment. Singing and dancing, the tenor of laughter and timbrels swelled through the crowd as people milled about everywhere. The smell of roasting meat mounted in the air. Bread and wine were being passed to all, shared in communal exaltation. Rejoicing and mirth, the sound of jubilation rent the atmosphere with some season of celebration.

So entered David, returned, the vanquishing hero, defender of the people. As he passed into the midst of the tumult, he looked about in confusion, searching his memory as to what occasion this must be.

"*Yom tov*, a good day," greeted David as he placed his hand upon the arm of a passerby. "*Mah Zeh*, what is this? Some festival?"

"It is a wedding feast."

"Whose wedding could this be, that it should be so grand a celebration?"

"Have you not heard? It is naught but the wedding of the king's daughter, Merab."

"How is this possible?" asked David. "For I have returned to claim Merab, my promised bride?"

"I know not of this, but that Merab has been given to Adriel, the Meholathite."

David released the man from his grasp, looking about in bewilderment. Then he knew. Merab had not been intended for him at all. It had been a ruse, a scheme to deliver him to some harm. Hurt flooded David's heart as the situation became clear in his mind. He had loved the king, trusted him. Now he felt the full force of royal manipulation.

What have I done to offend? There must be some words spoken or action taken, but what it may be, I do not know. The shepherd-captain glanced about him, lost in thought. The crowd worked its way around the stationary soldier, ignoring his intrusion upon their path. David lifted his chin in determination. *There is nothing for it but to seek words with the king and try the meaning of this affront.*

The courtyard of the palace was adorned, enhanced with flowing ribbons and banners and fragrant flowers that sent up a sweet perfume. Music floated on the air, delicate and ethereal, a covenant of dulcet tones, as the wedding guests talked and laughed.

David found the king in the royal court, which was set with many tables arranged in rows, his board at the head. The feast was in full progress. Food abounded, roasted meats and fine drink, fig cakes and vegetables seasoned with black cumin and coriander. The enclosure overflowed with many guests arrayed in fine garments and in good cheer.

King Saul espied David as he entered. With joviality, he raised his cup to the shepherd-captain and spoke, "Most worthy David, welcome home on this most joyous occasion. Come sit beside me and join us this day."

"My king, I thank you," answered David, bowing.

Working his way through the maze of seated guests, he came behind the head table. Saul had returned to his merrymaking. Little did he heed his captain's approach. As he drew near the king, David felt a wave of dread wash over him. Pushing his sheathed sword out of the way, he sat beside Saul. A servant poured him some wine; another set a plate of food before him. But he had no desire to eat nor drink, for his heart was wounded.

"Tell us how it fares upon the front," commanded the king. "Do we still hold well the border between our lands?"

David saw that Saul would not meet his gaze, but kept his eyes fixed upon the crowd.

"We have pushed the enemy beyond our borders in the west and north. Once more our lands are secure, at least for a time. The enemy has retreated out of the mountains beyond the eastern boundary of the Judean foothills. Captain Nagad and his men are holding back the tide of incursion from these Sea People. While the stay of arms is kept, I have brought my men home for some much-deserved rest, for they are weary from battle. Also, provisions are needed to replenish the ranks. I mean to return within the week."

"Good, good," spoke the king with genuine benevolence. "'Tis most excellent news for such a fine day. Come, drink to the happiness of the bride and groom."

David lifted his cup, but did not bring it to his lips. Saul's brow crumpled in false concern. Yet, secretly, the king admired his own devices, looking for David to become entangled in the snare.

"My son, what is the cause of your discourtesy? Is there something you require?"

"I lack nothing," answered David. "Only answer me this, for I am confused of mind. Was not Merab promised to me if only I displayed some honor for my king? And here I am, having returned from vanquishing the foe, to claim my bride, and yet I have heard she has been given to another."

"My son, do not be alarmed. We are most grateful for your valor in the name of the King. Only, much time were you away. We feared for your life, and in our distress for you, worried also about the welfare of our daughter's future care. Therefore, when the offer for marriage came, we reluctantly accepted to secure her a place in this world."

So spoke Saul, the fickle and faithless monarch, this nefarious king who meant to deeply wound, with indignity, his captain.

Seeing his intent, David answered with a pleasant tenor. "Then indeed, I will drink to this couple. May their union be long and happy."

The shepherd-captain raised his cup and drank deeply. Saul watched in disappointment as his plans fell into disarray. Even so, the king remained resolute in his purpose, though stifled for a time. A doleful spirit descended upon his mood. What should have been his triumph had turned to dejection. Poisoned by jealousy and bound by pride,[50] Saul had enwrapped himself in a rancorous temper that shrouded him in a thick gloom while yet his day still reigned.

Forcing a smile, Saul lifted his cup in reply and drank the bitter toast.

---

[50] Acts 8:23

CHAPTER 52

KINDLING TO THE FIRE

Stifling in the summer heat, the room felt like molten copper. Flames from the braziers and the fire pit added to the sweltering atmosphere. Sweat slid down Doeg's brow, his hands behind his back, listening as he stood beside the king. Saul slouched upon his throne, his arms lying upon the armrests, his legs bent and spread in front of him as he watched Abner with narrowed eyes. The general leaned over the pit, stoking the fire with a rod as he looked absently into the flames. A morose silence filled the room as the men broke off their speech.

The once barren walls of the throne room stood transformed, the murals having long since been completed. The fire cast shadows on the facade, bringing to life the images of the king's adoration: of his victory against Ammon, his annihilation of the Amalekites, and his most hated of enemies, the Philistines. Saul rose and walked over to the mural, looking upon his glory. In silence he stood, considering his life rendered before him. His chin he held within his hand, the other arm folded tight against his chest. The king's countenance was downcast.

"What has been the sum of my life? Is it not presented here before me? How I delivered God's people from the enemy? Have I not unified them as a nation and saved them from desolation? Is it a small thing that I have done?"

Abner looked up from the fire and rested his gaze upon his nephew, the king. "It is not a small thing you have done. The people needed a strong leader, and they have found one in you. Yet all that my king has labored to secure will be lost if he lose the heart of the people."

Dropping his hands, Saul turned to face Abner. "Flow gently, General. The tongue is a fire that can set the whole being to flame. It will ignite wrath. A word can render the affection turbid by stirring up the lees of ill sentiment."

Saul paced, a frown set deep upon his brow. "A faction is brewing. Fermenting, it incites turbulent and civil unrest. This David has taken the heart of the people; they have forgotten all I have done for them. He is a torch that kindles and burns everything in his path. I will not be left to drink the last dregs of bitterness."

Abner returned his gaze to the fire, stoking to rekindle flames that needed no assistance. "It is your sacred duty that you should carry with loyalty the full faith and trust of your people. The people have supported you, looked to you to lead them. But they have grown to love David. They see your treatment of him as a betrayal."

Saul halted in his trek, stayed beneath censure. Within, a conflagration smoldered.

Sensing a change in Saul's mood, Abner let the poker fall by the side of the fire and turned to face his king. "My king, the people are losing faith in you."

Saul wheeled about, and with swift haste strode toward the general, his face but a breath from Abner's own. "I hear their laments of discontent; I am not without hearing!" As water quenches fire, Saul released a long breath, his flame waning to embers. He withdrew from Abner, his back to the general, his eyes cast to the floor.

"All my plans go awry. How is it that for every move I make, he gains more esteem and my favor with the people dwindles?" Saul turned and looked at his uncle, a quiet plea pressed upon his visage. "We must find some remedy, something to restore the king to the favor of the people."

"Let righteous action bring you to the place you desire," advised Abner. "Choose well your next move."

Saul frowned as he walked back to his throne and let himself fall into the seat, his shoulders sinking.

Doeg approached Saul and whispered into his ear. At the words spoken, the king turned toward his servant, his eye brightening. "What is this you say?"

"My king, it is as I said." Doeg kept his voice low, for the king's ear alone. "Your youngest daughter, Michal, bears affection for the young man, David. I have seen them together, speaking softly in the shadows."

"Another of my children has knit themselves to this boy. Will there be no end to his power over my family?"

Saul stood and took a step, then stopped short. "Yet, I find this news pleases us. For now we see it, our mind begins to contrive a plan. Yes, this news will be quite useful." Returning to his throne, Saul spoke, "Doeg, we have need of your service."

"Yes, my king."

"Go and fetch our captain, David, and bring him before us, for we have a matter to put to him."

"As you wish, my king." Doeg bowed and took his leave.

"What purpose do you intend, my king?" questioned Abner.

"A way to use this revelation to our advantage. We can win back the good favor of our people and at the same time, rid ourself of the source of our distress."

Abner looked upon the king with doubt, suspicious of some ill-begotten scheme born of a malignant passion lurking behind those cold eyes.

Outside the fortress walls, wagons and pack animals gathered as men loaded them with supplies. The fields stood empty. No more were the tents assembled about the palace, alive with citizens in celebration. All had left, for the feast was past and life returned to its measured meter. Hot and dry the air remained, as the sky, calm and clear, stared down upon the men. The verdure of nature bent and withered in the summer heat.

Crates and sacks of grain and weapons, succor for the new recruits as they ventured to the outer garrisons of the kingdom, were being carried from the fortress storehouses. David himself, captain of the regiment, assisted in the loading of provisions, bearing what stores of food could be obtained.

"You mean to leave then?"

David looked up from the crate in his arms to see Jonathan approaching. "Yes, the men have need of provisions. It is better that I go."

"What cause do you have to leave so soon?" questioned Jonathan.

"You know why I leave," spoke David as he placed his burden upon a cart.

"I would that you were not leaving so soon after you have arrived," returned Jonathan. "Yet I know the confines of your heart. I do apprehend why you go. You must not take it to heart. The king acts without thought. He did not intend to injure you so."

"I do not hold against the king this injustice he has done me. Yet I know your father will not tolerate my presence much longer. As the stinging hair of the nettle burns, so too does my nearness chafe the king. But I do not leave because of Merab. There is another cause."

David paced back to the fortress wall to retrieve another bundle. Jonathan followed suit, taking up his own burden and placing it within the cart.

"Besides," continued David lightly, "I intend to brighten the hearts of the men with these much-needed provisions."

"You have another cause?" questioned Jonathan.

"I have a cause."

"What cause have you?"

"It was not Merab I wished to marry. There is another, but she I cannot have. It is better that I go. My soul wanders from heaven, suffering divine anguish. My heart, unblest, cannot endure the painful torment of love unconsummated. Weak and feeble, I fade under the glance her eye delivers me, which kindles love unattainable within my breast."

Jonathan marked the deep sadness behind David's eyes.

David smiled. "So see, my dear friend, I must go or languish here and die from woe."

"David, why have you not told me of your burden?" Jonathan rested his arm upon the crate he had just delivered into the cart. "Who could be beyond your reach, seeing that you are our nation's hero and held in such great esteem? You could take any to wife you desire."

David stopped and looked at the king's son. "No," he spoke thoughtfully as he shook his head, "there is one I cannot have, and she is all I desire."

Jonathan straightened, placing his hand upon David's shoulder. "My heart is thus divided. I—"

"My apologies, my prince," interrupted Doeg. "I have a message for the captain."

"Speak, then," answered Jonathan.

"Captain, my king wishes a word with you once more, before you leave. Please follow me."

David glanced over at Jonathan and espied a look of annoyance cross his friend's face. Turning to Doeg, he spoke, "Lead away, for I will follow." David inclined his head in farewell to Jonathan and followed Saul's servant into the palace.

As was his wont, the king received David within the throne room. Saul sat in regal array upon the dais, his crown upon his head. Looking down at the wary David, King Saul spoke with a gentle tongue. "My son, I have done you wrong in giving Merab to another. I wish to make amends. Please consider my younger daughter, Michal. She would make you a fine wife. For I love you as my own son and greatly desire you to be my son-in-law. Only delay your departure and think upon this offer."

A flutter rose in David's heart as hope rekindled in his breast. But the hurts of the past broke upon him, and caution grew within him once more. "I will consider your generous offer, my king." Bowing to Saul, David took leave of the king.

"My king, David doubts your word be true," spoke Doeg. "In mistrust he holds the king's offer, uncertain of the conviction of thy pledge, a residue after the last rejection. He wavers, for past offense is hard to forget."

"This is most unfavorable, yet not entirely unexpected." Saul sat for a moment, stroking his beard. Motioning to Doeg, Saul leaned over and spoke into the servant's ear.

"Go now and do all I have told you."

"As you wish, my king." Doeg bowed and in haste, left to attend the king's command.

Saul sat back, smiling, satisfied with all he had contrived. "The rope must be firmly fixed about his throat."

CHAPTER 53

CASTING THE NET

"Bring the livestock to the caravan," David instructed. "The time of our departure is fast approaching."

The servant bowed his head and went to the pens behind the stable. David walked into one of the stalls. Each stall, being separated from the others by pillared walls, housed several animals and a single manger. The smell of manure and straw stung his nostrils, yet he did not find it offensive. On the contrary, deep memory of earlier times filled his mind: of green pastures, and the sheepfold, and singing psalms as he cared for the sheep. It was a world away now. So much had changed.

What am I to do? How can I trust his word? What if I defy the king? What then? There is no right answer, no way to avoid what lies ahead.

David bent down to stroke the head of a lamb. As his fingers ran through the soft wool, he perceived voices coming from the next stall.

"I overheard the king today, speaking of his great love for David, his captain."

David recognized the voice of Doeg, the king's servant. Hearing his own name mentioned, he stood still and listened.

"He holds him in high esteem. He spoke freely of the captain's honor and truthfulness, how he places himself in constant peril for the sake of his people. The king is very grateful for all David has given and looks to make him son-in-law. It is a worthy honor."

"There is not another so worthy as he."

David could not identify the second voice, but he thought it must belong to another servant of the king.

"Yet," Doeg continued, "David has not agreed to this honor."

"Not agreed? Why be this so?"

"It is beyond my apprehension. For this honor is given freely and with great love. The king's daughter is fair to look upon. The king is generous in his offer."

"Does he forget what honor the king has already bestowed upon him, how he has lifted him from the sheepfold and made him captain of a thousand?"

"I do not think this is so," spoke Doeg thoughtfully, "for David is ever honest and upright. I believe it is his sense of duty to his men that holds him back."

"This should not keep him from becoming the king's son. For I have seen how King Saul looks upon David, as an intimate companion freely bestowing upon him true respect and friendship."

David could take no more. Stepping from the shadow of the adjacent stall, he revealed himself to the servants. "Does it seem to you a light thing to be a king's son-in-law, seeing I am a poor and lowly-esteemed man, unable to give a dowry worthy of the king's daughter?"

"My dear Captain," spoke Doeg, his voice slow and even, "I know none of this, but that the king has delight in you, and all his servants love you. Now therefore, become the king's son-in-law. The king holds you in great affection and, with good intent, pledges his daughter to you."

David frowned as he thought upon these words. He wanted to believe all the servant said, for truly, he loved the king as a father. Yet all that Saul had done of late spoke to another conclusion. Somewhere within his heart, hope kindled. To have the love of the king and to marry fair Michal would be to fulfill all of David's happiest longings, giving him occasion to lack nothing.

"My *adon*," spoke Doeg as he bowed, "we leave you to your thoughts."

With a wave, David dismissed the servants, his mind lost in deliberation, scarcely aware of their departure.

Lifting up his voice, speaking from within the depths of his soul, David spoke, his eyes turned upward. "O my God, I do trust in You; I lift up my soul. Let me not be ashamed. Do not let my enemies triumph over me."

David paused, swallowing back his emotion.

"Lord, I do not know who to trust; I do not know what to do. Show me Your ways, O Lord; teach me Your paths. For You are the God of my salvation. It is on You that I wait all the day, for You, O Lord, are good and upright. You guide the humble and teach the lowly."

David nodded as though he had reached an understanding.

"My eyes are ever toward You, O Lord, for You shall pluck my feet out of the net. Turn Yourself to me, and have mercy on me, for I am desolate and afflicted. The troubles of my heart have enlarged; bring me out of my distresses! Look on my affliction and my pain. Let integrity and uprightness preserve me. For I wait for You."[51]

Sighing deeply, David left the stable, still unable to decide what should be his course of action. Walking with heavy feet, he entered into the midst of men, and wagons, and cargo. Taking hold of a cord under which some crates were tied, he checked to see that all was secure. Jonathan, seeing David, ambled over to the wagon that engaged David's attention.

"Come," spoke Jonathan, "sup with me before you depart."

David looked up from testing the ropes and smiled sullenly at Jonathan. He nodded, and together they entered the fortress, side by side, alike in excellence. Passing through the gatehouse into the inner court, they were met by Doeg and the other servant of Saul, who were just leaving the palace keep.

"Ah, Captain," said Doeg, bowing. "I have spoken with the king concerning the manner of your words, and he told me to speak thusly to you. The king desires no dowry but a hundred foreskins of the Philistines, that vengeance may be taken upon his enemies. Only, you must do this swiftly, ere the time has expired."

"David—"

He stopped Jonathan with his upheld hand. "It may seem that I have misjudged the king. I have asked the Lord what I should do; now

---

[51] Psalm 25

it seems I have my answer. It pleases me well to become the king's son-in-law, for my heart already belongs to Michal, your sister."

Turning to Doeg, David gave instruction. "Tell the men to journey to the garrison without me. I must speak to the king. I will meet them upon the way."

"As you command, *adon*," spoke Doeg bowing, "so shall I do."

"Jonathan, supper must wait, my friend, for I must go to your father before this offer is withdrawn."

"I will go with you."

And so, David, with Jonathan beside him, once more returned to present himself before King Saul.

"My king," David bowed. "Your servant has informed me that you indeed desire me to become your son-in-law. Though I am unworthy, he spoke of the intent of your heart concerning the dowry for your fair daughter's hand."

Saul smiled warmly as he rose from his seat and stepped down from the dais. "Yes, yes, he has spoken true. Indeed, we do desire you to become son-in-law to the king. Do not concern yourself with dowries, my son, for you indeed are worthy in mine eye. Only this do we require: you shall slay one hundred Philistines, and as proof that indeed thou hast killed the uncircumcised enemy, you must bring us back their foreskins. Then indeed, you shall have our daughter's hand in marriage."

"My king," answered David, "to this offer, I do accept, for in slaying these Philistines I will achieve great honor for thee, and would provide opportunity to further destroy the enemies of Yahweh and His people."

Stepping forward, Jonathan spoke, "I shall accompany David upon this charge, *Abba*, for long has it been since I have ventured into battle."

Saul looked hard at his son, seeking to discern his intent. "This is decided then within your heart."

"Yes, *Abba*, I am determined to go."

Saul's brow creased in concern. He had not anticipated his son's part in this matter. The king turned and, with heavy steps, ascended the dais and sat once more upon his throne. Slouching upon his seat with his head resting on his hand, Saul spoke.

"Go then, and may Yahweh preserve you both."

The two companions bowed and withdrew from the presence of the king.

Saul sat for a time, stroking his beard, deep in thought. "The bait is set, the trap is sprung. May my weal be his woe."

And so it was that the king anointed his shield against David.

CHAPTER 54

NACHAL SOREQ

"Do you see them?" spoke Jishui, his tawny hair caught in the breeze that blew in from the west.

"Yes, just on the other side of the valley." Malchishua crouched beside his brother, hidden within the green scrub trees and brown grass upon the hill.

"How many?"

"Some hundreds are all I can reckon from this distance."

Looking across the wide Sorek Valley, west toward the border town of Timnah, the two men, full-bearded and tall, surveyed the Philistine garrison. Mount Baalah rose in the distance to the west, whose peak was used for the worship of Baal, lord of heaven, god of the Philistines. Bounded by chalky limestone hills, the valley was broader in the west, narrower in the east, following a perpetual stream that passed between the lofty hill of Zorah in the north and Beth Shemesh in the south, then coursed its way past Timnah to the northwest, and beyond the Shephelah to the Great Sea in the west. Timnah sat on the rise beyond the Sorek River at the western end of the crescent-shaped valley just north of Ekron. Here it was that the Sorek Valley, *Nachal Soreq*, the valley of the choice vine, opened into a broad alluvial plain well suited for vineyards.

Long ago in the city of Timnah, the Nazarite Samson came to court the Philistine maiden Delilah.

"What do you think?" queried Jishui.

Malchishua looked once more across the valley, studying the Philistine outpost. "It is as good a place as any, I should think."

"Then let us be on our way. We have lingered long enough."

Trekking through the scant trees and yellow-flowered hills, Jishui and Malchishua journeyed southeast toward Zorah, birthplace of Samson. The settlements of Zorah lay on the north side of the vale overlooking the confluence of three valleys. Trade caravans often traversed this valley, bringing goods from the coastal lands through the hills of Judea and into the interior of Israel. Hidden within the fold of the hills, cloaked among the forested surroundings, the men found the camp of Israel's army.

Nestled amongst the shadow of the trees, tents and makeshift shelters had risen. Great limestone boulders half-buried in the ground were strewn about as though some giant of old had carelessly tossed them there. The thick, twisting trunks of carob trees, brown and rough, lifted their spreading crowns upon sturdy branches. Bright sunlight and deep shade played within the broad, dark leaves. Long, leathery carob pods rattled in the breeze. Beneath the understory of brush and spiny thickets, the discarded seed cases, dry and brittle, crunched underfoot, announcing their arrival.

Standing outside the sheltered pavilion, Jonathan and David took their positions before Nagad. Helek, as was his wont, stood by his captain's side. Together, the four men were engaged in planning and directing the movements of their men, devising some stratagem with which to gain the advantage over their enemies. At the sound of Jishui and Malchishua's approach, the four looked up to see the two scouts heading toward them.

"*Sar*," Jishui half-bowed toward Nagad. "A small Philistine garrison lies but three miles to the west."

"How large?"

"Some hundreds strong."

Nagad took a stick and scratched in the dirt. Soon all could see the Sorek Valley unfold within the bare patch of earth.

"Here we are at Zorah." He pointed to a place on the ground with the stick. "Show me where you spied the Philistine garrison."

Nagad handed Jishui the stick.

Jishui took up the makeshift pointer and drew a circle around the desired place. "Here it is we found the enemy. The outpost is west of the valley beyond the river near the settlement of Timnah. Several sentinels could be spotted here, and here, and here." Jishui marked each place with the tip of the stick.

Nagad stood gazing thoughtfully at the coarse map, his arms folded, his brow creased, as he chewed the inside of his cheek. After a time, the old captain spoke without lifting his eyes. "Were they aware of your presence, these Philistines?"

"No, *Sar*, they did not see us," answered Jishui.

"Why should we settle for the outpost?" spoke Helek, looking toward his captain. "Why not set our sights on greater spoils?"

"What are you thinking, Helek?" Nagad unfolded his arms, placing his hand upon the hilt of his sword, which hung at his side, and met Helek's eye.

"Ekron. Is it not but a short span from Timnah? Let us strike at the heart of Philistia."

"You are over-brave, my friend," spoke Nagad with a laugh. "I have a liking for your enthusiasm; it puts me in mind of your father, but your aim is too lofty. We neither have the men nor the power for such a grand venture. Ekron is too big, its walls too strong. There is no victory there. We must stick to the outer garrisons on the borders of our land."

"What is to be done, Captain?" questioned Jonathan.

"This undertaking is Captain David's. Is it not?" With a grin upon his scarred face, Nagad turned toward him. "I believe it is he who should direct our actions."

The shepherd-captain looked up from the map and met the old captain's gaze. Glinting in the dappled sunlight, David's blue eyes spoke of youth and vitality in marked contrast to the battle-worn veteran at his side.

"The enemy has lost their confidence," spoke David. "King Saul has seen to that, and we shall use it to our advantage. Break camp, put every man's sword by his side. We leave at nightfall. In the morning light, we shall hold the upper hand."

Nagad smiled, for he understood his meaning.

So with the passing of the sun, the men of Israel broke camp and entered into their silent march west over the high plains, beyond the forested hills, hidden upon the eastern rim of the chalky heights that rose above the Sorek Valley. In the shadowy night, rank upon rank crouched under cover, overlooking the Philistine outpost, which was visible only as lines of scattered fires glowing in the moonless shade. Jonathan crawled to the position his brothers had taken. Jishui, the image of his father, with uplifted chin, knelt upon one knee as he looked out across the river. Malchishua, who favored his mother in form and spirit, took note of his older brother's presence with a nod of welcome.

"Brother," spoke Malchishua, "here we fight together again."

"So it is that we cross swords once more against the Philistines," answered Jonathan.

"And I will join you in this fight."

Recognizing his youngest brother's speech, Jishui turned from his task and looked upon Eshbaal, who had crept close. Unlike his brothers, Eshbaal did not have the stature of his father. His countenance was uncomely, his limbs long and thin, his face sallow with large, dull eyes.

"Why are you here?" Jishui's voice cut into Eshbaal.

"I want to fight."

"You are not made for fighting, little brother," replied Malchishua, more gently.

"It is my time to join you," spoke Eshbaal with his jaw set in determination. "Everyone else has come to fight. I do not want to be the only one not fighting. I, too, would gain honor in battle."

"Go home, little brother," remarked Jishui. "You are not ready."

"I am older than David was when he first went to war and he is captain over a thousand already."

Jonathan looked kindly at his young brother, placing his large hand upon his shoulder. "He is old enough, let him be. I will look after him."

"Hah," scoffed Jishui. "And who will tell *Ima* of her young one's death?"

After scowling at his brother, Jonathan turned toward the east. A faint glow rose over the mountains. "Soon it will be time."

"I wonder," spoke Eshbaal, barely louder than a whisper, "how do they know?"

Jonathan glanced sidelong at his brother. "Who knows?"

"The birds."

Jonathan lifted his gaze. Circling above the valley floor, great shadowy wings hovered silently, gliding upon some hidden thermal overhead.

"See how they circle the field waiting to dine upon our flesh. How do they know to come?"

Jonathan thought for a moment. "I do not know."

A great quietness fell over the valley. Eshbaal grew restless in the waiting silence.

Turning to his brother, Jonathan placed his hand upon the youth's shoulder. "Remove all feeling from your mind, for they have none in theirs."

Eshbaal nodded and peered again across the valley, hoping he had made a wise choice in coming to the battle.

The sky's canopy withdrew, unfurling morning's first blush upon the azure field, scattering dark shadows with glorious glowing embers of light that reached up over the eastern hills. Jonathan raised his head to look upon the dawn. His eyes met with David's.

"It is a good day," Jonathan spoke, smiling.

"That it is," returned David with a grin.

Helek crawled to where David bent low with his men. David turned toward him. "All ready?"

"Aye, *Sar*."

"Then let us begin."

David stood and unsheathed his sword. Lifting his blade skyward, crimson in the morning light, he spoke as his eyes passed over his crouching men.

"The Ancient of Days shall see us through. We need no bolster, for Yahweh is our Shield. Come, soldiers of God! Show yourselves, for Vengeance has come upon them!"

CHAPTER 55

THE HARVEST

The fire crackled in the silence of the night. A western breeze sent embers flying like fireflies fluttering in the dark. Four Philistine soldiers sat before the glowing flames speaking of home and of family left behind. Casluhim, Milkilu, Yabnilu, and Bua they were. Upon their backs, their shields were thrown; spears lay at their sides. Eat and drink were freely passed. No thought of danger lingered in their hearts. Young Bua shifted forward, listening as the older men recounted their tales, eager to learn all he could of past wars and feats of honor.

"There is an old story told," spoke Casluhim, his hands resting upon his knees as he leaned toward the boy. The fire glowed upon the old soldier's face, highlighting the lines etched by time, his eyes reflecting the radiance of the flame. "A story of a country north across the sea, a land green with grass, and mountains reaching to the heavens. That far country, the land of Caphtor, was our home long ago before the coming of our fathers in the great migration, which led us to Canaan, this rich and fertile plain. The Peleset, the Sea Peoples of old, came to this place, driven from their homeland by famine, and earthquakes, and invading tribes from the north. Our fathers pushed the great pharaoh out of this land, even to the doorstep of Egypt.

"And now we fight always to keep this country given to us by the gods. We struggle so that once more we will not be driven from our homes. We have bought this land with the blood of our people."

335

From the eastern hills, morning stretched her rosy arms, awaking from her slumber, breaking forth with unsullied courage to push away the bright stars, fading them into unknown realms. For is it not true that two lights cannot rule the sky even as two kings cannot share a crown. And so the dawn cast forth the shroud of night.

On a sudden, a shout was heard. The four soldiers stood, taking up their spears, looking east from whence the sound came.

"Did you hear that?" called out Bua.

"Quiet," spoke Milkilu. "Listen."

"Something approaches," added Yabnilu.

"Look to the hills!" cried Casluhim. "The enemy comes!"

All eyes turned east. Dust swelled upon the ridge above them. With a cry, the Hebrews rose as the disaffected night gave way, revealing in traitorous revelation the onrush of the adversary. The Chosen of God surged some five hundred cubits into the valley below. Crossing the river Sorek, with water lapping at their heels, the Hebrew host sought to crush the foe.

In confusion, the Philistines hastened to arm themselves. The insurrection of dawn rose in revolt against the band of Philistine soldiers, whose radiance would but last a moment, then fade into oblivion, for at that very moment, burnished beams broke across the valley as the sun shot over the crest of the hill, sending rays of light that pierced the sky, blinding the Philistines as their enemy came upon them.

The cohesive body of Hebrew soldiers crashed into the enemy, the two sides brought together by a force unseen, compelled as a mag-stone draws metal. The line of Philistine spears broke, knocked aside by the swords and spears of the invaders, as the Chosen of God entered into the fold of confounded warriors. Shield pushed against shield. Sword struck sword. Behind, javelins, stones, and arrows flew, killing many Philistines. The adversary came out to meet them as, with ruthless rancor, the Hebrews engaged in bloody battle, drenching the soil with the hemal flow, swallowing the enemy into its maw until they would but yield their place.

Fire arrows streaked against the bright sky, leaving trails of smoke arising from the rearguard of the Hebrew lines, setting the wooden shields of the Philistines ablaze. The soldiers of God were unwavering, pressing through the mass of bloodied soldiers and into the Philistine camp, overturning carts and tents, setting all to blaze. Smoke filled the valley, choking the men as on they battled.

Gripping his sword with both hands, David, captain of a thousand, entered into the fight, the bitter bite of his blade touching everything that moved. Arrows flew overhead as Jonathan, ever faithful, did battle at David's side; Eshbaal followed close behind.

Gray-haired Nagad fought, the old veteran, with earnest fervor, still powerful in war. Helek, Maʿaleh, Jarib the Reubenite, and Eyal the tall, ardent soldiers all, who strove for their captain and had oft known the sting of battle, joined the fray with alacrity. The sounds of conflict filled the air: the clash of swords and shields, the screams and shouts of men, the whir of arrows and the whizz of stones as they flew past their heads. The confusion of arms continued, slicing and hacking within the vale as every sword rose against another, an effusion of men bearing the ruin of war.

And so the battle raged, the Philistines unwilling to yield their arms, fed by the hatred that poisons men's souls. Battered bodies fell as smoke rose and spears clattered through a sea of soldiers, turbulent and tangled in a mass of undulating waves, surging here and there, falling off and rising again.

Up rose Casluhim, the awful lion, wreaking havoc across the valley, for none could touch him as he coursed through the field, devouring all who opposed him. The cry of battle sprung from his lips, his mind fixed to kill, lapping up his prey with his sharp teeth, seeking all to tear limb from limb. Who should dare to face him? For he would rend their life and free their soul.

One came, Jonathan, son of the king, who drew his sword against the lion of Philistia. Casluhim spied his quarry, circling the Hebrew with haughty strides, eyeing his prey through narrowed eyes. Poising his mighty spear beside his ear, Casluhim tested its weight, bouncing it in the palm of his hand. With a powerful thrust, the shaft took flight, driving for his breast. Back bent the prince, his shield to his chest. He heard the hiss, he felt the air; close over passed the shaft. It missed the mark and struck the earth behind his noble head.

Laughing, Casluhim approached Jonathan as he drew out his iron sword. "Pray now to your God, Hebrew, for I hear Him calling you to thy final home."

"If it is His will, let it be so," answered Jonathan as he circled to his right. "Yet first I will part thy soul from you, for I do hear another calling thee."

The Philistine lunged for the Hebrew, his life seeking to take. Yet Jonathan contended with Casluhim, tall as he was, meeting him stroke for stroke. With mighty blows, the two debated in earnest, each striving to deliver the final reckoning: the last line recorded and the account paid in full. Casluhim drove hard upon Jonathan; swift and near was his stroke. No use was his shield to turn the blade aside, but by the edge of his sword at the cost of his hold. Seizing his chance, the Philistine brought down his weapon, catching the Hebrew's edge. Well-landed the strike, for the sword was cast from his hand, leaving him perilously exposed.

Yet the king's son was not finished, for he rushed upon the Philistine, grabbing the enemy's sword arm with a strong grip. Jonathan could hear the sound of creaking leather and the grunt of effort as the two grappled for a time, until the prince could draw his knife from his belt and plunge it into the chest of Casluhim. Jonathan felt the blade enter the soft flesh and strike the hard bone. He felt the bone give way, heard it crack beneath his strength. Blood bubbled from the Philistine's mouth as the prince and the lion locked eyes. Sputtering, drowning in his own gore, the lion, whose pursuit was stayed, sank to the ground.

Jonathan stooped to take up his sword and shield. When he rose, he was confronted by a large Philistine, towering above him, breathing hard as a bull ready to charge.

"What is it with these Philistines? Are they all giants?"

The Philistine came at him with the strength of ten. Swinging his sword above his head, he brought it down. Jonathan blocked the stroke with his shield. Yet the force of the blow sent Jonathan staggering backward.

Assaulted by the smell of blood and sweat, Jonathan braced himself as the Philistine came at him again. With a mighty leap, the giant lunged at the king's son, sweeping his legs from beneath him as the two toppled to the ground. The enemy's weight pressed hard upon him. His chest constrained, Jonathan gasped for breath that would not come.

The Philistine sat upon the prince as he raised his knife. Jonathan grabbed the hand that held the knife, pushing with all his might against the iron will of the enemy. Beads of sweat rolled down his face, his lungs screamed for air, his muscles grew weak from strain, and still the powerful hand pressed the blade downward.

Then it was that David came upon the two grappling in the dust. Spying a spear whose point was embedded in the earth, he took it up and cast it toward the Philistine.

The Philistine's hand pressed hard against his enemy, leaning heavily upon the knife that was poised to kill. Jonathan's strength gave way. The blade jerked downward, the tip pricking the prince's breastplate. The Philistine froze, his expression faltered as his eyes looked to his own breast. Emerging from his lower chest, a bloodied point ruptured the leather armor. The Philistine toppled forward, pinning the prince under the lifeless weight of his enemy.

David hastened over and pushed the enemy off his friend. Stunned, the prince lay motionless until the shepherd-captain pulled him upright. Regaining his feet, he stood gasping, resting his arm on David's shoulder. The shepherd-captain looked upon him in horror.

"Where is thy wound?"

Jonathan glanced down at his breast and gaped, for it was thick with blood. He surveyed his flesh, searching for damage.

Jonathan shook his head. "It is not my blood."

David clapped him upon the back. "I am glad, my friend. Come then, we still have much to do, for many a Philistine yet remain."

The contest heated as the last flames of bitter contention burst forth, bearing the Philistines' final effort to shake off the chokehold of the Hebrews. A smoky brume filled the valley, wrapping the dead in an ethereal shroud. The sun sent rays of light that at times cut through the smoke, reaching out to collect the souls of those fallen. Men stumbled and fell over the dead and wounded, consumed by the misty mantle as though they had left the corporeal realm and entered into some insubstantial quarter dissolved in ether, until at length the last embers of battle were beaten out.

Jonathan stood for a moment, looking over the carnage wreaked upon the enemy, wisps of smoke circling about his feet. Not a Philistine remained who took in breath. Then the prince remembered his charge. In earnest, he turned his head, searching for the youth, but where he was, Jonathan could not discern.

"Eshbaal?" he cried. When no answer came, he moved through the field, turning over bodies, searching for his brother.

"Eshbaal!"

Movement drew the prince's eye whereupon he spied Eshbaal hidden among the equipment. Letting out a great sigh, Jonathan walked over to his brother.

"Eshbaal."

His brother's face was pale and he trembled with fear. Bowing his head in shame, Eshbaal spoke, "I could not bear it, Jonathan. Jishui was right. I am not made for war. I am ashamed."

Jonathan smiled, placing a hand upon his brother's shoulder. "Do not be ashamed. It was your first battle. I remember a time long ago when *Abba* hid among the equipment."

Eshbaal raised his face. "*Abba*? But he fears nothing."

Jonathan patted his brother on the shoulder. "*Abba* lives in fear."

Eshbaal looked hard at Jonathan, not grasping his meaning.

"Come, death has yielded a full crop and we have need to bring it in."

And so the costly harvest was gathered as the men waded through the sea of the dead, claiming the gruesome trophies. The Philistines, converted in death, their bodies giving what was asked, were set apart perforce to carry the badge of His chosen people.

CHAPTER 56

THE TROTH

On a hill near Gibeah, stairs cut from stone had been set that led to a throne upon a dais, under the shade of a tamarisk tree. Ridged and furrowed, the bluish-purple trunk of this saltcedar reached out its gnarled branches, terminating in a feathery canopy. Its scale-like leaves, salt-encrusted with spikes of pink blossoms, silently rose, enfolding the whole tree in a diaphanous blush of color. A sweet scent like honey clung to the faint breeze. Here sat King Saul, overspread by shadow within the open air as the morning waxed on, hearing cases and receiving petitions in an unending parade of suppliants as the ancient judges had done before him.

Coming forward, the beseecher bowed before King Saul, wringing his hands in agitation.

"Arise," spoke Doeg, motioning with his hand, "and plead your case before the king."

The man looked with furtive eyes at the Hebrew monarch, his fingers twisting upon one another. He seemed lost for words as he stood mute.

Growing impatient, Saul declared, "What charges do you bring before us?"

Regaining himself, the suppliant pointed an accusing finger at his neighbor. "His scales are dishonest. He has placed his thumb upon the scales."

"What proof have you?"

"None, my king."

"What does the accused say in defense?"

Bowing, the one under indictment rose. "My king, what this man says is false. I am an honest merchant."

"Do you have the ephah and the scale?"

"Yes, my king."

"Bring them here."

The accused yielded his scales for judgment.

"Doeg," Saul spoke, his voice hollow, "measure the ephah before us."

Doeg brought forth the balance and placed the vessel of grain upon the pan of the scale. Stone weights were set upon the opposite pan until the balance was level. Thus demonstrated, the merchant was found to have rendered less than was agreed, while exacting the full price.

"What say you to this charge? Shall we acquit a man with dishonest scales, who leans upon the pans? Your tongue is deceitful in your mouth. You must pay back the one you have cheated. Do you not know that the Lord hates the one who uses dishonest scales?[52] Take him out of our sight." Saul dismissed the suppliant with a wave of his hand.

"Doeg," Saul spoke, his voice low, "how many more are they? We cannot bear another moment of this tedious discourse."

"It appears many more, my king. I will number them."

Taking leave of the king, Doeg went forth to reckon those among the bystanders who had come to plead before the king.

Saul slouched down within his seat, his chin resting in his hand as he leaned upon his elbow. A murmur grew from within the crowd, at which Saul raised his head.

Doeg hastened to the king, his countenance grave.

"What is it?" queried Saul. "Not another petty squabble over goats, we hope."

"My king, David has returned."

"Returned? But how—" Saul sat up in his seat.

"He approaches."

---

[52] Proverbs 11:1

"Bring him to us."

As the king spoke, David walked past the line of people waiting, past the notable elders and scribes, past the gathered people arrayed in their best garments as they awaited their turn before the king; for this day, the king was holding court, and the multitude tarried in hope that their king would grant them mercy, that unmerited, he would deliver them favor for their cause.

As he drew near, David took note that Saul's visage was drawn and worn. Bowing before the king, he fell down to the earth upon his face.

"O king, may you live forever."

"Arise, my son. Tell us, how is it that you have come back to us, seeing so great a task was laid before you?"

David rose. "Praise be to the Lord our God! He has delivered up the men who lifted their hands against my lord the king. For see here this day, the king's host has prevailed."

Then David motioned for the baskets to be brought forward and set at the king's feet, and in doing so, he presented his dowry before all the people.

"I have come to claim my bride. The price was one hundred foreskins of your enemy, the Philistines. See here, twice over I have delivered the prize, for the full tale is two hundred, for surely the king's favor is highly esteemed by your servant David."

To his feet sprang the king, trembling fury rising at David's good fortune. Yet, sensing the eyes of the multitude upon him, Saul calmed himself, for in honor he could not refuse David's petition, seeing he had achieved the required condition.

Raising his hand toward his captain, Saul proclaimed, "This day, my servant David has fulfilled his obligation and shall take my daughter Michal to wife and become the king's son-in-law."

Yet in his heart, Saul vowed to destroy the young upstart who thought to be king.

CHAPTER 57

KETUBAH

When the time drew near that the two should be joined together, David and his witnesses came through the streets of Geba with great fanfare and the sounding of trumpets.

Jonathan went before David, crying out, "Behold, the bridegroom comes!"

As he spoke those words, the shofar sung, blaring out its unaltered tone. Primal and rich, the intimate voice reached beyond the system of words, expressing new life as it comes forth into the world and takes its first breath. Servants and friends and family gathered in the streets, following after the bridegroom, shouting and dancing in great celebration, for indeed this was a joyful day long-anticipated: the day David came to receive unto himself his bride. So through the streets the party progressed, until they presented the son of Jesse to the palace.

David waited outside in the courtyard of the king's stronghold, standing under garlands of flowers that were strung from wall to wall, making a floral canopy in the open air, heavy with the sweet fragrance of the perennial spray. Michal entered the court, attended by King Saul, arrayed in all his finery. Close behind followed Ahinoam and Merab, both with flowers and ribbons in their hair. Bride and Groom looked upon each other, each dressed in robes of sullen white, a double thread, clothes to espouse and entomb, hiding sweet alms in masks of sorrow.

Blue ribbons Michal had upon the border of her fringed robe, and in her hair a blue ribbon lay, for hers was of devotion and love and modesty.

David smiled as he saw his bride, his heart filled with gladness.

Jesse and Saul, father and father-in-law, escorted David forward to receive Michal. David reached up and took the veil in his hands. Pausing, he studied the comely face of his beloved, enraptured by her fair visage framed by rich dark hair, those dark piercing eyes that read his soul like a scroll. And in that moment, the two recanted liberty to the slavery of each other, their thralldom enacted as their hearts entwined.

Lowering the veil, David winked at Michal before her face was curtained in the light fabric. Together, the two walked before the priest, presenting themselves for the *nisu'in*. From this day forward, *Yahushua*, the Servant, would carry the burden of *Ruach Yahuweh*, the Bride.

Michal lifted her gaze to her groom, and, as was the custom, compassed him seven times as the *Hakafot* demanded, bringing low every barrier that yet lay between them. As she circled round each time, her eyes looked into the eyes of her beloved, her entwining path forging her thoughts to the center of her being, her love for David melding into the embers of her soul.

As the guests, arrayed in their finest garments, bore witness, David presented the betrothal contract, the *ketubah*, and a skin of choice wine. Receiving the contract, the priest read the promises written within before the presence of the people, and asked, "Has the *Mohar*, the Bride Price, been paid?"

"Yes, it has been fulfilled. It is finished," uttered the king.

Jesse, taking the wine, poured out the crimson offering into a silver chalice. The priest then lifted the wine and spoke the blessing. "*Baruch atah Adonai, Eloheinu Melech Ha-Olam Borey P'ree Hagafen*. Blessed are You, O Lord our God, King of the Universe, Who creates the fruit of the vine. Amen."

The priest handed the cup to King Saul. Giving his seal to the marriage, the king handed the cup to David; he received it and took a sip of the wine, then spoke words to Michal, saying, "All I have I give you. All I am is yours. I love you. I give you my body. I give you my life. I have paid the Bride Price; now enter into the covenant with me, for I have bought you with a price, even the price of the shedding of blood."

David extended the wine to Michal. "This cup of Redemption I offer to you. This cup is a new covenant between us. Do you take this cup, my sovereign pledge, and be my bride?"

Michal gladly received the cup into her trembling hands. Looking through the veil, she smiled at David and spoke, "*Da'ath*. I know that all you have is mine, and all I have is now yours. I lay aside my inheritance for your sake. I accept your life, and I give you mine. What you have given me, I now give back to you." She raised the cup to her lips beneath the veil and drank.

"Michal, you belong to me now, for see, you have been bought with a price."

Jesse took the hand of the bride and placed it in the hand of his son. At that moment, their bodies united, their hearts entwined, she became his wife. Swaddling bands the priest gathered and wrapped about the couple's hands, reserved thereafter when the fulfillment of love brought forth their progeny. Embroidered upon the band were the symbols of David's tribe: Judah, the lion, the lamb, and the tree of life, worked in blue and white. Each side perfect counterparts of the other, so that no right or wrong side could be discerned; for harmony was to reign between the inner and outer life of the two, now become one.

Then Michal spoke these words:

> My heart is overflowing with a good theme;
> You are fairer than the sons of men;
> Grace is poured upon your lips;
> Therefore God has blessed you forever.
> Gird your sword upon your thigh,
> With your glory and your might.
> And in your prosperity go, because of truth,
>   humility, and righteousness;
> And His right hand shall teach you awesome things.
> Your arrows are sharp in the heart of the king's enemies;
> The peoples fall under you.

Your throne, O God, is forever and ever;
A scepter of righteousness is the scepter of Your kingdom.
You love righteousness and hate wickedness;
Therefore God, your God, has anointed you
With the oil of gladness more than your companions.

A tear stole down David's cheek, and he smiled as he spoke, for his heart was light with joy and gladness:

Listen, O daughter,
Consider and incline your ear;
Forget your own people also, and your father's house;
Instead of your fathers shall be your sons,
Whom you shall make princes in all the earth.
I will make your name to be remembered in all generations;
Therefore the people shall praise you forever and ever.[53]

David lifted the veil with both his hands and cupped Michal's face in his palms as he looked into her glistening eyes. He breathed in her fragrance as he leaned forward to bind the contract. Gently their lips touched, sealing the promise with a kiss, their spirits exchanged with their breath, in part, each soul to dwell with the other, mingled spirits to abide forever. Then it was that he took her in his arms and laughed aloud as the bondage of love released him to liberty. A cheer went up from the gathered witnesses as they rejoiced in their union.

Music and celebration followed as Jonathan led the bride and groom to the wedding chamber and closed the door behind them. The king's son turned and faced the gathered people as he raised both arms into the air. Smiling broadly, he let out a shout of acclamation.

---

[53] Psalms 45

Behind the door, David beheld his bride as one looks upon a long-awaited dawn. A hush fell between them, tender and profound, as he drew her into his arms. The veil slipped from her hair beneath his gentle hand, her hair glistening in the lamp's warm glow. He bent to her, and their kiss came upon them like the fulfilling of an ancient vow. She softened against him, her heart answering his with a fervor that had ever grown between them, until at last it found its home in him.

"Michal."

Her name slipped from his lips, soft and low as a whispered breath. Warmth caressed her heart, overspreading her frame, as though she were unmade and made anew.

"Michal, you have entered the inmost chamber of my heart. Dwell with me there for all my days."

She kissed him upon the mouth, her arms tightening about his neck as though she would never let him go. He drew her near and laid her gently upon the bed, and in that quiet hour, the longing of their hearts was brought to its appointed fullness, and the covenant between them was sealed.

The guests watched Jonathan as he waited for the sign. He kept his post before the door, listening for a knock long in coming. The people stirred in their places, eager for the feast to begin.

Michal and David lay, cradled in each other's arms, lingering in the quiet sweetness of the moment, willing that hour to never end. Reluctantly, Michal rose and took up her robe, preparing for her duty to her guests. Stretching out his arm, David seized the end of her garment and pulled her back down upon the bed. He reached behind her head, the warmth of his hand upon the back of her neck, and drew her to him. He pressed his mouth onto hers and moved his lips down the side of her neck. Michal sighed at his touch, her body yielding.

She pulled away. "David, the guests—"

"Let them wait." He drew her to him and kissed her again.

"David, we must not keep them waiting so long. It is unseemly."

David pursed his lips and chewed the inside of his cheek, his eyes narrowing as he looked at Michal ruefully.

"After this day, our whole life lies before us. Then we can linger as long as you like." She leaned over him and kissed his brow, then ruffled his dark curls.

David smiled at Michal. He leapt from bed and rapped upon the door. Jonathan turned toward the crowd and gave the signal. All stood quiet in expectation. After a few moments, the chamber door opened. Michal and David appeared before the crowd of witnesses. A great roar went up from the wedding guests.

"Let the celebration begin, for the union is complete!" cried Jonathan over the rejoicing. A broad grin lit his face as he clapped David upon the back in approval.

Then followed seven days of feasting and of song, for the house of Jesse was bound to the royal house.

Michal and David reveled in each other, rejoicing amidst companions and kin. All the while, Saul watched, and as a cloud gathering before a storm, his mood darkened. Yet, David looked upon his wife, soaking in her beauty, unaware that this moment, as the tide of time runs, was destined to end, for one cannot breathe two breaths at once.

"Look how she fawns over him, how she brightens at his glance. I had hoped to use this marriage to my advantage," mumbled Saul as he raised his cup to his lips.

"Take heed of enemies reconciled, and of the vinegar of sweet wine, my king," spoke Doeg.

"In this marriage, I had thought to bring ruin upon my enemy, yet I fear I have opened the way for my enemy to come to the throne."

CHAPTER 58

NIGHT WATCH

Restless waves of thought surged over Saul's reason. He lay awake, watching the moonlight cast shadows upon the room. His mind, ceaselessly unquiet, was desirous of action, yet the gnawing hours strove on with a flagging pace. The weary groans of night were drowned by the constant droning of his hapless heart, filling his ears with unnumbered beats of the drummer's stroke. With a growl, Saul rose from his bed, strode across the floor, uttering oaths against David.

Stirred from sleep by the rising rage of the ruler, Rizpah lifted her head and propped herself upon her elbow, her hand set lightly beneath her cheek. Her dark hair in disarray, she regarded the agitated king with a measure of concern.

"What is it, my king? What disturbs your sleep?"

Standing in the shadows, Saul spoke, his throat tight, his voice strained. "All my steps are overruled. I strive to defeat my enemy, yet always it turns to his betterment. All my plans are thwarted. And though I seek to destroy him, it is he on whom I must lean to fight my battles. The princes of Philistia have ventured once more to wage war against us, to ravage and spoil our land, for their wrath is kindled. David has injured them, killing their champion and now slaying their two hundred, defiling their bodies. They thought to take advantage of our law. Believing David of no use to us, for he is newly married, they misinterpreted the custom, thinking he could not fight for one year. Thus, seeing what they deemed a favorable hour, they have again invaded Israel."

"Saul, do not think on this now. Cast your worries from your mind, and come back to bed."

Turning upon Rizpah, Saul lunged at her with wild eyes, his voice loud and savage. "Do you not see? For always we are permitted to defend ourselves against invasion, even to be taken from our marriage bed."

The king stood up, gripping the back of his neck. He began pacing. "And so, though newly married, I sent David to defend me against them. Yet he has behaved more wisely than any of my servants, more skilled than any of my captains. And he has returned again, a hero. The people love him, holding him in great esteem. It is as though everything he touches prospers. There is no one in the kingdom who can render service for me as David does."

Saul turned abruptly, grabbing his hair with his hands, clutching at his head. "It makes me mad! My thoughts grow more divided!"

Dropping his arms, the king looked at Rizpah, his voice lowering to a whisper. "It is a hard service given me, seeking shade from the all-seeing sun. So many wearisome nights have been appointed to me; months I have been given, months of futility."

"Saul, come back to bed. Let these troubles leave you for tonight. Come back to bed."

"There is no comfort for me this night. When I lie down, I cannot abide till morning; the night drags on and I cannot endure, longing for the night to be ended. No, I have had my fill of tossing till dawn."[54]

"I fear your fervor has clouded your judgment. For if David does such great service for my king, why do you wish to destroy him? It seems at odds with your needs."

Saul's voice rose as he glared down his nose at her. "Have you heard nothing I have been telling you? Do you not see? It is my throne he seeks! And as the people's love for him grows, they will gladly give it him!"

Once more Saul calmed. Looking out from the balcony, the king's voice faded. "A painful foreboding clouds my judgment, blighted and

---

[54] Job 7

withered in my desecrated fields. Even now I see the ax lying at the root of my tree."

Wheeling about, his voice found its strength, and with a finger thrust toward Rizpah's face, biting each word with wrath, Saul made his oath. "But mark it well, before the end, I will make the sword fall from his hand—No."

Saul turned away.

"I have had enough of tossing till dawn. I must act now, even with my own hands if it be necessary."

CHAPTER 59

TRAITOR AND USURPER

The solemn dignity of the throne room fell over all present, from the servants to the son, as they waited for their king to speak. The hush was disturbed only by the crackling hearth as the flame sent up sparks. Saul stood among the servants, his hand resting upon Jonathan's shoulder as he leaned forward, his face lambent in the soft glow of the fire.

Saul's voice was soft, personal and familiar, as though he were one of them. "My soul is cleaved within me. There is a deceiver in our midst, a traitor and usurper. There stands even now a threat to this very throne." Saul pointed to the seat upon the dais. "Bearing down on us by one we love. My son's succession to the throne is in danger. We must not let the crown pass to another."

He let his words settle upon them as he marked their response. Several stood with their mouths agape. Others looked from one to another, trying to discern who among them was the traitor.

"I speak of one you all know. I know not how to reveal it but to say it plainly. It is David who seeks to supplant me. He it is who desires to steal the throne. He will stop at nothing to claim it."

Jonathan pulled back as though struck. Frowning, he looked upon his father. "How can this be, *Abba?* David loves you like his own flesh. I do not believe this. You are mistaken."

"My son, I know that David is dear to you, but I am not mistaken. He seeks the throne. He may play the friend to you, but in secret he plans to take the kingdom from beneath you. He is no friend to you. He has no love for you."

Standing tall, Saul placed his hands upon his hips and stepped away from the stricken assembly. "Therefore," spoke the king as he turned and faced the men. "It is my desire to dispatch David. One of you must do this. There will be great reward for the one who accomplishes this task."

Jonathan shook his head and took a step toward Saul. "You cannot mean what you say, *Abba*."

"I am your father and your king. I would have hoped you, of all people, would listen to a father, rather than a forged friend." Saul placed his hands upon Jonathan's shoulders, smiling as he spoke. "Are you not wise enough, my son, to see where your true interests lie and abandon this David?"

Shaking his head, Jonathan backed away, his eyes fixed upon the floor. "No, this is madness. I will have no part in this." Turning, Jonathan stormed from the room. *My father has truly lost his mind.*

"I pluck thee for my love," spoke David as he reached down and picked a blue-petaled flax flower from the old stone wall of the courtyard. He breathed in the soothing fragrance and handed the bloom to Michal.

"It is a beautiful flower," said Michal.

"Is it?" questioned David, a mischievous smile upon his lips. "I cannot tell, for my eyes are blind to any other beauty than the beauty of thy fair face."

Michal lowered her head, color rising to her cheeks as she feigned to savor the fragrance of the flower. The two walked side by side, their hands barely touching, within the quiet enfoldment of love.

"You have defeated me, my love."

Michal stopped walking and looked at David, her brow knit, "Defeated you?"

David turned to face his wife, smiling. "Yes, your love has consumed me like a flame. I am slain by your love, dead to self, only to rise again, for you are the very breath of my life now." David reached up and placed his gentle hands upon Michal's arms, his eyes fervent. "My heart is banished from myself. Words cannot speak my thoughts, yet to not speak would perjure my love. My tongue is impoverished, vague in the translation of my mind."

Picking up David's thread, Michal spoke with emphasis, as she placed her hands over her heart with a dramatic flourish. "O, my Heart, I delight in you." Her voice grew serious as she gazed deep into his eyes. "You are a great happiness to me."

Together, they continued to stroll, their arms entangled, as Michal leaned her head upon David's shoulder. He kissed the top of her head. Spying the flower within her hand, David halted and reached for the bloom. Taking the flower, he placed it in Michal's hair, behind her ear. Smiling down at his love, he cupped her face in his hands and kissed her upon the mouth.

Whispering, he spoke, "Can you but hear the thunder of my heart every time you draw near? Love walks in your footsteps; it follows as you enter and leaves when you go. So stay or deliver treason to my heart."

"There is no power on earth that could take me hence from your sight, for when I am not beside you, breath fails me and the beat of my heart grows faint."

Enrapt in the presence of each other, the two were unaware Jonathan had intruded upon their juncture. Restlessly, he waited to be noticed. Feeling eyes upon him, David glanced over, struck by the look on Jonathan's face.

"What is it?"

"I must speak with you—alone."

"Why, Jonathan," cried Michal, "you are so pale. Are you ill? Has something happened? Is *Abba* ailing?"

Jonathan gave a queer, faltering laugh while shaking his head. "Please, Michal, I must speak with David."

"My love, give us a moment. I shall not be long." David leaned forward and kissed her once more.

"Jonathan..." Michal placed her hand upon her brother's face. Smiling, she kissed him on the cheek, then walked toward the palace.

Jonathan and David stood silent as they watched her disappear through the doorway.

The sun waned in the sky, elongating the shadows in the courtyard. A warm breeze brushed across Jonathan's face, bringing with it the scent of ripening grapes. He grabbed David by the arms, his voice urgent.

"David, you are in grave danger."

"Danger? By what am I endangered? I have only just returned from battle. The enemy has been put down. War has ceased for a time. There is no threat now."

"Foes take many forms. You have enemies from within." Jonathan glanced about and bent closer to David. "My father is—well, he suspects you of plotting against him for the throne and has conspired to have you killed."

David pushed away from Jonathan. "You are mad. I have ever loved the king. Take the throne? I would never usurp the dominion of God and force His hand. The Lord is He who chooses the one to sit upon the throne of His people."

"David, listen to me. There is no time. For even now, emissaries of the king seek an opportunity to take your life. Do not give it to them. Do not expose yourself to danger. You cannot return to your bedchamber tonight. You are not safe in your own house. You must seek a place to hide, a place where no one will expect to find you. Do this until morning. Keep strict guard over yourself this night."

"Hide?"

"Until dawn. In the morning, may it be that the mood of the king will have tempered and he will be more disposed to reason."

"Jonathan, I—" stammered David. "Where shall I go?"

"Each morning, just as the sun breaks over the ridge, my father is wont to walk in the fields. Hide there. I will walk with my father, and as we come to the place you are hiding, I will stand between my father and you. I will speak highly of you to him, endeavoring to reason with the king on your behalf. Listen to what is said, for may it be that you will hear what passes between us. I hope, with the dawn, I will be able to dissuade him from his desire to take your life. Look upon the king's countenance and read what it reveals, for then you will know how it goes with him. Then what I observe, I will tell you."

David placed his hand upon Jonathan's forearm. Jonathan matched the gesture, laying his hand upon David's arm.

"If what you say is true, then you do this at great risk to yourself."

"That is of little consequence." Jonathan embraced David.

Drawing back, he spoke, "Please, David, be on your guard until morning, and stay in a secret place and hide. Farewell, friend. I will see you at dawn. Now go quickly. I will tell Michal you cannot come to her tonight. Do not fear; in the morning we will see how this matter fares."

CHAPTER 60

THE VINEYARD

The night air cooled as he lay hidden in the field. Stars glistened in the clear sky. Above, Orion hunted with his sword in pursuit of the Pleiades until the heavens turned and the Great Bear charged across the celestial sphere. The waxing moon lifted its face to shine down upon the man, David, as he rested upon his back, eating a cluster of grapes he had plucked from the vine. Dampness settled about him as dew formed upon the ground with the passing of the night. Yet, sleep eluded him, for his troubled mind thought upon the wrath of his king.

Sighing deeply, David's heart felt heavy with the weight of grief. "Could what Jonathan said be true? Could Saul really intend to have me killed? After all these years of faithful service, is this the true character of the king, to betray one's friend?"

David rose to his knees, resting upon his heels. Overcome, the shepherd-captain bowed his head between his hands.

"Oh, how I ever loved and served Saul, my king, loved him as my own father, and yet, how is it that Saul has exposed me to treachery?"

He lifted his face toward heaven, his hands clasped in his lap.

"Is there something in my words spoken or my conduct done that the king has mistaken my deeds for treason? Is there some sin in me I am unaware?"

Shaking his head, he spoke, "No, I do not think it is so. Why then treat me so severely? Has he not shown some bent toward fits that unseat his reason? Has his mind not been perplexed by jealous rage before so that he cast his own spear at me? Then is this disposition an act of madness, or has it been his intention from the start to seduce me and then forsake me?"

David closed his eyes as he took in a deep breath, dropping his chin to his chest. "What escape is there for me? Who am I that I can stand against a king?"

Lifting his face once more to heaven, David implored, "O Lord, I cry out to You, for I know not which way to go! Will You not hear me?"

He searched the night sky, hearkening as though an answer he might hear, but only silence reached his ears. A slight breeze rustled through the vineyard, rattling leaves, rolling waves across the field. Yet even in the stillness, David sensed a Presence stirring about him as a fine brume overshadowing his being. His arms prickled as his skin rose to fine bumps.

"As certain as I breathe, faith stirs within my soul. And yet the spark of belief smolders within me, waiting to be fanned into flame."

David looked again at the stars laid out across the vast table of the aerial dome.

"Do not mine eyes teach me to trust, for look how majestic spreads the heavens before me. O Lord, how excellent is Your name in all the earth, who have set Your glory above the heavens! Out of the mouth of babes and nursing infants You have ordained strength, because of Your enemies, that You may silence the adversary and the avenger."

As he gazed into the abode of God, the wonder of the display lingered in his soul. "When I consider Your heavens, the work of Your fingers, the moon and the stars, which You have ordained, what is man that You are mindful of him, and the son of man that You visit him? For You have made him a little lower than the angels, and You have crowned him with glory and honor.[55] In You, O Lord, I will put my trust."

Smiling, David lay down upon his back with his hands behind his head. Peace settled over him as his mind calmed and his thoughts cleared.

---

[55] Psalm 8:1−5

The snap of a twig sent his heart racing. Sitting up, he realized that he must have dropped off to sleep. The sky had lightened in the east. Keeping his body close to the ground, he crept to a better vantage. The sun crested the hill. Hearing voices, David pulled himself nearer to where they were speaking. Lying low on his belly, hidden within the leaves of the vineyard, David waited.

The king and his son walked, side by side, as in times past, a time when Jonathan looked up with awe at his father. Now, anxious thoughts rested upon the son as he watched Saul and wondered at the man he had become. The king glanced over at Jonathan as a wave of nostalgia flooded over him, and he smiled.

Sighing, Saul spoke, his voice low and gentle, "We used to walk together among the fields at home. Do you remember?"

Jonathan nodded. "I remember."

Bending low, Saul took some soil in his hand and began kneading the rich loam. "This is good earth. I miss getting my hands dirty in the musky soil, tilling the field, sowing the seed, and watching it grow. Life was easier then. We were happy." Standing again, the king dusted the soil from his hands. "What has become of us?"

"*Abba*, much weighs upon you now. The welfare of a whole nation rests as a burden on your shoulders."

Saul sighed. "It is as the Lord wanted, yet there is a part of me that wishes none of this had come to me. I was content with the life I had. Yet, here we are." Shaking his head, Saul walked on. "Never mind, it is all the past. The question now is what to do with the future. Soon it will be you who walk in these sandals."

Looking down at the earth beneath his feet, Jonathan drew in a deep breath. "*Abba*, there is a matter about which I desire to speak with you."

"What is on your mind, son?" Saul walked tall and confident, breathing in the cool morning air.

"There is one among us who has been unjustly accused."

Saul stopped short and turned on Jonathan. "Are we to speak of this again? This matter has been settled! Speak not of this to me."

"*Abba*, please. Do not cut me off." Jonathan stretched out his arms before him. "Listen fully to what I have to say before you close this matter."

"Fine," Saul answered with resignation. "Continue with your plea, but I warn you, my mind is settled."

"*Abba*, you have a certain opinion of your servant, David. Yet I believe your anger has been kindled against him without cause. All he does, he does for his love of you. Always he places your will before his own, often risking all, willingly, for his king."

Shaking his head, Saul interrupted. "He may tell you he fights for his king, but he fights for his own glory. His reasons are not so righteous as to serve his king. You have seen how the people rally to him, and rejoice at his victories, slighting their own king for the joy of David."

Saul tossed his head to the side. "He is grasping for the crown. Can you not see it? All he does, he does to place himself in position to take the throne. He has the people in the palm of his hand."

Holding out his own palm toward Jonathan, Saul shook it as though he were demonstrating David's hold. Clenching his fist, he continued, "Do you not see that I have to kill him before he kills me? There is no other way."

"Oh, *Abba*."

Jonathan closed his eyes for a moment. "Listen to the sound of your own voice, to the words you have spoken. How have anger and jealousy filled your mind with thoughts of vengeance! You know David killed the Philistine. You were there; you witnessed it and were glad. How is it that now you hold all against him? Let not the king sin against his servant, against David, because he has not sinned against you, and because his works have been very good toward you. Has he not faithfully served you since he was a boy, with prudence and wisdom? He has fought for his king with courage and valor; integrity walks with him in all that he does."

Jonathan swept his hand in a broad gesture. "He has served you well, with goodness, often exposing his life to danger for the welfare of your people, for he took his life in his hands and killed the Philistine, and by his hand, the Lord brought about a great deliverance for all Israel. You saw it and rejoiced. Why then will you sin against innocent blood, to kill David without a cause?"

Saul was struck mute. He stood astonished, unable to think clearly. In that moment something changed in the heart of the king, and he heeded the voice of Jonathan. Tears stung his eyes as the love he bore David welled up within him. "As the Lord lives, David shall not be killed."

Jonathan let out his breath in relief. Then, father and son, walked quietly together. Saul looked ahead through the rows of ripened grapevines. Jonathan gazed upon his father, once more seeing the man he called *Abba*. It seemed to Jonathan that they had been separated by a long journey, but had now returned home. And he gloried in the moment as, with hearts rejoined, they tarried for a time.

"I must get back, for the duties of state cannot wait forever," spoke the king. "It has been good, son, to walk together as once we had."

"*Abba*."

Saul turned to go, but stopped.

"Oh, and Jonathan, you can tell David he has nothing to fear from me."

Smiling, Jonathan answered, "I will, *Abba*."

When Saul had gone, Jonathan called to David and told him all that had passed between the king and himself. David once again came before Saul and was in his presence as in times past. Orders were issued that if anyone touched the man David, death would be their reward.

Peace reigned in the heart of the king, yet often it is said, peace lasts but a moment. And as the threat of war rose in the west, so too, dark clouds warned of a coming storm.

PART THE FIFTH

The wicked plots against the just,
And gnashes at him with his teeth.
The Lord laughs at him,
For He sees that his day is coming.

PSALM 37:12–13

CHAPTER 61

TWILIGHT

As the summer waned, there was war again, for the Philistines sent out bands to harass the people residing upon the outer settlements. Although the season for battle was almost over, King Saul had no choice but to dispatch David and his thousand to reinforce the border. Taking his men along the Ridge Route, David marched south, from Gibeah through Bethlehem to Hebron, then turning west, to Beth-Tappuah in search of the place where Captain Nagad and his thousand waited. His plan was to join forces to root out the Philistine war-host before the early rains began. Thirty-five miles, he pushed his men, traveling the distance in just one day.

The light was fading as the exhausted soldiers came to the garrison. The camp was set within a clearing encircled by orchards. The sweet scent of apples clung to the air, stirring the appetite of the travel-weary men. David raised his arm to halt his men as he saw Captain Nagad hastening in his faltering gait to meet him. The gray-haired captain extended his hand. David reached out and they clasped forearms in a firm and friendly greeting. Nagad looked as though the life had drained from his face.

"How are you, Captain?" questioned David.

"*Tov Me'od, Todah.* I am good," answered Nagad. "Word has come to me that congratulations are in order. May Yahweh bless your union."

"*Todah*, Captain. I thank you."

Surveying the soldiers, Nagad lifted his chin toward David's troops. "Dismiss your men, Captain, for I know they are weary from the forced march; then we have much to discuss. The Philistines are on the move and we have not a moment to spare."

David nodded. Turning to face his thousand, the king's son-in-law dispersed his men. Eager to retire, the troops set to work pitching their tents.

"Now, tell me," spoke David, "what have you heard of the Philistines' next move?"

With a stick, Nagad scratched a rude map upon the ground. Helek stood watching, as always, faithfully by Nagad's side. Jonathan and Cabbal, the prince's armor-bearer, were beside David as the old captain's marking took shape.

"The Philistines are situated north in the Valley of Zephathah." Before their eyes, the spine of the Judean hills appeared in the dirt. West of the mountains was the valley. Next, the old captain sketched lines down the extent of the lowlands. "River beds stretch the length of the valley, running north-south, cutting the land in two: the strong line of mountains to the east and the fertile green hills of the Shephelah to the west." Indicating places with his make-shift pointer, Nagad continued, "The land is further bounded by the desert to the east and south. Altogether, the pass through the mountains is only accessible from the north, right where our enemy is encamped."

Nagad straightened and stretched, wincing as he placed his hand on the small of his back. Taking a deep breath, the old captain looked at David. "Here it is that the enemy will enter into our lands." Nagad forcefully struck the map at the gap in the mountains. "At Mareshah."

"Word has reached the king that the Philistines have not sent out their full force," replied David as he studied the map. "This is good, seeing we have not either. Yet, we are still outnumbered, about three to one."

"Ah, no problem, *Sar*, we have dealt with worse odds," spoke Helek with his usual zeal. "All the more for each of us. It will make for a more interesting battle."

Nagad gave Helek a sideways smirk.

"Here it is that the gap through the mountains tapers to a narrow pass." Taking his stick, the gray-haired captain pointed to places on the map. "The latter rains, being severe, have left a brackish marsh at the base of the mountain, further restricting the passage through the ravine. A small brook runs from this fen, which passes west toward the sea. Libnah lies here, to the north, outside the hill country, connecting directly to the coastal plain. The Philistine city of Gath lies just eight miles to the northwest. To the south is Lachish. The main thoroughfare north passes through Lachish, then into the pass at Mareshah."

Nagad looked intently into David's eyes. "It is imperative that the Philistines not gain control of this passage."

The shepherd-captain stood without a sound, rubbing the end of his chin as he studied the map. A smile broke across his face as he reached for Captain Nagad's make-shift pointer.

"You have a plan?" Nagad grinned as he relinquished his stick to the young captain.

"I have."

The sun had not yet breathed upon the night sky as the old captain rose stiffly upon his cot. He groaned as his joints gave an unwelcome snap. For a while, he just sat on the edge of his bed massaging his sore left leg. Years of battle had taken its toll. He felt weary. He stretched his neck to the right, then to the left. His neck answered with a crack. Looking down at his naked leg, Nagad ran his fingers over the scar. The skin puckered awkwardly forming a sunken irregular line. He rubbed the depression in his flesh where the spearhead had entered. His leg ached; it always ached.

The old captain drew in a deep breath and let it out. He reached for his tunic and pulled it over his head. It fell loosely across the long scar that ran from the middle of his back, just below his shoulder blade, extending to his side under his left arm. Slowly, he stood, feeling the pull in his lower back. Taking a measured step, he tried his leg, working it to loosen the muscles.

Nagad sighed. "I am not what I used to be."

371

After donning his armor and strapping his sword to his side, the old captain opened his tent flap. The morning air struck him with the fresh scent of apples. Memories flooded his mind, of an earlier time when he was young. It was near Tappuah in the north, beneath the pink-petaled apple trees, that he first met Orach. The sting of grief bit into Nagad's heart.

So long has it been, yet it lingers still. Would that you were again fighting by my side, old friend.

Now, here he was, all these years later at Beth-Tappuah, the place of apples, with Helek, Orach's son. A tear welled in his eye, threatening to escape. Nagad blinked several times, driving sorrow from his sight.

The shroud of memory that haunts our thoughts is the vice of old age. Sentimental fool. There is no time for this.

Shaking his head to chase the memory away, Nagad walked out into the dark. David saw the old captain emerge and bounded over to meet him.

"*Boker tov*, Captain."

Nagad smiled as he inclined his head toward David. "Good morning to you also."

The two captains looked upon one another for a while, each taking the other's measure. David was agile and lively. Nagad grinned at his vigor and wished for the youth he once had. Then, gazing at the clear sky of the coming twilight, Nagad spoke, "The day shall be fair. The time draws upon us quickly."

"The men are up and ready, eager to begin."

"Good. You and your men should move out. Dawn will be upon us soon."

"We will make haste," agreed David. "Remember, you must give us time to get into position. I am afraid you and your men will be alone in this fight for a while. You must hold them. By noon we should be in play."

"We will hold them."

The shepherd-captain nodded, his hand resting upon his sword. "*Tov me'od*, very good."

David reached up and plucked an apple from a nearby limb. Half chuckling, he sank his teeth into the crisp flesh, causing juice to drip down the sides of his mouth. As he chewed, he wiped his face with the back of his hand. With his mouth full, David spoke, the smile still etched upon his face. "I will see you then, at Mareshah."

David turned and walked away, taking another bite of apple.

"Do not be late," Nagad called after him.

Grinning, he nodded and, with a half wave, left the old captain standing in the shadows.

CHAPTER 62

MARESHAH

From Beth-Tappuah, Nagad took his men along the winding path, due west, toward Mareshah. A few ragged trees sprung from scrub brush, dotting the hills with their faded green foliage. Beneath, chalky limestone boulders emerged from the pale sandy soil. Through the narrow ravine the regiment strove, until they entered into the open lowlands just west of the Judean ridge. The sun was full in the eastern sky, casting long shadows before them, when the Hebrew troops spilled onto the fertile rolling plains. Yellow blooms and tall green grass caressed the valley floor, graceful waves swaying in the breeze.

Though the ground-waters had waned in the summer heat, a shallow marsh remained pressed against the north side of the pass. Tall swamp reeds reached up from the mire of the brackish bog. The putrid smell of decay rose into the air, embittering the nostrils. Trickling southwest, a small stream filtered through the hollow marsh grass, struggling to gain the sea. The Hebrew company moved south of the swamp, keeping clear of the murky waters.

Word of their coming had reached the ears of the Philistines, for as the old captain and his thousand entered into the valley, there stood the enemy, ready to do battle. In haste, the Hebrews formed ranks, preparing to meet the imposing host. The wondrous array of well-clad soldiers waited, striking spear to shield in a brazen proclamation of war. The rhythmic beat of the taunting malice quickened the mettle of the Hebrew forces. Soon the beat of their own hearts kept time with the metrical cadence of the Philistine host.

"Ah," complained Helek, "that is a foul-smelling bog."

Nagad grinned as he nodded, but he was relieved the swampy mire had endured through the dearth of summer.

"We have come in the name of the Lord, our God!" cried Nagad. "Against Him, mere men cannot prevail! To battle!"

"To battle!" The men raised spear and sword at the ready.

Nagad took off sprinting toward the enemy. His men joined him in his charge as the Philistines answered in kind. The two great lines of warriors surged forward, closing the gap until, with a concussive wave, the sides collided. Interwoven in a tangled mass of sword and shield, the war-hosts fought with frenzied fervor. Every sword received an answer, every thrust a biting reply. In the thick, raging battle, the clash of arms ran red. Bloody deeds of valor sprung from the heart of conflict—the tide of battle rising.

They fought before the Judean hills until the sun rose to its full height. The intensity of the onslaught mounted with the heat of day. Then the thundering line of battle broke. With measured steps, the Hebrews relinquished ground, enticing the enemy to follow, as the Chosen of God filtered through the pass and into the narrow entrance of the Israelite territory. The Philistines were elated with the ground gained, sensing they were driving their adversary before them, ready to comply as the Hebrew lines gave way.

With his shield, Nagad pushed against a Philistine combatant, pressing hard to throw the enemy off his balance. The soldier took a step, yielding his position. He growled at the Hebrew captain and charged him, sword at the ready. Stabbing, slicing, biting, he came, raging at the gray-haired foe. Nagad was forced back, the attack bearing heavily upon him. With such fervor the enemy came at him, full of youth and vitality, that Nagad could only raise his shield to meet the striking sword. Useless lay the sword in his hand as the Philistine beat him down. The old captain's leg gave way, and with a crash, he fell to his right knee, his shield yet lifted to ward off the hammering blade.

Nagad struggled to gain his feet, his left leg lacking the strength to raise him. Driving through the pain that tore through his old wound, groaning with the effort, the old captain forced his battered frame to stand. Yet, even as he rose, the enemy beat him down again. The Philistine's blade was relentless, striking against the old captain's shield. Each blow sent a tremor of agony coursing through his body.

Flashes of memory clouded his mind as the enemy battered him. His thoughts turned to Riyphah, his wife. *All these long years she had waited for me. And now—*

A sharp kick struck his shoulder, casting him hard to the earth with his shield pinned fast beneath him. Above him stood a second foe, smirking as he looked upon the stricken Hebrew captain. Lifting his sword, Nagad blocked both blades as he strove to regain his feet, but his left leg failed again to raise him.

His sword grew heavy; a tremor ran down his arm. He rolled to his right and lifted his shield to ward off the blows of the coupled enemy. From his back, he struck out at the twain, his shield arm raised against their battering blades. He swept his blade to either side as he fought to rise, and with that stroke of defiance he drove them back. Laying his clenched sword to the earth, Nagad heaved himself upward, his shield alone holding back their blows. Drawing from the last shred of his might, he hoisted his weary frame to retake his stand.

A sandaled foot drove into his side, forcing Nagad to take a step back. From his left, the Philistine struck, catching him in the gap beneath his shield. He gasped as pain seared across his breast. With the two closing upon him, Nagad arced to his right, his blade finding the foe's belly. His sword bit deep, gutting the enemy. He had no time to glory in his success, for to his left, the other Philistine drew nigh.

As he turned to face his foe, Nagad was struck full in the face with the pommel of his enemy's sword. The skin over his left eye split, laying open his brow. Blood flowed freely, shrouding his sight with a crimson veil. With the back of his sword hand, Nagad wiped his brow. But upon him sprung the mighty Philistine ere his eye could see.

Seizing Nagad's sword arm, the enemy pressed his blade against the captain's throat. Nagad roared as he pushed back with his own sword, wrenching the sharp edge away from his neck.

With arms locked in unyielding contention, the Philistine drove his knee into the old captain's left side with three brutal blows. He heard the bones within him crack beneath the crushing force. Yet the strike loosed the enemy's hold upon his sword arm. Nagad drew his arm back and thrust his weapon forward, sinking the point into the foe's belly, ending him.

Stunned, the gray-haired captain stood transfixed, gulping for air, but his lungs would not open. The weight of his shield bore heavily upon him. Unable to brook the pull on his arm, he let his shield fall to the ground, the sound ringing against the hard earth. He clasped his left arm against the pain searing through his breast. He strove to straighten his frame, but the burning in his side bent him forward. The roar of rushing waters filled his ears, and the world fell away from him.

Within the severing hush, Nagad stood watching, removed from the fray about him. Hard pressed, the enemy came against his men. All around him, he saw the waste of war, and he wondered why men fight. Young men dying before their time; fathers burying their dead sons. What was the point of it all? It sickened him.

Stooped, gasping for air, his lungs yet refused to take in breath. His sight blurred, forcing him to yield an unsteady step back. Staggering, he teetered on the edge of darkness.

The spasm ceased, and air rushed in. His vision cleared; his hearing returned. And in that moment, Nagad, with a mighty roar, spun about, and by his blade he struck off the head of a Philistine that had come upon him.

The brutal battle raged as the Hebrew lines gave way, and still David had not come. The gray-haired captain knew his men could not endure long unaided. Sensing their failing resolve, Nagad cried in a loud voice as pain tore through his breast. "Our land! This is our land! And we do not yield!"

Sword gripped tight, his left arm yet held to his side, Nagad charged toward the enemy. His men took up their captain's iron will and pressed forward into the fray.

A horn rent the air, sounding from behind the Philistine lines.

"That is no enemy war-song," cried Helek.

Glancing over at the stout Hebrew, Nagad was startled to see his body so battered. Blood was matted upon his helmless head. A large gash extended the length of his naked shield arm.

Nagad nodded. "It seems our shepherd-captain is true to his word."

David's war-band, having taken the small mountain path through Lachish, then turning north, had entered into the valley, closing off the pass at Mareshah, and in so doing came upon the Philistines' rear.

Roused by the sudden change in fortune, the Hebrew ranks raised a resounding cheer, and with renewed vigor, entered once more into the fray. Surrounded, the Philistines' courage gave way. Many turned to meet David's men. Others fought on against the mighty hand of Nagad's troops. The Philistines were a divided host, pressed within a vise that would not relent.

Hard-run and nearly spent, Nagad rushed forward with his men, pressing the enemy between the mountains that guarded the gates of the pass. The Philistines had no choice but to retreat into the narrow strip between the steep slopes and the swamp. Caught in a gauntlet, the foe was hemmed in with nowhere to flee. Bowmen and slingers let loose from the cliffs above, sending arrows and stones, and rolling boulders into the ravine below. For it was that David had stationed some of his men there to lie in wait until their skill was needed. Benjamin, Saul's own tribe, bearing shields and wielding bows, valiant warriors all. Their skill now put to the test; their aim answered true.

The sudden onslaught proved too much. The mighty war-host of Philistia broke. The way was shut, and with no place to turn, the Philistines were driven toward the swamp. Feet sank into the swarm-ridden bog. A sucking pull rose from the mud as each foot was wrenched free of the miry earth. Water flowed and filled their tracks, their passing vanishing until no trace remained. The scent of death clung to every breath. Strange movements brushed against their legs, hidden creatures disturbed by the intrusion upon their murky lairs.

Knee-deep, the enemy spilled into the marsh, their legs bound fast within the grasping mire. Cold and slick, the cloying earth would not yield. The rooting weight hindered their steps, and many fell. As the Hebrews pressed them further, those whose footing failed were trampled by their own men and drowned beneath the sullied waters. Seeing their comrades taken by the swamp, the Philistines turned in the only way left to them: back into the Hebrew lines.

Easy prey they were, those Philistines, stuck in the mud among the swamp reeds. With spear in hand, the Hebrews stood, plunging their weapons into any who dared venture from their murky grave, until not a one was left upon his feet. The crimson carnage of the spear-point stained the fen with the red ruin of battle. It was a heavy blow struck upon the Philistines as dark clouds gathered in the west, warning of a coming storm.

The Hebrew troops sent up a hearty cheer, glad they were of the victory wrought over these enemies of old. All that was, except Nagad, the gray-haired captain, who stood unmoved as he looked upon the Philistine desolation.

"*Sar*, we have victory," spoke Helek, still alight with the thrill of battle. "Why do you not rejoice?"

Shaking his head, Nagad answered in a hoarse whisper, "I have grown weary of battle."

"*Sar?*"

"War is the providence of the young. Somewhere in the thick of battle, I have lost my youth." The old captain sighed. "I am old, Helek. My time is passed, and I have seen enough of war."

Bewildered, Helek looked hard at his captain. "What are you saying?"

The gray-haired captain shook his head. "Nothing." A wan smile touched Nagad's lips as he lifted his blood-stained sword toward the shepherd-captain watching them. "Let us go, David waits upon us."

And so, the Philistine harassment was quelled before it took flight. In triumph, David returned, having once again defeated the enemy, a victorious conclusion before the winter rains set in. From his balcony above, Saul looked down as the people rallied to David and hailed him their great hero.

"O wretched man that I am that I should have the people bow before this David. Yet I perceive this victory of his is dearly bought—I cannot look more upon this boy."

Turning from the window, Saul spoke to the empty room. "It stirs my blood and inflames my terror. Enjoy your day, yet look to your laurels, for this fire shall be quenched and the pride of this glory will be your last."

CHAPTER 63

WRETCHED

The early rains swept gently in from the southwest. The work of ploughing the earth and sowing the fields with winter wheat and barley began. Slowly, Saul slipped into his former spirit; a gray melancholy hung like a cloud over his thoughts. And as the winter rains crept in upon the plains, so too the great torment of his past swept over his soul, filling him with the heat of jealousy. In the hidden chambers of his mind, suspicion and distrust lay to roost until at last he feared even to leave his rooms.

"My king," spoke the servant, "here is some food prepared for you." The attendant placed a plate upon a table beside the king's couch.

Saul looked upon the food, then the servant. His eyes narrowed. "You have brought me this food, but who has touched it? It is tainted, is it not?" Saul thrust his arm across the table, dispatching the contents onto the floor with a loud clamor. Food and drink flew across the room.

Startled, the attendant sprang back, crying out, "My king, I assure you, no one has tainted the food. You have to eat, do you not?"

Saul lunged for the servant, taking him by the robes. "They will stop at nothing. I cannot trust anyone. Surely, they will try to slay me, even my food can be used against me." Saul looked hard into the eyes of the attendant. "Ah," he exclaimed as he thrust the man aside.

The king turned toward the balcony, his gaze far off. He stroked his beard as his mind drew apart, wandering in false fields of delusive thought.

"It will be some secret plan or sudden attack. I must not let my guard down, for that is when it will happen. Yes, must keep watch—the wind has shifted. See, it comes from the north. The full force of the coming rains shall fall now upon all of Israel."

The storms came hard, mingled with fine hail, as thunder and lightning raced across the swarthy sky. A chill mounted in the air. His mind overthrown by waves of mistrust, Saul grew more distracted. His humor waxed dark as black bile, while a spirit of dejection gave rise to an agitated and somber pensiveness. Often he walked his endless gyre with spear in hand, as though hunting an invisible prey.

"All I feel, like the unfurling wind upon the shore, is the roar of my grief."

"My king?" Saul startled at the sudden intrusion. Wheeling about, he found Nagad standing before him.

"What cause have you, Captain, to come upon us so abruptly?" Saul had a wary glint in his eye.

Concern washed over the old captain as he regarded the king, noting his disheveled look and the spear he bore in his hand.

Half-bowing, Nagad spoke, "I sought you in your hall, but I was instructed to meet you in your chamber. I am told you no longer venture from your quarters."

"Tales told are often exaggerated," quoth the king. Saul sat upon his couch, leaning upon his spear. "Tell me, why do you seek after us?"

"For many years I have faithfully served you. Of late, I have come to conclude that my allotted time is nearly spent. I seek to withdraw, for the strength of my youth has departed. I respectfully request to be relieved from active duty."

Saul looked upon his steadfast captain and recalled the years they fought and bled together. Even now, the gray-haired captain bore the wounds of his recent battle. Overwhelmed by the memories, the heart of the king grew soft and his mind calmed. "Yes, you have ever shown honor and loyalty before me. I will miss your presence here. What will you do?"

"I seek only to withdraw to some quiet place, some place where no war will touch." Nagad sighed deeply as he dropped his gaze and traced his battle-scarred hands. "I grow weary of battle."

"*Tzetech leShalom veShuvech leShalom*, go in peace and come in peace. Be at your ease as the sun sets upon your day." Saul's eyes drifted afar, as though longing for something outside his reach.

Nagad's chest grew heavy as he sensed the king's sorrow. "Is there some final service I can do to ease your mind and free my king from this prison?"

"No, nothing can be done for me that I can ask of you. You have served me well and your task is accomplished."

Saul stood and walked over to Nagad, placing a hand upon the old captain's shoulder. "Remember me, my friend." The eyes of the king betrayed the doctrine of doom that ruled his thoughts.

"My king," bowed Nagad.

With a wave of his hand, Saul dismissed Nagad. The captain left the king alone in his chamber.

Unsettled by what he had just witnessed, Nagad's steps were heavy as he limped down the corridor with his head lowered.

"*Shalom uv'racha*, peace and blessing, my dear Captain Nagad."

He lifted his eyes to find Ahinoam drawing near. Weary and worn she appeared. *What has happened here, for so much is altered?*

Ahinoam placed her hands in his and smiled up at him. Yet sorrow dwelt upon her countenance.

"My *G'biyrah*, my queen, how is it with you?"

Ahinoam gazed knowingly at Nagad. "You have seen the king?"

"I have just left his presence. How long has the king been in this state?"

"Since the onset of winter, yet this is not the first he has plunged into agitation and suspicion. He has for years been harassed by periods of depression and anxious thought. Each time he lapses into these unseasonable apathies, it is deeper. I fear one day he will go so far from me that there will be no returning."

Nagad took a step closer to Ahinoam and grasped her hands. "I am saddened by your misfortune. How may I serve my queen?"

"You are very kind, but I fear there is nothing anyone can do. The king is in the hands of Yahweh, if only he would lean on Him."

Shaking her head as though throwing off some ill omen, Ahinoam smiled. "My dear Captain, tell me, why have you come to see the king? I hope all is well with you." She looked upon his wounded and battle-scarred face.

"My *G'biyrah*, I have come to withdraw from active life. I fear I have grown old in the king's service."

"Where will you go?"

"I will go to Ramah, to offer aid to the prophet Samuel. He has been my friend for many years. There, at the Naioth, I will find peace. My wife has waited long for me to return to her. She has been staying with the prophet in my absence. It is time I went to her with no fear of leaving. She deserves some peace before the end." Nagad smiled as he cast his eyes toward the distance, nodding as though affirming the truth he had spoken.

Roused from his thoughts, the captain's visage grew serious. "Yet, if I could be of some service to you, I will stay if you but ask."

"Captain, you have done much for your king and your people. Go and rest from your labors. Tell the prophet all you have seen of your king. May it be that he can intercede in some way."

"What will you do, my *G'biyrah*?"

"I will walk forward from this day. Go now in peace."

Nagad bowed his head and gave her hand a gentle pat, his heart heavy with her burden. Ahinoam watched as the old captain lumbered down the hall, his footsteps echoing off the stone walls.

Taking a deep breath, she opened the door to the king's chamber and peered within. Saul paced the room, his spear ever in his hand as he muttered inaudible maledictions. Ahinoam backed out of the chamber and, taking care not to make a sound, closed the door.

"Come, servant," spoke the queen, "summon David, for I have need of his service once again."

And so David, captain of one thousand, came to the aid of his queen, once more taking up his harp to play before the king. Yet the melodious strains, which in past times had calmed the spirit of the king, yielded no solace, for the harp had lost its charm. Oaths of the past forgotten, love proclaimed overthrown, in his ears a most unnatural strain, the song became as a stone that makes one stumble. Saul gripped his spear tightly, each strum of the harp grating at his mind, a harsh and discordant rasping, galling at his senses as a coarse file drawn across rough wood. In a sudden outburst of ungovernable aberration, Saul cast his spear, seeking to pin David to the wall.

"Saul!" exclaimed Ahinoam as she leapt to her feet.

Saul glared at the empty place where David had been, for in that moment, the shepherd-captain had dodged the spear and slipped away from the king's presence, preserved for a time. With such force did the king hurl the spear that it entered into the wall, the point of which lodged in the stone masonry.

So David, having narrowly escaped death at the hand of the king, fled into the night, a fugitive and outcast.

"Saul!" cried the queen as she grabbed the king's arm. "What have you done?"

Saul flung Ahinoam aside, so that she stumbled and fell. Turning his back on her, Saul growled, unmoved by his wife's tears.

Rising to her feet, Ahinoam admonished the king. "Your jealousy has gotten out of hand. This cannot continue. As a moth goes to the flame, so you go to your own destruction. Can you not see it? You are your own torturer—Saul, David would do anything for you. He would give his life for you, and yet all you see is distorted by your jealousy!"

Saul looked out the open window, his gaze far off as the cold air washed against his impassioned face. "On the contrary, I see everything clearly now. I will not torture myself any longer with the fantasy that David loves me. It is all so clear. I know what must be done."

"What are you thinking? What are you going to do?"

"I have abandoned all remorse, all timidity. This lingering and consumptive ardor that has tortured me, will no longer flail under my restraint, but freely I will engage the passions of my heart. Only then will I be relieved of this madness that plagues me, for David is the cause of this morose spirit."

"You are the maker of your own madness." Ahinoam walked over to the king and rested her hand upon his arm. Reaching up, she stroked his hair, tears still flowing down her pale cheek. "Come back to me, Saul. Let us live as once we did. Do not leave me here without you. I love you. Please, Saul—"

The king turned to face his wife and met her eyes. His own were hard. Startled, Ahinoam took a step back as a chill ran through her.

Saul stepped toward her, his brow furrowed and his eyes dangerous. "*He* has been after my throne since he first appeared in my court. *He* has wormed his way into the hearts of my people, poisoning their loyalty, turning them to his own designs. It will not be long now before he makes his move. Do you not see? None of us is safe. He will not rest until our entire family is destroyed and he sits upon the throne of Israel."

Backing away as Saul walked forward, the two led a trek across the floor. Ahinoam trembled, her knees growing weak under her. "David is your son, your daughter's husband. How can you speak of him this way? You know he loves you like a father. He would never hurt you. He is loyal to you. We are all loyal to you. I love you."

Taking her by the arms, Saul shook her hard. "Be silent, woman! Hold your tongue." Throwing Ahinoam roughly to the ground, the king walked away, trembling, as his wife sat on the ground crying, reaching out to him still.

With cold eyes he glared at her. "So even you, Ahinoam, are against me. You, who hold my heart in your hand." Saul stepped closer to his wife and thrust his clenched fist before her face. "See how you squeeze it in your hands until the blood bursts forth. How can you claim you love on one side, while you betray me on the other?" Saul shook his head as he turned away.

"Saul, do not say such things. You know my love is true. I would do anything for you."

"Even kill my enemy?"

Ahinoam gasped. Crawling over to Saul, she clung to his legs, lifting her gaze to him, her eyes pleading. "You do not mean such a thing! I tell you, he is not your enemy. Saul, we all love you."

"Speak not of love!" Shoving her aside, Saul looked with hard loathing into Ahinoam's eyes. "Leave me. Do not ever come before me again or I shall slay you as you have slain me!"

"Saul, do not say this!" Clutching her chest under the crushing weight, Ahinoam cried, "Your sword has entered my heart!"

Pointing toward the door, Saul spoke coldly. "Go, or your life is forfeit!"

Stricken, Ahinoam knelt unmoving before the king. Seizing her by the back of her robes, Saul thrust her through the door.

"Saul!" she cried, her hand yet pressing into her chest. He glared at her for a moment, then turned and slammed the door.

"My heart—"

Ahinoam's knees gave way. She crumpled to the ground and wept.

CHAPTER 64

BEGUILED

"David, David, wake up."

Opening his eyes, he smiled as he saw the silhouette of his wife leaning over him. He reached up in an attempt to draw her to him, yet she resisted.

"David, I have come to warn you. You must get up."

"What are you saying? Whatever it is, never mind. Come back to bed, my heart."

"David, listen to me." Michal was moving fast, grabbing clothes and staples, shoving them into a goat-skin bag.

"Are you going somewhere?"

"No, you are."

"Where am I going?"

"David, you are not listening to me. You must do as I say. My father's violence has no restraint of conscience to hem him in, but openly he plots against you. He has laid a trap. The king's men will surround the house tonight. The guards have orders to kill you the moment you appear in the morning."

David threw his legs over the side of the bed. "How do you know this?"

"I came upon my father as he and his men were making preparations. At once I understood their intentions. You must flee,

David. You must go, before they surround the house and there is no escape. Quickly, David, get dressed while there is still time."

David rose and walked over to his harried wife. Reaching out to her, he took her arms in his hands and turned her toward him. As his lips pressed against her brow in a gentle kiss, he could feel her body trembling under his touch.

"Michal."

She closed her eyes and took in a deep breath. The sound of David's voice speaking her name still thrilled her heart. Surrendering to his embrace, she stood, allowing him to hold her close.

"Michal. If you help me, you risk your father's wrath. I cannot leave you to face him alone."

"Oh, David, you must. If you do not save your life tonight, tomorrow you will be killed. Do not fear for me. If anything happens to you, my love, then I am done anyway. Please, David, save yourself."

"I will do as you say." David threw on his clothing and took the bag from Michal.

"Here, tie this rope to something sturdy," instructed Michal as she handed David a large cord. "I will lower you down from the window. Sneak out through the garden entrance."

He did as his wife bade him, climbing out the window and clinging to the rope that led to his freedom, as Michal followed close and leaned out after him. Yet before he could descend, he drew himself back toward her, and there, upon the threshold between safety and loss, he kissed her.

"Go," Michal breathed.

He lingered, his eyes fixed upon her.

"David, please, go."

He started down the rope, then climbed back up and took his wife's face in his hand, kissing her, long and fiercely. "I'll come back for you."

"Go."

Smiling, David nodded and descended the rope. From above, Michal watched until her husband's feet touched the ground. She watched as he waved up to her. She watched as he disappeared into the shadows and vanished from her sight. Just as Rahab long ago lowered the spies of Israel from the walls of Jericho[56], so too, Michal let David down from the window of the palace.

As she strained her eyes at the empty garden below, her heart sank. A dreadful foreboding settled over her as though her very life was stole away.

Yet Michal was not done. Turning back to the room, she sprang into action. Taking a household god made in the image of a man, a *teraph*, she laid it in the bed and threw the covers over it. The king's daughter then placed a net of goat's hair upon the idol's head. She stepped aside and looked at her work with a critical eye. In the shadows of the night, it seemed as though a body lay sleeping within the bed. Satisfied, she waited.

Dawn crept into the room as Michal stirred. With a start, her eyes flew open. She must have fallen asleep on the floor, leaning against the bed. Darkness withdrew as the morning advanced. Her heart pounded. Her breath came in short pants. Fear filled her mind as she waited, quietly, until at last she heard the footsteps she had been expecting.

The pounding of a fist against the wooden barrier startled her to her feet. Taking a deep breath, Michal tried to calm herself as she, with hesitant steps, walked to the hinged entrance.

Leaning toward the wooden barrier, Michal called out, "Who is it that calls so early in the morning?"

"Open the door in the name of the king!"

"What do you want?" answered Michal. "It is still early and we are not ready to entertain visitors. Go away. Come back later."

The door reverberated again as the guard beat on the wooden barrier. "Open the door. We have come to bring David to the king for he has been summoned."

Michal opened the door a crack and looked out.

Pushing the door open, the guard entered the room, shoving the king's daughter aside.

Michal grabbed the man's arm and leaned close to his ear, whispering, "Please, David is not well. See how soundly he sleeps." Michal pointed to the image in the bed. "He cannot rise to go to my father today. Tell the king of our regret."

---

[56] Joshua 2:1–15

Looking at the bed, the guard stood still, as though thinking of what to do. The king's man walked toward the bed. With haste, Michal stepped in front of him, her hands upon his chest, holding him back.

"Do not go near him, for it may be that he has some sickness that will pass to you."

The guard stopped short and looked again at the bed. Turning to the man at his side, he gave instruction. "You there, go tell the king that his son-in-law is too ill to come to him."

The man nodded, then strode down the corridor, his footfalls echoing in the distance. The other guards left the room and stood as sentinels before the door. Michal remained beside the bed, her breath held as she watched their movements.

Surely this ruse will not last much longer. I hope it is enough to see David to safety. Her heart ached at the thought of him running for his life. *Where will he go?*

Moments later, the guard returned. "*Sar*, the king has commanded that the man David, being too sick to come on his own, must be brought to the king even upon his bed."

The guards entered the room and lifted David's bed. Michal gasped as the goat skin fell from the idol's head. To the guards' great surprise, it was not David who lay upon the bed, but a *teraphim*.

"What is this!" cried the guard as he turned to Michal. She stood pale and trembling before him. He grabbed her by the arm, his fingers digging into her flesh, and forced her along with them. The sound of rushing feet echoed down the corridor as Michal struggled to get away.

Into the king's chamber they went. Saul looked upon his men sternly, his head cocked to one side. Bowing slightly before the king, the guard shoved Michal at his feet.

"She has deceived you, my king."

Saul looked with scorn at his daughter weeping before him.

"Where is David!" commanded the king as a chill ran down his royal spine.

"He has escaped with the help of this woman," reported the guard. "For she has aided his escape by placing an image upon the bed to beguile us. Now, where David is, we do not know."

Saul grabbed Michal by her hair and lifted her to her feet. "Why have you deceived me like this, and sent my enemy away, so that he has escaped?"

"*Abba*, I had no choice," cried Michal, clinging to her father's hand at the back of her head. "It was you who gave David to me as husband. You knew he was a soldier and a violent man. His sword is sharp. He said to me, 'Let me go! Help me escape for why should I kill you?' So I let him down by the window for I was afraid of him."

Saul growled in his daughter's face. Violently, he thrust her to the floor. Turning to the guards, the king's impassioned voice boomed out his orders, snarling as he spoke. "Seek this David. Search until you find him. Do not venture to come before us again until you bring word of where he is to be found. We shall see who shall beguile whom."

CHAPTER 65

A Safe Haven

Shadows awoke in the moonlight as David passed from the palace grounds through the garden wall. The night air was crisp and cold; his breath came in bursts of steam. In quick haste, he gained the hill. The drumming of his heart filled his ears with the measure of doom. He turned and looked upon the king's fortress. Dark and quiet the palace stood as those safe within its walls slept, content to rest upon their beds. He stood watching, waiting as his thoughts reeled. The dew was heavy upon him, dampening his tunic, and in that moment of uncertainty, he shivered.

It cannot be that I must leave Michal. Surely the king's anger will abate, as always it has. He will quiet as the day awakens. It is how it has often been with the mood of the king. This is no different.

Finding a tree, he sat down upon the sodden earth. Drawing up his legs, David rested his arms upon his knees and waited.

The chill eased as golden beams filtered over the eastern hills. Taking in a deep breath of fresh air, the shepherd-captain smiled upon the growing village of Geba. Many houses and structures had sprung up around the fortress, as trade prospered near the palace grounds. All seemed quiet in that moment ere the people rose from their rest. In the depths of the suspended silence, within that hour just before daybreak, it was as if the dawn held its breath in anticipation of the coming travail.

A man called out, trailed by a press of voices and a host of footfalls. David leapt to his feet, his heart beating wildly. Dogs barked in the wake of soldiers scouring the city below.

"O God! What unrelenting happenings betide! Could it be that the mournful pride, the hostile craft of the king has not dissipated with the coming day? O God! Sheol has looked me in the face!"

Gazing up into the heavens, tears stung the eyes of David as he cried, "Deliver me from my enemies, O my God! Defend me from those who rise up against me. Lift me on high, set me upon a lofty tower, beyond the reach of the adversary. Rescue me from the workers of iniquity, and save me from bloodthirsty men. Awake to help me, and behold! Put forth Your might and look upon me!"[57]

The shepherd-captain turned, glancing over his shoulder at the home he had to leave. The sound of soldiers drew nearer. Swiftly moving, David made haste along his foot track, each step measured by the beat of his heart. Confusion and hurt filled his soul like a crushing blow. Yet, a shadow of hope remained, for often the king's moods have changed with the course of one day.

Soon I will be back home in Michal's arms. For now I will seek the counsel of the prophet.

So west he fled as the sun chased after him until he entered into the land of Ramah, to the place of Samuel the prophet. The lone mount rose upon the grassy field, veiled in the silver-green foliage of gnarled olive trees.

Large wooden doors stood gaping, welcoming the day's visitors into the city. The shadow of the great tower gate loomed over the entrance as people pushed their way through the crowd, bringing with them items to sell and to trade. Upon entering the city of Ramah, David searched for Samuel.

He came upon the market square. Temporary awnings, in a multitude of colors, were set up over carts to shade those selling their wares. People hurried to and fro in a flurry of movement. Children ran in the narrow streets, dodging carts and people, as they yelled in their exhilaration. Engulfed by the throng that ebbed and flowed as they pursued ordinary life within the dust of the streets, David stopped to take in his surroundings. The pleasant aroma of bread and fish and

---

[57] Psalm 59:1–2, 4

honey cakes wafted through the air, stirring the ache of hunger within his belly.

"Have you seen Samuel the prophet?" David called out to a passerby. Ignored, David was not discouraged, but sought after another person. "Where can I find the prophet Samuel?"

Stopping to see who addressed him, the man spoke, "He would be at his Naioth at this time of day, taking his midday meal I suspect."

"Naioth? Where can I find the Naioth?"

"There." The man pointed to the outskirts of the city. "Within the lower level, set aside, you see, beyond those buildings."

"*Todah*, thank you." He patted the man upon his shoulder and gave a grateful nod.

David made his way down the narrow alley toward the lower city. There he found a complex of buildings just as he had been told. The Naioth would offer refuge with its olive trees and springs of water and a cluster of separate dwellings built back to back and side to side. As he approached, a sense of holy reverence descended upon him. This was a sacred place, a place to draw near to God. Here, he would find a safe haven.

Through the gate, he came into the courtyard of the Naioth. The music of the lyre could be heard, coming from some distant recess of the school. In the center of the yard, under a large ash tree, sat Samuel at a table placed in the open air. With him was a gray-haired man. The two sat together in deep conversation over the remains of the afternoon meal. The old friends did not hear David's approach for they hung on each other's words, speaking of some earnest matter. They both looked up in surprise to see the shepherd-captain standing before them.

As Samuel's companion turned his face, David's eyes were opened. Nagad it was who sat there, clad in the robes of a civilian. David fixed his gaze firmly upon him. He had never seen the gray-haired captain out of uniform, and now, seeing him so, he seemed out of place.

Nagad rose, the table shifting slightly beneath his weight. Each looked upon the other. David marked the old captain's weariness. And as Nagad beheld the pale and unsettled face of David, concern swept over him.

"Captain, come, join us," Nagad spoke lightly.

Without a word, David did as Nagad bade. Taking hold a chair, he sat and let out his air.

"Eat, my boy," spoke Samuel as he pushed the dish of boiled eggs toward him. Nagad poured a cup of water and placed it before the shepherd-captain.

David sat there, his eyes upon the eggs. It was true he was hungry, yet at that moment, he had no stomach for eating. The table was arrayed with sundry clay bowls offering figs, green onions, and golden honey cakes. Under normal circumstances, he would have relished such fare. But there was nothing normal about today. As he regarded the food before him, his belly churned.

Sensing David's grief, Samuel asked, "What sorrow do you carry? Tell us, and we will share in this burden."

"I come not for bread nor water, but for truth. My faith needs strengthening, for I fear in this present danger, my soul will grow to waver. Give me words of comfort, Samuel, lest I fall into the shadow of despair."

"What has happened?"

"The king has it in his mind to slay me. For what, I do not know. I have always loved him. I have served him in all that I do."

David spoke of all that had transpired: how Saul, the king, had twice cast his spear at him, and how this very morning he had sent soldiers to David's house to take him. "Yet vain was their watching, for the quarry has been delivered by the daughter of the one who desired blood."

A ragged breath escaped. For the first time in his life, David knew fear. "Samuel." He leaned forward, his hands pressing against the table. "See how they lie in wait for me! Fierce men conspire against me for no offense or sin of mine. Like wild beasts they wait, ready to spring upon their prey!"

David paused. The wound of betrayal struck hard. With his voice low, he continued, looking across the table at the old prophet. "I am guilty of no wrong against the king. I have done nothing to warrant such violent treatment. Unjust suspicions have filled his mind with vengeful lusting. I am innocent; I have not offended Saul. Yet he holds me accountable for some unknown wrong."

A tremor ran down the shepherd-captain's spine. "They came in the night growling like dogs, searching the city, surrounding the house, ready to spring upon me, howling and hungry for their prey. Indeed, they belch out with their mouth; swords are in their lips." David took in a deep breath. "Every word is as a sword, for they fear neither God nor man."[58]

Samuel sat quietly for a time. Then slowly he spoke in a gentle voice, "Has not the Lord already shown you, that you, David, are under His divine protection? He has chosen you for a special service. Yahweh will not forsake you. Have faith that what God promises, He will fulfill."[59]

David looked hard into Samuel's eyes. Concern washed over the young captain's face. "Could it be that Saul has found out that you, Samuel, have anointed me king in his place?"

Nagad gasped, his eyes wide. Samuel had not revealed this detail to him, and the knowledge of this sat heavy upon the old captain.

"I have told no one, so how could he have found out?" continued David.

"What did you say?" questioned Nagad as he found his voice. "Anointed king? Maybe Saul is not too far off the mark!"

"Nay," answered David as he turned his gaze to the gray-haired captain. "I have done nothing to carry this forward. I have not plotted nor schemed to obtain the throne. If Yahweh wishes this, He it will be that must supplant Saul. I will not lay a hand on the anointed of God. I will not be the cause of our king's downfall."

"And yet, as we sit here, that is exactly what has transpired." Nagad looked at David, not with loathing, but pity, for he could sense that he was tormented. What the shepherd-captain spoke, Nagad deemed was true.

The three sat together in silence. Nagad gazed upon David with concern, disappointed that his hero-king had changed so much over the years. This noble son of Benjamin, who had bound a band of fractured tribes into one nation, this thundering bear who saved his men at Jabesh-Gilead, now himself a raving self-seeking tyrant.

How did this happen? He had made such a good start. Now what shall become of Israel? And Nagad regretted his old age, for what strength did he now have to fight for his people? *No, this task is not mine. The burden*

---

[58] Psalm 59
[59] Deuteronomy 7:9

has been passed to David and his generation. I grieve that I cannot go to my grave knowing that I leave behind a better world. It seems that peace never lasts.

"It is so peaceful here. And quiet," spoke David, breaking the silence.

Samuel nodded. "Yes. I think it best for you to remain here at the Naioth for a time. Do not return to your home, David. Here you shall wait for comfort and direction. In safety you shall tarry, for even our king would be ashamed to execute his bloody schemes in my presence."

David shook his head. "It has been long since last you gazed upon the person of our king. He is a man undone. Samuel, I do not think even your presence would hinder his designs."

"Yet, one knows not what may betide, save Yahweh."

CHAPTER 66

PERDITION

Ahinoam looked up at the balcony of the king's chamber, a deep ache pulling at her heart. She could see no sign of Saul. A cold breeze brushed past her face, toying with the wisps of hair that had escaped her dark plaits. Taking the wayward strand, she tucked it behind her ear. The courtyard was empty, save for the two sentinels who guarded the gate. She was alone, forsaken. Gathering her resolve, she turned to leave.

"*Ima.*"

Ahinoam stopped. Jonathan was coming toward her, his mouth pressed thin.

"*Ima*, have you seen David? I have searched, but I cannot find him anywhere."

"David is gone." Ahinoam's face was hard.

Jonathan stared at his mother. He noted her jaw muscles working as she looked past him toward the gate. "I do not understand. What has happened? Why has he left?"

Ahinoam smiled, but there was no joy in it. She turned her gaze upon her son. There was a shadow behind her eyes.

"Your father has sought David's life. Even now, soldiers are seeking to slay him."

Jonathan took a step back, recoiling in disbelief. "I knew he had threatened this, yet he swore to me David had nothing to fear from him. He promised me. I cannot believe that *Abba* could stoop to such cold-hearted violence. Not *Abba*."

"Jonathan, it is as I say, and he has sent me from his presence. I am no longer permitted before the king. There is nothing more I can do to turn away his wrath."

"*Ima*—" Jonathan looked at his mother. "*Ima*, I—"

Jonathan's face fell; a tear ran down his cheek.

"My dear son." Ahinoam raised her hand to his face and cradled it as she cocked her head and smiled. "Life is full of sorrow—and joy. If you deny it, you will only be haunted the more. I am going home." Removing her hand from his cheek, she gathered her robes and turned to leave.

"You—you are leaving? But *Ima*—"

"I cannot stay here and watch this unfold any longer. Jonathan, it is over."

"*Ima*—"

"Your father loves you, Jonathan. Do not forget that."

Ziba, the family servant, met her outside the gate. In his hands were the queen's personal belongings. "My *G'biyrah*." His voice was sober as he bowed his head.

She gave a gentle nod.

The two traveled toward Gibeah and the home that held so many happy memories. Long it had been since last she saw the house where Saul, her husband, brought her; endless time since last she felt the joyful bliss of love fulfilled in bonded union. Now she meant to end her days in lonely solitude; no husband to fill the ebbing days of her life. The plans made in hopeful youth, now dissolved into disappointment.

Ahinoam's eldest son watched as she faded into the horizon. Then, she was gone. Jonathan was left standing before the fortress gate, alone with a fire burning within him. His breath became ragged as his anger ignited into a savage rage. Clamping hard his jaw, the prince wheeled from the gate and rushed through the courtyard. He stormed into the palace, up a flight of stairs, and down the hallway. With each step, the inferno grew, heating his heart with rebellion.

He flung open the door to the king's chamber and burst in, ready to do battle. He stopped cold in his tracks. Before him stood the king with a small detachment of soldiers. Jonathan knew these men. These were not weak nor faint-hearted men, but the best in Saul's service. Stalwart soldiers, full of strength and courage. As the king and his armed men turned to see who entered so abruptly, Jonathan's own courage failed him. He stood there dumbfounded, the flame of indignation smothered by confrontation.

The silent stalemate continued until Doeg entered the room. He paused at the sight of the king and his soldiers facing the crown prince. Coming to himself, the Edomite crossed over to the king and spoke for all to hear.

"My king, take note, David is at the Naioth in Ramah!"

Saul left off gazing at his son. His spirit rose to elation as he took in the news. "Harrumph! That does not surprise me! Two conspirators under the same roof!" Saul placed his hands upon his hips as he lifted his chin. "This is good news indeed."

Facing his men, the king gave command. "Go to Ramah and collect this son of perdition! Bring him to me. Do not allow anyone to restrain you from this task!"

"As you wish, my king, so it shall be done." Bowing, the company of men left the presence of their king.

Jonathan stood gaping. Saul looked at his son with an air of satisfaction.

"Well," spoke the king. "What has brought you to enter my chamber so boldly?"

"*Abba*—" But a stranger stood before him.

Shaking his head, Saul dismissed his son with the wave of a hand. "I have no time for your games. Leave me."

Saul turned away smiling. "My snare is nearly sprung."

CHAPTER 67

REFUGE

The crisp air filtered in through the lattice-framed window as David looked from his chamber into the courtyard. The garden slept sullen in its hibernal season, mirroring the malignant wretchedness of his mind: of lifeless being and shadowed images of barren days, brief and dark, that concealed the blissful memories of spring. He was kindred to the somber yard; his thoughts brooding upon the oppressive vapors harbored in his soul. With helpless striving, his meager faith struggled to issue forth in unabated strength.

Yet in the bleak of winter's gray, the sky burst forth in vibrant azure rays. The atmosphere arrayed so clear that nature showed halcyon and pure, unstained by the seasons that lay behind; reset and rinsed clean by the winter rains, a canopy devoid of color, awaiting the artist to take brush to canvas, raising a spectrum of vivid hues, painting the earth anew.

And though the garden was open to the lucent sky, a half-wall marked the confines of the yard, a barrier that circumscribed the edge of the cloistered grounds. Rising beyond the stone barrier, cracked and faded, the wooden beams of a grape arbor endured. The vine was bare, the wood twisted and weathered, and heavily pruned in preparation of the coming spring.

Likewise, the ash tree, which resided in the center of the yard, stood unadorned against the winter chill, its gnarled roots reaching into the diamond-ridged trunk. The durable, straight-grained hardwood was encased in a mantle of silver-gray, the color so like the remains of a hearth-fire. Carried by the upward curve to the shoot, the bony skeleton of the leafless branches stretched out toward sunlit skies. The fingered limbs were dotted with black winter buds, the sooty offshoots arranged in opposite pairs, the promise of returning green.

Little shade was offered under the old ash tree, yet here Samuel stood as sunlight wove through the empty branches. Each ray filtered and reflected, an interplay between light and shadow that diffused in a radial pattern across the prophet's robes. Within this curtain of light, Samuel directed his pupils in lifting up songs of praise to Yahweh. Melodic voices rose and fell on a wave of acclamation, filling the body and soul with jubilant exaltation.

David's heart stirred within him as he listened through his chamber window. He turned away and looked into the room. The cell was sparsely furnished. A simple bed of sound construction, a network of cords stretched across a wooden frame upon which a mattress rested, sat in the corner of the room. Next to the cot resided a small square table bearing a single lamp. The limestone block walls were bare, save the small lattice window that opened onto the garden.

The voices of the students filtered clearly into the room, echoing off the chamber walls. It was too much to be contained. David dropped to his knees beside his bed, groaning under the weight of his despair.

"Deliver me from my enemies, O my God," cried the shepherd-captain. "Defend me from those who rise up against me. O save me from these bloodthirsty men." David lifted his face toward heaven as he rested there upon his knees. "For look, they lie in wait for my life; the mighty gather against me, not for my transgression nor for my sin, O Lord. They run and prepare themselves; they come for me, but what have I done?"

In anguish David pleaded, "Awake to help me, and see! Stay the hand of the one who seeks my life. You therefore, O Lord God of all the hosts of heaven, the God of Israel, awake to punish; do not be merciful to treacherous men."

David sighed a ragged breath as he looked down at his hands. He bore several scars from his last battle, wounds that had healed over. These scars he knew he would carry for the remainder of his life, for one can never be the same after overcoming trials. All things change, are shaped by what is suffered. David ran his thumb over the length of the longest scar. His face crumpled in distress.

"With swords they come for me. But You, O Lord, shall laugh at them; I will wait for You, my Strength, for You, O God, are my defense. Without fear I shall face my enemy. Though I am buffeted all day long, I will trust in You, O God. Not alone shall I confront my adversary, but You, O Lord, shall be with me. For I have tried You and found You to be a faithful protector. My path You shall clear. My God of mercy shall come to meet me; God shall let me see my desire on my enemies. Hinder all they do. Disappoint their counsels. Send them with shame upon their heads, exposing them to ridicule."

David knelt in silence, thinking upon his words. Taking a deep breath, he took up the thread again. "Yet, do not whet Your glittering sword, nor with Your hand slay them, lest Your people forget. Do not kill, but scatter them by Your power, O Lord, my shield. In the peak of their power, bring my enemy low with the words of pride still fresh upon their lips. Consume them in wrath, consume them. Frustrate their plans, bring them to naught, and let them know that God rules in Israel, even to the ends of the earth."

He heard the sound of several footfalls and the unmistakable ring of armor. His heart's pace quickened. Springing from the floor, David hurried to the window. His breath drew up short. Soldiers were advancing toward Samuel.

What do they intend? The prophet—is he in danger? "They are here," whispered David, "growling like dogs, wandering up and down for food. O how they howl when not satisfied!"

Yet as David looked on from the shadow of his chamber, he noted that Samuel did not react to the approaching soldiers. He continued leading his students in songs of praise, undeterred by the presence of Saul's men.

"But who are these men who mean to ambush me? And who is their master who seeks my life? For my God walks beside me. What power then do my enemies have?"

The pupils and the prophet lifted their voices, drowning out all thought, the chorus soaring toward heaven proclaiming Yahweh as a vanguard of the soul. The music spilled over and diffused within the courtyard, infusing the garden with a sense of the sacred, as though the very presence of God filled the yard. And the enemy could not stand. David watched in amazement as the men fell down worshiping, undone by the Spirit of God. The soldiers laid down their arms as the euphoric release overcame them. They began to prophesy with Samuel and his students, as though they were one of the prophets.

David gasped, elated; he too was overcome. His soul could not contain the liberty of unfettered grace. And he sung out praise to his Shield and Strength, "But I will sing of Your power; yes, I will sing aloud of Your mercy in the morning; for You have been my defense and refuge in the day of my trouble. To You, O my Strength, I will sing praises; for God is my defense, my God of mercy."[60]

---

[60] Psalm 59

CHAPTER 68

By the Hand of the King

"What?" bellowed Saul.

"It is as I told you, my king," spoke the attendant with trepidation. "When the detachment of soldiers saw the band of prophets prophesying, and Samuel standing as leader over them, the Spirit of Yahweh came upon the men and they became as one of the prophets."

Saul sat upon his throne, shaking his head. "How is this possible? What power does the old prophet hold, that my men should be so easily disarmed?"

"These men were weak in spirit, my king." Doeg's voice slid low. "Though they proved strong in battle, their hearts were not fashioned for matters of prophets and kings."

"Will this thorn ever be taken from my side?" Saul exclaimed. "How is it that so much distress should be wrought by one man?"

The king looked across the throne room into the vacant air. He did not move or speak. Those present grew anxious as the moment stretched, fearing the mind of Saul had broken.

"Send another detachment." The king's words echoed off the stone walls, startling the attendant as his voice ruptured the silence. "Tell them to be wary of the old prophet so that they, too, shall not fall under his spell."

The attendant bowed. "It shall be as you have spoken, my king."

Doeg smiled as he glared down his nose at the king.

Twice more word reached the king that yet again his men had succumbed to the Spirit of Yahweh. Three times he sent detachments of soldiers, and three times the men were lost in the euphoric dispensation of praise, casting down their weapons and becoming as one of the prophets.

"My king, they had no power to contend with God, but were struck down by His mighty presence. There is no one who can overcome the effects of the prophet's sacred acts, no one who is capable of discharging their commission. David, my king, is out of reach."

Saul's face flushed in anger; his body trembled with seething fury. The king sprang to his feet, his eyes raging and nostrils flaring as a beast let loose from a cage. He railed in anguish as foul oaths vented from his mouth. The attendant took a step back. Saul shuddered. He released a long breath. The furrowed lines of vexation smoothed from his face. The change was audible. A sudden hush fell over the room as when a violent tempest is extinguished.

Saul looked evenly at the attendant, his eyes hard. "I will go myself. By my own hand, David shall fall."

The king stood fixed before his throne. "Yes, it is better this way," Saul mumbled softly. "It is better that I should be the one." The king smiled, yet no mirth touched his face. It was not the look of a sane man, but of a vexed spirit cloaked in an eerie calm.

CHAPTER 69

MANTLE OF THE KING

Accompanied by ten personal guards, the king had abandoned his throne for a time, leaving behind the citadel, and the safety of those stone walls. Outside, the world was dormant, waiting in slumbering expectation. A frosty mantle covered the otherwise bleak landscape, coating the earth with a thin crystalline sheen. The ground crunched under their feet. The air was cold; breath came in puffs of steam. Saul wrapped his cloak tightly around himself.

As the sun rose, it warmed the king's back. He shivered as a biting breeze ruffled through his robes, nipping at his face. He drew his cloak in tighter. The road to Ramah was familiar. He followed the unbroken ridge through the hills of Ephraim. The vast landscape stretched before him, boulders embedded within the barren hills, thickets of bare bark reaching up to cloud-draped skies.

The wandering king's heart stirred. Saul remembered the time before he was king, when he had ventured along this road searching for lost donkeys. It was at Ramah that he had first met Samuel. He had loved the prophet like a father. Now the thought of him brought rancor to his soul.

"I wish I had never met the old prophet. He should have left me alone," Saul mumbled under his breath. "I was happy."

His mind traveled the distant hills to his home in Gibeah, and to his fertile fields of golden grain. He longed to stand upon his hill, to look out across his land, to feel the breeze caress his face. The king let out a long steamy breath.

It was a lifetime ago. So much has changed, so much lost.

Then his thoughts reached Ahinoam, and the life they had shared. He saw her face, felt her warmth. His heart ached with the weight of memory.

Now everyone he loved had turned against him. He shivered and his heart hardened. Drawing his hand through his hair, Saul pushed the memory aside.

I am king. No one can stand against me. David has ruined everything. The shepherd-captain will pay.

When Saul came to himself, he found he was at Sechu. There was a great cistern where the people gathered, for it was the time of day the inhabitants of the land came to water their flocks. Many convened, talking jovially to one another, sharing the local gossip. They were just ordinary people living their lives without concern for the matters of the kingdom. That was the burden of the king, not theirs. Saul envied them their simple lives.

As he and his bodyguards walked toward the well, the civilians parted, making a path for the king. Many bowed as a hushed murmur ran through the crowd.

"My king." A man knelt before his sovereign.

Saul regarded this shepherd as loathing rose in his mind. *David.* But this shepherd was not the lowly dog he sought.

The king stood proud before the people. Lifting his chin, he looked down his nose at them.

"Where are Samuel and David?" spoke the king in a loud voice. "Can they yet be found at Ramah?"

The shepherd answered with confidence, "Indeed, they are at the Naioth in Ramah, even now as we speak, my king."

Saul smiled. "Very well." He narrowed his eyes as he turned his face west. "Soon, David, very soon."

The royal retinue rejoined the road as the citizens of Sechu watched in wonder. Rumors of his passing filtered through the town while questions arose as to why the king had ventured from his citadel. Little could the people imagine the purpose of this grand excursion, or the malevolent intent within their sovereign's heart.

Just beyond the horizon, the rise of Ramah soon came into view. As a chalky limestone sea, the land flowed in undulating waves. Overhead, the sun centered in the clear sky. The day had warmed to a more comfortable clime. No longer shivering, the king let his mantle hang loosely about him. The crystal coating had all but faded, leaving the damp earth exposed. Weariness settled on Saul as the road sloped in an upward grade.

On either side of the path, fields lay brown and empty. The silvery-green of olive trees added color to the muted countryside. Fused at the base of the thick leathery leaves, clusters of nubby buds reached out with the promise of a fruitful crop.

Turning south, the royal procession veered toward the village, which resided upon the height of a limestone hill. Stone cisterns dotted the landscape, glimmering pools that pierced the stark swells of barren earth, embellishing the countryside with dazzling jewels. Saul recalled the well where he had paused to inquire about the seer, and in his mind, he cursed the maidens who had made known where the prophet was to be found.

As the king and his men drew near the walls of the village, melodic strains reached their ears. It seemed to be arising from the lower city. Saul felt drawn to a cluster of buildings just beyond the city gates.

The Naioth, thought Saul.

The company approached the school of instruction. With each step, the music grew louder. Something stirred in Saul's breast, as though the love of his youth had entered into his presence. Etched in the air, the pure intonation of the students transfigured the atmosphere in unbroken goodness. The mystery of creation unfolded upon the blending harmonies, as one voice in sweet accord rose toward the heavens.

Saul gasped, drawing deep the manifold richness of the song.

Calm transcended. The king walked as in a trance through the gate and into the courtyard of the Naioth. There the prophet stood, standing before his pupils. Saul looked upon Samuel. He had aged since last the king had seen him. His hair was no longer ash, but white as snow. And though Saul loathed the prophet, it saddened him to see how Samuel had grown old.

Samuel beheld the king, but did not halt the mounting notes of worship. The prophet smiled at him, as though he was pleased to see a friend long absent.

Saul was disconcerted. He had not expected so fair a welcome. He stood transfixed as the music reached out and caressed him. Encapsulated, circumscribed, the euphonic waves encircled him as though he converged with the measured song, bodily contained within the folds of melodic rhapsody. The intonation came forth as though the very stones cried out praises to the King of kings: sound beyond time, marked through the ages.

At first there was pain, a sensuous searing of the soul as though his very Being was torn from him. Then, quiet peace settled within his mind. His thoughts calmed and became clear. He was Saul again, not the doomed and ruthless king, just Saul.

But the music was not yet finished. Deeper it penetrated, piercing beyond the seat of understanding. The voice of God spoke, as though saying, "Saul, I am with you more than you know. Turn to Me and I will hold you, heal you. Only let go of the past, let go of your haughty spirit, and come back to Me."

The breath of Yahweh was upon his face. He could not breathe. The world tilted around him. All that had happened, all his fear just melted away in the presence of the Holy One. And he was undone, unmade before God. Tears flowed from his eyes. His clothes were stifling, the atmosphere so close that he could not take in air.

He unclasped his cloak and let his royal robe fall from his shoulders. Then he fell down upon his face, lying within the crumpled folds of the kingly mantle. Dethroned before the great *I AM*, Saul became as one of the prophets.

All day and all night, he lay there humbled, worshiping Yahweh.

As the night gave way to the morning light, Saul stirred. He was aware that Samuel stood before him. Rising to his knees, the king bowed his head, unable to look upon the prophet. Samuel placed his hand upon the king's shoulders as he once was wont to do. Saul lifted his face, tears tracing the ruin of his pride.

Samuel's kind eyes reached into Saul's soul. "My son, this is how the Lord could work within you at all times, if you would but let Him, if you were but humble and willing. Let it go, Saul, for glorifying God leaves no room for pride. Come back to God and be the man you were meant to be."

CHAPTER 70

MISHPACHAH

Sealed in his chamber, David sat upon his cot with his back resting against the wall. Mindlessly, he strummed his lyre, the strings singing in harmonic chords. Divided by the lattice slats that covered the window, ribbons of light filtered in across the bed. His thoughts ran deep. Seeing Saul in the court of the Naioth had shaken him. And though he was safe for now, David wondered how long it would be before the king came back for him.

He sighed. The hollow ache in his heart deepened. The knife of separation plunged far into the fathomless reaches of his Being. It had been many weeks since he had seen Michal, and the absence of her made each moment an eternity. The walls pressed in upon him. He was a prisoner and his room a prison cell.

Thrusting his lyre aside, David sat upright and threw his legs over the side of the cot. "I cannot just sit here waiting to be arrested."

His mind was settled. Heedless of the consequences, he was going home. After saying his goodbyes, David left the sanctuary of the Naioth and the counsel of the prophet, and began his journey back to Geba. Samuel was not sure of the wisdom in young David's choice, but did not endeavor to dissuade him from his determined enterprise. It had been a week since the incident with Saul, and no further attempts had been made to take him.

Maybe the king's heart has softened. Well, there is but one way to find out. I must seek the answer.

Upon reaching Geba, David hid behind a boulder that rested on a hill just within view of the citadel. His heart pumped wildly in his chest. For a time he stood watching, hunched down so that he was barely visible. There was not much activity coming and going from the fortress gate. David continued to wait. Then, finally, he saw the one he sought coming through the portal of the citadel. Jonathan walked the path that led up the hill, which would take him past the place David hid.

David's heart quickened. *What if Jonathan is in league with his father? After all, he had not warned me of the king's intentions. This may be a bad decision, but I have to know.*

As Jonathan drew near, David took his chance, risking all for the sake of his heart. Stepping from the shelter of the rock, David called, "Jonathan."

The king's son glanced about, and as he saw David, his face lit up in a smile. "David, where have you been?"

"In hiding."

"In hiding?" repeated Jonathan. His expression melted into confusion. "Father came back saying all had been forgiven. His anger has left him, David. It is time for you to come home."

"I wish it were so. He may have been deterred for a time, but I do not believe it will last." David looked down at his hands as though examining some mar. "Jonathan, I do want to come home." His voice broke; his gaze remained fixed upon his hands. Unsure of where Jonathan's loyalties lay, he took a deep breath and met Jonathan's eyes. "Tell me, what have I done? What is my iniquity, and what is my sin before your father, that he seeks my life?"

Jonathan's brow furrowed as he shook his head. "By no means! You shall not die! There is nothing to your account." Smiling, he reached out and placed his hand upon David's arm. "After all that has happened at Ramah, my father will not persist in his malicious intent toward you. David, the king tells me all that is in his heart. Whether great or small, my father tells me all. Nothing is hidden from me. The wrath he felt toward you sprung from the spirit of despair that has plagued him. Since the Naioth, his mind has been returned to him. There is nothing left to fear."

David made no reply. Chewing the inside of his cheek, he stood looking off toward the citadel, unsure of what to believe.

"Why should my father hide this thing from me? It is not so!"

Narrowing his eyes, David turned his gaze to the king's son. "I am sorry, Jonathan. I know you want this to be true. The Lord knows, I desire this, but sane or insane, I am convinced the king is determined to slay me."

"You are wrong, David. I promise you."

"Jonathan, your father certainly knows of our friendship. How can you be sure he would tell you anything regarding me? I swear to you, as the Lord lives, and as your soul lives, there is but a step between me and death!"

"Whatever you desire of me, I will do it."

"I have a plan. Tomorrow is the festival of the New Moon, and as son-in-law to the king, I should not fail to sit with him to eat. Only let me go, that I may hide in the field until the evening of the third day. If your father misses me at all, then say, 'David earnestly asked permission of me that he might go to Bethlehem, his city, for there *mishpachah*, the yearly sacrifice, is being held for all the family.' And in this way, we can try the motives of the king. For if he gives his blessing, then his heart is good and I can come home. But if he goes into a rage, we will know that his intent is to harm me."

David clasped Jonathan's shoulder. "Remember our covenant, one to another, and deal kindly toward me, for we have taken an oath before the Lord. Yet, if you find some treason within me, if you believe I have been unfaithful or untrue to the king, then do not take me to your father." David held out a knife, hilt first, toward the prince. "But kill me yourself."

Jonathan gaped. Brushing the knife aside, he took a step back. "Do you doubt my fealty? Far be it from you! I could not bring harm upon you. There is no breach. Our oath holds true. If I were certain of any evil scheme determined by my father against your person, would I not tell you?"

David returned the knife to his belt.

"I do not doubt you, Jonathan. It is only that so much has happened, and you, being the king's son, and the crown prince—I know you are caught in the middle, pressed on both sides for loyalty. I am sorry you must bear this burden. Now, tell me, who will inform me of the king's reaction? What if your father answers you roughly?"

"Come, let us go out into the field," suggested Jonathan. "We are too visible here."

Into the green waves of winter barley they went. Though first of the crops to harvest in the spring, the striking awns had not yet emerged, leaving the barley spears uncrowned. But the field was out of the main thoroughfare and here the two conspirators would be less exposed. Midway into the flowing grain, Jonathan halted and faced David.

"By the Lord God of Israel, I swear to you, that by this time the day after tomorrow, I will sound out my father and send word to you regarding his intentions. If he has a mind of evil toward you, I will report it to you and send you away, that you may go in safety. And the Lord be with you as He has been with my father."

With both hands upon David's shoulders, Jonathan looked down at the ground between them. He sighed deeply. The son of Saul tightened his grasp on the shepherd-captain. When Jonathan raised his gaze to meet David's, there were tears welling in the prince's eyes. "I ask one thing of you, only show me the kindness of the Lord while yet I live, that I may not die. Remember me when you come to the throne and do not cut off your charity from my house forever, no not even when the Lord has struck every one of the enemies of David from the face of the earth."

"It is as you desire." David's voice was solemn. "I vow that no harm will come to your house as long as I have power to see it so."

Jonathan smiled weakly and nodded as he let go of David. "Tomorrow is the New Moon; and you will be missed, because your seat will be empty."

David returned the smile. He doubted little that Saul would note his vacant chair.

"This is how it will be," continued Jonathan, "hide somewhere until the third day. The day after tomorrow, toward evening, go to the place where you hid when this trouble began, and wait by the stone of Ezel. Stay out of sight. There I will meet you. I will shoot three arrows to the side, as though I were shooting at a target. Then I will send a lad, saying, 'Go, fetch the arrows and bring them back.'

"Now if I say that the arrows are on this side of you," Jonathan gestured with his hand, indicating the place before David. "Get them yourself and come, for this will mean there is safety for you and no harm will come against you. But if I say to the lad, 'Look, the arrows are beyond you,'" again, Jonathan motioned with his arm, indicating a place behind David. "Flee for your life, for evil is intended toward you. And as for the matter of which you and I have spoken, indeed the Lord be between you and me forever."

CHAPTER 71

THE NEW MOON

The moon in silhouette hung in the dark sky, cradled by the first sun-kissed sliver that touched the outward senses. Her beauty reached out in muted display, beckoning the onlooker to welcome the arrival of the new month. The celebration was a joy-filled festival. The appearance of the burgeoning evening light was greeted with the sounding of trumpets. Burnt offerings and a sin offering were presented to Yahweh to call forth blessing for the coming lunar interval.

And so sat the king at feast in his usual place of honor upon his couch, which resided in the left-hand corner of the upper room. Jonathan was on Saul's left, pinned in, as it were, between his father and the wall. As the evening breeze caused the curtains of the balcony to flutter, the crown prince noted the spear resting against the wall behind the king's seat. Jonathan grew uneasy as he eyed the weapon.

When Abner entered the room, he saw his chance. As the general presented himself to the king, Jonathan stood and beckoned him to take his seat next to the king, feigning honor to his elder. Abner tipped his head to the crown prince, smiling as he took his place against the wall. Jonathan then sat across from his father. Here he was unrestricted by the confines of the wall and could better observe the king's face.

Jonathan watched his father's every move, hoping to find some insight into the king's mind. Saul ate his meal with vigor as he laughed at something Abner said. Standing by the door, Doeg, Saul's attendant, guarded the exit.

This Edomite was always in the king's presence. Once the king's chief herdsman, Doeg had risen to Saul's most trusted advisor.

Jonathan eyed him with loathing. Often he had seen this man whispering into his father's ear, giving counsel to the king. *Why does Abba listen to this man? What wisdom does he possess? What craft to beguile? Would that he were struck from the king's side.*

Saul's gaze fell upon the couch to his right: David's vacant seat. Jonathan held his breath as Saul's eyes lingered on the forsaken couch. No change affected the king's expression, yet he looked long at the empty seat as though working through some thought.

Then, when Jonathan could take no more, Saul turned his attention back to the feast. The king said nothing; he took no action. David's absence was left unaddressed.

Jonathan pondered the meaning. *Maybe the king thinks David has been defiled and could not come to the feast, being unclean.*

He sighed in relief.

The evening progressed without incident and Jonathan's mind was encouraged that he had believed correctly. *David will be able to come home and all will be as it was.* Jonathan's mood lightened. He smiled as he partook of the feast with his family.

The next evening began much as it had the previous night. Everyone took their seats. This time Jonathan procured the place across from his father as soon as he entered the room so that each person was positioned exactly as before. Again, Jonathan eyed his father, watching his expression for any sign of agitation. It was not long before the king's gaze fell upon David's vacant couch. And as the peace offering was placed before the participants, Saul grew restless.

He turned toward his son and asked, "Why has the son of Jesse not come to eat, either yesterday or today?" Saul's words sounded indifferent, as though his question was a passing curiosity.

Jonathan smiled at his father, his voice calm despite the disquiet in his soul. "David earnestly requested liberty to go to Bethlehem. It seems his family has a sacrifice in the city, and his brother has commanded him to be there. He asked if he had found favor in my eyes, would I please let him get away and see his brothers. I granted his petition. Therefore, he has not come to the king's table."

The air grew still. The room was silent. Saul sprang to his feet. With violent waves of pent-up passion, the king's anger burst forth in a savage tempest of rage against Jonathan. His voice roared as a mighty storm, "You son of a perverse, rebellious woman! Always you resist my will! Do I not know that you have chosen the son of Jesse to your own shame and to the shame of the mother who bore you? You are a fool to be so benevolent to the one who would supplant you! For as long as the son of Jesse lives on the earth, you shall not be established, nor shall your kingdom. Now therefore, send some men and bring him to me, for he shall surely die!"

"Why should he be killed? What has he done?" pleaded Jonathan.

Saul trembled. His face reddened. Reaching behind, he took hold his spear and cast it at his own son to slay him. The king's aim was not true. The spear fell to the ground with a clank against the stone floor.

In fierce anger, Jonathan rose to his feet. As he did so, he bumped into the table overturning several bowls of wine. A crimson tide bled across the board. Forsaking the feast and the astonished guests, Jonathan stormed from the chamber.

There was no longer any question. The king would have David's life.

CHAPTER 72

THE MORNING OF THE THIRD DAY

Jonathan's heart was heavy at the breaking of the day. No food had he taken since his father's wrath had broken forth. Deep sorrow seethed through his soul as he went into the field at the appointed time. He brought with him a little lad, innocent and without need of explanation. For the task at hand was of great importance, a secret tending toward treason. There had been so much promise, such hope when his father had become king. He remembered walking beside his father behind the old ox cart and the conversation they had had about kingship.

"What is it to be a king?" I had asked. And what had Abba answered?

"A king must be honest and just. A good heart is not enough. A king must be wise and know his people, his land, and the needs of all his subjects. He must know evil and yet not yield to it."

Jonathan peered across the field at the stone of Ezel. He knew David was hiding just beyond it. Sighing, Jonathan mumbled to himself, "To know evil and yet not yield to it. How did it come to this?"

"*Sar?*"

Jonathan shook his head. "It is nothing." He looked down at the lad. "Now remember what I told you, run and find the arrows as I shoot."

The boy nodded, his frame eager to take flight.

Raising the bow, the prince took aim. The lad sprang forward. An arrow flew straight beyond the boy's path. Marking its descent,

Jonathan dispatched two more in quick succession. He called out in a loud voice, "Is not the arrow beyond you?"

Swift of foot, the youth found the arrows, one after another. Jonathan cried out after the lad, "Make haste, hurry; do not delay!"

The boy gathered the arrows and ran back to his master. "Here they are, *Sar*."

But the king's anxious son did not take hold the arrows, but gave his bow and quiver to the lad. "Go, take these to the citadel."

With a nod, the boy did as he was bade.

Jonathan watched until the youth was out of sight, then turned toward the field.

From behind the stone of Ezel, David had seen all. It had been a small matter, the flight of an arrow, but it told everything. His entire life had changed in a single moment. David would no longer be welcome to live in the palace. He could no longer be captain of his men. He could not return to his wife. He was now a fugitive, exiled, fleeing an angry king whose jealous mind was bent upon his destruction.

As soon as the lad was gone, David arose from his hiding place. He felt weak as he walked toward Jonathan, who stood pale and stone-faced among the swaying stalks of barley.

David fell on his face before the king's son, bowing three times to the crown prince of Israel. Jonathan reached down and lifted him to his feet. Together, they embraced, weeping as they clung to each other. Jonathan moved to separate from David, fearing lest they linger too long. But David would not let go. He was broken, an outcast, driven from all he knew, from all he loved, and he loathed the parting.

Jonathan took hold of David's arms and pushed him away. He looked into his friend's blue eyes, glazed with tears, and said, "Please, David, go in peace. Do not fear. The Lord will not forsake you. It may all work out in the end. But for now, you cannot linger here overlong. Soon I will be missed and I stand not well with my father at present. They will seek me in their attempt to find you. You must make haste away from this place, and do not return until some sign comes to you. My father is beyond reason. There is nothing I can do to alter his will against you."

David closed his eyes, anguish written upon his face. He had no voice to speak.

"Go, go in peace, David. Remember, we have sworn an oath. That oath still holds. The Lord is our witness between you and me, and between our descendants, forever."

"You risk much for me." David shook his head as he held onto Jonathan's arms. "I have never understood. Why do you hold to me when it is your throne that is in question? I am he who stands in your way."

"I know that I will never be king as my father wishes. That fate has been lost to me. It is you who shall be the next king. Be a good king. Remember me. Do not forget."

"Come with me. Stand by my side." David fixed his gaze upon Jonathan as he grasped his arms.

"He is my father." Jonathan laid his hand upon David's shoulder, and took a step back, breaking their connection. "I cannot leave him if there is any chance for his redemption. I must stand by him. There may still be hope though it fades quickly."

David nodded and spoke his final words. "Thank you for all you have done, my brother. May it be that God will see fit for us to meet again. I will never forget you nor our covenant."

David grasped Jonathan's arms, then let go, and walked away. Jonathan went back to the fortress. Yet when he had gone, David turned and followed Jonathan's path back toward the citadel.

"There is one thing I must do before I leave."

From a ridge that overlooked the window of Michal's chamber, David watched. It had been risky, but he could not leave without making contact with his wife. He waited for what seemed a long time, but finally he spied her coming to the window. She was lovely as she peered out across the garden court, and his heart longed to go to her.

After a time, her gaze fell to the windowsill. There she noticed a small blue flax flower resting upon the ledge. Amazed, she picked it up and lifted it to her mouth. Her lips brushed against the pale petals.

The hairs on the back of her neck rose as she felt David's eyes upon her. Looking up, she scanned the distant hills for a sign of him, but he was gone.

CHAPTER 73

THE NATURE OF JEALOUS MALICE

Inside the fortress, all was in turmoil. Men hurried about grabbing equipment and taking hold of arms. Fear gripped Jonathan's heart. He backed into the shadows so as not to be seen, following the outer wall until he reached the entrance to the citadel. The stone masonry was cool against his body as he slunk through the hallways that led to the king's chamber. The door was ajar. He pressed himself flat against the wall as he peered into the room. Soldiers hastily strapped on armor and weapons. Then Jonathan saw his father standing in the midst of his men. He too was donning armor. As he slid his sword into its scabbard, Saul had a look of thirst in his eyes. Jonathan had seen that look before, and he knew David was in grave danger.

"Abner," bellowed Saul, "take your men west. Jishui, you go north, and Malchishua take your men east."

Jonathan's heart paused as he saw his brothers taking part in this madness. He alone remained faithful to David.

"I," continued Saul, "I will head south. Together we shall hunt this dog down. He cannot escape us for we are many." The king stood proud, his hand upon the hilt of his sheathed sword as he smiled with satisfaction.

Jonathan felt sick.

"When one of you finds David, come and report to me. It shall be my hand that ends his life."

Jonathan could not believe what he was hearing. His breath drew up short; sweat formed on his brow. The sound of his pounding heart was so loud he feared he would be discovered. He had to leave. *If the king's men find me—I need to keep away, to give David enough time to escape before my father's men get hold of me. Through me, they could find David.*

Jonathan backed out of the doorway and stole down the hall. Staying in the shadows as much as possible, he made his way through the web of harried men. No one noticed him as he rushed past the frenzied activity within the court. With ease, he passed beyond the gatehouse and entered upon the road. He hurried west until the fortress was lost to his sight. His only thought was to get to Ramah. There he would seek the counsel of the prophet. *I have nowhere else to turn, for who can I trust but the old seer?*

West he trekked along the Ridge Road, the same path David had taken just weeks before.

Jonathan's mind had a single purpose: get Samuel to stop Saul. *If anyone can get through to my father, it is the old prophet.* But doubt plagued his thoughts. Was it too late? Was Saul so far down his path that he was beyond reaching?

Soon, Jonathan found himself standing outside the Naioth. He had no recollection of how he had gotten there. He had been so fixed on the trouble at hand that he had lost all perception of place and time. But he was here, so he entered through the little gate. There the aged prophet sat at a table under the ash tree, looking at a scroll that was stretched out before him. Jonathan could see his lips moving, but no words were spoken. He was afraid his approach would startle the old man, so he lingered for a bit, wondering what he should do.

"Come, sit beside me. You have come to seek advice regarding your father, have you not?" Samuel spoke without looking up, but motioned Jonathan to an empty chair.

"But how—"

As Jonathan settled himself in his seat, Samuel rolled the scroll and pushed it away from him. "I have been sitting here waiting for you, my son. It is a lovely day, is it not?" Samuel gazed at the sky, a gentle smile upon his face.

"I do not understand. You have been waiting for me? But how could you—"

"My son, I see many things."

Jonathan, who had been driven by his purpose, sat mute before the old prophet. A slight breeze ruffled the ends of his hair as he looked with unseeing eyes at Samuel. The prophet poured a cup of water and handed it to Jonathan. Without awareness, the son of Saul took the cup and drank.

"Now, that is better, is it not?"

Jonathan nodded.

"You have come to ask me something," continued the prophet. "Well, you are here, as am I. What is it that you desire? Though I fear you have come too late."

Jonathan found his voice. "Samuel, *Sar*, my father—he has lost his mind! He needs you. You have to do something. He is bent on destroying David, the one you anointed to be king. You cannot let that happen."

"David shall be king," spoke the prophet. "You can be assured of that. But answer me, why do you want to spare David? For if he lives, he will be king and not you. Does that not disturb you?"

"Kingship means nothing to me. I have always known I was not to be king. The Lord has chosen David. I wish only to do what is right in the eyes of our great God. I could not live if any harm were to befall David. He is dear to me."

Samuel smiled. "You are a good man and a better friend. What would you have me do? I have fallen out of favor with the king."

"David tried to warn me of my father's wrath, but I just could not believe my father had so greatly fallen. Now, he has gone too far. He is at this very moment scouring the countryside with his armed guards, searching for David. There are too many men; they will find him. My father desires to take his life by his own hand. I cannot abide this; it is too terrible to fathom!"

"It is the nature of jealous malice," replied the prophet. "I am sorry, my son, there is nothing I can do."

Jonathan was overcome. If Samuel would not help, he had nowhere to turn. "How can you change so quickly? You loved him once. How is it that your heart has grown so cold?"

"Ceased to love? I have not ceased to love Saul, your father. My heart is rent within me. Well do I still love the king. That has never changed."

"Samuel, you cannot leave him!"

The old prophet placed his hand upon Jonathan's arm. "He is beyond all reach now. There is nothing I can do. I cannot go to him."

"I cannot accept that. There must be something that can be done, some help you can offer him. Some hope you can give me." Jonathan's voice trailed off.

"There is no more I can do for him. He has turned his back on Yahweh. The Lord speaks no more concerning your father. My part in this is over."

"Then there is no hope. All is lost."

"Lost? The Lord is still on His throne. All is not lost. He will work it out as He sees fit. But I fear that, yes, your father is lost. If he would but relent to the will of God, he would have a chance to be saved. But I deem he will not. He has become a proud and stubborn man."

Jonathan studied Samuel. He had not noticed before how tired the prophet looked. His eyes bore the greatest burden.

A flutter of dried leaves, remnants of a lost season, swirled against the garden wall. Jonathan released his breath and lowered his head. Together they sat, prophet and prince, in silence, waiting out the hours in helpless resignation.

CHAPTER 74

NOT BY BREAD ALONE

David fled south, along the Great North-South Ridge Road; the unbroken spine through the central highlands lay before him. He did not think; he just ran, pushing all thoughts from his mind. He did not note the kestrel circling overhead, or its quick descent to claim its prey. He did not heed the chamois grazing on the green hillside where patches of wildflowers dusted the dew-kissed landscape. He did not notice the vast view of the Judean Desert to his east, or the sun painting vibrant hues of deep orange and rich gray upon the barren uplifts and wind-swept ridges. Nor did he take note of the deep ravines that fell away on either side of the road. He just ran, unseeing of all that enveloped him, blind to all else save the path ahead.

Soon he saw what he was looking for, the height of Nob. It was located on a plateau just east of the road, built upon a rise that broke into a lower ridge then sloped into the ravine at the head of the Kidron Valley. Ascribed to the tribe of Benjamin, Nob lay north of the Canaanite city of Jebus. Here the Tabernacle stood, raised upon this elevation after the destruction of Shiloh. This was a city of priests, the remnant of the house of Eli.

David hastened toward the Tabernacle in search of the priest, Ahimelech, for he hoped this servant of Yahweh could aid him. The Tent of Meeting rested upon the high place, poised above the village.

The path up diverted from the main road. The trail narrowed as it wound along the plateau's ridge, swerving to miss boulders and brush that stood in the way.

As David turned a bend in the road, *Adonai's* portable shrine came into view. The sun shone behind the Tabernacle, casting a halo of light that radiated beams as a crown of glory. David halted, awed by the sight of the illuminated structure. The dwelling place of God. This was the same Tabernacle erected by Moses, and here within, for more than four hundred years, it was that Yahweh chose to meet His people.

The Tabernacle resided within a rectangular enclosure, a courtyard that housed the brazen altar and copper laver. David parted the curtain at the gate and entered into the Outer Court. The Tent of Meeting stood before him, its canvas roof fastened down by cords fixed into the ground with pegs. As David looked upon the walls of the Holy Place, it struck him that Yahweh had no permanent residence among his people, as though His stay was but temporary.

While the Children of Israel wandered, the Tabernacle, fashioned of canvas, served a purpose. But Israel had long ago settled this land. Each one had his home, built upon a solid foundation and made of stone, a perpetual dwelling place. Yet the Lord had no permanent house in which to abide. *It does not seem right that we should have better than the Lord.* But for now, that could not be helped.

David had more pressing matters. He had journeyed unprepared, hoping that this trial would not be necessary. He could not return home, so he must continue, seeking help wherever it might be found.

Several steps led the way to five brazen pillars marking the entrance of the Tabernacle. Here upon a level platform before the doorpost sat Ahimelech. As David walked toward him, the priest rose. He looked with wariness upon the disheveled captain and wondered that he had no men with him. How strange that seemed. Even a captain in the king's service would not wander these parts unaccompanied.

"Why are you alone, and no one is with you?"

David sensed the priest's discomfort. Taking on an air of indifference, the shepherd-captain explained. "The king has ordered me on some business, and said to me, 'Let no man know anything about the mission on which I send you, or what I have commanded you.' Have no fear, I am not alone, for I have directed my young men to a place hidden and kept. But we lack provisions and need your aid. Now therefore, what have you on hand? Give me five loaves of bread, or whatever can be found."

"There is no common bread on hand; but there is holy bread," answered the priest. "Yet if the young men have at least kept themselves from women, and are clean, then I will give you the shewbread that has been taken from before the Lord."

David chuckled to himself. "Truly, women have been kept from us about three days since we came on this mission. And the young men are holy as always before a campaign, and the bread is in effect common since it no longer rests before the Lord's Table. Even if it was consecrated in the vessel this day, it would be right to give in our need, for nothing stands in the way of preservation of life. Mercy is to be favored over sacrifice."

Ahimelech wondered why these men would have ventured on so great a charge thus ill-prepared. *Would not the king have given provision for his men before sending them? This cannot be rightly so. Yet he is David, the king's captain. What he says must be true. The mission must be urgent, the men not taking time to gather supplies.* "As you wish, I will do. Wait here; I will return with what you require."

The priest withdrew, leaving David alone. All was quiet. He squeezed the back of his neck with his hand. His muscles were tense as he shifted his weight from one foot to the other. A quick glance confirmed that there was no place to shield him from view as he stood waiting on Ahimelech. With his hands resting on his hips, David looked upon the entrance to the Holy Place and upon the five pillars that supported the porch of the Tabernacle.

It brought to mind the columns of fire and cloud and of the Lord's leading in the wilderness before the Children of Israel settled Canaan. Yahweh had been faithful to His people in the desert.

Now, I am to wander as my forebearers had. An outcast, exiled from my home, forced to become a ranger in the wilderness. I wonder, will the Lord lead me as He did my fathers before me?

An uneasiness of mind stirred David to glance over his shoulder. He felt exposed, as though a predator was stalking him, waiting to pounce. The walls of the court closed in upon him. Aware there was but one exit, he turned to face it. He fixed his gaze upon the gateway until movement drew his attention back to the Tabernacle. Ahimelech returned, emerging through the cloth gate carrying a parcel under his arm. David took a deep breath. *None too soon.*

The priest handed David the satchel. "This bread I give you has been replaced by the day's hot bread. May your fellowship with Yahweh remain fresh as new bread. Enjoy the Lord's hospitality."

David tipped his head at Ahimelech as he received the parcel. "I am grateful."

There it was again; on the fringe of his awareness he sensed eyes upon him. David jerked his head toward the gate. He caught a glimpse of a face as it darted behind the veiled entrance. But it was enough: Doeg, Saul's trusted servant. He was sure the Edomite had seen him.

Restless urgency filled David as he turned toward the priest. "Is there not here on hand a spear or a sword? For I have neither brought my sword nor my weapons with me, because the king's business required haste."

Ahimelech looked upon David with doubt. *A soldier without his weapon?* Nevertheless, the priest spoke, saying, "The sword of Goliath the Philistine, whom you killed in the Valley of Elah—there it is," Ahimelech pointed his finger toward the Tabernacle, "wrapped in a cloth behind the ephod. None has a better right to it than you, for you it was that took it from the Philistine. If you would wield it yourself, take it and use it as you desire. You will find no other weapon here."

"There is none like it; give it to me." David shifted with anxiety. *Doeg will run straight to Saul. I do not have much time.*

Ahimelech nodded. "Very well." The priest turned, walked up the steps of the Tabernacle, and disappeared into the Holy Place.

David paced the court. Sweat beaded upon his brow. The air grew thick around him, catching in his throat. Overwhelmed, David wheeled about, searching for escape when Ahimelech returned. Across his open palms lay the sword wrapped in a linen cloth, a relic of faith in action.

The priest extended his hands toward David. "Behold, the sword of Goliath."

A thrill ran through David as, with careful reverence, he uncovered the sword. The blade shone in the midday sun, unblemished by time. David reached out, and with his hand, took up Goliath's sword. He raised it into the air and looked upon the quality of the iron blade. The shepherd-captain tried the sword, slashing the air this way and that. It was a good sword. Then, tenderly, David rested the side of the blade on the palm of his hand and studied its gleaming edge.

Memory returned of his encounter with the giant. His belief in Yahweh had served him well. Once he had trusted in his shepherd's tools, now he was relying on the weapon of a Philistine. He had not needed deceit and lies to protect him then, and he felt ashamed by his lack of faith.

"I will use this blade with honor," vowed David.

Ahimelech saw the truth in the young captain's eyes and nodded his head in approval. "May it always be so, my son."

David took leave of the priest and flew south toward the mount that overlooked Jebus. There, he chose a path through a garden where olive trees rose into the sky. This was a place of solitude, and he desired to linger, to enjoy the beauty of the landscape and the splendid view of the old Canaanite city. But time would not allow, for danger pressed him onward.

His hand rested on the hilt of Goliath's sword as he breathed in the fragrant air of the garden of olives. Reaching with his sword arm, David slid the blade part-way from his belt, for there was no sheath. Often as he looked upon the sword, his faith was strengthened. And in the months that followed, his trust in Yahweh would be all he had to sustain him.

CHAPTER 75

BY WHATEVER MEANS

After a futile search, Saul had returned to Gibeah. He was discouraged, for nothing had come to his ear regarding the whereabouts of his shepherd-captain, David. The air was warm, so the king found solace under the shadow of the tamarisk tree, as he so often had, upon the dais cut from the earth. Sitting in the evening shade of the branching tree, Saul perceived its pleasant coolness. The gauzy pink blooms engulfed the wispy canopy, casting waves of fragrant honey across the breeze. Even so, the king found no reprieve from the restless agitation in his soul. Somewhere, David was out there, free to conspire against the king's person. Until the shepherd-dog was captured, Saul knew in his heart that his reign was in question.

With his spear firmly grasped within his hand, Saul sat with his servants standing about him. A decision needed to be made: what to do to rid the kingdom of this threat. He was ready, ready to defend his throne and have revenge upon his enemies. The men before him waited to receive his orders, to serve their sovereign in any way they could. Or so they thought. Little did they foresee how far their king would go to end this matter.

"Hear now, men of Benjamin! Will the son of Jesse give every one of you fields and vineyards, and make you all captains of thousands and captains of hundreds?" Saul looked hard at the men before him, his eyes narrowed in suspicion. "All of you have conspired against me, and there is no one who reveals to me that my son has made a covenant with this shepherd-dog. There is not one of you who is sorry for me or made known to me that my own son, my own flesh and blood, is in league with this," Saul could hardly bring himself to say his name, "*David*, and has stirred up my servant against me, to lie in wait, as it is this day. For surely, my son wishes to supplant me with this shepherd boy of Judah!"

Saul looked upon the men of Benjamin, his own tribe whom he had favored above all other tribes with possessions and positions of power—he looked upon them now, with loathing. For his mind was diseased with suspicion, his reason unseated, so that his actions were without conscience. And like many tyrants before him, his mind was tortured by thoughts of sedition.

Then it was that Doeg, the Edomite, came before the king, for he had news that would incite such treachery, the shock of which would be felt through many generations.

"My king, forgive my delay, but I have information that you will be glad to hear. I saw the son of Jesse going to Nob, to Ahimelech the son of Ahitub. I followed him. I watched all he did. There, the priest inquired of the Lord for him, gave him provisions, and handed him the sword of Goliath the Philistine."

Saul stood, gripping the arms of his royal seat until his knuckles paled. He roared as he bared his white teeth against his bronzed skin. His face burned; his neck prickled with a raging fire.

And even at the mention of Goliath's sword, Saul forgot all that David had accomplished for him: how he had slain the giant and fought many battles to secure the king's throne. All Saul could see was conspiracy, for his eyes were blind to reason. The jealous malice harbored in the heart of Saul was well watered by the ambitions of the Edomite, who daily fed into the fears of the king.

"My king, may it be that the priest is in league with this outlaw, your servant David?"

"Bring me the priest! And all his father's house!"

With haste, messengers were sent to Nob to summon Ahimelech, the son of Ahitub, and all the priests who resided within the city. Now Ahitub was the brother of Ichabod, whose father, Phinehas, was killed upon the field of battle when the Ark of God was taken by the Philistines. Ahimelech, and these priests of Nob, were the last of the house of Eli.

And they all came to the king, unencumbered, to stand before Saul, each with conscience clear.

"Hear now, son of Ahitub!"

Noting that Saul had stripped him of his due title, Ahimelech, the high priest, responded, "Here I am, my king."

Yet the priest knew nothing good was in the heart of Saul. He stood before the king poised with honor, preparing for what was to come.

Saul wasted no time, but leveled his spear at the heart of Ahimelech. His eyes narrowed. "Why have you conspired against me, you and the son of Jesse? Why have you given him bread and a sword? You mock me, for was it not Goliath's sword you placed in his hand? You have even inquired of God for him that he should rise against me, to lie in wait, as it is this day. Tell me, why have you committed treason against your king?"

Ahimelech gasped. "My king, who among your servants is as faithful as David? He is your son-in-law, who does whatever you ask of him. He is without guile, but has acted with honor in all that he has done for the king and his household."

Extending his hands, palms up, the priest pleaded with Saul. "Often he has come to me for advice, to seek the will of Yahweh. This was not the first I have gone before the Lord on behalf of your servant David." Ahimelech shook his head as he lowered his eyes. "Far be it from me to go against the word of my king. I had no knowledge of my king's dispute with the son of Jesse. Let not the king impute anything to his servant, or to any in the house of my father. For as the Lord lives," the priest looked into the eyes of Saul, "your servant knew nothing of all this, little or much."

Saul's heart was hard, unmoved by the testimony of Ahimelech. And as the heathen kings of other nations, Saul uttered his decree.

"You shall surely die, Ahimelech, you and all your father's house!"

Ahimelech took a step back as though struck. "But my king, we are innocent. What proof do you have?"

Saul stood upon the dais, an opposing figure towering over his charge. His spear was but a breath from the priest's breast. "I need no evidence but my own."

Turning to the guards who had encircled the body of priests, Saul commanded them, "Turn and kill the priests of the Lord, for they, also, are in league with David. They knew when he fled and did not send word to me."

Not a one moved.

Saul faced his men, his spear pointed at Ahimelech. "Kill them!"

But none would lift their hand against the priests of the Lord, for they feared God more than their king.

Saul growled. Then, unabashed, he turned to his servant, Doeg. "You kill the priests!"

The false accuser had no qualms complying with this bloody decree. Doeg, the Edomite, that whispering snake, drew his sword and struck the high priest of the Lord. Ahimelech fell to the ground, bleeding as his life left him. The other priests looked on wide-eyed. Panic seized them as they sought escape. But the encircling Benjaminites closed ranks. And though the men would not strike down the priests, neither would they lift a hand to help them.

The cries of the holy servants filled the air as the ruthless hand of the Edomite fell upon the defenseless priests. The glint of the crimson-stained sword flashed. Gore spilt from gaping wounds, bathing the ground in red. Saul watched the slaughter with satisfaction; the one who dared in false mercy to spare Agag from destruction had no mercy for the anointed priests of Yahweh, nor for the remnant of Eli's house.

So all should fear who stand against the designs of their monarch. This was Israel's king, for whom they asked. And now, they felt the full force of his sovereignty. A tyrant bent on his own wild will. Justice by might, judgment by the whim of the crown.

It did not take long for the Edomite to accomplish his task. His breath came heavy as he stayed his sword. His face, hands, and clothes marred by the day's work. As he wiped the back of his arm across his brow, trailing a sanguineous smear, Doeg looked upon the yield of his carnage. Eighty-five of the Lord's priests lay before Saul, their linen cassocks stained with crimson, the holy garments evidence against the savagery of the king.

"It is not finished," spoke Saul as he regarded his faithful servant. Doeg nodded.

CHAPTER 76

BLOODLETTING

Something stirred in the north; a murmur in the wind that bore down, whipping through the trees, bringing ill bodings of a coming storm. The breeze surged over the hills, racing through the valleys, catching the garments of the priest as he fought to keep them in place. A piercing shriek cut through the air as a lone kestrel struggled against the wind. As Abiathar looked up, he caught a glimpse of the bird as it soared overhead. The clouds were moving swiftly, stretching out in serpentine swirls. Holding the linen mitre on his head, the young priest watched as the bird met a thermal and was lifted beyond sight.

The morning had been busy, for he was alone to tend the people. Summoned by the king, the other priests had traveled to Gibeah to appear before Saul. Abiathar had only just entered into the service of the Tabernacle, and he felt ill-prepared to be left on his own. He was young, and inexperienced, but the others were needed and he, being the youngest, was left to serve the people.

"Trial by fire," spoke the priest under his breath.

"I am sorry, my *adon*, I did not hear you."

Abiathar shook his head. "It was nothing. Now, bring me your peace offering and we shall begin."

The citizen of Nob lifted the goat onto the table. Placing his hand upon the head of the perfect animal, the suppliant watched as

Abiathar took his knife to the throat of the beast. Blood flowed from the wound. The priest then placed a basin under the stream to collect the crimson dower, for the blood was the Lord's. But before Abiathar could sprinkle the offering upon the altar, cries from the street ruptured the troubled calm.

The two men, suppliant and priest, hurried to the gate and looked outside the court of the Tabernacle. Horror filled their vision. Raiders molested the people; havoc flooded the streets.

A flash of recognition scraped against Abiathar's memory, for in that moment he spied their leader: *Doeg, the king's own servant.*

"What is this?" cried the suppliant of Nob. "These are not Philistines!"

"No, these are the king's men," returned the priest.

"I must go. My family."

In fear, the citizen ran into the street. And as the young priest stood in witness, the man was cut down, taken mid-stride with the edge of a sword. Abiathar did not linger, but turned back into the courtyard. His breath came in ragged waves as his body, with trembling limbs, raced toward the Tabernacle.

Into the Holy Place he bounded. Tripping over the threshold, he fell headlong into the inner sanctuary. Stunned, he lay where he was as sweat dripped into his eyes. He blinked hard as he shook his head.

Get up! his inner voice commanded. Abiathar sprang to his feet. He rushed to the altar, reached behind the sacred *chamman*, and took up the ephod of the High Priest. He grabbed the table linen from beneath the shewbread, and with fumbling hands, wrapped the garment in the fine cloth and bound it about his waist with his girdle.

Abiathar looked around the lamp-lit chamber. *What has happened? Where are the other priests? My father? I do not understand.* He stood trembling. Screams of slaughter echoed through the Sanctuary. *What can I do? How can I help the people?*

Grief tore at his heart, for he knew he had no power to save them. Taking one final look, he forsook his service to the Tabernacle and fled through the curtained doorway. The young priest ran toward the gate of the courtyard. There he paused and peered into the street. No sign of marauders, so he slipped out and headed to the outskirts of the village.

Death and destruction were all around him. Children lay bleeding in the street; women fallen beside their young, run through with the sword—their lives given to shield their offspring. Old men littered the ground, stricken as they tried to defend the city. But they had no power to resist the strong arm of the Edomite and his cohorts.

Tears blurred his vision as he stumbled through the street. He caught his foot and tripped over a body that blocked his passage. Unable to recover, he reached out to brace his fall. Even so, he landed hard beside a woman whose empty eyes looked back into his. Blood leached onto his linen cassock, marring the pure cloth with crimson stains. He could not breathe; the wind was knocked out of him; whether from the fall or the image of the dead woman, he did not know.

As he lay there gasping for air, he heard the rancor of the intruders returning. He remained still, drawing in shallow breaths.

The noise of their revelry resounded through the streets. Abiathar lifted his head just enough to see them running toward where he lay. And there was Doeg, leading the savage slaughter, elated by his bloodlust, his ambition greater than his humanity. The brutal butchery continued until the bloodletting consumed the entire village. When no people were left, Doeg and his wicked men turned to killing the livestock. Abiathar did not move as he bore witness to the merciless massacre.

What does it take for a man to kill innocents? How does a heart grow so cold as to decimate an entire people? What evil must have entered into the soul of such a man?

"Make sure they are all dead," bellowed the Edomite to his men.

The brutal marauders stabbed bodies with the point of a spear, walking among the dead, taking whatever life was left in those cast upon the ground.

Abiathar felt a wave of panic. The men drew closer to where he lay. *What do I do?* Then they were upon him. He held his breath, feigning death. The woman's body beside him was thrust aside, flipped over by the bloodied foot of the assailant. The man turned up his nose at her corpse, disgusted by the gaping wound in her chest.

"They are all dead. We are wasting our time."

"Let us move to the other side of the village," Doeg commanded. "Take whatever spoil you can find. It is payment for your loyalty to the king."

"Blood money, that is what it is."

"Aye, you do not see the king dirtying his hands now, do you?"

And then they were gone. The young priest dared not move. He lay beside the cold corpse of the slain woman, taking breaths in small gulps. Flies swarmed over the slain. He heard the call of the kestrel as it circled above the city. As the day warmed, the stench of death hovered, giving testimony to the trial inflicted throughout the village.

Abiathar's belly churned. Bile rose in his throat, burning as he swallowed. Lifting himself to his knees, he strained to stand. His limbs were heavy as though the life had drained from them. Gore covered the ground. His feet slipped as he stepped over the dead, weaving his way to the edge of town. All was silent.

The birds had descended upon the slain, relishing the bounty before them. The young priest turned his head. He had aged, his youth lost in a single afternoon. He had witnessed the horror of man's inhumanity, and he was marred by the memory.

The road lay long before him as he struggled to move his feet. Numbness encircled him along the empty path, leading him away from the carnage that was Nob, the priestly city of Jehovah. As he crested the hill that broke into the next valley, Abiathar looked back, over his shoulder, at the silent city. He let out a long breath, for he understood. The priests would not return.

"I am the last of my father's house and all that remains of Eli."

Then, with one final look, he turned his face west and entered into exile—he alone carrying the ephod with him.

CHAPTER 77

ENEMY OF THE STATE

The wind picked up from the north as David surveyed the vast landscape of the hill country. Though it was mid-summer, the heavens rumbled with a brewing storm. David turned his gaze to the sky. He sympathized with the struggle within the clouds, drawn toward the contention above. Somehow he had stumbled into this place of opposing forces, a place he could not escape. He had a choice to make, one that would alter his course.

David stood upon the cusp of two nations. To the east lay the sun-painted hills tumbling toward the Judean Wilderness. It was a region in constant turmoil, ever reviving as though with each passing season the wind-swept countryside was created anew. To the west, the Shephelah and the Plain of Philistia, the territory of the enemy. Beyond the low hills and rolling valleys, the vast fertile expanse stretched to the sea. Young as he was, David had traversed much of this region defending his nation against the Philistines. His blood had been spilt; he was a part of this land.

And now, he was cast out, exiled from the very place for which he had crossed swords. All that he was, all he had fought for, was stripped away. He had only ever tried to do right. How short a time ago he had been praised by the multitude. Now he was a fugitive, hunted by the ones he had struggled to preserve. How quickly it had all changed.

He had come to a decision, though he loathed what he was about to do. His mind reeled against it, contending with his conscience. But desperation often leads to rash deeds. And so it was with David. Seeing Doeg had shaken him, driving him toward reckless acts.

"There is no place else to go. I cannot stay in Israel, for there is no one to defend me. The servants of Saul will ferret me out and hand me over to the king. All other lands are at peace with Saul. They would eagerly deliver me up to him rather than go to war with Israel."

Shaking his head, David heaved a heavy sigh. "No, I have no choice. I must go to the enemy. May it be that they will not recognize me, or rather, that I could be of use to their king? Either way, if I am to die, would that it be at the hand of the enemy and not my king."

David looked over his shoulder at the nation he loved. "Ta," David mused. "The great hero of Israel defecting to the enemy of his people." He shook his head. "What will they think?"

Then with one last glance, David turned his back on his nation, on his people, on his king, and entered into the land of the Philistines—he their greatest foe, and in his hand, the sword of Goliath.

CHAPTER 78

THE COMING STORM

Dark clouds formed over the throne of the king, yet no rain followed. The wind raced across the rise, whipping banners that danced wildly about the clearing. As though a drummer incited an army to advance, a thundering crescendo rumbled across the mountains. And in the gathering storm, Doeg came to Gibeah and to Saul, his king, who sat upon his outdoor dais as though he had waited, unmoving, for the servant's return.

The king's heart skipped a beat at the sight of Doeg. He leaned forward. "Well?"

"It is finished."

"All?"

"Every last one of them."

Nodding his head, the tyrant king spoke, "Good, good."

"I have report, my king, of David's whereabouts."

A rising thrill coursed through Saul. "Yes? Where is he?"

"I am told he has been sighted traveling west over the mountains."

"West?"

"Yes, my king, into Philistine territory."

Saul laughed as he leaned back in his seat. "Let the enemy have him. I do not care who ends him, as long as he is dead."

"My king, if David can get the Philistines to back him, what chance do we have? What will prevent him from gaining the throne of Israel?"

Saul thought on these words as he ran his hand down the side of his beard. "Indeed, that would be a problem." Taking hold his scabbard, the king rose to his feet and stepped off his dais to stand among his servants.

"Come men, bolster your courage." Saul smiled as he strapped his sword to his side. "We seek a traitor."

APPENDIX A – GLOSSARY

Ark of Covenant – Aacred chest where the Hebrews kept the two tablets containing the Ten Commandments; the symbol of God's presence; the throne of God on earth. The Ark was captured by the Philistines at the battle of Aphek, but returned after a disastrous plague struck all of Philistia. *Ark of God; Ark of Testimony.*

Balm of Gilead *(bahm - uh v - gil-ee-uh d)* – A healing compound made from the resinous gum of a small evergreen tree, Commiphora gileadensis, of the family Burseraceae, known for its medicinal properties.

Early Rains – The "early" or "former" rains commence in autumn in the latter part of October or beginning of November and continue to fall heavily for two months; *former rains.*

Ebenezer *(eh'-ben haw-e'-zer)* – A memorial stone placed by Samuel near Mizpah after the battle of Mizpah to commemorate the divine assistance given to Israel in their great battle against the Philistines, whom they totally routed.

Ephod *(ay-fode')* – Girdle; sacred vestment worn by the High Priest, resembling an apron, made of fine linen twined of gold, blue, purple, and scarlet, intricately embroidered, in two parts fastened together at each shoulder by a large onyx clasp.

Former Rains – See early rains.

Latter Rains – The "latter" or spring rains fall in March and April, and serve to swell the grain then coming to maturity.

Mitre *(mahy-ter)* – Headdress most often worn for religious purposes.

Tent of Meeting – Sacred tent, a portable and provisional sanctuary, where God met His people; resting place of the Ark of the Covenant prior to its capture by the Philistines. *Tabernacle; Sanctuary.*

Urim and Thummim *(yū'rĭm, thŭm'ĭm)* – Sacred stones carried inside the breastplate of the High Priest of ancient Israel and used as an oracle to divine the will of God.

Wadi *(wah dee')* – A perennial water-course that leaves a channel carved in the earth during the dry season.

Abba *(ab-bah')* – Father.

Achi *(awkh ee')* – My brother.

Ad me'ah ve'esrim shanah *('ad may-aw' ve'es-reem' shaw-naw')* – May you live to be one hundred and twenty.

Adon *(aw-done')* – Master, lord.

Aleichem shalom *(ah-le-khem shaw-lome')* – Upon you be peace; a greeting of peace.

Arnebeth *(ar-neh'-beth)* – Hare; an ancient rabbit that chews its cud, probably extinct.

Attah *(at-taw')* – Now.

Avi *(ah vee')* – My father.

Azov oti *(ah-zohv' oht-i)* – Leave me (alone).

Bamah *(baw-maw')* – High place.

Barchot ve Tefillot *(ber-aw-kot' ve tef-il-law')* – Blessings and prayers.

Baruch atah Adonai, Eloheynu Melech Ha-Olam Borey P'ree Hagafen *(bah-rooch ah-tah ah-doh-noye eh-loh-hay-noo meh-lehch hah-oh-lahm bo-rei per-ee' hag-gah-fen)* – Blessed are You, O Lord our God, King of the Universe, Who creates the fruit of the vine.

Belial *(bel-ee'-al)* – Wicked; lawless; worthless.

Benayim *(bay-nah'-yim)* – Man of the space between armies; champion.

Boker tov *(boh-kehr tohv)* – Good morning.

Chadesh yameinu kakedem *(khaw-dawsh' ya-me-nu ke-ke'-dem)* – May we renew our days like the days of old.

Chamman *(kham-mawn')* – Incense altar.

Cherem *(khay'-rem)* – Devoted to destruction.

Cukkah *(sook-kaw')* – A booth; pavilion.

Da'ath *(dah'-ath)* – Knowledge; understanding.

Drishat shalom *(duh-ree-shaht shaw-lome')* – Kind regards.

Ela mai *(e'-la mahee)* – What then?

Édut *(ay-dooth')* – Testimony; bracelets affirming the king's adoption by Yahweh.

Ephah *(ay-faw')* – Approximately one bushel or about 33 liters.

G'biyrah *(gheb-ee-raw')* – Queen.

Hakafot *(hak-kah-foht)* – To encircle; during the marriage ceremony, the bride circles the groom seven times; symbolism of bringing down any barriers between them.

Ima *(eem'aw)* – Mother.

Ketubah *(ke-too-baw)* – A written thing; betrothal contract.

Kinnor *(kin-nore')* – Harp; lyre.

Lakad *(law-kad')* – Trap; to capture, take, seize.

Le'an atah nose'a *(le'awn aw-taw' no-se-a)* – Where are you going?

Lehabah *(leh-aw-baw')* – Flame; tip of a weapon; spearhead.

Lielah tov *(lye-lah tohv)* – Good night.

Mah atah o'mer *(maw aw-taw' o'-mer)* – What are you saying?

Mah zeh *(maw zeh)* – What is the meaning of this?

Meshiah Adonai *(maw-shee'-akh a-do'-nī)* – God's anointed one.

Mishpachah *(mish-paw-khaw')* – Clan, family; the yearly sacrifice held for the entire family clan.

Mishpat *(mish-pawt')* – Manner, judgment, law, ordinance.

Mohar *(mo'-har)* – Dowry; the bride price.

Na'ar *(nah'-ar)* – Lad.

Nesicha *(nee si kah)* – Princess.

Neshama *(nesh-aw-maw')* – Breath; soul; spirit; my little darling.

Nezer *(neh'-zer)* – Crown; diadem.

Nisu'in *(nee-soo-een)* – To carry; marriage ceremony.

Owphan *(o-fawn')* – Wheel.

Reggah *(reh'-gah)* – Wait; in a moment.

Rofe *(roh-feh')* – Physician, doctor; one who heals.

Ruach Yahuweh *(roo'-akh yah-oo-we)* – Spirit or breath of God; the Bride.

Sar *(sar)* – Sir, captain, ruler.

Sarah *(saw-raw')* – Noble lady.

Shalom *(shaw-lome')* – Peace; a greeting of peace.

Shalom aleichem *(shaw-lome' ah-le-khem)* – Peace be unto you; a greeting of peace.

Shalom uv'racha *(shaw-lome' oov-rah-khah)* – Peace and blessing.

Shalom uv'racha leYisrael *(shaw-lome' oov-rah-KHAH le yis-raw-ale')* – Peace and blessing to Israel.

Shelem *(sheh'-lem)* – Peace offering; voluntary sacrifice of thanks.

Shelet *(sheh'-let)* – Shield.

Teraph *(ter-awf)* – Idol; household idol in a human shape.

Terufot *(teru`fot)* – Medicine.

Tzetech leShalom veShuvech leShalom *(tse-tekh le-shaw-lome' ve-shoo-vekh le-shaw-lome')* – Go in peace and come in peace.

Tzinnah *(tsin-naw')* – A large shield.

Todah *(to-daw')* – Thank you.

Tov me'od *(tohv mē' od)* – Very good.

Yahushua *(yah-oosh-ah)* – The servant; groom.

Yom tov *(yohm tohv)* – A good day

APPENDIX C – PEOPLE

Aaron *(air-uhn)* – Light bringer; the first High Priest of the Israelites; a Levite who was the older brother of Moses and a prophet of God. (Exodus 4:14)

Abiathar *(ab-ee-ath'-ar)* – Father of abundance; priest, son of Ahimelech the High Priest. (1 Samuel 22:20)

Abijah *(a-bi'-ja)* – Samuel's second son; judge over Beersheba with his older brother, Joel. (1 Samuel 8:2)

Abinadab *(ab-ee-naw-dawb')* – Father of nobleness.
1. A Levite of Kirjath-Jearim, in whose house the Ark of the Covenant was placed after having been returned by the Philistines; Eleazar's father. (1 Samuel 7:1)
2. Second son of Jesse and brother of David. (1 Samuel 16:8)

Abner *(ab-nare')* – Father of light; Saul's uncle; the younger brother of Kish, Saul's father; general of Saul's army. (1 Samuel 14:50)

Achan *(aw-kawn')* – A man of Judah who violated God's specific ban against taking any spoil from the captured city of Jericho; he and his family were stoned to death for this sin. (Joshua 7:1)

Achish *(aw-keesh')* – I will blacken or terrify; only a man; the Philistine king of Gath. (Samuel 21:10)

Abraham *(ab-raw-hawm')* – Father of a great multitude; the son of Terah, and founder of the Israelites; after hearing the voice of God, he left Ur of Sumer and traveled to Canaan, where he entered into a covenant with Yahweh. (Genesis 12)

Adonai *(a-do'-ni)* – My Master; title for Yahweh meaning sovereign.

Adriel *(ad-ree-ale')* – Flock of God; the son of Barzillai the Meholathite. It was this man to whom Saul gave his daughter, Merab, though she was already promised to David. (1 Samuel 18:19)

Agag *(ag-ag')* – I will overtop; king of the Amalekites. (1 Samuel 15:8)

Ahijah *(a-hi'-ja)* – Brother of Jehovah; son of Ahitub; brother of Ichabod; grandson of Phinehas, the son of Eli; a priest of the house of Eli who served Saul after his estrangement from the prophet Samuel and wore the ephod when Saul inquired of God. (1 Samuel 14:3)

Ahimelech *(akh-ee-meh'-lek)* – My brother is king; son of Ahitub; priest of Nob; father of Abiathar; slain by order of King Saul following David's visit to Nob. (1 Samuel 21:1)

Ahinoam *(akh-ee-no'-am)* – Delight; pleasant; daughter of Ahimaaz, and wife of Saul. (1 Samuel 14:50)

Amah *(aw-maw')* – Maidservant; handmaid to Michal, daughter of King Saul.

Amalek *(a-mal'-ek)* – Dweller in a valley; the grandson of Esau, the patriarch Jacob's twin brother; people descended from Amalek.(Genesis 36:12)

Amalekites *(a-mal'-e-kītz)* – inhabited various places in or near southern Canaan; a semi-nomadic people descended from Amalek, the grandson of Esau, the patriarch Jacob's twin brother. (Genesis 36:12)

Ammonites *(am-mone' nahytz)* – A people descended from the incestuous relationship of Lot and his daughter. The people of Ammon, who dwell east of the Jordan River. (Genesis 19:38)

Amorites *(am'-o-rīts)* – Highlander, hill men; one of the principal kingdoms in Canaan, east of the Jordan River valley; descendants of one of the sons of Canaan. (Numbers 13:29)

Anakim *(an'-a-kim)* – The descendants of Anak that dwelt in the south of Canaan near Hebron; said to have been a mixed race of giant people. (Deuteronomy 9:2)

Aphiah *('Aphiyah)* – I will make to breathe; an ancestor of Saul. (1 Samuel 9:1)

Asher *(aw-share')* – Happy; the eighth son of Jacob and ancestor of one of the twelve tribes of Israel.

Asherah *(ash-ay-raw')* – Groves: Canaanite fertility goddess; cohort of Baal; "she who walks on the sea"; *Ashdoda; Anoth.*

Baal *(bey-uhl)* – Lord; Canaanite god, son of Dagon, cohort of Asherah; Rider of the Clouds; god of thunder and storms and fertility. *Aliyan Baal; Baal Hadad; Athar-Baal; Baal-Zebul.*

Balaam *(ba'-lam)* – Devourer; not of the people; the son of Beor; he had the gift of prophecy; paid by Balak, king of the Moabites, to curse Israel, but instead, he blessed them. (Numbers 22:5)

Barak *(baw-rak')* – The military commander who, with the prophetess Deborah, destroyed the Canaanite army under Sisera. (Judges 4)

Bedan *(bed-awn')* – In judging; judge of Israel who followed Gideon.(1 Samuel 12:11)

Benjamin *(ben-juh-muhn)* – Son of the south; son of the right hand; the youngest son of Jacob and Rachel, and the brother of Joseph. One of the twelve tribes of ancient Israel traditionally descended from him. *Ben-oni*, son of my suffering. (Gen. 35:18)

Benjaminite *(ben'-ja-meen' īt)* – From the tribe of Benjamin. *Benjamite.*

Boaz *(bo'az)* – Fleetness; young conscript of Jabesh-Gilead who fought with Captain Nagad against the armies of Ammon. (Ruth 2:1)

Bua *(boo-uh)* – Asked for; Philistine conscript who fought at Timnah where David attempted to gain his dowry for Michal.

Cabbal *(sab-bawl')* – Burden-bearer; Jonathan's armor-bearer.

Casluhim *(kas-loo'-heem)* – Fortified; Philistine soldier who fought at Timnah where David attempted to gain his dowry for Michal; *the lion of Philistia.*

Children of Belial *(bel-ee'-al)* – Worthless men who stood against Saul.

Dagon *(daw-gohn')* – A fish; Philistine god of agriculture and the earth, represented as half man and half fish; the national god of the Philistines.

Dan *(dawn)* – A judge; fifth son of Jacob; one of the twelve tribes of ancient Israel traditionally descended from him.

David *(da'-vid)* – Beloved; the youngest son of Jesse. (1 Samuel 16:1-13)

Delilah *(del-ee-law')* – Feeble; the Philistine maiden who betrayed the secret of Samson's strength, cut his hair, and gave him over to the Philistines. (Judges 16:4)

Doeg *(do-ayg')* – Fearing; the Edomite; chief herdsman of Kish, who later became Saul's trusted adviser. (1 Samuel 21:7)

Edomites *(ed-ome' itz)* – Red; descendants of Esau, Jacob's older brother whose birthright he stole. (Genesis 36:1)

El-Elyon *('ēl 'elyōn)* – The Most High God.

Eli *(ee-lahy)* – Ascension; descendant of Aaron through Ithamar; high priest and judge of Israel; guardian of Samuel. (1 Samuel 3)

Eliab *(el-ee-awb')* – My God is father; eldest son of Jesse and brother of David. (1 Samuel 16)

Ephraim *(ef-rah'-yim)* – Double ash-heap; I shall be doubly fruitful; second son of Joseph; one of the twelve tribes of ancient Israel traditionally descended from him.

Eshbaal *(esh-bah'-al)* – Man of Baal; fire of the ruler; the fourth son of Saul; *Ishbosheth (man of shame)*. (1 Chronicles 8:33)

Eyal *(eh-yawl')* – Strength, help; a hardened warrior commissioned with Captain Nagad during the siege of Jabesh-Gilead.

Ezer *(eh'-zer)* – Treasure; aid, support, help; the aged elder of Jabesh-Gilead during the siege by Nahash of the Ammonites.

Gad *(gawd)* – Troop; seventh son of Jacob; one of the twelve tribes of ancient Israel traditionally descended from him.

Gadowl *(gaw-dole')* – Elder; haughty; a member of the council of elders present during the battle of Aphek in which the Ark of the Covenant was lost.

Garah *(gaw-raw')* – To cause strife, stir up, contend; one of the sons of Belial.

Gideon *(gid'-e-un)* – Hewer; youngest son of Joash from the Abiezrite clan in the tribe of Manasseh, fifth judge of Israel who led the Israelites against the Midianites; *Jerubbaal.* (Judges 7)

Gileadites *(gil-ee-uh d īts)* – People of Gilead.

Goliath *(go-li'-ath)* – Splendor; a man of Gath, champion of the Philistines, whose height was six cubits and a span; he was a descendant of the Anakim; killed by the boy, David, in the Valley of Elah after a protracted standoff between the Israelites and the Philistines. (1 Samuel 17:4)

Haddabar *(had-daw-bawr')* – Counselor, minister; Elder of Israel who met at Bethel.

Hannah *(han-naw')* – Grace; the mother of Samuel, one of the wives of Elkanah. (1 Samuel 1:2)

Hebrew *(he'-broo)* – See Israelites.

Helek *(hay'-lek)* – Traveler; a Hebrew soldier, son of Orach, who befriended Nagad during the battle of Mizpah; *Helek ben Orach.*

Israelites *(iz'-ra-el-ītz)* – Name given to the members of the Hebrew people. A people who made up twelve tribes descended from the line of Jacob; *Children of Israel; Hebrews; Chosen of God.*

Issachar *(yis-saw-kawr')* – There is recompense; the ninth son of Jacob; one of the twelve tribes of ancient Israel traditionally descended from him.

Jacob *(ja'-kub)* – Supplanter; son of Isaac, grandson of Abraham, and father of the twelve patriarchs of the tribes of Israel. (Genesis 25)

Jarib *(yaw-rebe')* – He contends; a Reubenite soldier who served under Captain Nagad at Jabesh-Gilead.

Jehovah *(je-ho'-va)* – The personal name of God.

Jephthah *(jef'-tha)* – Opener; ninth judge of Israel who defeated the Ammonites; because of a rash vow, he sacrificed his daughter as a burnt offering. (Judges 11:1)

Jesse *(jes'-ē)* – Wealthy; Yahweh exists; son of Obed, grandson of Boaz, and father of David. (1 Samuel 16:1)

Jishui *(jish-vee')* – He resembles me; the second son of Saul. *Abinadab* (1 Samuel 14:49, 31:2)

Joel *(jo-ale')* – Eldest son of Samuel; judge over Beersheba with his younger brother, Abijah. (1 Samuel 8:2)

Jonathan *(jon-aw-thawn')* – Jehovah has given; eldest son of Saul. (1 Samuel 14:49)

Joshua *(jeh-ho-shoo'-ah)* – God is salvation; leader of the Israelites during the Conquest, distribution and settlement of Canaan. He led in the covenant renewal at Mt. Ebal and Mt. Gerizim. (Joshua 1)

Judah *(joo'-da)* – Praised; the fourth son of Jacob; one of the twelve tribes of ancient Israel traditionally descended from him.

Kish *(keesh)* – A Benjamite of the family of Matri, father of Saul. (1 Samuel 9:1)

Levi *(le'-vī)* – Joined to; the third son of Jacob; the ancestor of the priestly tribe of Levi.

Levite *(le'-vīt)* – Of the tribe of Levi, set aside by God for His service.

Lot *(lote)* – Covering; the nephew of Abraham who dwelt in Sodom. He was delivered from the destruction of Sodom. Father of the nations of Moab and Ammon through the incestuous relationship with his two daughters. (Genesis 19)

Ma`aleh *(mah-al-eh')* – Ascent, incline; tribal chief under the command of Saul and Abner during the battle of Jabesh-Gilead.

Malchishua *(mal-kee-shoo'-ah)* – My king is wealth; third son of Saul. (1 Samuel 14:49)

Manasseh *(men-ash-sheh')* – Causing to forget; eldest son of Joseph; one of the twelve tribes of ancient Israel traditionally descended from him.

Maoch *(maw-oke')* – Oppression; father of King Achish of Gath. (1 Samuel 27:2)

Marad *(maw-rad')* – To rebel, revolt, be rebellious; one of the sons of Belial.

Matri *(mat-ree')* – Rain of Jehovah; family in the tribe of Benjamin to which Kish and Saul belong. (1 Samuel 10:21)

Meholathite *(me-ho'-la-thīt)* – One belonging to a place called Meholah, an inhabitant of a city in Issachar.

Merab *(may-rawb')* – Increase; eldest daughter of Saul. (1 Samuel 14:49)

Michal *(me-kawl')* – Who is like God; youngest daughter of Saul. (1 Samuel 14:49)

Milkilu *(mil-kē-loo)* – Moloch is king; Philistine soldier who fought at Timnah where David attempted to gain his dowry for Michal.

Moloch *(mo'-lok)* – Mountain devil; Canaanite god who required propitiation by sacrificing children.

Moses *(mo'-ziz)* – Drawn out: chosen by God to lead the Children of Israel out of bondage from Egypt. (Exodus 3)

Nahash *(naw-hawsh')* – Snake; king of Ammon. (1 Samuel 11)

Nagad *(naw-gad')* – Messenger; a Hebrew soldier who brought word to Eli of the loss of the Ark following the battle of Aphek *(Eben-Ezer)*; later portrayed as a captain in Saul's army. (1 Samuel 4: 12)

Naphtali *(naf-taw-lee')* – Wrestling; my struggle; the fifth son of Jacob; one of the twelve tribes of ancient Israel traditionally descended from him.

Orach *(o'-rakh)* – Way, path; traveler, wayfarer; the Hebrew soldier of the tribe of Naphtali who befriended Nagad the Benjaminite; father of Helek; he was killed at the battle of Aphek *(Eben-Ezer)*.

Orel *(or'el)* – The light of God; elder from the city of Jabesh-Gilead who met with Nagad and Helek to decide the fate of the city during the siege of Nahash.

Peleset *(pe-lé-set)* – See Philistine. *Sea People.*

Philistine *(fil'-is-tinz)* – A member of an Aegean people who settled ancient Philistia around the 12th century B.C., who made war on the Israelites; *Peleset; Sea People.*

Phinehas *(pee-nekh-aws')* – Mouth of brass; son of Eli; priest at Shiloh; one of the two corrupt sons of Eli; slain with his brother Hophni at the battle of Aphek. (1 Samuel 1:3)

Rachel *(rā'-chel)* – Daughter of Laban, wife of Jacob, and mother of Joseph and Benjamin. She became mother of the Benjaminites, Saul's tribe. (Genesis 29)

Rahab *(rah'-hab)* – Breadth; harlot of Jericho who helped the Hebrew spies escape by letting them down the wall of the city with a rope. (Joshua 2:1)

Reuben *(reh-oo-bane')* – Behold a son; the eldest son of Jacob; one of the twelve tribes of ancient Israel traditionally descended from him.

Riyphah *(ree-faw')* – A grain or fruit (for grinding); a woman of Beth Shemesh who witnessed the return of the Ark of the Covenant; wife of Nagad the Benjaminite.

Rizpah *(rits-paw')* – Hot stone; handmaid in Saul's household; a concubine of King Saul; mother of Armoni and Mephibosheth. (2 Samuel 3:7)

Samson *(sam'-sun)* – Like the sun; a Nazarite from the tribe of Dan, whose strength was renowned, until he was betrayed by his mistress Delilah; judged Israel for twenty years. (Judges 13-16)

Samuel *(sam'-u-el)* – God has heard; last judge of Israel; a prophet of Yahweh. (1 Samuel)

Saul *(Saoul)* – Desired; asked for; the son of Kish and the first king of Israel. (1 Samuel 9)

Shamgar *(sham-gar')* – Sword; son of Anath; a judge of Israel; killed six hundred Philistines single-handedly with an ox goad. (Judges 3:31)

Shammah *(sham-maw')* – Astonishment; the third son of Jesse and brother of David. (1 Samuel 16:9)

Simeon *(sim'-ē-on)* – Heard; the second son of Jacob; one of the twelve tribes of ancient Israel traditionally descended from him.

Sisera *(sis-er-uh)* – Battle array; general under King Jabin of Hazor and slain by Jael. (Judges 4:2)

Tiphcar *(tif-sar')* − Captain; captain in the Hebrew Army, during the battles of Aphek and Mizpah; member of the Council of Elders.

Yabnilu *(yab nil-oo)* − God made; Philistine soldier who fought at Timnah where David attempted to gain his dowry for Michal.

Yahweh *(yah-weh)* − YHVH; the name of God; I am.

Yogev *(yow' gehv)* − Farmer; one of the citizen defenders of Jabesh-Gilead during the siege by Nahash, king of the Ammonites.

Zalal *(zaw-lal')* − worthless; vile; one of the sons of Belial.

Zaqen *(zaw-kane')* − Elder; one of the Hebrew elders who met at the council of elders at Bethel.

Zebulun *(zeb'-u-lun)* − Exalted; tenth son of Jacob; one of the twelve tribes of ancient Israel traditionally descended from him.

Zeruiah *(tser-oo-yaw')* − Balsam; daughter of King Nahash of Ammon.

Ziba *(tsee-baw')* − Statue; servant of Saul. (2 Samuel 9:2)

APPENDIX D – PLACE NAMES

Abel-meholah *(aw-bale' mekh-o-law')* – Meadow of dancing; a place west of the Jordan River, south of Beth-shan.

Aijalon *(a'-ja-lon)* – Field of deer; city of Dan, fourteen miles northwest of Jebus; a city under the control of the Philistines within the Shephelah.

Aijalon Valley *(a'-ja-lon val-ee)* – Field of deer; the northernmost valley within the Shephelah, or lowland, just south of the Plain of Sharon; appointed to the tribe of Dan, but under constant pressure by Philistine invasion, surrendered the valley. Here it was that Joshua commanded the sun and moon stand still; *Valley of Aijalon; Vale of Aijalon.* (Joshua 10:12–13)

Ammon *(am-mone')* – The land east of the Jordan River.

Aphek *(ay' fehk)* – Strength; a rapid torrent; Aphek is located northeast of Joppa near the source of the Yarkon River in the Sharon plain. The Philistine armies encamped at the stronghold during the battle of Aphek in which they captured the Ark of the Covenant.

Aram Zobah *(ar-am' tso-baw')* – Exalted station: exalted conflict; the land northeast of Damascus.

Ashdod *(ash'-dod)* – Powerful; a Philistine city about midway between Gaza and Joppa, and three miles from the Great Sea. It was one of the chief seats of the worship of Dagon and a capital city within the Philistine pentapolis.

Askelon *(ash-kel-one')* – The fire of infamy; I shall be weighed; on the shore of the Great Sea between Joppa and Gaza and a capital city within the Philistine pentapolis.

Azekah *(az-ay-kaw')* – Dug over; a town in the Elah Valley, west of Gath, where Joshua defeated the southern coalition of Amorite kings led by Adonizedek of Jebus.

Beersheba *(be-er-she'-ba)* – Seven wells; the uttermost reaches of Judah; twenty-eight miles southwest of Hebron.

Beth-aven *(bayth aw'-ven)* – House of vanity; a place on the northern border of Benjamin, east of Bethel and northwest of Michmash.

Bethel *(bayth-ale')* – House of God; ancient place and seat of worship south of Judah; a border city between Benjamin and Ephraim twelve miles north of Jebus.

Beth-horon *(bayth kho-rone')* – House of hollowness; Upper and Lower, two towns in the mountains of Ephraim built by Sheerah, the daughter of Beriah.

Bethlehem *(bayth'-le-hem)* – House of bread; a town in the territory of Judah, five miles south of Jebus; the village resides upon the sloping sides of a prominent limestone ridge within the Hill Country of Judah.

Beth-shan *(bayth she-awn')* − House of ease; a place in Manasseh, west of the Jordan.

Beth Shemesh *(bayth sheh'-mesh)* − House of the sun; named for the Canaanite sun-goddess Shemesh; given to the Levites, a border town between Judah and Dan upon the south side of the upper Sorek Valley; the most important town in the Sorek Valley; here is where the Ark of God returned after being taken by the Philistines; *Har-cherec.*

Beth-Tappuah *(bayth tap-poo'-akh)* − Place of apples; a town in the mountainous district of Judah, near Hebron. Also called *Tappuah.*

Bezek *(beh'-zak)* − Lightning; rendezvous place for Saul's army before he faced Ammon at Jabesh-Gilead; general place of assembly northeast of Shechem on the road to Beth-shan, nearly opposite the ford of the Jordan River, at Jabesh-Gilead.

Bozez *(bo'-zez)* − Surpassing white; glistening; the white cliff that stands on the north side of the gorge at Michmash.

Canaan *(key-nuhn)* − Lowland; the land between the Jordan, the Salt Sea, and the Great Sea, promised to Abraham by Yahweh, subsequently conquered by the Israelites under Joshua. *The Promised Land.*

Carmel *(kar-mel')* − Garden-land; a town in the mountains on the west side of the Dead Sea and south of Hebron; the mount where Saul erected his pillar in honor of his triumph over Amalek.

Damascus *(da-mas'-kus)* − Silent is the sackcloth weaver; capital of Syria; in the plain east of Hermon.

Eben-Ezer *(ehb'-ehn-ee'-zehr)* − The stone of help; place name where the Israelites camped during the battle of Aphek in which the Philistines captured the Ark of the Covenant.

Ebenezer *(ehb'-ehn-ee'-zehr)* − The stone of help; the memorial stone placed by Samuel near Mizpah after the battle of Mizpah to commemorate the divine assistance given to Israel in their great battle against the Philistines.

Edom *(ed-ome')* − Land south and south-east of Israel.

Ekron *(ek-rone')* − Torn up by the roots; in the lowlands of Judah, it is the most northerly of the capital cities within the Philistine pentapolis; place of the noted sanctuary of Baal-Zebul.

Elah River *(ay-law' riv-er)* − An oak; the river that transverses the Elah Valley; it was here that David chose five stones before slaying the giant Goliath.

Elah Valley *(ay-law' val-ee)* − Valley of the oak; a flat triangle-shaped valley, located on the western edge of the Judean hills near Sochoh and Azekah; it was within this valley that David slew Goliath; *Valley of Elah; Vale of Elah; Emek ha-Elah.*

Ephes Dammim *(eh'-fes dam-meem')* − The end of bloodshed; a region six miles southwest of Jebus, between Sochoh and Azekah; the place where the Philistines encamped against Israel, sending out their champion, Goliath, to harass the Hebrew army; *Happas-dammim.*

Ephraim *(ef-rah'-yim)* − Double ash-heap; doubly fruitful; second son of Joseph, blessed by him and given preference over first son, Manasseh; mountainous area in the center of Canaan, west of the Jordan, south of the territory of Manasseh, and north of the Tribe of Benjamin.

Gath *(gath)* – Winepress; one of the five royal cities of Philistia located near Israelite territory at the end of the Elah Valley.

Gaza *(gah-zuh)* – The strong; the southernmost of the five royal Philistine cities located on the Great Sea; *Azzah.*

Geba *(gheh'-bah)* – A city in Benjamin set on a steep precipice six miles northeast of Jebus and three miles from Gibeah, lying south across the gorge from Michmash; a Philistine garrison was stationed there.

Gezer *(gheh'-zer)* – Portion; between the lower Beth-horon and the sea, a Canaanite city on the border of Ephraim.

Gibeah *(ghib-aw')* – Hill, height; a city in Benjamin, upon a height that overlooks Kirjath-Jearim. Saul's home.

Gibeath-elohim *(ghib-ath' e-loh-him)* – The hill of God; a Philistine garrison was located in this region; *Geba.*

Gibeon *(gib-ee-uhn)* – Hill-city; a Levitical city in the territory of Benjamin.

Gilead *(gil-ee-uh d)* – Rocky region; a mountainous region east of the Jordan River, south of Bashan, and north of Moab and Ammon.

Gilgal *(ghil-gawl')* – Wheel; the first Israelite encampment in the Promised Land, west of the Jordan, and east of Jericho.

Great Sea – An inland sea that lay to the west of the Philistine coastline and north of Egypt; later it was renamed the Mediterranean Sea. *Western Sea.*

Havilah *(hav-ee-law')* – Circle; within the Negev, one of the far reaches of the territory ruled by the Amalekites.

Hazor *(ha'-zor)* – The royal city of Jabin within the territory of Naphtali.

Hebron *(he'-brun)* – A community; alliance; a Levitical city south of Jebus.

Israel *(yis-raw-ale')* – God prevails; Promised Land; land of the Israelites. See *Canaan.*

Isle of Caphtor *(kaf-tore')* – Land of origin for the Philistines. *The island of Crete.*

Jabesh-Gilead *(yaw-bashe' gil-ee-uh d)* – Hill of testimony; a town east of the Jordan in the hills of Gilead; its inhabitants refused to join Israel against Benjamin during the civil war and were later besieged by the Ammonites.

Jabesh, Valley *(yaw-bashe' val-ee)* – Region surrounding the city of Jabesh-Gilead east of the Jordan River; *Vale of Jabesh.*

Jebus *(jee-buhs)* – Threshing place; Canaanite city that was later renamed Jerusalem.

Jericho *(jer'-i-ko)* – Its moon; north of the Salt Sea, this was the first city to be taken in the Conquest. *City of Palm Trees.*

Jezreel *(jez'-re-el)* – God sows; city on the northwest spur of Mount Gilboa.

Jordan River *(jawr-dn riv-er)* – Descender; river in northern Canaan, flowing south through the Sea of Chinnereth to the Salt Sea.

Jordan Valley *(jawr-dn val-ee)* – Part of the Great Rift Valley, this low-lying land divides the land east and west; it follows the Jordan River from the Sea of Chinnereth to the Salt Sea.

Judah *(joo'-da)* – The land inherited by the tribe of Judah in southern Canaan.

Judean Mountains *(joo-dee-uhn moun-tn)* – A north–south mountain range running through Judah, extending east and west of Jebus (Jerusalem) to Mount Hebron; forming the natural divide between the coastal plains and the Jordan Valley; *Judean Hills.*

Kidron Valley *(ked-rone' val-ee)* – Turbid; a valley with a winter torrent that runs through it, east of Jebus, it breaks through the region until it reaches the Salt Sea.

Kirjath-Jearim *(keer-yath' yeh-aw-reem')* – City of woods; a Gibeonite town on the border of Benjamin, eight miles northeast of Beth Shemesh; the Ark was brought to this place from Beth Shemesh, placed in the care of the Levite, Abinadab.

Lachish *(law-keesh')* – Invincible; a city lying south of Jebus within the foothills of the Shephelah on the border of the Philistine plain.

Land of Jackals *(land ov jak'-olz)* – Desolate; three valleys that converge into a great ravine near Shalisha; Saul traveled within this depression in search of his father's donkeys.

Lebanon *(leb-aw-nohn')* – Whiteness; the celebrated white mountains of Syria, whose highest peaks are perpetually covered with snow, located north of Canaan extending north-east running parallel with the Great Sea; famed for its spectacular beauty and large cedar trees.

Levant *(le'vant)* – The area east of the Great Sea; Lebanon, Syria, and Israel.

Libnah *(lib-naw')* – White; storax tree; located on the eastern edge of the Elah Valley, a Levitical city of Judah bordering Philistia.

Lod *(lode)* – Travail; a city eleven miles southeast of Joppa in the Plain of Sharon in the territory of Benjamin; established by Shemed, the son of Elpaal, a Benjamite.

Mareshah *(mar-ay-shaw')* – crest of a hill; a city in the Shephelah of Judah on the Zephathah River south of Beth Shemesh.

Michmash *(mik'-mash)* – Hidden; a city in Benjamin near Ramah, 10 miles north of Jebus. The town lays north of a deep gorge across from the Philistine garrison at Geba.

Migron *(mig-rone')* – Precipice; Saul's outpost upon the southern brow of the ravine, on a precipice west of Michmash.

Mizpah *(miz'-pa)* – Watchtower; an old sacred place in Benjamin near the Valley of Aijalon. Here it was that Samuel led the people in a great reformation. After routing out the Philistines, Samuel set up the memorial called Ebenezer near Mizpah.

Moab *(mo-awb)* – Of his father; the land inhabited by a people descended from the incestuous relationship of Lot and one of his daughters, east the Jordan River and the Salt Sea, and south of the Arnon.

Mountain of Shen *(moun-tn ov shane)* – Tooth; crag; the tooth-shaped projection across the plain from Mizpah.

Mount Baalah *(mont bah-al-aw')* – Mistress; mountain west of the Sorek Valley, near Ekron, whose peak was used for the worship of Baal, god of the Philistines.

Mount Ebal *(mont ay-bawl)* – Stony; is one of the two mountains that border the city of Shechem, forming the northern side of the valley in which Shechem resides, the southern side being formed by Mount Gerizim. The mountain is one of the highest peaks within Canaan.

Mount Gerizim *(mont gher-ee-zeem')* – Cutting off; is one of the two mountains that border the city of Shechem and forms the southern side of the valley in which

Shechem resides, the northern side being formed by Mount Ebal. The mountain is one of the highest peaks within Canaan.

Mount Gilboa *(mont ghil-bo'-ah)* – Swollen heap; crescent-shaped mountain range encircling the southeastern end of the plain of Jezreel.

Nahal Besor *(naw-hal' bes-ore')* – Cheerful; good news; the largest water source in the Negev, which ran a course from the mountains east of Beersheba through the western plains until finally draining into the Great Sea to the west.

Naioth *(na'-yoth)* – House of instruction; located in the city of Ramah, this was the school for prophets established by the prophet Samuel.

Negev *(né geb)* – A rocky desert region in southern Israel; a land ruled by nomadic tribes.

Nob *(nobe)* – High place; a priestly city in Benjamin upon a hill north of Jebus.

Ophrah *(of-raw')* – A village in Benjamin five miles east of Bethel.

Philistia *(fi-lis'-ti-a)* – Land of sojourners; the southwestern coast of Canaan, the territory of the Philistines.

Promised Land – See *Canaan*.

Ramah *(raw-maw')* – Height, high place; *Ramathaim-Zophim*, the birthplace of Samuel the prophet. Situated on the eastern side of the Central Benjamite Plain, opposite Gibeon, about halfway between Bethel and Jebus.

Rehob *(rekh-obe')* – Broad place; a broad plain west of the Jordan River, northwest of Jabesh-Gilead.

Rock of Rimmon *(rim-mone')* – Pomegranate; a rock that sheltered six hundred Benjaminites during the civil war with the other tribes, west of Michmash at Migron; here it was that Saul sheltered his troops in watch of the Philistine garrison at Michmash.

Salt Sea *(solt)* – The gathering of waters at the terminal end of the Jordan River; a land-locked body of water with a high mineral content; *Dead Sea*.

Sechu *(say'-koo)* – A city near Ramah that has a great cistern; here it was that Saul inquired of David.

Seneh *(seh-neh')* – Thorny; the shadowy cliff covered in thorn bushes that stands on the south side of the gorge at Michmash.

Shaalim *(sha'-a-lim)* – Land on the west side of the mountain range of Ephraim on the slopes to the east of Lod. Saul passed through this region as he searched for his father's donkeys.

Shaaraim *(shah-ar-ah'-yim)* – Double gate; a city in the Shephelah or lowland of Judah; through this area, the Philistines fled after the slaying of their champion, Goliath.

Shalisha *(shaw-lee-shaw')* – Three; the third; a highland region of Ephraim twelve miles west-south-west of Shechem in the Plain of Sharon; a district near Mount Ephraim through which Saul passed as he searched for his father's donkeys.

Sharuhen *(shaw-roo-hen')* – Refuge of grace; capital of the Amalekites; eighteen miles west of Beersheba, between the Way of Shur to the east and the Way of the Philistines to the west; this fortress controlled trade between Egypt and the Levant.

Shechem *(shek-em')* – Shoulder; the city within the narrow sheltered valley between Mt. Ebal on the north and Mt. Gerizim on the south. Here is where Abraham received Yahweh's covenant of the Promise Land and later Joshua gathered the twelve tribes of Israel to renew their covenant with Jehovah.

Sheol *(sheh-ole')* – The underworld, the abode of the dead.

Shephelah *(shef-ay-law')* – Low place; the Judean foothills in south-central Israel stretching between Mount Hebron and the coastal plain; the in-between land bordering the territory of the Hebrews and the domain of the Philistines.

Shiloh *(shī'lō)* – Place of rest; tranquil, secure; a meeting place and sanctuary for the Israelites and the site of a tabernacle where the Ark of the Covenant was kept until its capture by the Philistines. The city and its tabernacle were destroyed after the battle of Aphek.

Shiloh Valley *(shī'lō val-ee)* – The valley surrounding the ancient city of Shiloh where the men of Benjamin lay in wait for the daughters of Shiloh, stealing them to be their wives; *Valley of Shiloh; Vale of Shiloh.*

Shual *(shoo-awl')* – Jackal; a region in Benjamin north of Michmash.

Shur *(shoor)* – Wall; a place southwest of Israel within the Negev on the eastern border of Egypt.

Sochoh *(so-ko')* – Lupine hill; a region in the Shephelah, between Adullam and Azekah that lay along the southern hillside of the Valley of Elah; *Givat Ha Turmusim.*

Sorek River *(so'-rek riv-er)* – Choice vines; river within the Sorek Valley that borders the realm of the Philistines and the territory of the Hebrew tribe of Dan.

Sorek Valley *(so'-rek val-ee)* – The valley of the choice vine. A crescent-shaped valley in the Shephelah between Zorah and Ekron; *Vale of Sorek; Valley of Sorek; Sorek River Valley: Nachal Soreq.*

Spring of Harod *(khar-ode')* – A stream west of the Jordan, south of Beth-shan, near the hill of Moreh; a place where Gideon and his army were encamped; *Ein Harod.* (Judges 7:1)

Stone of Ezel *(stohn ov eh'-zel)* – Departure; a memorial stone within a field near Geba.

Syria *(sir'-i-a)* – Country that lies to the north-east of Phoenicia.

Tappuah *(tap-poo'-akh)* – Apples; located in the hill country, on the border of Ephraim and Manasseh, northwest of Shiloh. See *Beth-Tappuah.*

Telaim *(tel-aw-eem')* – Lambs; within the Negev, a city on the outskirts of Judah, between Israel and the land of Edom; here it was that Saul mustered his forces before attacking Amalek.

Timnah *(tim-naw')* – Portion; a town on the rise beyond the western end of the Sorek River Valley, just north of Ekron.

Way of the Sea – The main road that ran north-south through the coastal plain; later became known as the Via Maris; *the Way of the Philistines.*

Wilderness, the *(wil'-der-nes)* – The Judean desert; an arid desert arising from the Negev that sweeps east of Jebus and extends to the Salt Sea; *Judean Wilderness.*

Zeboim, Valley of *(tseb-o-eem')* – The valley of hyenas; valley in Benjamin between Jericho and Jebus.

Zelzah *(tsel-tsakh')* – Shadow; a place on the boundary of Benjamin five miles from the Canaanite city of Jebus. Rachel's tomb is located within this region.

Zephathah Valley *(zef'-a-tha val-ee)* – A valley in western Judah near Mareshah. *Valley of Zephathah; Vale of Zephathah.*

Zorah *(tsor-aw')* – Hornet; birthplace of Samson; a town on the crest of a hill overlooking the valley of Sorek in the low country of Judah, allocated to the tribe of Dan.

Zuph *(zuhf)* – Honeycomb; a district in Benjamin, northwest of Jebus.

REFERENCES

Brown, Francis, S. R. Driver, and Charles A. Briggs, with additions by Wilhelm Gesenius. *Hebrew and English Lexicon of the Old Testament*. Keyed to Theological Word Book of the Old Testament. Public domain. Accessed February 12, 2015. http://www.biblestudytools.com/lexicons/hebrew.

Easton, M. G. *Illustrated Bible Dictionary*. 3rd ed. 1897. Public domain. http://www.biblestudytools.com/dictionaries/eastons-bible-dictionary.

Orr, James, ed. *International Standard Bible Encyclopedia*. 1915. Public domain. http://www.biblestudytools.com/encyclopedias.
— "Abijah."
— "Adonai."
— "Ahijah."
— "Aijalon."
— "Amalek; Amalekite."
— "Amorites."
— "Anakim."
— "Aphek."
— "Ashdod."
— "Balaam."
— "Beersheba."
— "Bethlehem."
— "Bozez."
— "Caphtor; Caphtorim."
— "Children of Israel."
— "Dan (1); Dan, Tribe of."
— "Eben-Ezer."
— "Elyon."
— "Gibeah."
— "Gideon."
— "Gilead (1)."
— "Hazor."
— "Hebrew; Hebrewess."

— "Hebron (1)."
— "Jericho."
— "Jehovah."
— "Jephthah."
— "Jesse."
— "Judah (1)."
— "Levi (1)."
— "Levites."
— "Moloch."
— "Moses."
— "Naioth."
— "Philistia."
— "Philistines."
— "Rachel."
— "Samson."
— "Samuel."
— "Saul."
— "Shiloh (1)."
— "Simeon (2)."
— "Sorek, Valley of."
— "Syria (1)."
— "Wilderness."
— "Zebulun."

Chayim, Orach. "Jewish Phrases." *Headcoverings* by Devorah. Accessed February 12, 2015. http://www.headcoverings-by-devorah.com/Hebrew_Phrases.htm.

———. "Jewish Blessings." *JewishYellow.* Accessed February 12, 2015. http://jewishyellow.com/jewish_blessings.html.

BIBLIOGRAPHY

Alter, Robert. 1999. *The David Story: A Translation With Commentary of 1 and 2 Samuel.* New York: W. W. Norton & Company, Inc.

Anderson, Robert. 2011. "Egypt: Who Were the Sea People." Tour Egypt. June 9. Accessed on or before 2011. http://www.touregypt.net/featurestories/seapeople.htm.

Arnold, Bill T., and Bryan Beyer. 2002. *Readings from the Ancient Near East: Primary Sources for Old Testament Study.* Grand Rapids, MI: Baker Academic.

Baldwin, Joyce G. 1988. *The Tyndale Old Testament Commentaries, I & II Samuel.* Bristol: Inter-Varsity Press.

Benner, Jeff A. 1999-2012. "Numbers 6:24-27." Ancient Hebrew Research Center. http://www.ancient-hebrew.org/40_numbers1.html.

—. 1999-2012. "The Aaronic Blessing." Ancient Hebrew Research Center. http://www.ancient-hebrew.org/12_blessing.html.

n.d. "Bethel." Bible-history.com. Accessed January 3, 2013. http://www.bible-history.com/geography/ancient-israel/bethel.html.

Brooks, Simcha Shalom. 2005. *Saul And the Monarchy: A New Look.* Burlington, VT: Ashgate Publishing Company.

Campbell, Antony F. 2003. *Forms of Old Testament Literature: 1 Samuel. Vol. VII.* Grand Rapids: Wm. B. Eerdmans Publishing.

Campbell, Lee. n.d. "Idolatry in the Ancient Near East." Xenos Christian Fellowship. Accessed 2008. http://www.xenos.org/classes/papers/aneidola.htm.

Clark, John David. 1995. "The Nations of the Bible: Amalekites." Isaiah 58 Broadcast & Tracts Amalek. January. http://www.isaiah58.com/broadcasters/amel.htm.

Clarke, Adam. 2002. *Commentary on 1 Samuel.* Concord, NC: Wesleyan Heritage Publications.

David M. Howard, Jr. n.d. "PHILISTINES." http://people.bethel.edu/~dhoward/articles/articles2/PhilistinesPOTW.htm.

de Geus, C. H. J. 2003. *Towns in ancient Israel and in the southern Levant.* Bondgenotenlaan, Leuven: Peeters.

Deffinbaugh, Bob. 1995 - 2012. "The Fellowship Offering." bible.org. http://bible.org/seriespage/fellowship-offering-leviticus-31-17-711-34-195-8-2229-30.

DeMaris, Richard E. 2008. *The New Testament in Its Ritual World.* New York: Taylor & Francis.

Easton, Matthew George. 2008. "Easton's Bible Dictionary (1897)/Samuel." Wikisource. Accessed 2009. http://en.wikisource.org/wiki/Easton's_Bible_Dictionary_(1897)/Samuel.

Ellicott, Charles John, ed. 1883. *An Old Testament Commentary for English Readers.* Vol. II. London: Cassell, Petter, Galpin & Co.

Gabriel, Richard A. 2003. *The Military History of Ancient Israel.* Westport, CT: Praeger Publishers.

Geikie, Cunningham. 1888. *The Holy Land and the Bible: A book of Scripture illustrations Gathered in Palestine.* Vol. II. New York: James Pott & Co.

Guzik, David. 2004-2010. "David Guzik's Commentary on 1 Samuel." Enduring Word Media . http://www.enduringword.com/commentaries/09.htm.

Henry, Matthew. 1838. *An Exposition of the Old Testament.* Vol. II. Philadelphia: Haswell, Barrington, and Haswell.

Henry, Matthew. 1997. *Matthew Henry's Concise Commentary on the Whole Bible.* Nashville: Thomas Nelson Publishers.

Iain William Provan, V. Philips Long, Tremper Longman, III. 2003. *Biblical History of Israel.* Louisville, Kentucky: Westminster John Knox Press.

Josephus. 1930. *Jewish Antiquities,* Volume I: Books 1-3. Cambridge: Harvard Press.

Kitto, John, D.D., FSA. 1859. *Daily Bible Illustrations Being Original Readings for a Year, on Subjects from Sacred History, Biography, Geography, Antiquities, and Theology.* New York: Robert Carter & Brothers.

Knapp, Christopher. 2006. *Life and Times of Samuel the Prophet.* Believers Bookshelf, Incorporated.

Lockyer, Herbert. 1959. *All the Prayers of the Bible.* Grand Rapids, Michigan: Zondervan.

Meyer, Frederick Brotherton. 1895. *David: Shepherd, Psalmist, King.* New York: Fleming H. Revell Company.

Mills, Watson E. 1997. *Mercer Dictionary of the Bible.* Macon: Mercer University Press.

Orr, James. 1915. *The International Standard Bible Encyclopaedia.* Vol. II. Chicago: The Howard-Severance Company.

Pinson, Rav Dovber. "Rosh Hashanah: The Sounds of the Shofar Explored." IYYUN Center for Jewish Spirituality. http://iyyun.com/holidays/rosh-hashanah-the-sounds-of-the-shofar-explored.

Rich, Tracey R. 2006. "Sukkot Blessings." Judaism 101. http://www.jewfaq.org/prayer/sukkot.htm.

Robinson D.D., Edward. 1865. *Physical Geography of the Holy Land.* London: William Clowse and Sons.

Stewart, Robert Laird. 1899. The Land of Israel. New York: Fleming H. Revell Company.

Thomas, Kelly Cheyne, and John Sutherland Black. 1901. *Encyclopædia Biblica: A Dictionary of the Bible.* II vols. London: Adam and Charles Black.

Woodhouse, John, and R. Kent Hughes. 2008. *1 Samuel: Looking for a Leader.* Wheaton, Illinois: Crossway Books.

ABOUT THE AUTHOR

Susan Van Volkenburgh is an award-winning author of Christian fiction and nonfiction, celebrated for her lyrical style and immersive reimaginings of biblical history. Her *Trilogy of Kings Saga* brings ancient Scripture to life with depth and spiritual resonance; the first edition of the opening volume, *The Stone of Ebenezer*, received the Grand Prize in the New Look Writing Contest sponsored by WestBow Press and HarperCollins.

Shaped by personal loss, Susan began her literary journey after the death of her father in the September 11, 2001 attacks. Her experience of grief and faith is poignantly explored in *Silent Resolve and the God Who Let Me Down (A 9/11 Story)*.

With experience as an oncology nurse, homeschool educator, and member of the gospel music group *The Van Martins*, Susan draws from a well of empathy and understanding, crafting stories that resonate with emotional and spiritual truth. She formerly owned *Savannah's Meadow*, a treehouse bed and breakfast that embodied her love of beauty, wonder, and rest—a spirit that continues to shape her storytelling. Now living in Northeast Texas, she and her husband raise Texas Longhorns, embracing a life rooted in tradition, perseverance, and grace.

Through every page, Susan invites readers into timeless narratives of hope and transformation—stories where the broken find purpose, and the past speaks into the present with eternal significance.

Susan would love to hear from you. Visit her online.
www.susanvanvolkenburgh.com

Other Books by
Susan Van Volkenburgh

www.ingramcontent.com/pod-product-compliance
Lightning Source LLC
Chambersburg PA
CBHW052330110726
47901CB00005B/1185